Dutch anthropologist Jeroen Windmeijer (1969) writes thrillers in which Roman and biblical history and the history of his hometown, Leiden, are brought together. His first book was very well received by both the press and booksellers, in the Netherlands and beyond. With *The Pilgrim's Conspiracy* he claims his place among the great storytellers. Jeroen's thrillers are plot driven, smart and authentic.

Also by Jeroen Windmeijer

St Paul's Labyrinth

The Pilgrim Conspiracy

ST. PETER'S MYSTERY

JEROEN WINDMEIJER

Translated by
HAYLEY WAKENSHAW

One More Chapter
a division of HarperCollins*Publishers*
1 London Bridge Street
London SE1 9GF
www.harpercollins.co.uk
HarperCollins*Publishers*
1st Floor, Watermarque Building, Ringsend Road
Dublin 4, Ireland

This paperback edition 2021
1

First published in Great Britain in ebook format
by HarperCollins*Publishers* 2021

Translated by Hayley Wakenshaw

A catalogue record of this book is available from the British Library

ISBN: 978-0-00-845515-6

Printed and bound in the UK using 100% Renewable Electricity
by CPI Group (UK) Ltd

MIX
Paper from
responsible sources
FSC™ C007454

This book is produced from independently certified FSC™ paper
to ensure responsible forest management.

For more information visit: www.harpercollins.co.uk/green

Then Jesus summoned his twelve disciples and gave them authority over unclean spirits, to cast them out, and to cure every disease and every sickness. [...] These twelve Jesus sent out with the following instructions: `Go nowhere among the Gentiles, and enter no town of the Samaritans, but go rather to the lost sheep of the house of Israel.'

Matthew 10:1, 55-6

Prologue

The old man stared into the distance, gazing across the water that stretched out endlessly in front of him. As the wind tugged at his beard, the waves lapped gently over his bare feet, soaking the hem of his woollen robe. He watched as though he expected the sea to open up before him, as the Eternal One had parted the Red Sea for Moses when the pharaoh and his army were at his heels.

But no one was chasing him now. They had escaped the terrible destruction of the city of the Lord in time. Yeshua had foreseen it. Hadn't He foretold that not one stone would be left upon another, that all would be thrown down? Who could have thought that it would come to pass so soon? But where was He now? What had happened to his promise that this generation would live to see his glorious return?

'Oh Lord,' he murmured to himself, 'help me overcome my unbelief...'

Had Judas been right after all?

He clutched the little ivory casket tightly to his chest. He hadn't been able to bring himself to throw it away.

The end was near. Hadn't they escaped the massacres in the city by the skins of their teeth? Watched from the brow of a hill as the Temple went up in flames? Hadn't there been wars and rumours of war? Had nation not risen against nation, and kingdom against kingdom? There had been famines and earthquakes – the beginning of the birth pangs, as had been prophesied. Hadn't many followers of the Way been handed over to councils, flogged in their synagogues, dragged before governors and kings to bear witness because of Him?

He heard his horse snorting behind him. He looked over his shoulder and saw clouds of steam escaping from the beast's nostrils. His companion, Archippus, held the reins tightly in his hands. As if the animal would ever take it into its head to run away from its master! No, this animal had always been loyal to him. An animal would never desert you...

Archippus beckoned to him. He was right. It was finished.

After the Disaster, they had planned to go as far away as they could from the devastated city. Thaddeus and Bartholomew were to go to Armenia. Matthew to Ethiopia. Lazarus, Martha, and Mary would go to Gallia with Yeshua's children. Joseph of Arimathea would go to Britannia... Paul had gone to Hispania many years earlier after being acquitted at his trial in Rome, and he had died there.

He took one last look at the sea.

Perhaps this was all part of a divine plan to proclaim the good news in every corner of the world. If that was true, then the journey he and Archippus had made would end here in Brittenburg, one of the furthest corners of the Roman Empire. What trials they had endured on the way! The hardships they had suffered, crossing the Alps, more often on foot than on horseback... And always haunted by the fear of discovery.

They had kept up their courage by singing: 'The cords of death encompassed me; the torrents of perdition assailed me; the cords of Sheol entangled me; the snares of death confronted me.'

But God was good and had kept them safe.

There had been unrest here too: the Batavi and the Cananefates had risen up against the Roman oppressor. Theirs had been a bold revolt, but ultimately, a doomed one, a fire that blazed fiercely all too briefly, extinguished with the blood of many young men. The city was still being rebuilt, and before long, everything would be as it had been before.

'Cephas!'

He heard Archippus calling him. Even now, he was often slow to respond to his name, even though the Master had given it to him over forty years ago. He had been young then, not much more than twenty and in the prime of his life. The muscles of his arms had been like cables; he'd worked with his nets from dawn to dusk.

His parents had named him Simon, but Cephas was a beautiful name, a name with a promise. 'On you, I will build my church,' He had said.

But what had come of that?

A few boats bobbed near the shoreline, waiting for a new day and the promise of a good catch. They reminded him of home. He looked up again and signalled to Archippus that he was coming.

He walked back up the beach, his feet sinking into the soft sand. He heaved himself onto his horse and gave the animal a reassuring pat on its neck. They had agreed that they would ride to the settlement near Matilo and find somewhere to stay there. He sensed that his own end was approaching, and he wasn't sure what to feel or think about that. Had he failed miserably? Or had he taken an important step in keeping his Master's legacy alive?

He had given his faithful companion detailed instructions of what to do when he died. Archippus should bury him in accordance with the funeral rites laid down by the Patriarchs. But it wasn't his earthly body that concerned him most now. And since he had already received the keys to the Kingdom of Heaven from the Lord himself, nor was it the salvation of his soul. No, what concerned him were the letters he was carrying, which Archippus had transcribed and translated into Greek.

The ingenious construction of the ivory box would ensure that neither wind nor water, earth nor fire would ever defile its precious contents. He had left his other writings, the Source, behind in Jerusalem for others to base their own versions of the Good News on. But the contents of the casket were different, not meant for everyone to read. Whether or not it should be discovered, he would leave up to God. Then the people could judge for themselves if he had made the right decision or not.

As the sun sank slowly into the sea behind them, the travellers' horses trudged over the dunes through the shifting sand. Ahead of them lay a yellow-green landscape of low scrubland, and in the distance, they could see the sun shimmering on the surfaces of many lakes.

As if by some silent agreement, they both began to quietly sing the same song: 'To you, O Lord, I lift up my soul. O my God, in you I trust. Do not let me be put to shame. Do not let my enemies exult over me. Make me to know your ways, O Lord; teach me your paths.'

Chapter One

LEIDEN, 1996

This was his favourite part of the day. Peter de Haan sat on the sofa in his office, put his feet up on the well-ordered coffee table, and lit a cigarillo. He looked out at the Witte Singel canal and the University library beyond it. It was half-past five, and the University of Leiden's Archaeology department was more or less deserted.

Although he wasn't breaking any rules by smoking in his office, he'd opened the window an inch or two to expel the worst of the smoke. He'd always found the smell of cigars relaxing, but he knew that not everyone appreciated it. The open window would trigger the alarm system as soon as the clock struck six, but it was safe for the moment.

Right now, many of his students – and probably some colleagues too – would be next door in the LAK, the arts academy building, eating dinner together at the long tables in the canteen. But Peter prized these moments when he could sit alone in complete silence, mulling over his day, watching clouds of cigar smoke swirl up to the ceiling where, now and then, a sudden draught would burst them apart.

It had been a quiet day with only two lectures on his schedule: An Introduction to Archaeology for his first-year students in the morning, and a seminar on the history of Leiden for the final-year students in the afternoon.

Being a historian rather than an archaeologist, Peter was something of a square peg in the faculty. But as the author of several books on the history of the 'City of Keys', he was increasingly involved in the region's archaeological digs. There had been a few disgruntled faces when he, an outsider, had taken up the post of lecturer in Regional Archaeology, and that feeling of resentment still hung around the faculty now. These days, he shuttled back and forth between this building and his other faculty, the History department, where he also didn't entirely fit in. He had always preferred to avoid conflict and sometimes found it challenging to navigate the rocky waters of university life with all its different groups, opposing interests, and peers who were envious of each other's successes.

Peter looked around his room. One wall was entirely covered with shelves full of books. Stacked in front of them were tidy piles of professional literature that he'd not got around to reading yet, and on top of one of those was a heap of student papers waiting to be marked. On the wall next to his desk, he had thumbtacked huge strips of wallpaper where he jotted down ideas. The result was a jumble of squiggles, arrows in various colours, diagrams, and summaries all crisscrossing over and around each other. For him, this was a way of creating order from chaos.

Three framed posters were hung above the sofa where he sat. On the left, a reproduction of Gustave Wappers' famous painting of Burgomaster Pieter van der Werff offering his body as sustenance to the starving citizens of Leiden a few weeks before the end of the Spanish siege. It had been a gift from Leiden's councillors, a token of their gratitude for Peter's services to the city. Below the image were the words known to all true Leideners: 'I have no food for you, but I know that I shall die one day. If you will be helped by my death, take this body, cut it into pieces and share it among yourselves as best you can. Then I shall be comforted.'

In the middle was a poster of *The Last Supper* by Leonardo da Vinci depicting a dramatic moment when Jesus and Judas, the latter clutching a bag of money, both reach for a piece of bread at the same time. Peter had bought it in Milan just before work began on the restoration of the fresco, during his first trip without his parents after his final exams in the summer of 1978.

And on the right was a large black-and-white photograph of Pope John Paul II on his first ride in the new, armoured Popemobile, which had been fitted with bulletproof glass.

He heard footsteps in the corridor and guessed from the click-clack sound they made that it was a woman in heels. The sound stopped every few seconds as if whoever was wearing them was pausing to read the nameplate on every door. She obviously wasn't familiar with this department. The footsteps came closer, and he saw through the frosted glass pane in his door that the woman had stopped outside

9

his office. She seemed to hesitate for a moment, then knocked timidly, as though she didn't expect to find anyone behind it at this hour.

'Come in!' he called.

The door opened to reveal a young woman with dark blonde, shoulder-length curls, and cheeks flushed pale pink. She was dressed in an elegant but slightly mumsy blouse with a bow at the collar, tight jeans, and pumps with – yes – high heels. She was clutching an oversized shoulder bag, more practical than stylish, easily big enough to hold a binder.

Peter recognised her. She was one of the students in his History of Leiden seminars. She always took notes diligently during the sessions, but she never said very much. However, the same could be said of most of his students; they were often too shy to speak, or too ill-prepared to offer anything constructive.

What was her name again? Ah, yes, Judith. Judith Cherev.

'Come in, Judith,' he said. 'What can I do for you?'

He sat up straight, like a schoolboy caught around the back of the bike shed, waving his hand in the air to disperse the smoke.

'Sorry to bother you without making an appointment first. I wanted to catch you after the seminar, but you left so quickly. I sent you an email last week. Do you remember? I'm sure you get lots of messages. It was about my dissertation; I was working on a rough draft of the research proposal.' She was still standing in the doorway, quite unassumingly, but at the same time, she had a determined look about her.

The university had recently switched to an electronic mail system. It was pointless, innovation for innovation's sake in Peter's opinion, but time would tell.

'Yes, I saw your message,' he fibbed. 'Remind me what it was about?'

He invited her to come into his office and sit down.

'So, I'm in the final year of my history degree, and I've decided to write my dissertation on the history of Judaism in Leiden. I want to focus on one man in particular, a Jewish merchant who fell under the influence of Rabbi Zevi.'

'Ah, Sabbatai Zevi, the Messiah.'

'No, he wasn't the Messiah!' she said, apparently with more ferocity than she had intended because she apologised immediately. 'Many people thought he was the Messiah, though. I want to paint a broad picture of early Judaism in the Netherlands and then focus back in on Leiden and this merchant again.'

'You're Jewish yourself?'

'Yes, that's right. I suppose the name Judith gives it away.' She gave him a little smile.

'Judith beheaded someone, didn't she? Quite a dangerous woman. Doesn't she appear in that story about—'

He was interrupted by the telephone.

Peter motioned to Judith to stay in her seat. When he walked past her to pick up the phone, he caught a faint hint of perfume that almost took his breath away. The scent seemed familiar, but he couldn't quite remember why.

'Hey, Peter, you need to get over here, quickly,' Thomas Konijnenberg said excitedly. 'We've found something incredible!'

Thomas was in charge of the day-to-day supervision of the excavation of the Roman fort Matilo on the border between Leiden and Zoeterwoude. The municipal archaeologists had been allowed to excavate the site before the land was developed into the new suburb of Roomburg. The area had been part of the Roman Empire's northern border, and relics from the period were often found there. The newly discovered remains of a Roman fort – similar to those of an early Roman army camp recently excavated in Nijmegen – were unique to the region. But Peter had never heard Thomas sound as excited as he did now.

'I'm running out of the door as we speak,' Peter joked. 'But can you give me a hint about what it is already?'

'A mask! Bronze, a visor mask, and it's in wonderful condition. It might be the most beautiful thing ever found in Germania Inferior. It's stunning. It's like a Roman soldier is looking right at you, face-to-face with history. You really have to see it for yourself. We've christened it Gordon.' He laughed.

'Gordon?' You've named it after that curly-haired crooner from Amsterdam?' Peter started singing theatrically: 'If only I could have one more moment with yooouuu.'

'Exactly. It's the spitting image of him. I'm going to give Hoogers a call. He's going to be thrilled that this has been found so close to his retirement. But come over right now, and you can see it for yourself! It's only me here. Everyone else has gone home already. They've all got the day off tomorrow for the October 3rd festival. Come over now and I'll wait for you. And there's more, Peter. There's more! That's why I'm calling you. I've found him, and I wanted you to be the first to know.'

'That's great, I... What do you mean, "There's more"? Who did you find? Do you mean—' But Thomas had already hung up.

Seconds later, Peter heard the telephone ringing in the office next door. Thomas didn't waste any time.

Peter stood for a moment with the receiver still in his hand and felt a pang of jealousy. But he couldn't complain. He didn't work in the trenches, ankle-deep in clay, so he was never going to make a find like this. The romantic notions he'd had in his youth about archaeology had never entirely left him. The idea of going on adventures like Indiana Jones ... the possibility that you might uncover a fantastic ancient treasure that had been hidden for hundreds of years.

Judith coughed.

Peter had forgotten she was there, perched on the edge of the sofa as though she might jump up at any moment, with the light falling on her hair and making it shine...

Suddenly, he remembered who she reminded him of. Israel, 1978. After he'd finished high school, he'd spent a few months working in a kibbutz. Sabrina. God, how in love he'd been with her...

'Magie Noire?' he asked. She gave him a puzzled look.

'Magie Noire, your perfume. Lancôme. That's what you're wearing, isn't it?'

She laughed delightfully. 'Yes, it is! Impressive. Not many men would know that. Are you some sort of expert?'

'It just reminds me of someone I knew a long time ago. Anyway, that phone call I just had – you know the dig at Roomburg? They've found something. They want me to go and have a look.'

She looked disappointed.

'Why don't you come with me?' he suggested. 'You can tell me more about your dissertation on the way. It shouldn't take long. And I can drop you off in town afterwards.'

She paused for a second or two, looking at him with her head cocked to one side as though she was trying to gauge his intentions. 'All right,' she said. 'I didn't have any other plans for the evening anyway. If you could give me some pointers, I might be able to finish my proposal tonight.'

Peter picked up his car keys and put on his jacket. Since he planned to return to the office to work later that evening, he left his computer running. As they walked down the corridor, Peter noticed that the light was still on in his old tutor Pieter Hoogers' office. The professor would usually have gone home by this time, but Hoogers was due to retire in two days, and he was probably dotting the i's and crossing the t's on his farewell speech.

Peter knocked on the door and opened it without waiting for a response.

Hoogers looked up, agitated, clasping the telephone receiver tightly to his chest.

'Professor Hoogers, I'm going to Matilo,' Peter told him.

'Thomas Konijnenberg called. Found a visor mask in beautiful condition.'

'Yes, yes, I know... Good, good,' Hoogers replied distractedly. 'Tell me about it later. I'm in the middle of a conversation. Come by and give me a report when you get back... I assume you will be coming back.'

He glanced past Peter at Judith and gave her a brief nod of acknowledgement. Then he turned his back to them, indicating that the conversation was over.

'He seemed a bit annoyed,' Judith whispered after Peter had quietly closed the door.

'I probably shouldn't have barged in like that. It was quite rude. Oh well. Let's put it down to excitement.'

They crossed the Witte Singel canal and headed for the car park underneath the building that housed the Modern Languages department, next to the university library.

'Is Thomas a good friend of yours?'

'Thomas? Not a friend exactly, no. We had the odd lecture together when we were students. He's a colleague of sorts, although he doesn't work for the university. We've been out for drinks a couple of times, but we have more of a professional relationship, really. He's good at networking, so I suppose you could see it more as being part of each other's networks than a friendship.'

They descended the stairs into the car park.

In the more intimate and confined environment of Peter's car, Judith's perfume was even more noticeable.

Peter closed his eyes.

'Are you okay?' Judith asked him. She was smiling.

'Oh, yes, I'm fine.' He started the car. 'So tell me about

15

your dissertation. Judaism in Leiden? Not much has been written about that yet. That could be a problem.'

'I know, but I came across some documents in the city archives that belonged to the merchant I want to look at. Letters, bills, that sort of thing. They haven't been used before, and that piqued my interest.'

'What period are we talking about?' He turned the car onto the Witte Singel, the wide, serpentine canal winding through the city centre. They drove past the observatory with its distinctive dome. The dig site was less than ten minutes' drive away.

'I found some papers belonging to this merchant, Moshe Levi. The earliest is dated 1660, and the last one is from 1666. That in itself is pretty unusual because, if you look in the archives from the sixteenth century, you'll hardly find any mention of Jews. It wasn't until the beginning of the eighteenth century that something resembling a Jewish community began to emerge in Leiden.'

'And why are you so interested in this man? It could be quite a short dissertation if you have to rely on just a handful of documents.'

'I won't only be writing about him. So little has been written about Judaism in Leiden, so I actually want my dissertation to give an overview of the development of the Jewish community in Leiden, from its earliest beginnings in the sixteenth century to the present day.'

'Do you live in the Jewish student halls on the Levendaal?'

'No,' she said. 'I live in one of the *hofjes*, the Groot Sionshof. It's one of the loveliest courtyards in Leiden.

Another student told me that one of the little almshouses was up for rent there, so I jumped at the chance to move in. I loved the idea of living in that particular courtyard because it has such a Jewish-sounding name. And now I do. It's close to the town centre too.'

'Anyway, back to your dissertation...'

'Yes, the history of Judaism in Leiden with a particular focus on Moshe Levi. But maybe that's too big for a dissertation,' she said uncertainly. 'What do you think, Meneer de Haan?'

'I – you can call me Peter, by the way – I think it might be a bit too broad, yes. You have to ask yourself what you want. You said earlier that Moshe, the merchant, was under the influence of Rabbi Zevi, right?'

'Yes. That's why Levi's correspondence stops after 1666. I think he was convinced that Zevi was the Messiah, and he sold everything and went to Turkey.'

'Then I would concentrate on that. Start your paper with the story of the Jews arriving in the Netherlands and eventually settling in Leiden. Then you can write about your merchant, which will allow you to discuss the Jews' position in society at that time: trade, how they interacted with gentiles, that sort of thing. Then you devote a chapter to Rabbi Zevi. After that, you write about your merchant who sells up and follows him, as many other European Jews did at the time. Then I think you'll have a well-defined subject that's original but still manageable enough at bachelor level. And what I especially like is that you'll be using documents that haven't been used before. You could try to get one or two articles published about it. And if you want to explore it further, you can start thinking about a PhD.'

Peter stole a sideways glance at Judith. He thought she might be blushing, but it was getting dark, and he couldn't tell for sure.

The roads were busy. The traffic was at a standstill on the Levendaal and the Hoge Rijndijk leading out of town. It was often bumper-to-bumper here at this time of day, but now the town centre was closed for Leidens Ontzet, the annual commemoration of the Spanish Siege of Leiden and the relief of the city in 1574.

After about twenty minutes of slow, stop-start progress, they finally arrived at the Roomburg construction site. It was gone six-thirty, and the place looked deserted. The only light still burning was in the large tent where the day's finds were washed, classified, and packed into crates.

The ground looked boggy, so he decided it would be wiser to leave the car parked on the side of the road. They walked over to the tent, their feet sinking into the sodden grass. It would have been difficult to find less suitable footwear for this terrain than Judith's pumps, but she seemed not to mind that the mud was ruining her shoes.

Suddenly, one of the two flaps at the front of the tent was moved aside, and a man appeared. Peter couldn't make out who it was because of the bright light behind him. Peter waved and called Thomas's name, assuming it was him. The man looked startled, froze for a second, and then ran off.

Peter started to run too.

Chapter Two

Peter reached the tent first and flung back the flap on the opening.

Inside, he found Thomas lying on the floor with what looked like a severe head injury. A pool of blood had formed next to his head. The field telephone was completely spattered with blood; it looked like it had been used as a bludgeon. The cable had been pulled out, so there was no chance of using it to call for help.

Peter knelt down next to Thomas on the dusty wooden decking that formed the floor. Thomas was breathing heavily and was clearly in a great deal of pain.

'What happened? Thomas, can you speak?'

When Judith came into the tent, her hand flew to her mouth in horror.

Thomas tried to say something, but it came out as little more than a weak murmur. His cheek was streaked with a mixture of saliva and blood, and Peter could see a sticky patch of red in his hair. They couldn't move him; who knew what other internal injuries he might have?

'Can you drive, Judith? Take my car and drive to the nearest house and ask them to call an ambulance. And the police.'

'I'm sorry... I don't drive.'

'All right, then you stay here and look after Thomas. I'll be as quick as I can. Will you be okay?'

'But what if that man comes back?' she asked anxiously. 'What should I do? You can't leave me here alone.'

'I don't think... I think that whoever did this has got what he wanted. He was about to leave just as we got here. I'll be as quick as I can. We don't have much choice.'

Judith nodded. Nothing was left of the blush that had been on her cheeks just moments ago. All the blood seemed to have drained from her face.

'All right,' she said. 'But please hurry.'

Peter was about to go outside when he spotted the bronze mask on the floor. It had to be the mask Thomas had called him about. When he'd found Thomas lying on the ground, he'd assumed that this had been a robbery related to the discovery of such a spectacular artefact. But the visor mask was still here, tossed carelessly aside as though it was of no more value than a fairground prize.

Peter picked up the mask; it felt surprisingly heavy.

The metal caught the light, giving it a strange glare except for the two dark holes for the wearer's eyes.

It was remarkable to think that it had probably been made to measure for someone two thousand years ago, that a real, living person had worn it.

'Peter!' cried Judith. 'What are you doing? This man is seriously injured. You need to hurry. Go!'

He stared at Judith for a moment without really seeming to see her.

Then he carefully put down the mask on one of the tables and went outside. The darkness seemed even blacker after the bright light inside the tent, and at first he could hardly see anything at all. He blinked a few times and started to run through the marshy grass. He landed in puddle after puddle, and the muddy water seeped into his shoes.

Peter searched his pockets for his car key then realised that he had left it in the ignition. When he reached the car, he opened the door and swore: his keyring was gone along with the car key.

What should he do? In the far distance, he saw lights in the windows of the houses on the city's outer limits.

Peter decided to run straight towards them.

'Your word is a lamp to my feet and a light to my path,' he said out loud.

Psalm 119, the longest Psalm in the Bible; he knew all 176 verses by heart. It had been years since he'd spoken them – it felt as if they were being sent to him now.

In the darkness, he stumbled on the uneven ground. His shirt was already sticking to his sweaty back, and he tried to take off his tie as he ran. His jacket fluttered and flapped behind him.

Before long, he reached a long, quiet street where a handful of houses stood, but as he approached it, he realised to his dismay that there was a ditch between the construction site and the road. It was probably too wide to jump over but going around it would take too long.

Peter took a half-hearted run at the ditch and launched himself into the air. He almost made it, but only one of his feet found purchase on the other side, causing him to lose his balance and end up waist deep in the water. He felt something sharp slice into the flesh on his shin.

He scrambled up the side of the ditch and rolled up his trouser leg, revealing a nasty gash. The oozing blood mixed with the watery mud coloured the top of his sock a reddish brown.

Lights blazed in the first house he reached, but no one answered when he rang the bell. He held down the doorbell at the next house and pounded on the door too, and then when that took too long, he banged on the window. A light came on in the hallway, and a man's voice asked who was there.

'I'm... We need to call the police...' Peter said, gasping and out of breath. 'An ambulance... There's been an accident. Someone's been injured. Please!'

He leaned forwards with his hands on his knees.

The door opened a crack. Peter tried to push it open, but it was secured with a chain. Frightened, the man slammed the door shut again.

Peter realised that his appearance wasn't exactly likely to be inspiring the man's trust and confidence.

'Sir,' he said, almost desperately now, 'there's been an accident. I had to run across the field to get here, and I ended up in the ditch. Someone's been attacked on the construction site. He needs medical help urgently.'

This time, the door opened wide. A portly man in his fifties appeared. He had a drooping moustache, and he was wearing a blazer set off with the distinctive red and white tie of the October 3rd Society. He looked Peter up and down. Whatever he saw seemed to convince him that Peter's distress was genuine.

'Uh ... you'd better come in. You can use my phone. You're in quite a state!'

The man pointed to a telephone on a side table in the hallway. Peter left a trail of dirty, wet footprints on the parquet floor. He dialled the emergency number, 06-11, and waited.

He thought back to a conversation he'd recently had with Thomas. Thomas had been raving about the convenience of having a field telephone at the excavation site. He sometimes used it on the sly to call home if he was going to be late. He'd predicted that everyone would have some sort of field telephone within the next ten or fifteen years. Eventually, a way would be found to reduce the size of their huge batteries, and the technology could be made available to the general public.

Peter had laughed and replied that he couldn't imagine a conversation being so urgent that you would need to conduct it on the street where everyone could listen in. And anyway, there were phone boxes all over town, weren't there?

But now he had to agree with Thomas. A personal telephone would have been a godsend in this case. Perhaps even a lifesaver.

The dispatcher on the other end of the line asked if he needed the police, the fire brigade or an ambulance.

'An ambulance,' Peter shouted into the phone. 'And the police. Someone's been attacked. I think he's dying. Please, come quickly!'

'What's the address?'

'The address?' Peter realised with panic that there was no address. 'It's in Leiden, on the site where they're building the new suburb. Roomburg.'

'Could you be a little more precise? Which building site is it exactly?' The woman was so perfectly calm and professional that she could have been performing a role-play as part of a job interview.

'Tell them it's the Spaarnestraat,' the man said from behind him.

'The Spaarnestraat in Leiden, near the Hoge Rijndijk. I'll be standing on the side of the road to show them the way.'

'That's an excellent idea, sir. The police and the ambulance have been notified, and they're on their way. Is the victim seriously injured?'

'I don't know. It looks serious. But I'm sorry, I have to hang up now,' Peter said, and he put the phone down.

A puddle of water had formed on the spot where he was standing. The man stared at it for a moment and then looked up at Peter.

'Don't worry about that. Go outside and wait for the ambulance. I was just about to set off for the fair.'

Peter looked at him and tried to give him a friendly-looking smile. 'Such a pity,' the man began again.

'What's a pity?'

'That they're going to build over there. I've always liked having all that wide, open space on my doorstep. But what can you do?'

'I'll wait outside,' Peter said. 'Thanks for your help.'

The man nodded and showed him out. Peter heard the chain being replaced as soon as the door was closed.

It was chilly outside, especially now that Peter was soaked from his feet to his waist and his shirt was sodden with cold sweat. He pulled his jacket a little tighter around him, but it didn't help much.

He heard sirens in the distance. That was fast! The three-tone horn of the ambulance sounded louder than the two-tone wail of the police cars.

Only now did Peter realise that he'd not given a moment's thought to Judith.

He had to stop himself from jumping over the ditch and running back to her. What if the man had come back as she'd feared? After all, he'd not left straightaway but had taken the time to remove the key from the car's ignition. It was odd, now he thought about it, that he'd not stolen the car altogether.

'God of Israel, give her strength,' he muttered.

He saw the ambulance turning into the street. Peter stood in the middle of the road and waved his arms wildly until it stopped just in front of him. Two police cars pulled up behind it.

Before the paramedic had a chance to open the passenger door, Peter was at the driver's side of the ambulance. The EMT lowered the window.

'He's not here!' Peter said urgently. 'He's on the construction site. I'll show you the way.'

The paramedic gave him a strange look, but then he jumped out of the ambulance. 'Take my seat and show my colleague how to get there. I'll sit in the back.'

He pushed open the side door and got in so that Peter could take his place in the front. The driver turned the flashing lights back on.

Peter hurriedly told them about what he and Judith had encountered at the dig site.

Fortunately, they made swift progress. The driver stopped at the edge of the construction site to assess whether he would be able to drive across the muddy field; he quickly decided that he could. The police cars followed behind them.

Peter opened the door and jumped out before the ambulance had even come to a standstill. Searing pain from his injured leg shot through his entire body.

He ran to the tent and opened the flap, prepared for the worst.

He was relieved to see that Judith was still there, and apparently still unharmed. She was sitting on the floor with her legs outstretched, cradling Thomas's head in her lap. Together, the two of them looked like a real-life pietà. A professional photographer could not have lit the scene more dramatically. She gently stroked his hair with one hand. Peter felt a fleeting pang of jealousy, which he knew was patently ridiculous.

She looked up at him helplessly with tears in her eyes.

'His breathing is so weak. I don't think he's going to make it.'

The ambulance crew came into the tent and took over.

They carefully lifted Thomas's head so that Judith could get up. One of the paramedics quickly assessed him while his colleague left and returned not long afterwards with a stretcher. Thomas, moaning weakly, was lifted onto it with great care.

Judith fell into Peter's arms, and he held her tightly, breathing in the scent of her hair and the perfume that brought back memories of Sabrina even in this awful situation. In the departure hall at Ben Gurion Airport, he and Sabrina had stood wrapped in each other's arms for perhaps as long as an hour, holding on until the very last moment. The final call for boarding had already been announced. Then, one last kiss. Their last kiss ever, as it would turn out.

Two police officers entered the tent, accompanied by an older man who had an air of weariness about him. Somewhat incongruously, he was wearing a red and white October 3rd scarf around his neck.

Following behind them was a younger, eager-looking man who acted as though he had somehow just stepped into an episode of a thrilling television series. Peter and Judith told them what had happened. They weren't able to give a description of the man who had run away. When the older officer pressed them to try to remember, they almost started to doubt whether it *had* been a man.

When Peter told the officer that his keys had been stolen from his car, Judith gave him an anxious sideways look.

'But how will we get home?' she asked.

'Don't worry,' the older officer reassured her. 'We'll take you home. But first, we need to call in the CSI team so they can collect the forensic evidence. Although I'm afraid they won't find very much. There'll have been too many people stomping around here today, no doubt. But with a bit of luck, they'll be able to get something from that phone.'

He clapped his notebook shut and put it away. His colleague had gone outside.

The police officer rocked back and forth on the balls of his feet. Then his eye fell on the bronze mask on the table. He picked it up then quickly realised that there might be fingerprints on it and put it down again. 'This is beautiful. I can't believe they didn't steal it!'

His colleague returned and reported that the forensics team was on its way. The senior officer told Peter and Judith to ask his colleagues to take them home in the other car. The two detectives would stay behind and wait for the crime scene investigators.

Judith and Peter went outside and approached the police car. The two officers inside had apparently already been given instructions.

'Where would you like to go?' one of them asked.

'I live in the Groot Sionshof,' Judith said, 'but it will be hard to get to because of the fair.' She thought for a moment and pointed at Peter. 'I'll go wherever he's going.' Then, so quietly that only Peter could hear it, she said, 'I'd rather not be alone just now.'

He nodded.

'I live on the Boerhaavelaan,' said Peter, 'near the Leidse Hout. I think it should be easy enough to get to.'

They got into the back of the car.

As they drove away, Peter looked out of the rear window. What sort of crazy story had he got himself into?

The car bumped over the rough terrain. The radio was tuned to what must have been a local station. Who else would play the song '3 Oktober' by the Leiden parody band, Rubberen Robbie?

Judith sank back into the seat and leaned into him. He assumed that she'd done so because she was tired, but then she reached into her bag and took something out.

'Besides, I wanted to show you this,' she whispered. The rosy glow had returned to her cheeks.

On her lap was a small ivory casket.

Chapter Three

Extracts from the diary of Thomas Konijnenberg

Monday, July 1, 1996

I t is so good to be back here in this place where I always feel so at home. I'm looking forward to the next three months, away from the bureaucratic red tape at the office, three months of doing exactly what I became an archaeologist for: spending my days ankle-deep in the wet clay, excavating the past, layer by layer...

These feelings are hard to explain to an outsider. There's an almost zen-like concentration that comes effortlessly when you're focused on carefully scraping away soil or sand. A constant hope that all that scraping will reveal something spectacular. And the possibility that it actually will. Knowing that, bit by bit, you're forming a clearer picture of the lives of real people, people whose flesh and blood have long since turned to dust, but who once lived their lives here with all their hopes and desires, their failures and sorrows. Two thousand years from now, will someone else look at our lives in this way, wonder what was going on in our heads?

I still cling on to some of those romantic ideas about this work, even though the thrills are often in short supply when you're stuck in a draughty tent, rinsing off your finds with numb hands at the end of a long day. Especially when those finds might, at best, be nothing more than slightly larger-than-usual chunks of an amphora or plate.

But it's not just about the finds, of course. It's also about working out where the fort's boundaries were, solving the puzzle of how each space was used, and so much more.

Soon, this year's team will all be together for the first time. Some of them were here last year, but there are new faces too, mostly archaeology students hoping to get some practical experience and earn a bit of extra money.

We have until the first week of October – Friday, 4 October, to be exact. Although I'm not counting on many of us being here during that last week. The students will be back in lectures by then, and most of the others will want to go into town to celebrate the Relief of Leiden. (I wonder what would happen if the giant Ferris wheel were to be dug up centuries from now by people who'd never seen one before? What would they think it was? Some sort of giant machine for a ritual, where initiates sat in its gondolas to experience the eternal cycle of life?)

Friday, July 5

The first week has flown by. Everything aches! But it's not like I wasn't expecting that. I'm looking forward to cycling home and taking a long, hot shower. Although, no matter how much I scrub, I never quite manage to get all of the dust out of my pores. I'll have a permanent crescent of black under my nails for the next few months too, but it's all part of the deal. Suus teases me about it all the time.

We have a good team again this year. Serious, but not overly so. Focused, driven. They get along with each other well, from what I can tell. The couple who met at last year's dig will celebrate their first year together this summer, which is just fantastic. We've got a young German man joining us this year, Herman. Bit of a loner. Joins in, talks to everyone, but doesn't seem to actually connect with anyone. He was swaggering about quite cockily last Sunday because of Germany's win in the Euros, but I'm not sure that even that was genuine.

Friday, July 12

Just completed this week's dig report. There are a few minutes left before our traditional boozy Friday afternoon get-together starts. After that, I'll be going home for the weekend. So I'll use this time to jot down a few personal notes. We're concentrating mostly on the village next to the army camp again this year, so we're uncovering everyday objects that belonged to the non-Romans who lived there. It looks like the village was populated by a colourful mix of traders and craftsmen, judging from our finds, which have included many things that clearly weren't originally from this region, like glass, hairpins, and beads.

Thursday, July 25

Today has been an extraordinary day. We found a burial ground next to where the village must have been. It falls just outside the area where we officially have permission to dig, but I think I can defend it to the commission.

All the clichés about the thrill you get when you think you're about to find something big – the dry mouth, your breath catching in your throat, the pleasant tightness in your chest – they're all true.

My excitement was evident to everyone, but no one could have guessed what I was really excited about.

I've talked to Peter a few times about my theories. He always listens to them with a sort of mild amusement. Ever the scientist, he pokes as many holes in my argument as he possibly can, but eventually, even he's had to admit that there might be something in it...

I'm going to explore the site myself when nobody else is around. Suus is used to it by now. I already know the look she'll give me when I tell her I want to spend my weekends at the dig too: the head cocked to one side, the narrowed eyes, the smile. And then a wink to let me know I have her permission.

Sunday, August 25

That German man, Herman, is really starting to get on my nerves. He's more of a hindrance than a help. He came to 'keep me company' again today without being asked, so I had to be careful not to reveal what I was really looking for. I got him to help me with the tedious tasks still left from Friday, like cleaning last week's finds. Obviously, I would rather have left that until tomorrow. This isn't the first time I've lost precious time because of his unwanted assistance.

Monday, September 2

It's much quieter around here now that the students have all gone back to university. Only Jantien, Theo, Ronald, and I are still here – and, of course, Herman, who apparently has nothing better to do.

We only have one month left before it's all over for this year. I know there's another digging season next year, but I'm closer now than I've ever been, I'm sure of it... The commission has turned a blind eye when we've gone outside our assigned site to excavate the burial ground this time, but I've heard through the grapevine that they won't be so accommodating next year. So it's now or never.

Imagine what might happen if I actually find his grave! Part of biblical history will have to be rewritten. How will the Catholic Church respond? What would be left of the mandate the pope inherited from Saint Peter if Saint Peter's grave was actually here in Leiden? Because isn't every pope considered to be the direct heir of Saint Peter, upon whose tomb the Basilica was built in Rome?

Friday, September 27

My frustration and anxiety are starting to take on epic proportions.

We have just one week to go before this excavation season ends. We've more or less started to dismantle the whole operation over the last few days.

I'll be staying here tonight, just as I did last weekend and the weekend before that. I'll be here until the last possible minute, working by flashlight if I have to. After all, Carter discovered Tutankhamun's tomb just before he was supposed to return to England, didn't he?

Sunday, September 29

I think the combination of exhaustion and excitement might be making me hallucinate. I'm convinced that someone is watching me constantly. Am I losing my mind? Last night, as I tossed and turned on the uncomfortable cot in the tent, I dreamt that a Christ-like figure spoke to me: 'Thomas, Thomas, why do you persecute me?'

Wednesday, October 2

Great excitement! Theo has found a visor mask! It's in fantastic condition. A truly incredible find, but I'm struggling to swallow my disappointment.

We opened the champagne that we were supposed to be keeping until Friday. My frustration aside, this has to be the prize find of all the excavations at Roomburg, and it will be a fantastic showpiece for the National Museum of Antiquities. I can already see it in its display cabinet, gleaming under the spotlights.

I'll make one last attempt this afternoon when everyone has gone home.

5:30pm – What has just happened might almost make me believe in God... I'm lost for words. It's the last day, only me left on the site. Went to the burial ground where we'd been digging random trenches in the hope of finding something. Lots of human bone fragments, shards of earthenware – grave goods probably – but found nothing as spectacular as a sword or helmet. It's likely that only commoners were buried there.

Against my better judgment, I went back to the site. I took the long, sharp stick that I use to prod the ground to see if it hits anything. A primitive method, but an effective one.

I spent most of the morning stabbing it into the earth in the sides of the trenches we'd dug, without success. I was about to give up, but I pushed the tip of the stick into the soil one last time, not really expecting anything to come of it. I felt it hit something hard. I tried again a little further along: same result. Prodding higher and lower, I determined the shape and size of what was hidden beneath the surface.

It could have been a big rock, of course, but that didn't seem very likely to me. The dimensions seemed too uniform for that.

I tried to dig it out with my hands, but my fingers scrabbled uselessly in the clay. I ran back to the tent to get a trowel, a spade, and the wheelbarrow. I was overcome with a sudden fear that someone would beat me to it – absurd, obviously, because there was nobody but me left on site.

When I'd collected the tools I needed, I ran back and found everything just as I'd left it: the stick lying next to the trench and the holes in the trench wall indicating that whatever lay hidden there was about fifty to sixty centimetres long and about forty centimetres high.

I removed the top layer of soil with the spade, and, as I'd suspected, it revealed a rectangular piece of stone that looked a lot like it might be a lid of some sort. Once I'd worked out its exact size, I was able to dig out the sides with the trowel. As soon as I'd dug it free, I recognised it as an ossuary, a stone chest in which the exhumed bones of the dead were collected a year after burial. Whoever it belonged to, they must have had someone, a companion perhaps, who could take care of this for them.

The earth seemed reluctant to let go of the treasure that it had been hiding for nearly two thousand years, and it took quite a bit of effort to work the chest free. In my haste, I didn't see if there were any inscriptions on it, but the sides were still caked with soil and mud, of course. I put my find in the barrow, and then, out of nowhere, I started to cry. Whether from relief or nerves, I'm not sure.

It wasn't easy to push the wheelbarrow back across the uneven ground to the tent with the heavy stone ossuary on top. It was still broad daylight, and anyone could have seen me walking over that wide, open terrain. I hoped and prayed that no one would come to the site. It couldn't have been more than ten or fifteen minutes before I was safely back in the shelter of the tent, but it felt like it had taken hours. My back was drenched with sweat, and my breaths were rasping.

I filled a bucket with water and cleaned the soil from the chest, first with a stiff brush and then with a softer one. I worked slowly, trying to calm my breathing and prepare myself for a disappointment. I cleaned one long side of the chest as well as I could, then I started on the other side, where I uncovered something that looked like an inscription. Intriguingly, it was clear that it had been carved by an untrained hand. Now, I forgot all about being careful – I rushed to remove the dirt that had hardened onto it over many centuries.

I don't think I'll ever be able to describe how I felt when I saw the first rough letters of the inscription. I was filled with a sudden regret that there wasn't a single person here with me to witness the moment. 'What do you see, Mister Konijnenberg?' that person would ask when they saw the astonishment on my face. 'Wonderful things,' I would stammer.

I stared at the chest in front of me. It was still filthy and covered in earth, but the area around the inscription was scrubbed clean, and the effect was amazingly dramatic, as if a light had been deliberately cast on that particular spot. The letters could easily have been deciphered by a grammar school student who was only just mastering the Greek alphabet:

πετρος κεφας

Petros Kefas!

I'm going to call Peter. And I suppose I should call Hoogers and tell him about the visor mask. He'll be put out if he finds out that he wasn't one of the first to know. I wouldn't want to do anything that would risk spoiling the good relationship we have.

Chapter Four

Peter looked at the casket and then back at Judith, dumbfounded. She put it back in her bag and then stared into the distance with an expression that Peter thought could equally be either shame or excitement.

The casket was about twenty-five by twenty centimetres in size and about five centimetres high. Peter couldn't tell which part was the top and which was the bottom, and at first glance, he couldn't see where it might open; it appeared to have been hermetically sealed in some way. It looked like a thick, lustrously polished, rectangular tile.

Peter tried to swallow the sudden annoyance rising inside him. Removing artefacts from an excavation site! That was outrageous! It went against the basic rules of archaeology, and of decency too. How many precious finds had already been lost because someone had pocketed them and sold them on the black market for enormous sums of money?

They sat in silence for the rest of the journey, but luckily, it didn't take long. The police officers used a bus lane for a large part of the route, sailing past the long line of slow-moving cars trying to get into the city. They soon reached his street and pulled up outside Peter's apartment block, a low, three-storey building that took up about a quarter of the Boerhaavelaan. The entire complex was owned by Leiden University, and all the residents were connected to the university in one way or another.

Peter tried to get out of the car, but the door wouldn't open. One of the officers looked over his shoulder and said, 'Child lock.'

The officer got out and opened the nearside door to let Judith out. Only then was Peter's door opened. Peter apologised for the damp patch he had left on the back seat, but the officer dismissed his apology with a wave of his hand.

'My colleague has taken your details already, hasn't he?'

'Yes,' Peter answered, and he was suddenly overcome by a feeling of utter exhaustion. 'I'll come to the station tomorrow anyway to report the theft of my car keys. My head's not up to it just now, if I'm honest.'

'I can imagine. There's only a skeleton crew at the station tonight anyway. We need all our officers in town. Things can get out of hand on the 2nd of October.' He sounded like he was actually looking forward to it. He got back in the car, and the two police officers drove away down the street.

The noise from the funfair was loud, even from here, but they were only three or four hundred metres away from it as the crow flies. Peter looked up at the apartments and noticed that all the windows were dark. It looked like his neighbours had gone out for the evening.

He fished around in his pocket for his house key and unlocked the lobby door. Inside, he opened his letterbox as usual and took out the NRC *Handelsblad* and his mail. When he reached the stairs in the hallway, he stopped so abruptly that Judith almost bumped into him. He turned around.

'You shouldn't have taken that casket, Judith. For a start, you can't just remove things from a dig. But a crime was committed there, and that casket could be evidence. I didn't want to make things difficult for you in the car just now, but we're going to go to the police station together shortly and hand it in.'

Judith sighed and attempted a smile.

'I understand why you're angry, Peter, but I've not been completely honest with you. I couldn't tell you earlier because I was scared that the police would hear.'

'Tell me what?'

'Just before you came back, Thomas started to come round. He was so weak, but he opened his eyes wide, and then he managed to lift his arm up and point at the roof of the tent. So I climbed onto a table to see if something was hidden up there. Thomas closed his eyes and put his arm back down again then, as though he felt reassured that I'd figured out what he meant. I felt around up there, and I found this casket, Peter. It was on the ridgepole. I don't know how, but I knew right then that it was something to do with the robbery, and that Thomas had deliberately hidden it up there. When I heard the ambulance coming, I panicked and put the casket in my bag without thinking.

Then, when I heard you calling my name, I relaxed a bit. So I sat back down on the floor with Thomas's head on my lap. You came in with the ambulance crew and the police, and I thought, I'll tell him later, I'll show it to him then.'

'But even so...' Peter said, still annoyed. 'That was no reason not to hand it over there and then. Now we're stuck with it. I'm going to call the police later and explain everything, and that will be the end of it.'

'Listen...' Judith began, but she didn't finish her sentence.

Peter turned away, and they climbed the stairs to the first floor without speaking. He could hear his cat meowing before he'd put his front door key in the lock.

'Oh, you have a cat!' Judith said, glad to be able to switch to a lighter subject.

'Yes, I do. He's called Oedipuss. I thought the name was brilliantly original at the time, but it turns out that quite a lot of other Dutch people think so too.' They went inside, and Oedipuss wrapped himself around Peter's legs. Then he ran into the kitchen and waited next to his empty food bowl. Peter filled the bowl with dry cat food and refreshed the water. Then, out of habit, he put the chain on the front door before hanging up his jacket.

'If you don't mind, I'm going to take a shower,' he said, 'and put on some dry clothes. Then we'll talk about what to do next. Make yourself comfortable in the living room. I won't be long.'

His bedroom floor was littered with piles of clothes where he'd dropped them after getting undressed. A single duvet was rumpled on the large double bed that filled most

44

of the room. Peter rummaged through the piles on the floor to find a collection of things that resembled an outfit and carried them to the bathroom. When he looked through the glass partition wall in the hall, he saw Judith perched on the edge of the couch, fidgeting with her bag. She had put the casket in the middle of the dining table. The lamp over the table was the only light in the room that she'd switched on. It illuminated the casket like an artefact in a museum.

In the bathroom, he kicked off his shoes and stripped off his wet clothes. The hot shower began to restore his mood. He tipped his head back and let the water stream over his face. On closer inspection, the wound on his leg was less serious than he had thought. It was an ugly scratch, but the bleeding had already stopped.

Why on earth did she take that casket? he thought with irritation. As if the situation wasn't bad enough. She should have just left the damn thing where it was or given it to the police. On the other hand, if Thomas had wanted that, he wouldn't have shown her where the casket was...

He dried himself off and got dressed. Normally, he would have walked back to his bedroom naked and put his clothes on there, but he could hardly do that now with Judith in the apartment. That wasn't something he'd ever had to consider when Hanna lived here. It had already been two years since she'd left. He still had a bin bag full of her clothes that he'd promised to take to the charity shop.

When he was dressed, he went back into the living room where he found Oedipuss curled up on Judith's lap. Judith was stroking him and tickling his chin.

'I wouldn't mind getting cleaned up myself,' Judith said.

Peter apologised for not having suggested it. Her trousers were caked in clay and blood. There was even blood on her hands and a muddy red smudge on her forehead.

'Of course, go ahead. I'll get you a towel. Actually, I have some clothes here that belonged to my ex. I think you're about her size.'

He found the bag of clothes and tipped it out onto the middle of the living room floor. He'd vaguely hoped that they would still smell like Hanna, but he was disappointed. All he could smell was a musty cloud of dust.

Here was the blouse she had worn so often in Greece. *The one that I gave her*, he thought.

He handed it to Judith, along with a pair of jeans and a pair of stockings. Judith went to the bathroom.

Peter stuffed the rest of the clothes back in the bag and put it in the corner of the room. He picked up the casket and realised that it was heavier than he had expected for something so small. Holding it close to his ear, he shook it but heard nothing. There was a faint line running around the circumference of the casket, but he still couldn't see where it might open.

He put the casket back on the table and stood indecisively for a moment. Then he remembered that he needed to call the police about his car. Thomas's attacker had probably stolen the key, so they would have to process the vehicle for evidence before giving it back. Peter wanted to know what would happen to it afterwards. The police couldn't just leave it unattended on the side of the road when someone else had the key.

There was no chance now of going back to his office to work this evening. And tomorrow he planned to go and see Thomas in the AZL, the university hospital.

Peter heard Judith turn the shower on. The bathroom door was slightly ajar, and he stood next to it, listening to the water splash onto the tiles as Judith softly hummed a tune.

He briskly turned around and went back to the kitchen where he poured himself a whisky. He added a couple of ice cubes to the tumbler, and they tinkled pleasantly as he rolled the whisky around the glass. He sniffed the peaty aroma and took a sip.

Thomas must have had a good reason for showing Judith where the casket was. He would have had other, more immediate concerns on his mind, given what had just happened to him. Making sure that nobody else got their hands on the casket must have been vitally important to him.

Of course, what they could do, Peter thought, was open the casket first to see what was inside and then hand it in to the police. Maybe that was the best option. They could tell Thomas if they found anything, and then give the casket to the police for further investigation. But if they were going to open it, they should do it at the institute, where they could use the low-oxygen cabinet that his colleague Verbeek had constructed that allowed him to work with old documents. Whatever was inside this casket, it hadn't been exposed to the air outside it for two thousand years, so they needed to be very careful. Verbeek's cabinet resembled an incubator with two long-sleeved gloves on the inside attached to holes in the glass casing. A camera was mounted above it so that the documents inside it could be photographed.

Peter heard the shower being turned off.

He walked back to the living room and glanced briefly at the bathroom door on the way. He could see Judith drying her hair through the frosted glass window in the door. Shortly afterwards, she emerged with a towel wrapped around her hair.

Peter held his breath. Hanna's blouse and Hanna's jeans... It was as if Hanna herself had just walked into the room.

It was only now that Peter realised what a beautiful face Judith had. It had been hidden behind her long hair, but now he could see her properly: a sprinkling of freckles on her cheeks, and bright green eyes beneath neatly tweezed brows. With those sharply defined cheekbones, there was something Slavic in her features. He finished his whisky and felt his annoyance flare up again.

But Judith beat him to the punch. 'Okay,' she said. 'You're right. I shouldn't have done it.'

Peter smiled and nodded.

'But there was more to it than that. And now I need you to listen while I tell you everything because I didn't get the chance to earlier.'

She walked past him and sat down on the sofa. Peter sat in the armchair opposite her.

'So Thomas was staring at the casket, and he pointed to where it was, but just before he lost consciousness again, he mumbled something as well. I couldn't hear him very well, but it sounded like "Peter, Pt... Pss..." I assumed he meant you. That this casket might have been meant for you.'

'So it wasn't about the mask at all? That wasn't actually why he called me?'

'Apparently, it wasn't about the mask for whoever attacked him either. He just left it there.'

'And he said my name?'

'Like I said, it sounded like: "Peter, Pt..." At least, it started with a P, and I heard a T.'

'That's quite mysterious. Well, I was planning to visit him tomorrow anyway. Hopefully, he'll have regained consciousness by then, and I can ask him what he meant. I might call the hospital later and see how he's doing.'

'I'm absolutely certain he didn't want the casket ending up in anyone else's hands. Why not wait until you've spoken to him before you call the police and hand it in? I'm sure he'll be well enough to talk to you by tomorrow, won't he? What if you gave it to the police tonight and that messed up whatever Thomas was planning?'

Peter thought it over. 'That's a good point. I was thinking about trying to open it first. My colleague has built a special low-oxygen cabinet that he uses to examine old documents and take photos without damaging them. But I think your idea is more sensible.'

Judith visibly relaxed, and Peter felt a sense of relief too. He stood up and went over to the dining table. Judith came over and stood beside him.

Peter picked up the ivory casket and asked Judith to look at it with him. She peered intently at it with her face close to his. Just as Peter had done earlier, she noticed the thin seam running around the outside.

Judith straightened up. 'I should head home. It's not like we can do anything more tonight.'

'No, no, stay awhile. I'll make us something to eat, a sandwich or something. Stay and have supper with me.'

Judith tilted her head to the side and thought about it.

'You need to eat anyway. Come on.'

She relented, and they went back to the kitchen where a small table with two chairs was set up in front of the window. Next to the window was a door leading to a small balcony at the back of the apartment. Peter never used it, except as a convenient spot for Oedipuss's litter tray.

Judith put on her stockings and shoes, which she had apparently cleaned up in the bathroom.

A short while later, as they sat eating supper at the table with steaming cups of tea in front of them, Peter started to unwind a little. 'The dig at Roomburg is fascinating, you know,' he said. 'The Roman Empire's northern border ran along there two thousand years ago. It followed the Rhine from roughly where Katwijk is now all the way to Germany. But this area where we are now wasn't actually controlled by the Romans in those days. This area belonged to the Batavi, or the Cananefates, to be precise.'

'Ah, hence the Latin name for Leiden? Lugdunum Batavorum, right?'

'No, actually. That's what everyone thinks, but the real Lugdunum was Katwijk. Leiden took the name Lugdunum later and added "Batavorum" to it. That's just cod Latin. Historically speaking, it's nonsense. Anyway, there were other places in the Roman Empire called Lugdunum, like Lyon in France.'

He picked up his cup of tea, wrapped his hands around it, then blew across the top before taking a sip. 'But where Thomas and his team are excavating, there was a Roman *castellum*, a fort, called Matilo. There were similar forts along the length of the Rhine, built at exactly the right distance for them to communicate with each other using beacons. They were clever, the Romans. And now, the local authority is planning to preserve the entire space that the original fort occupied, which will be fantastic. There are even plans to put up some earthen walls to mark out where it was.'

'And has much been found there yet?'

'Lots of the usual things. Pots, pans, arrowheads, pieces of pottery. And the mask that Thomas called me about. But that's not been the main aim of the dig. What they're actually interested in is determining the exact site where the fort was, working out its size and layout and how many people were likely to have been stationed there. And they were hoping to find traces of the Batavian Revolt.'

'Ah, right. That was in AD 70, right?' Judith seemed pleased she was able to contribute something to the conversation at last. 'Although, that's pretty much all I know about it.'

'Yes, that's right. There was a major uprising here in this area. The Cananefates crossed the Rhine near where Valkenburg is now, and they attacked the Romans. They took them completely by surprise. It appears that they'd had some sort of tacit agreement to leave each other alone.

They traded with each other, and there were even young Cananefates serving in the Roman army. In any case, they respected each other's territory – until the revolt. The Cananefates left a trail of destruction behind them; they burned many Roman forts, including Matilo. But the Romans hit back hard, and eventually, they crushed the rebellion. The forts were rebuilt, and everything was peaceful for the next two hundred years.'

'Should I be taking notes, professor?'

Peter smiled. 'Sorry. I'm fascinated by all this stuff, so I get carried away sometimes. Let me tell you the rest, though... From about AD 250 onwards, Roman power slowly but surely crumbled, and increasingly, Germanic tribes crossed the border to plunder the wealthy villas on this side of it. And of course, the Roman Empire itself was torn apart by all sorts of internal disputes. The area we know as Leiden disappeared into the mists of time, as we historians say, for many, many years. It wasn't until around 1100 that another settlement developed, more or less along where the Breestraat is now. The Counts of Holland took up residence in the area, and a church was built, which was the predecessor of the Pieterskerk that stands there today.'

'Well, thank you for a very informative history of Leiden in a nutshell.'

'But there's another thing. Thomas was a bit cryptic about it, but I got the impression that he was actually looking for something else, something that wasn't specified in the project brief.'

'What was he looking for?'

'He didn't want to say too much about it,' Peter said. 'But he hinted at—'

Peter's doorbell rang, loud and piercing. Both were startled by the harsh disruption of the peaceful atmosphere in the apartment.

Peter went to the intercom and asked who was there.

'Good evening. Meneer De Haan?'

'That's right.'

'This is the police,' said a tinny voice. 'I understand that your car keys were removed from your vehicle this evening without your consent. Is that correct, sir?'

Peter couldn't help laughing at the policeman's formal tone. It sounded like he was reading the words from a form. Peter detected a slight Teutonic accent.

'That's correct.'

'Then I have some good news for you, sir. Your keys have been recovered from the immediate vicinity of your car. Would you be so kind as to allow me to come in? Then I can inform you of the appropriate procedure.'

'Yes, all right.' Peter said and pressed a button to open the entry door downstairs.

'The police,' he told Judith, who had come over to stand next to him. 'They've found my car keys. What a relief. I'll just put my shoes on. I, or we, might need to go with him to pick the car up. That's going above and beyond, isn't it, coming all the way over here?'

There was a knock on the apartment door.

As Peter moved to open it, the person on the other side rammed it with his shoulder as if he was trying to knock

Peter down. But the chain on the door was strong enough to hold the door back.

In the seconds before Peter managed to wrestle the door closed again, Judith caught a glimpse of the man behind it.

'That's not a policeman at all,' she hissed. 'He's wearing normal clothes.'

'What do you want?' Peter shouted through the door.

'Meneer De Haan, open the door,' said the man. His voice was chillingly calm. 'Let's just have a chat, and I can explain it to you. Open up. I believe you have something that doesn't belong to you.'

'Go away!' Peter yelled. 'Leave now, or I'll call the police.'

'Sir, you have no idea what you're dealing with here. No idea! Just hand it over, and we'll forget this little misunderstanding.'

Peter gave Judith a questioning look, and she shook her head emphatically. She went back into the living room, took the casket from the table, and put it back in her bag. Then she put on her coat and handed Peter his jacket.

It had gone quiet on the other side of the door. Peter and Judith both held their breath. Was the man still there or had he gone?

Then they heard two sharp, deafening bangs that shattered the lock. The man hurled himself at the door again with his full weight, using more force than he had in his initial attempt. The screw holding the chain onto the door frame was sticking loosely out of the wood.

Judith looked at Peter with wide eyes. She curled her fingers tightly around the handles of her bag.

Peter grabbed her hand, led her to the balcony at the back of the apartment, closed the door behind him and blocked it with a broom. Then he climbed over the railing and slid down on the ledge, holding onto a rail with one hand. He jumped and landed in the dense bushes two and a half meters below. The impact sent a sharp pain through the wound on his leg.

What kind of crazy situation had he got himself into?

By now, Judith had climbed over the railing too. She threw her bag down to Peter, then she hung from the edge of the balcony and let go. She landed well, losing her balance for just a second before Peter caught her. He looked up and saw the intruder in his kitchen.

The man, who had pulled his hood over his head to obscure his face, caught sight of Peter and Judith and began to push frantically at the balcony door.

'Come on!' Peter shouted, and they started to run.

Peter looked back and saw that the man had given up trying to open the door, and he had apparently decided that shooting his way through it would be too risky. The man turned around and left the kitchen.

Judith and Peter were swallowed up by the darkness.

Chapter Five

They ran towards the Leidse Hout, a large park on the edge of the city. Their assailant would no doubt run around the apartment building and soon be on their heels.

'The police station, Peter,' Judith said raggedly. 'We need to report this.'

'No!' Peter shouted. 'No, we can't do that!'

'Why not? Someone broke into your apartment. He fired a gun!'

Peter stopped. 'And what then?' he asked, sounding hopeless. 'What would I tell them? That we took an ancient casket from a crime scene where a man had been seriously injured? Do you know what would happen to me if that got out? What it would do to my reputation? I can already see the headline: "Leiden University Archaeology lecturer steals Roomburg find". Even if we could explain everything, that headline would stick to me forever. But more importantly: Thomas wouldn't be keeping that casket secret without good cause. He hid it up there on the ridge pole for a reason. Who knows what sort of trouble we might be landing him in by going to the police? Not to mention what it might do to his reputation. But come on, we need to keep going.'

'Okay, Peter, we won't go to the police. But what do we do now? Where can we go? There's a madman with a gun chasing us.'

'Let's...' Peter said, thinking quickly. 'There's only one person who can help us. We'll go to the AZL. Let's hope Thomas has come round already. Maybe he can tell us what's going on.'

Without another word, they set off again, running past the Diaconessenhuis general hospital and the Visser 't Hooft Lyceum and towards the grand houses on the Rijnsburgerweg. They glanced back occasionally, but it didn't look like they were being followed.

Feeling safe enough to slow down, they stopped running and started to walk, although they still kept up a brisk pace.

They crossed the Rijnsburgerweg and passed the Faculty of Social Sciences, which students still called 'Building 5', the name it had had when it was still part of the AZL hospital.

'What time is it?' Peter asked.

'Almost half-past eight. Do you think he'll still be allowed visitors?'

'If we're lucky, yes. Visiting hours are from seven to nine, I think. But we're almost there. Look, there it is already.'

The brightly lit, cream-coloured building was located

behind the recently rebuilt Central Station. An enormous, long expanse of lawn spread out in front of the hospital.

Inside, an electronic information board in the hospital's entrance hall told them that visiting hours were indeed from seven to nine.

Peter went to the information desk.

'Excuse me, could you help me?' he asked.

The receptionist, a matronly lady, gave him a friendly smile. 'Of course. What can I do for you?'

'I'm looking for Thomas Konijnenberg. He was brought in tonight with a head injury.'

'I'm terribly sorry, but I can't give out information about our patients.' The smile was gone. She looked at him with a combination of surprise and mild irritation that he wasn't aware of this rule.

'I understand, but it's—'

'It's really quite urgent,' Judith jumped in. 'Meneer Konijnenberg was the victim of a crime tonight. We found him after the attack, and we're very worried about him.'

'That may well be, mevrouw, but I still can't give you any information. It's simply not allowed.' She folded her arms, ready to parry any further attacks on her professional ethics.

'Is there anyone else we can talk to? A doctor or someone else who can tell us something?' Peter asked.

The receptionist seemed to thaw slightly. 'What's your relationship to the victim?'

'He's a colleague.'

She frowned theatrically.

'I work at the university, and he's leading the

59

archaeological dig in Roomburg. We sometimes work together. It's... He called me and asked me to come to the dig site, and when we got there, we found him lying in a pool of blood. He'd been attacked. We called the police and the ambulance, and they brought him here. We just want to know how he's doing.'

She shook her head.

'I'm sorry. I'm sure you're telling me the truth, but I can't give you any information if you aren't a close family member. Strictly speaking, I can't even tell you if he's actually here.'

Peter heaved a deep sigh and turned to Judith, defeated. Just then, the detective he had met in Thomas's tent came into the entrance hall as he talked to a doctor walking beside him.

Judith noticed him too and saw an opportunity. Without another word, she strode up to the detective as Peter followed behind her.

The detective looked a little irritated when Judith interrupted their conversation, but quickly recognised her, and his expression softened.

Peter joined them. 'Can you tell us how Thomas Konijnenberg is doing?' he asked.

'And you are?' the doctor asked.

'These are the people who found Meneer Konijnenberg tonight and called us. Things might have turned out much worse for him if it hadn't been for them.'

The doctor hesitated for a moment. 'I can reassure you that his condition is stable. But I can't tell you any more than that.'

'Could we see him for a minute or two?' Judith asked.

'That will be difficult,' the doctor said.

'Not least because he's not well enough to talk yet,' said the detective. 'I came here to see if he could tell us anything, but I'm going to have to come back tomorrow.'

'If we could just have a little look at him, just a peek from around a corner,' Judith said plaintively. 'It was so awful, finding him in the tent like that. I...' Her voice trembled.

The detective looked imploringly at the doctor, who smiled and narrowed his eyes a little.

'All right. I'll make an exception, but only because the man probably owes his life to you. I'll have someone go with you, and you can have a quick look at him from around the corner. Meneer Konijnenberg is in a separate, secure ward where he's being well guarded.'

Relieved, Judith and Peter shook hands with the detective who saluted them with an odd little tap on his forehead. They followed the doctor to the reception desk, where he had a conversation with the lady sitting at the computer. She picked up the phone, and shortly afterwards, a security guard came marching towards them.

The doctor gave him some instructions. After Peter and Judith had shown the guard their IDs, they said goodbye to the doctor and followed the guard down the hall.

Judith gave Peter a furtive, worried look. He put his hand on her shoulder and kept it there until they arrived at the secure wing. The guard announced his arrival on an intercom. He swiped a card through a slot next to the door, and a green light flashed.

The automatic doors opened noiselessly, and a wide corridor stretched out in front of them, similar to the ones they had just walked through. Gleaming linoleum reflected the light from the fluorescent strips hanging from the ceiling in a regimented line.

Stationed outside a door at the end of the corridor was a police officer sitting on a chair.

He stood up as they approached, making his gun holster bump against his thigh and the chain on his handcuffs jangle.

The man who had accompanied them briefed the policeman in an almost overbearing tone, then took his leave with a tap on his cap.

'I believe that you are the individual who found Meneer Konijnenberg at the scene of the crime this evening. Would that be correct, sir?' the officer asked officiously.

Peter tried and failed to stifle a chuckle. Do they teach them how to talk in this pompous way at the Police Academy? he wondered as he tried to compose himself.

'That is correct,' he replied.

The police officer nodded. 'An initial examination of Meneer Konijnenberg has shown that he sustained no injuries except for blunt force trauma to his head,' he explained. 'He appears to have quite a severe concussion, but he's expected to make a full recovery.'

Peter and Judith nodded like attentive school children listening to their teacher.

'I understand that you have permission to briefly enter the room?'

They nodded again.

He opened the door and waved them in.

Peter and Judith entered the room and closed the door behind them. The room was dimly lit, making the intermittently flashing lights on the machines next to the bed easier to see. Thomas was lying on his back with his eyes closed. He looked like he was asleep.

Peter gulped and blinked hard. 'Thank goodness, he's...' he started. He swallowed again. 'Thank goodness he's going to be all right.'

He stood next to the bed, and Judith stood close behind him. Peter put his hand on Thomas's arm and squeezed it gently.

Suddenly, Thomas's eyes sprang wide open.

Peter jumped backwards in fright, treading on Judith's foot.

Very slowly, Thomas turned his head to the side. When he saw Judith and Peter, he raised his eyebrows, as if he was trying to tell them to come closer. He mumbled something, but they couldn't make out the words.

Peter leaned down and held his face close to Thomas's. 'Calm down, Thomas,' he said. 'They say everything's going to be fine. Don't worry now. You need to rest. You're safe here. No one can hurt you.'

Thomas's face contorted with the effort of trying to speak. Peter turned his head so that his ear was closer to Thomas's mouth.

'The cssk... c... cas....ket,' Thomas muttered gaspingly. 'Where?'

'We've got it, Thomas,' Peter whispered in his ear. 'Don't worry. We'll look after it for you.'

That seemed to reassure Thomas. He relaxed a little, but then he tried to raise his head again. 'No... po... no...' But he didn't have the strength to get the words out.

'No police,' Peter finished for him. 'No, no police. Don't worry. You'll be out of here in a day or two, then we'll deal with this together. We'll look after the casket for you until then.'

'Open,' said Thomas. Or was it a question?

'Open? No, it's still closed. We'll keep it cl—'

With a strength that took Peter by surprise, Thomas grabbed Peter's arm and gripped it tightly. 'Open... You ... open.'

'You want me to open it?'

Thomas nodded.

Judith jumped in.

'Are you sure?'

Thomas nodded again.

'Okay. Then I'll take it to the institute,' Peter said to reassure him. 'I'll use Verbeek's cabinet. It'll be fine. Nothing will happen to it. Everything will be all right, Thomas.'

Thomas let go of his arm. 'Petrus,' Thomas said.

Peter was surprised to hear Thomas call him that. It was his baptismal name, but nobody – except for his father, sometimes, in jest – ever called him by it.

'Found... We found him,' said Thomas, struggling for breath. 'Petrus.' His voice was growing weaker.

'Yes,' Peter tried to reassure him. 'It's a great find, Thomas. The find of your life. We'll work this out together. I'll open the casket. I'll do it tonight. And I'll visit you again tomorrow. I'm sure you'll be feeling better by then. Then we'll come up with a plan and get this all sorted out.' The door opened, and a male nurse came in, pushing a tall metal cart.

'Good evening,' the nurse greeted them cheerfully. 'I've come to prepare Meneer Konijnenberg for the night. It's time to say goodbye now, yes?'

Peter looked at Thomas, but he had closed his eyes again.

His chest rose and fell in a steady rhythm.

The man picked up a syringe and held it with the needle pointing upwards. He flicked the barrel smartly a few times and smiled. The smile seemed forced.

Judith frowned and looked nervously at Peter.

Without any further ceremony, the nurse pushed the needle into Thomas's arm and injected the contents into his veins.

Suddenly, Judith noticed the muddy shoes sticking out from under the nurse's too-short white trousers.

'So,' said the nurse. 'We won't be hearing anything more from him.' When he turned towards them, his smile was gone.

Now Judith recognised the man she had caught a glimpse of when he'd broken down Peter's front door.

And Peter recognised the German accent that he had detected in the fake policeman's conspicuously formal Dutch earlier that evening.

'What have you done?' Judith wailed. 'Peter, he's not a nurse at all! That man...'

Now Peter also saw the man's muddy shoes and

realised the man had followed the same thought process that had brought him and Judith to the hospital. But how had he managed to get in? An ID card was clipped onto his jacket, but the photo on it didn't look even slightly like him. The man must have overpowered someone and put their uniform on over his own clothes.

'Listen to me carefully, and there will be no need for anyone else to die.' He said it so coolly that it sounded even more threatening.

'Anyone else? What have you done to him?!' Judith cried. Her voice caught in her throat.

'Let's just say that right now, he is meeting his maker and giving an account for all his earthly deeds. And the same fate' – he looked at Judith and Peter in turn – 'is waiting for both of you if you don't return what belongs to us.'

'Us? What are you talking about? Who is "us"?' Peter said fiercely.

Judith started to head for the door to warn the police officer outside.

The man let out a short, mirthless laugh. 'Oh, he's going to be in dreamland for a while. You really are on your own here. So come on. Hand it over. Then we can all forget this unfortunate incident and be on our way.' He moved his hand to his hip as if to grab his gun.

Judith opened her bag and grabbed the casket.

The man's eyes lit up, and a grin spread across his face. 'Very good,' he said. 'You're a smart lady. Now, give it to me.'

Peter shouted. 'Judith! Don't!'

But Judith walked over to the man, holding the casket out to him. He reached out a hand to take it. Suddenly, she lashed out with a ferocity that took their attacker by surprise, swinging the ivory box hard into his jaw. The man grabbed his face and fell to his knees. Judith and Peter ran out of the room before he had a chance to recover.

The policeman they had just spoken to was slumped in his chair in what looked like a deep sleep.

Now Judith took the lead. 'Come on,' she said. As they neared the ward doors, which fortunately opened automatically from inside the ward, they heard the door to Thomas's room being opened again. The man staggered out, clutching his injured jaw with one hand.

The doors closed behind them, and they dashed to the stairwell.

'What now?' Peter whispered.

Judith saw a sign indicating that the hospital had a prayer room on the floor above them. She pulled Peter up the stairs with her. 'Come on. I've got an idea. He's going to be expecting us to leave the hospital. Let's sit up there for a while. He'll go outside, and meanwhile, we can try to decide what to do next.'

They ducked into the prayer room and found that they had it to themselves. It was a small chapel that reflected the AZL's Catholic origins. There were wooden pews with prayer cushions, and a faint smell of incense hung in the air. A beautiful wooden crucifix was illuminated from above by two spotlights, drawing the attention of anyone who came into the room to the crucified figure of Jesus.

'Are you sure this is a good idea, Judith?' whispered

Peter. 'So far, he's followed the same line of thought as us. What if he comes upstairs? There's nowhere to hide in here.'

Judith walked over to the altar and beckoned Peter to come closer.

There was a space about half a metre wide behind the wooden panelling on the back of the altar.

'Quick, we're going to hide behind there,' she said. Peter grimaced.

Suddenly, they heard footsteps in the corridor. Without saying a word, they both dived behind the wooden panel and sat down on the floor. It was dusty, and Peter's nose started to itch.

They heard the door to the prayer room swing open.

Chapter Six

The door closed again, but it wasn't immediately clear whether someone had come into the room or not. Then they heard slow, steady footsteps coming towards the altar.

Peter and Judith both held their breath.

Whoever it was sat down on one of the pews. Judith gripped Peter's hand. Then, they heard the voice of an elderly woman reciting the first words of the Lord's Prayer, and their mouths fell open with relief. They exhaled at last.

'Our Father, who art in heaven, hallowed be thy name...' The woman recited the rest of the prayer silently.

But their relief didn't last long. Soon afterwards, the door opened again, and they heard footsteps in the aisle. This time, they came right up to the altar.

'My dear lady,' a voice said, and they recognised the unmistakable accent of the gunman. 'Please accept my sincere apologies for disturbing your private moment of prayer, but I'm looking for two people most urgently. May I ask how long you've been in this room?'

They couldn't make out what the woman said in reply.

'Thank you very much, and once again, my sincere apologies for disturbing your prayer. I only did so because it was very urgent.'

He paused for a moment, and then they heard his footsteps moving away. The door to the prayer room opened again and then slammed shut.

Just as Peter was about to shuffle backwards and stretch out his legs, he heard footsteps coming towards them again.

'I thought you had left,' said the woman, now clearly audible.

'And I shall leave, dear lady, don't worry.'

Shortly afterwards he moved away again. They heard the door open and close.

'Well, and about time, too,' the woman grumbled. 'You can't get five minutes peace anywhere these days.'

About ten minutes later, she got up and left the chapel. Peter and Judith both scooted backwards and stretched out their legs.

At least ten more minutes passed before Peter dared to peer around the wooden panel. He was sure that the prayer room really was empty now.

They both got to their feet and emerged from their hiding place. The old chapel felt safe, at least for the time being.

'What now?' Judith whispered.

'Let's stay here for a while. There's something I have to tell you.'

'What do you mean?'

'I'm afraid I haven't told you everything.'

Judith looked at him and furrowed her brow.

'Come over here,' Peter said, crossing to a corner of the room and taking a seat on one of the pews.

Judith sat down beside him. 'You haven't told me everything? What does that mean?'

'It's complicated, Judith,' he said. A look of anguish had appeared on his face. 'Do you remember what I told you at my house, just before the phoney police officer rang the bell and broke my door down?'

'No, sorry. My brain is a little fuzzy right now.'

'I told you that Thomas had been secretive about the excavation in Roomburg. And he hinted now and then that he was looking for something that wasn't described in the original brief.'

'Ah, yes, now I remember. So you know more about it than you said?'

'He told me this in confidence. It's...' Peter stared at the crucifix; he looked as if he was trying to gather the courage to speak. 'It's... Thomas kept saying, "Petrus". Do you know who he meant?'

'Petrus?' she asked. 'Did he mean Saint Peter the Apostle?'

'Yes.'

'Saint Peter was Jesus' most important apostle, one of his confidants. Fisherman. Hot-tempered,' Judith began to reel off. 'Cut off that Roman's ear when Jesus was arrested. Appears in lots of important New Testament stories. Jesus gave him the name Petrus, or Peter, meaning "rock", and said he would build his new church on him. Uhm...' She thought for a moment. 'After Jesus was arrested, Saint Peter denied him three times before the cock crowed, just as Jesus had predicted. Then, after Jesus' death and resurrection, Saint Peter became the new leader of the Christians. Went to Rome to preach the gospel and was crucified there, upside down, because he didn't think he was worthy of dying in the same way Jesus had. That's about all I know.' Judith paused and then said, 'I've only just realised... Your name, Peter de Haan, it means "Peter the cockerel". That's not just a coincidence, is it?'

Peter smiled.

'Actually, it is just a coincidence in as much as I was named after my grandfather, who was called Petrus. I wasn't usually called that though. I've always just been Peter. There was the odd smart-aleck at school who thought it would be hilarious to crow like a cockerel during the Bible readings at Easter, but apart from that, it's never bothered me.'

Judith smiled.

Peter sighed deeply and then he began to speak, fast and low, and Judith had to lean in to hear him properly.

'The things you just said about Saint Peter, Judith those are the stories we've been told since we were children. But when you look deeper into the gospels and how they came about, and if you compare them, you'll see that the traditional story taught in churches and schools doesn't hold water. The gospels themselves contradict each other so often that there's no way of knowing what actually happened.'

Judith nodded.

'I mean, what were the last words that Jesus really spoke? How many people went to his tomb on Easter Sunday, and who were they? Who did Jesus appear to, and where did he appear? Was he born in Nazareth or Bethlehem? There's not a single point where the four accounts agree, and they can't all be right. Not to mention the fact that the oldest account, the gospel of Mark, was written somewhere around AD 70, about forty years after Jesus died. The gospels are all completely unreliable as historical evidence. But they were never meant to be historical accounts. They're stories of faith, written to convince people that Jesus was the Messiah promised in the Old Testament.'

'I know what you mean. I talk about this all the time with my friend Mark. He's studying at Leiden uni too.'

Peter didn't seem to hear her.

'Have you ever noticed, for example, that...' Peter picked up a Bible that had been left on the pew and started leafing through it. The words *Holy Bible* were printed on the front in large white letters.

'Do you know Greek too, by the way?' Peter asked.

'Yes, I passed my Greek exam at grammar school, and of course, we read parts of the gospels in Greek in the first year of my degree. But I was specialising in Judaism, so I concentrated more on Hebrew after that.'

Peter opened the Bible at the fifteenth chapter of Acts. 'Right. Here, look at this,' he said. 'Did you never wonder why the Apostle Peter disappears about halfway through the Book of Acts? Or why the lion's share of what follows is written by the Apostle Paul or at least attributed to him?'

'Well,' Judith countered, 'Peter went to Rome, didn't he?'

'Where does it say he went to Rome? That's all apocryphal, Judith. It says he went to Rome in the Acts of Peter, but that's pure myth-making, hagiography, the idealised biography of a saint. It describes Saint Peter going to Rome to give the keys to the gates of heaven to the Bishop of Rome. It's a fantastic tale, and by that I mean it's literally a tale full of fantasy. It even has talking dogs!'

'Then why is that story about Saint Peter's time in Rome told as if it's a historical account?'

'The Bishops of Rome wanted to reinforce the legitimacy of their authority by claiming that they were given their sovereignty by an apostle. And not just any apostle. No, it had to be Saint Peter, the disciple who had been at Jesus' side during many important events.'

'So what's the real story then? Or what does Thomas think happened?'

'That's... I'll get to that later,' said Peter. 'Don't forget, Judith, that history is written by the victors. It's always their story we read, their version of events we hear. And in those versions, they always come out on top, and their enemies are portrayed as people who tried in vain to prevent the inevitable course of history. That goes for the New Testament too... Saint Peter simply disappears from the story. It's really very odd when you think about it. After the fifteenth chapter of Acts, we just don't see him anymore.'

'But what about his letters then? First and Second Peter

in the New Testament?' Judith argued. 'Did he not write those?'

'They're attributed to him, yes. But do you really think that a simple fisherman like Peter could have written in such fluent, meticulous Greek? And about such sophisticated theological ideas – ideas, moreover, that weren't actually developed until the second century? Saint Peter was long dead by then. And in those letters, he was supposedly able to quote from the Septuagint, the Greek translation of the Old Testament. No, no serious Bible scholar would ever attribute those letters to Saint Peter. But in ancient times, it was fairly common to do just that to give a letter more authority.'

Peter tapped the page with his finger. 'So Saint Peter appears just one more time, during the meeting described here when Paul, his helper Barnabas, the apostles, and some other leaders meet in Jerusalem. A group of Jews who had converted to Christianity have just told some Christians from Antioch that they wouldn't be saved unless they were circumcised. And circumcision was a dangerous procedure back then. This is a crucial point because some people thought that the Mosaic law regarding circumcision was still in place, even for Christians. But of course, that would have seriously hampered the expansion of the new faith. The apostles Paul and Barnabas didn't agree with this idea at all, and they went to Jerusalem to discuss it with the others. So at the meeting, Peter makes an impassioned speech. It starts at verse seven.'

He started to read out loud.

'After there had been much debate, Peter stood up and

said to them, "My brothers, you know that in the early days God made a choice among you, that I should be the one through whom the Gentiles would hear the message of the good news and become believers. And God, who knows the human heart, testified to them by giving them the Holy Spirit, just as He did to us; and in cleansing their hearts by faith He has made no distinction between them and us. Now therefore why are you putting God to the test by placing on the neck of the disciples a yoke that neither our ancestors nor we have been able to bear? On the contrary, we believe that we will be saved through the grace of the Lord Jesus, just as they will."'

Peter closed the Bible but kept the index finger of his right hand tucked between the pages.

'But I thought you were a Catholic?'

'Yes, I was raised as a Catholic. I lapsed many years ago, but I've been fascinated by the figure Jesus since I was a teenager. I've talked about this with Thomas a few times. Our relationship was sometimes... How should I put it? Our conversations sometimes went beyond the purely professional. But the point is that, for most Christians, like the lady who was praying here just now, it doesn't matter if Saint Peter preached in Rome or not. It makes no difference to her belief. She feels Jesus' love in her heart. If you told her that those letters weren't written by Saint Peter, that the Acts of Peter is pure legend, that, from a historian's perspective, you can find fault with just about everything written in the gospels – none of it would change her faith.'

'And what about Thomas's faith?'

'Oh, he lost it in high school, long before he even started

to examine the Bible more deeply. He still considered studying Biblical Archaeology, but then his chief reason for doing so would have been to show that the Bible was wrong. He decided against it, in the end. He didn't want to go digging in the desert for years just to prove himself right by finding nothing. So then he started to focus on the archaeology of the Low Countries, and that's how he got involved in the Roomburg dig.'

'Wait a second. Saint Peter disappears from the story,' Judith reiterated. 'And you're right, that is quite odd. I never paid much attention to it, but the fact that one of the major characters from the gospels is unceremoniously written out of the story is quite strange. It's like reading a book about the Roman Empire and finding that the chapter on Julius Caesar ends before he's even been murdered.'

'Exactly. And, according to Thomas, there was even more to it than that. As I said, it's a fact that history is written by the victors. The losers are either dead or not in a position to be able to tell their story.'

'And the victor here is...'

'The victor is Saint Paul, obviously. The version of Christianity we know today is based on Paul's ideas. And *his* story suddenly stops at the end of the Book of Acts, but that's a subject for another day. According to Thomas, Saint Peter was written out because his version of Christianity didn't fit in with Saint Paul's plans and ambitions. Thomas says that Peter's words, the words I just read, were never spoken by him. Whoever wrote the Book of Acts put Paul's words in Peter's mouth. And I suspect the same can be said of Saint Peter's vision in Acts where God suddenly tells him there are no dietary restrictions anymore and he can eat whatever he wants. So, just like that, one more obstacle, one more thing that was hindering the spread of the message to other nations was removed. I know I don't have to tell *you* how many laws there are prescribing what Jews can and cannot eat.'

Judith sighed and smiled. Perhaps she was thinking of her mother's kosher chicken soup, Peter thought.

'Thomas didn't believe any of it. Saint Peter was a Jew who spent his entire life within the Jewish tradition. He followed a rabbi who claimed on more than one occasion that he didn't want to change a single iota of the Law. Peter, of all people, is going to suggest breaking with Jewish customs? Thomas thinks that he agreed with Jesus and wanted the message to be given to Jews and only Jews. You'll find plenty of evidence to support that view in the New Testament itself. Thomas wasn't the first to come up with it.'

'So what was Saint Paul's agenda then?'

'Paul is quite a remarkable character. He never even met Jesus. He actually persecuted Jesus' first followers. He was supposedly converted on the road to Damascus, on his way there to arrest Christians. But it's very unlikely that he had any authority to do that, so that story isn't very plausible either. I'm not sure what really happened.'

'Perhaps he was a spy for the Romans, working on some sort of undercover operation to weaken the new cult. Change it from a revolutionary movement to a group whose members would be obedient to the government and be content to wait for an everlasting reward in the afterlife.'

'A spy? Like a biblical 007?' Peter joked. 'Who knows? But I don't think it was likely. That's more the stuff of fiction. Personally, I think Saint Paul's conversion was genuine, and he really did believe in Jesus. Like most converts, he was eager to spread the message to as many people as possible. And to do that, he had to remove a few obstacles that were in the way of preaching the message more widely.'

'So you don't think it's likely that Saint Peter would distance himself from the Jewish Law, but a learned orthodox Jew like Saint Paul would?'

'You have to remember,' Peter said, stabbing the air with his index finger, 'Paul never met Jesus. That meant he could be freer in his interpretation of the good news. I think he was just very enthusiastic, and probably swayed by the vanity of someone who wanted to play an important role in the new movement. Maybe it gave his life a purpose. Or maybe it was pure vanity. Who can say?'

'So what did Thomas believe?'

'Well, there's a tradition that tells of a trip that Saint Peter made to Britannia – to England.'

'I suppose that's apocryphal too?' Judith asked.

'Yes, but it's probably as important as the other tradition that puts Saint Peter in Rome. Thomas was convinced that the stories about Peter's journey to our part of the world were historically more correct. According to his theory, Peter was just a simple fisherman who lost the debate with Paul, a learned man who had a gift for words. Maybe Peter stayed in Jerusalem while Paul travelled around the Roman Empire with his version of the gospel. Saint Peter could have come this way towards the end of the sixties, just before Jerusalem was destroyed by the Romans in AD 70.'

'But how does this fit into our story?'

'There was one idea that Thomas couldn't let go of. Suppose that Saint Peter was here, at Brittenburg, where Katwijk is now, and intended to cross the channel to England, but changed his mind. Maybe there were no boats available. Or maybe it was because he was an old man by then, exhausted from the long, dangerous journey across mainland Europe, and he decided not to risk making the crossing. Like Jesus, he was probably born around the year zero, so he must have been about seventy years old.'

'Yes, so...' Judith looked at him, clearly not understanding where Peter was going with this.

'So ... so, according to Thomas, it could be possible that Saint Peter isn't buried in Rome at all, but here in the Netherlands. And since Matilo was the largest Roman fort in the area, Thomas had pinned his hopes on the Roomburg excavation proving his theory.'

'But that ... that's absurd.' Realising that the words had come out louder than she had intended, she clapped her hand over her mouth. 'That's pure conjecture, Peter,' she said, more quietly now. 'You're kidding, right? You don't actually believe that, do you?'

'I don't know what to believe anymore, Judith. He's looked into it pretty deeply. He's shown me things in ancient manuscripts, cryptic references that suddenly make sense when you read them in the light of his theory. But above all...' Peter paused. 'This is the last thing I'm going to say on it for now,' he said, 'because we really do need to get out of here. But above all... It's strange that the first little chapel built in Leiden, which eventually became the Pieterskerk, was dedicated to Saint Peter. Thomas reckons it's an indication that, for whatever reason, people at that time believed Saint Peter had a connection with this region. He's always been Leiden's patron saint, but not many Leideners realise that their city is known as the "*sleutelstad*" – the "City of Keys" – because of the keys Jesus gave to Saint Peter. Despite the Reformation, and even after the Relief of Leiden, when you might assume that the city would have been cleansed of all traces of the stain of Catholicism, the importance of the Pieterskerk was undiminished. Nothing was done to it; not even its name was changed. Thomas went so far as to say that the real reason the Spaniards laid siege to Leiden was that they were searching for something, and they believed they would find it within the city's walls...'

'That all sounds like a conspiracy theory, Peter.' Judith shook her head in disbelief. 'I don't know...'

'What to think about it? Me neither, Judith, me neither. But now it looks like there might be some truth in Thomas's theories. Otherwise, we wouldn't be in this situation.'

'But we'll only know for sure if...' Judith hesitated.

'If we open the casket. I don't know if that's what you were about to say, but it *is* exactly what I intend to do. We owe it to Thomas. He gave his life for this. Before I go to the police – because we are going to have to tell someone about this eventually – I want to know for myself why Thomas died.'

'And how are you going to do that?'

'In that low-oxygen cabinet that I told you about that my colleague made. It's ingenious; you can study brittle, centuries-old documents in it without the acid in the air affecting the paper. There's a Polaroid camera fixed above it so that you can take photos of them but only expose the paper to the light for a second.'

'Do you think there are documents of some sort inside the casket?'

'Documents, a letter... Or it could even be a new, undiscovered gospel...'

'Or a Roman soldier's last will and testament...' Judith suggested. 'I'd prepare myself for a huge disappointment if I were you, Peter.'

'Who knows? We'll see,' he said resignedly. 'But come on, let's go. We'd better go out by one of the doors at the back of the hospital.'

At the chapel door, Peter stopped and peered cautiously around the corner. He couldn't see anyone. Judith tucked her arm through his, and they walked calmly along the corridor. They looked like a pious couple who had stopped into the chapel to pray for the swift recovery of the family member they had been visiting.

When a doctor in a white coat appeared at the end of the corridor, walking briskly towards them, Judith and Peter ducked down a narrow passage. It looked like a dead end. But when they got closer to the bottom of it, they realised there was an emergency exit with a door that could be opened by pushing down on the long horizontal bar across it. Judith looked back and realised that the doctor they had just seen in the corridor had followed them into the passage. He stopped and called out to them, 'Hey! What are you doing down there? Didn't you hear the announcement? All visitors have been asked to assemble in the central hall.'

The doctor continued walking down the passage, somewhat hesitantly at first, but he gradually grew more confident and marched smartly towards them. The distance between them quickly shrank.

'Would you come with me, please? Then we can...' he began.

'Come on, Judith!' Peter said, turning around and putting his hand on the bar of the emergency exit.

Judith faltered for a second and gave the approaching doctor an apologetic smile. Then she turned away from him too.

Peter pushed down on the bar. The door flew open, and a loud alarm bell began to ring.

Chapter Seven

Judith could hear the footsteps of the doctor running behind them. She glanced back and saw him standing in the doorway, staring at them, evidently thunderstruck. He was holding a small device in his hand, probably a beeper that would alert the hospital's security guards.

Peter turned to Judith. 'Come on,' he said under his breath.

They walked along the back of the hospital to the bicycle tunnel that connected Plesmanlaan with the plaza in front of Central Station.

'We can use the crowds in town to our advantage,' Peter said, taking Judith's hand. They walked hand-in-hand along the Morsweg in the direction of the Morspoort.

Judith's palm was clammy. But after a while, Peter felt her hand start to relax in his. To the outside world, they looked just like everyone else making their way to the fairground.

Peter heaved a sigh and looked sideways at Judith. She gave him a little smile. She squeezed his hand, and despite the situation they were in, he felt a not altogether unpleasant tingling in his abdomen.

They were nearing the bridge in front of the Morspoort. A constant stream of people was crossing the canal, moving towards the centre of town. Judith and Peter stopped next to the large cannon at the gate, unsure where to go. The gate was usually open, but today a podium on the other side blocked the archway. The crowd flowed around the building like a river. Peter and Judith were the only ones standing still.

Suddenly, they heard the sound of a siren in the distance. Startled, Judith looked back towards the tax office on the plaza and saw two police cars approaching with their blue lights flashing.

'We'll go to the institute,' Peter shouted in Judith's ear. But the band that was playing outside Café Het Huis De Bijlen was making so much noise that he could barely hear his own voice. He pulled Judith out of the crowd and into the quiet seclusion of De Put Park. They walked along the little path next to the water that came out at the bridge over the Galgewater canal. The sails of the windmill next to it were festooned with red-and-white Leiden flags.

They continued on through the Weddesteeg and past the modern building occupying the spot where Rembrandt was believed to have lived before moving to Amsterdam.

There's so much history here, Peter thought. *Perhaps even more than we're aware of...*

They walked down Rembrandtstraat towards the

Institute of Archaeology. The wrought-iron gate that led to the courtyard garden was open, as usual, so they walked straight up to the entrance. A lamp next to the front door glowed brightly, and inside, the lights were still on in the hallway.

Peter swiped his pass through the slot on the wall, and the door unlocked with a soft click. He looked at his watch. Ten o'clock precisely. It was hard to believe that, less than five hours ago, he'd been sitting in his office, contentedly smoking a cigarillo.

He hadn't even locked his door before leaving, thinking he'd be back within the hour. In Peter's office, Judith took off her coat, dropped onto the couch and rested her head on the wall behind it. Neither of them had spoken since they'd left the Morspoort.

'Right,' Peter said. 'Listen, this is what we're going to do.' But Judith had closed her eyes.

'Are you still awake? We've got to keep going. I promised Thomas.'

Judith nodded but didn't open her eyes.

'You just sit there for a while, and I'll fetch Verbeek's cabinet. I'll wheel it back down here, and have it set up in about ten, maybe fifteen minutes, and then we'll see if we can get the casket open.'

Peter left the room.

A heavy stillness hung over the building. It wasn't unusual for Peter to work at the institute late into the evening, and he usually appreciated the hush that fell over its corridors then. But now, the deep silence felt different, almost ominous. He hoped that whoever was chasing them wouldn't think of coming here.

But perhaps the man was busy dealing with the police, who had no doubt been alerted after what had happened at the hospital. He was likely to be more circumspect now.

Verbeek's room had been left unlocked, and Peter could see his device standing in the corner. Peter's colleague had developed and built it himself, and it was brilliant in its simplicity. An ingenious system extracted the air inside its thick glass walls, creating a pH-neutral – or acid-free – environment. Two spotlights with UV-filters were attached above it. Fragile documents stored away from daylight, perhaps for many centuries, could be examined inside the cabinet without any danger of them being damaged.

Peter was relieved to see that the Polaroid camera had been left inside the cabinet. Verbeek used an instant camera because it spat out the photo almost immediately, allowing you to see whether or not the text on a document was legible within moments. With an ordinary camera, you wouldn't know how useful your images were until after the film had been developed. For Verbeek, the advantages of instant results and the shortest possible exposure to light and air far outweighed the disadvantage of not having negatives of the photos. He enlarged the Polaroids on a photocopier immediately after taking them and using these images to study the documents.

Peter carefully wheeled the contraption back to his office.

Judith seemed to be more alert now. She was standing in front of the Gustave Wappers painting.

'What an awful situation. Just so ... grave.' Judith said without turning to look at Peter.

'Brave? There's no truth to that story, you know. That's all apocryphal, too. And anyway, what would the starving people of Leiden have done with the burgomaster's emaciated body?'

'I said grave, not brave.' Judith turned around.

'Ah, I misheard you,' Peter said apologetically. 'It *was* a grave situation. Thousands of people died during the siege. Leiden had eighteen thousand citizens, and more than six thousand of them died of hunger or the plague. What most people don't know is that there were actually two sieges. The first one lasted five months. It was lifted for two months, but then the Spaniards came back. The city had stockpiled enough supplies the first time around, but they were completely unprepared for the second siege, despite having been warned about it by the Prince of Orange. And that was the siege that cost so many lives in the end.'

'So what's the story about Burgomaster Van der Werff?' Judith asked.

'Van der Werff wanted to do something that would give his burghers the courage to hold on. So, supposedly, he offered his body to them. Like a modern-day Christ, I suppose, his death would have allowed the people to live. But if you look closer...' He stood next to Judith. 'Now this was one of Thomas's jokes,' Peter said, 'but according to him, Van der Werff isn't offering up his own body in this painting at all. He's actually suggesting that the burghers eat this child in the foreground. Look at how the terrified mother is wrapping her arms around her child to protect him.' He smiled.

'But what Thomas didn't joke about,' he continued, 'was his belief that the Spanish had very different reasons for laying siege to Leiden than the ones most historians assume. Leiden was a relatively unimportant town at the time. Thomas thought there must have been something here that made it worth going to the trouble of laying siege to it for a year. He was convinced that the Spaniards were aware of a secret that was of vital importance, either for them or the Catholic Church.'

'And that secret was connected to Saint Peter in some way? Once you've convinced yourself that a conspiracy exists, I'm sure you can connect it to just about anything,' Judith said.

'That's what I thought too, at first,' Peter agreed. 'But the deeper you dig into history – and that was something Thomas was very good at – the more you'll see all sorts of inconsistencies that his theory could explain. And now it looks like he really was on to something after all. Of course, when he called me this afternoon, it wasn't to tell me about the mask they'd found. "And there's more, Peter. There's more! I've found him, and I wanted you to be the first to know." That's what he said just before he hung up.'

'And the man who was chasing us? Or is still chasing us?' Judith felt a faint shiver move through her whole body.

'I don't know,' Peter said uncertainly. 'That German accent... It sounded vaguely familiar. I felt like I'd heard it somewhere before. Maybe at the dig, or even here at the institute. Thomas told me about someone working on the dig who he had a bad feeling about. A German student who'd been introduced to him by Hoogers. I didn't think it was important at the time. And anyway, how could he be mixed up in all of this?'

Peter stared into space for a moment, lost in thought. 'Come on,' he said. 'Let's get this machine connected up. It shouldn't take more than ten minutes, and then we can get to work. Could you pass me the casket?'

Judith walked over to the sofa where she'd left her bag next to her coat. She appeared to hesitate for a second before she gave Peter the casket, and when Peter tried to take it from her, she held onto it for just a brief moment before letting go. 'Are we doing the right thing here, Peter?'

Peter looked at her determinedly. With one hand still holding the ivory box, he put his other hand on her shoulder and squeezed it gently. 'I know this is all completely crazy, but it will be over soon. I just need to do this. We'll open the casket, take some photos of it, and close it straight back up again. Then we can decide what we're going to do next. Although... We don't really know what we are up against, or even who we're up against. Anything could happen. Whatever this is, it must be worth a great deal to them if they were prepared to kill Thomas for it. And if there's even a shred of truth in Thomas's theories, then we're onto something huge here. Who knows what will happen to this thing once we've handed it over to the authorities? Who knows how powerful our opponent is? Everything we've done so far has been entirely defensible. But this, what we're about to do... I want to have these photos in case we need some sort of backup. Suppose it turns out later that this is something much bigger than we could ever have imagined, and this evidence somehow vanishes. I don't want to regret not having taken photos when I had the chance. I think I owe it to Thomas. Otherwise, he died for nothing.' He lifted his hand from Judith's shoulder.

She nodded and let go of the casket.

Peter carried it over to the cabinet and placed it inside. He checked that there were enough shots left in the Polaroid camera. There were.

'How are you going to open it? It looks like it's hermetically sealed to me. And you can't justify damaging it just because we're in a hurry. Surely it would be better to bring everything out into the open first and then open it under proper lab conditions?'

'Honestly, Judith, I know this thing looks a bit makeshift, but you won't find a better machine than this anywhere. Not even in the most advanced laboratories. This is state of the art.'

Judith said nothing.

'But you're right. We need to find a way to open this casket. I don't get the feeling that we need a code or anything like that. It's just a very skilfully made box with two halves that fit perfectly together. I think Verbeek had something in here...' Peter opened the drawer underneath the glass cabinet.

A huge array of tools were laid out neatly inside. There were tweezers, knives in various shapes and sizes, files of some sort that tapered into sharp points, and even a small hammer.

'These should do the trick.'

He chose a few instruments and placed them inside the cabinet next to the casket. Then he closed the lid, tightened the clamps on the outside to create an airtight seal, and fastened the camera into the holder positioned above it. The two long-sleeved gloves protruded into the cabinet like amputated forearms.

Peter pushed the plug into the electricity socket, and two lights blinked on, emitting a soft blue glow. The small extractor fan started to hum as it created a gentle stream of expelled air next to the cabinet.

'There,' he said, relieved. 'Everything seems to be working. I've used this before. Not with anything as old as this, naturally, but I have looked at some very fragile documents with it.'

He sat down on the sofa and patted the cushion next to him, inviting Judith to do the same.

'Why did you choose that particular picture?' Judith asked, pointing to the poster of Pope John Paul II in his Popemobile.

'Ah, that poster,' he smiled. 'Beautiful, isn't it?

'It's all right, I suppose,' she said doubtfully. 'I can't see anything special about it. But I'm surprised to see this particular picture hanging in an ex-Catholic's office.'

'Not many people know this, Judith, but the day that photo was taken was the day I lost my faith in God. My first day as an ex-Catholic, as you call it.'

Judith looked at him quizzically. 'What do you mean?'

'You probably know that there was an attempt to assassinate the pope?'

'Yes, I remember it actually. In 1981. I was eleven at the time.'

'Exactly, May 13th, 1981. A Turkish man called Mehmet Ali Ağca managed to fire a few rounds at the pope at close range. He was hit in the stomach, hand, and arm, but miraculously, he survived the attack. For the faithful, of course, it wasn't a miracle. It was perfectly "simple".' Peter gestured with his fingers, making quotation marks in the air. 'It was proof that, obviously, God intervenes in people's lives. According to the pope himself, the Holy Mother guided the bullets past his vital organs.'

'And he forgave the gunman afterwards, didn't he?'

'Yes, he visited Ağca in prison and gave him his forgiveness, which was fantastic PR for the pope. But that car, the Popemobile... He already had a similar vehicle with a glass box raised up on the back so that the crowds could get a good view of him as he blessed them. But that was made of ordinary glass. After that attack in May 1981, it was replaced with bulletproof glass...'

'Yes? And? I still don't understand what that has to do with the beginning of you losing your faith.'

'It was strange. Something suddenly struck me. I remember watching the news reports about the pope's first procession in his new Popemobile with the bulletproof glass. They showed footage of the crowds, going wild, all cheering for him. Lots of them were in tears, raising their hands up to heaven to thank God for saving their pope. And I thought... I just thought: Well, if Pope John Paul himself doesn't have enough faith to believe that the Almighty would protect him from harm, what hope is there for me, just a simple Christian? If even the pope has to resort to bulletproof glass because he's not absolutely certain that God will guide the bullets past his vital organs next time... And if the next attempt on his life was successful, would that have been God's will?'

The hum coming from the machine started to grow quieter.

'And I thought,' Peter said, almost whispering now. 'Didn't the Bible say that God has counted even all the hairs on my head? Wasn't God so concerned with humankind that nothing happened to us unless he wanted it to? Didn't he have the whole world in his hand? And if the Vicar of Christ doubted God's omnipotence, who was I, an ordinary believer, to cling onto such unwavering faith in him? It wasn't that I completely lost my faith on exactly that day, but...'

'And now?' Judith asked.

'And now? Now I don't know what to think anymore,' Peter said. 'There was a period, when I was a student, that I went looking for meaning in my life. I visited different churches on Sunday mornings trying to find one where I could belong. I ended up at a traditional Protestant church for a year or two. I even went down the path of becoming a proper member. Nothing came of it, but their intellectual approach appealed to me: the long sermons, their Bible knowledge, singing the psalms and the hymns. I read the Bible from cover to cover twice with one of those reading plans, and I learned some of the most beautiful psalms off by heart just for the fun of it. Most of what I know about the Bible comes from that time.'

'But that faith faded too?

'Yes, exactly, you could put it that way. It didn't stick. And actually, I couldn't even tell you why. Maybe it was like that parable about the farmer who sows his seed on rocky ground. Do you know it? The seeds sprout, but the crop shrivels up through lack of water.'

Judith nodded. 'I know that one, yes.'

'I heard the word and received it with joy, but apparently, it didn't take root in me.'

He glanced at Judith.

'That was the short version of the story,' he said. 'When we find ourselves in better circumstances – and I hope that's soon – I'll tell you the long version. And then I want to hear more about you. What you think about things. What you believe.'

They heard the cabinet make a short clicking sound, and then it stopped making noise altogether. A green light at the front of it blinked on.

Suddenly, the phone rang, shattering the stillness in the room. Frightened, they both held their breath and stared at the phone on the desk.

'Don't answer it,' said Judith.

'No, of course not. Nobody knows we're here, do they? It's probably a coincidence, just one of my students calling. I'm sure it's nothing.'

The ringing stopped.

But then it immediately started again. It rang eight or nine times before whoever was trying to reach Peter gave up.

Judith and Peter sat perfectly still, like children playing musical statues.

Peter stood up, checked the glass cabinet and gave its lid an approving pat. 'Looks like it's ready,' he said, obviously doing his best to sound lighthearted. He rolled up his sleeves and stuck his arms inside the long gloves. 'Nothing is covered up that will not be uncovered, and nothing secret that will not become known,' he said quietly. He picked up the casket and turned it on its side. 'The moment of truth,' he said, picking up a chisel.

Judith had got up from the sofa to stand next to the cabinet where she leaned over, peering through the glass lid.

'Normally, you'd do this with tweezers,' Peter said as beads of sweat started to form on his forehead. 'Some documents are too fragile to be touched with your bare hands, and you use tweezers to turn the pages. But sometimes...' He gently chiselled at the faint line that ran around the sides of the casket. Nothing happened. He struck the chisel with the hammer again, slightly harder this time. A tiny chip of ivory flew into the air.

He mumbled a curse.

'Do you want me to have a go?' Judith asked.

Peter shook his head emphatically. 'This was only my first attempt. If this doesn't work or if I can't do it, then you can try.' He placed the chisel in the same spot as before and gave it another short, sharp tap. Now a larger piece broke off.

'Ah!' Peter said, sounding delighted despite having damaged the casket. 'This is where it opens. Of course, I could also... No, I don't want to break it open. It would be the easiest option, but...'

'Come on, let me try,' Judith said, putting a hand on his shoulder.

Peter gave the casket another half-hearted tap with the hammer, but he realised that he was only likely to damage it even more in his eagerness to get it open. He took a step back, allowing Judith to come forward and stick her arms inside the gloves. A furrow of concentration appeared on her brow as she picked up the casket and explored it with her hands as if she was seeing it for the first time.

'If this has been sealed shut for two thousand years,' she said uncertainly, 'I don't know if we're going to be able to open it. But, luckily, I think it may just be a question of prising off the lid. Imagine if we had to crack a code or something first, and that we'd end up bursting a tube of ink or acid inside it if we got it wrong.'

She positioned the chisel close to the place where Peter had just chipped off a little chunk of ivory and carefully tapped at the seam. She repeated this action over and over, moving the chisel a fraction each time.

'Maybe this will just loosen it a bit,' she said, focusing so hard on the task that she paused between each word. 'It feels like it is loosening, actually.' The very tip of her tongue was poking out of her mouth.

Peter stole a glance at her. He noticed the resemblance to Hanna again, but that was probably mostly because Judith was wearing Hanna's clothes.

Or no, actually... She was more like Sabrina...

He remembered the letters they'd sent each other after

he'd gone back home. Two or three letters a week. The depth of his disappointment on the days when there was nothing on the doormat. Waiting for the postman to come by at the same time each day. Going downstairs sometimes four, five, six times because he thought he'd heard the letterbox clatter. Reading the letters at lightning speed, always reading the last lines first because that was where she told him how much she loved him, confessing her desires in myriad ways without ever repeating herself. 'Kisses, wherever you want.' And a rare telephone call every now and then, but neither of them could really afford international calls, and hearing each other's voice only increased their longing. Making plans to meet up the following summer.

And then, the slow, steady decline in the frequency of the letters, which, in hindsight, had always been inevitable. The memories that faded over time until, eventually, it seemed as though he had never actually experienced those things himself but had read about them or seen them in a film. They felt like someone else's life. The tone of her letters had become more distant, more ordinary. But, even so, the letter she'd written to tell him she'd met someone in the army had caused him such pain. Like all women in Israel, she was obligated to do national service in the army for about eighteen months. She had sent him one last photo, of herself in full military gear with the Golan Heights in the background. God, what he would have given back then to be in her unit and standing there beside her...

'Yes!' Judith said, drawing the 'y' out for a second or two.

Peter was jolted out of his daydream.

'I think it's about to...' she said, giving the casket few more little taps with the chisel. What had been a faintly perceptible line had now become a clearly distinguishable crack.

She grabbed a chisel with a slightly thicker blade and began to gently pry at it. The lid moved a fraction, and the crack grew wider. She continued the same way, gingerly tapping the chisel around the casket.

'I think,' she said, more to herself than to Peter, 'I think the lid is pretty much loose now. Do you want to take it off?'

Peter hesitated. 'No, I'll leave that honour to you. You've done it so neatly.'

'All right then. Here goes.'

She put down the chisel and hammer and started to remove the lid.

At that moment, they heard the front door at the end of the corridor slam shut. They looked at each other nervously.

'It's after eleven,' Peter whispered. 'Who on earth could that be?'

'One of your colleagues? Someone who has a key card like yours?'

'It must be, but what are they doing here at this time of night?'

They heard footsteps coming towards Peter's office. It sounded like whoever was coming down the corridor was in no hurry and making no effort not to be noticed.

'Quick!' said Judith. She had pulled her hands out of the gloves. 'Do you have anything we can throw over this? A blanket or something?'

Peter grabbed the blanket that he kept under his desk. He liked to have a blanket over his legs when he worked at the computer. It was something that had infuriated Hanna towards the end of their relationship. 'It makes me feel like I'm living with an old man!' she'd complained.

He threw the blanket over the cabinet, hiding it from view.

There was a knock at the door. 'Peter?' someone said. 'Peter, are you there?'

It was Hoogers' voice.

Peter opened the door. Standing before him was his old tutor, his neck blotched red as it always was when he was wound up about something. Without asking, he barged inside, placing his hand on Peter's chest, pushing him backwards into the room. He slammed the door closed behind him.

'Who's she?' he said, nodding towards Judith without looking at her.

'That's Judith, Professor Hoogers. Judith Cherev, one of my students. Judith, this is Professor Hoogers. Judith and I were just...'

'I came by this afternoon to talk about my dissertation,' Judith said, trying to help him out. 'We went to the dig in Roomburg and then came back to...'

'Shut up, both of you,' Hoogers said with barely restrained fury. 'Do you think I'm an idiot? I just rang you, and you ignored your telephone even though you were here.' The red blotches had spread up to the lower half of his face. 'Do you know' – and it was only now that he addressed Judith too – 'Do either of you know how much trouble you're in? What you've got yourselves into? The chief of Leiden police just called me at home. He wondered if I could provide him with any information on your whereabouts.'

'But why would the police call—' Peter began, but Hoogers didn't let him finish his sentence.

'Because they're looking for you,' he said, speaking the words with staccato fury. 'Because they were hoping that I, as your boss, might be able to enlighten them. They're looking for you in connection with a murder, Peter. What was I supposed to tell them? You reported to the front desk at the hospital, you were seen by the security cameras. Just before the murder was committed, someone sprayed a liquid of some sort on the camera aimed at the door to Thomas Konijnenberg's room, and then he was murdered in his hospital bed. The unfortunate officer who was on guard in the hallway is still unconscious.' Professor Hoogers' voice grew louder as he spoke.

'Yes, but we didn't have anything to do with that,' Peter said, raising his own voice now too.

Judith jumped in. 'Really, Professor Hoogers,' she said softly. 'Let's all try and stay calm. Peter and I can explain everything. But first, we just need to...' She looked at Peter, who nodded.

'There's something we still need to discuss, or rather, need to do,' she continued. 'Trust us. We'll go straight to the police afterwards. You have my word. It's all been very distressing, and I know the evidence seems to be stacked against us, but it's not what it looks like.'

'Peter,' Hoogers began, as if he hadn't heard Judith at all.

'Thomas is dead. Murdered. And the police think you did it. Why did you run away from the hospital if you had nothing to do with it? Why didn't you alert the security guards?'

'Listen, Professor,' Peter tried. 'Pieter. I understand how it looks, but just give us a little time. You can wait in the next room if you like, but Judith and I really need to discuss something very urgent, right now, with each other, alone. So much has happened today. Yes, Judith and I will have to own up to some of it later, but we will be able to explain everything. Eventually.'

Now it was Peter who laid a hand on Hoogers' chest, pushing him gently but determinedly backwards towards the door. This seemed to startle Hoogers, who meekly obeyed.

Relieved, Judith let out a barely audible sigh.

Hoogers narrowed his eyes as if he still didn't trust them. 'If I don't see the pair of you within the next half hour,' he said in a threatening tone, 'I'll call the police myself. Understood? I will be waiting for you next door in my office. And your time' – he looked pointedly at his watch – 'starts now.'

Just before he closed the door, he turned around to look at them. 'Oh yes, and I understand that you two have stolen something from the excavation site. Do you still have it?'

Peter nodded. 'Give us half an hour. Then we'll go to the police together and hand it in. And explain everything.'

Hoogers left, closing the door behind him without another word. They heard him enter his own office. 'It's a bit odd, isn't it, that he's willing to give us half an hour?' Judith wondered. 'If the police did call him, and he came over to the institute especially to see if you were here, you'd think he'd have called them straightaway once he'd found you, wouldn't you?'

'Well, we have known each other for a very long time, Peter said in a conciliatory tone. 'I know he's angry now, but I'm sure he trusts me. I've known him since I was eighteen when I was one of his students. He's worried about what this might do to the reputation of his institute. He's retiring the day after tomorrow, so he's probably afraid that this is going to tarnish his life's work in the last few days of his career.'

'Well then,' Judith said, pulling the blanket off the glass cabinet. 'Let's get a move on, shall we?'

She put her hands back inside the gloves and managed to remove the lid without too much trouble. She held on to it for a moment, like a magician keeping her audience in suspense during a vanishing trick.

Peter came back over to the cabinet and put his arm around her.

Judith put the lid down.

Inside the casket were two double rolls of paper of some sort, either parchment or perhaps very thin vellum. There were wooden handles at either end of each roll, giving them the appearance of miniature Torah scrolls. They both seemed to be in astonishingly good shape.

Peter and Judith held their breath.

Very carefully, Judith picked up one of the scrolls as Peter exhaled slowly through his teeth.

'The casket's construction is ingenious,' he said. 'It's protected the contents for centuries from anything that could have damaged them... Can you unroll one? We'll take some photos and then put them straight back inside.'

Judith moved the casket, its lid, and the tools to one side to make room. She painstakingly unrolled the first document, and they both saw that its 'pages' were covered in very neat writing, like the words on a Torah scroll.

'This is so neat. I think it must be a transcription,' Peter remarked. 'It looks like it's possibly a clean copy of something else. Letters, maybe? Can you keep it rolled out and weigh the corners down with something to stop it rolling back up? Then we can take the photos.'

Judith did what Peter asked.

'It's Greek,' he said. 'Can you read this?'

'Well, I might be able to decipher bits and pieces with a dictionary,' Judith said dubiously. 'But this is the original text, of course, so it hasn't got any commas, full stops or capital letters.'

'Oh. That's a pity,' Peter replied, disappointed.

'But I know someone who would have no trouble translating it,' she said delightedly. 'He's kind of a genius. Mark. He was two years ahead of me originally, but life got in the way, and he fell behind in his studies. He says, "Punctuation is for dummies."' She smiled, but she wasn't looking at Peter. 'Did you know spaces weren't added between individual words until somewhere in late antiquity? Experienced readers wouldn't have needed them, but then suddenly, there was a need for word dividers to make texts easier to read.'

Judith had arranged the scroll so that the first page was completely open. She withdrew her arms from the gloves and took the first picture with the Polaroid camera. The photograph came out of the camera almost as soon as she pressed the button. It was completely white, but within a minute or so, a hazy image began to appear. They waited for the photograph to fully develop, and when it did, the quality of the image surprised them both.

'Wow!' said Judith. 'I did not expect it to be so clear.'

'I told you it was state of the art,' Peter said triumphantly. 'But come on, let's not waste any time.'

Judith put the photo aside and unrolled the next page. 'It looks like ... what I just said – like a neat copy. Look, it's all written in the same handwriting, all uniform, without any corrections or crossings out. I'm curious,' she said as she took another photograph, 'about whether that other scroll is in the same handwriting.'

'Can you say anything about what's written on it?' Peter asked.

'It seems to be a letter. It doesn't look like an official document or anything like that. But sorry, apart from that, I can't tell. I would really need a dictionary.'

'Let's take these pictures as fast as we can, then. We'll have a chance to translate it later.'

'Okay.'

The first scroll was twelve pages long. It contained what appeared to be separate letters – if they were indeed letters – because every now and then, there was a blank space separating two blocks of text.

When Judith had taken the last picture of the first scroll, she gasped.

'What is it?' Peter asked.

'Look!' Judith pointed at the final line. 'Look at that! That name turns up a lot. I've only just noticed it. See?'

She carefully hovered her finger over the name to show Peter where it was.

Ἰούδας

'Judas. And here, at the beginning of this next letter, in the first sentence, it says... Wait a minute... I can read this! It says: "*Cephas, a servant and apostle of Yeshua, greets*"... "Cephas", that's Simon, Peter... And then, look, here it says: "*you, good Judas*".'

Judith looked up in amazement at Peter, who was staring intently at the document in front of them. 'Could it be...? Letters from the Apostle Peter to Judas Iscariot? But then...'

'Then this would be even more explosive than Thomas ever dared to imagine,' Peter added.

'This might be something much bigger than we can handle, Peter,' Judith stammered. 'Is that what the man who broke into your flat meant when he said that we didn't realise what we were getting into?'

Peter nodded.

'Who knows, Judith? But then, how could he have known that Thomas had found something? If Thomas had hidden it in the tent, wouldn't we be the only ones who knew about it?'

The telephone in Hoogers' room rang. They heard him answer it, and then the muffled sound of him speaking to someone. He hung up again a few moments later.

'We don't have much time,' Judith said. 'Let's photograph the other scroll, and then we'll go to the police with Professor Hoogers, all right?'

She rolled the first scroll back up, returned it to the ivory box, and took out the second one. This scroll also appeared to have twelve 'pages'. The handwriting was identical to that of the first.

'I get the impression,' Judith said when she reached the end of the scroll, 'that this is someone's copy of a series of letters between two people. The letters from the Apostle Peter in the first scroll and the letters from... My God, Peter. Now I see it! These were written by Judas! The letters on the first scroll are from the Apostle Peter and the letters on the second scroll are from Judas Iscariot. Look at this! They're even signed with his name!'

'Or,' Peter suggested, 'they were written by someone else who used Judas and Peter's names. Just like those letters in the New Testament weren't actually written by Saint Peter either.'

'But Thomas was convinced that these letters were authentic. Didn't he say to you: "I found him"? "I found him," those were his words, weren't they? He must have found something that could only have belonged to Saint Peter. He was trying to make it clear to you that he was absolutely certain that the casket belonged to him.'

She rolled the second scroll up tight again and put it back in the casket. Then she replaced the lid and tapped it gently to seal it just as tightly as it had been when they found it.

Judith stacked the two sets of photos into a single pile,

found a pen in Peter's desk, and numbered the back of each one.

Meanwhile, Peter unplugged the cabinet and unfastened the clamps around it.

He lifted out the casket and gave it back to Judith. Then he took an envelope from his desk drawer, put the Polaroids inside, folded it over, and tucked it into his inside pocket.

They put on their coats.

'Well done, Judith,' he said. 'We've done as much as we can. Now we'll go back to see Professor Hoogers, and then we'll hand ourselves in to the police. We'll give them the casket, but we'll keep the photos, just in case. I don't want to think about that casket falling into the wrong hands. What if it really is an exchange of letters between Saint Peter and Judas Iscariot? What an insight that would give us into the beginnings of Christianity ... through the eyes of Jesus' apostles.'

They heard the door to Hoogers' office being opened. Hoogers went into the corridor, but he didn't come into Peter's office as they expected him to. His footsteps seemed to be moving away, towards the institute's front door.

Peter went to open his own office door, but Judith suddenly grabbed his arm.

'There's something strange going on here, Peter.' The words tumbled out of her in a frantic rush. 'I couldn't put my finger on why, but after Professor Hoogers left, I felt really unsettled. I had this feeling that something wasn't right.'

'What do you mean?'

'Do you remember what the professor said just before he closed the door?'

'Yes. He wanted to know whether we still had the thing we'd stolen...' He didn't finish his sentence; it was starting to dawn on him too.

'How did he know we'd taken something from the dig?' Judith asked with rising panic. 'Thomas had hidden the casket up on the ridgepole of that tent. We were the first ones to reach him after he was attacked. I'd already put the casket in my bag when you came back with the paramedics and the police. So somehow...'

They heard Hoogers' voice in the distance. It sounded like he was in conversation with someone.

'The only person who knows we took something is the man who attacked us. Peter, no one else could possibly be aware of that. No one.'

They heard the front door slam shut, followed by two sets of footsteps coming towards them. Whoever it was, they were no longer talking.

'The only way he could know is if...' Judith looked at the window. 'Does that window open?' she asked, grabbing the chair from behind Peter's desk. She rolled it over to the door and jammed it under the handle to jam it. 'Come on! We've got to go!' she whispered. 'The only way Professor Hoogers could have known is if he had spoken to the man who attacked us.'

Hoogers and his companion had arrived at Peter's door. Someone rattled at the door handle but failed to push it down. Then Hoogers knocked a few times and said in a low, calm voice: 'Will you open this door? My patience is wearing thin. We had an agreement. So please open this door.'

'We're coming,' Peter called to him as he nodded towards the window.

Hoogers knocked on the door several more times. Peter saw through the frosted glass that the other figure was moving backwards away from it.

Judith opened the window, immediately triggering a flashing red light on the outside of the building. For a moment, they were both frozen by indecision, but then Judith jumped into action, grabbing Peter's hand.

'Come on,' she said. 'We're going to blend in with the crowds out there.' And she dragged him out of the window and led him towards the Rapenburg.

Chapter Eight

'But this doesn't make any sense, Judith. Professor Hoogers would never do such a thing. He's a professor!' Peter stopped. 'For God's sake, surely you don't think someone with his reputation would get mixed up with a character like that, do you? Come on, let's go back. We'll tell him that we panicked because we didn't know who was in the corridor with him. He's bound to understand that we were suspicious after what happened to us earlier tonight.'

Judith marched on without looking back at him.

Peter was forced to follow her. 'Judith!' he shouted. 'What are you doing?'

'Going to the fair,' she told him, still not looking back.

'But it's swarming with police there.'

'That's right.' Now she stopped at last. 'Swarming with police who'll all have their hands full trying to control crowds of people who've been drinking all day. On a night like this, the police won't have the manpower to send that many officers out looking for us. They know who we are; I mean, they know who *you* are. And they also know that you won't be able to avoid them forever. The police will be more interested in making sure tonight goes smoothly, and then tomorrow, you'll be the first person they go after, believe me. Anyway, I have a plan. Come on.'

She led him to the corner of the Rapenburg and the Breestraat, and then on to Kort Rapenburg. The short street had been closed to traffic, and both sides of the road were awash with trampled plastic beakers, paper, and empty French fry trays.

A great stream of people, most of them clutching plastic cups of beer, were moving through the street towards the fairground. Many had decked themselves out with comical wigs or cowboy hats or had draped big feather boas around their necks. When they reached the Blauwpoortsbrug, Peter and Judith found the bridge full of food vendors and colourful market stalls selling clothes, watches, and perfumes.

Judith pulled Peter over to one of the stalls where she found a huge, curly, orange wig that the stallholder was selling off for next to nothing now that the European football championship was over. She twisted up her long hair and tucked it under the wig. She picked up a wide-brimmed red and white cowboy hat emblazoned with the two crossed keys featured on the city's coat of arms and put it on Peter's head. Then she found a red stick of face paint, and, steadying his face with a hand on his chin, she wrote on both of his cheeks.

'There. Now you do me.'

'What should I write?'

'I wrote "03" and "10" on your cheeks. I'm sure you can think of something,' she said, laughing.

Peter looked at her. With her hair tucked up under the wig, he could see her whole face, and he noticed again how beautiful she was.

He held her head still, cupping a hand under her chin and resting his fingers on the side of her face. On one cheek, he drew a heart and coloured it in, and on the other, he drew two crossed keys.

The seller had watched all of this with amused interest, but now he wanted his money. Judith took her purse from her bag and paid him. On the next stall, she ordered two large beers. They both took a few big gulps before continuing on to the fairground. They passed some policemen on the way. Just as Judith had predicted, they were far too busy paying attention to the groups of high-spirited revellers around them to notice two well-behaved nobodies passing quietly by.

The alcohol began to make Peter relax a little, and if they hadn't been in such a bizarre situation, he might even have been able to enjoy it. They walked arm-in-arm past the fairground rides which were all spinning and twisting at full tilt.

October 2nd had always been Peter's favourite part of the festival. The street bands, the hustle and bustle of the fairground, the smells of all those food stalls... He'd enjoyed the festival to its fullest ever since his earliest student days. Usually, he and his friends went to the Antonius Clubhouse where they'd sing rousing sentimental ballads about love and life with the 'real Leideners'. Afterwards, they'd move on to Burgerzaken in the Breestraat to dance the night away. Sometimes they literally danced all night, and occasionally they went straight from the café to the Reveille outside the city hall to sing the national anthem and hear the trumpeter wake the city. From there, it was on to the Van der Werffpark where hymns were sung from eight o'clock in the morning. Then, finally, to the Waaggebouw, once the city's weigh house, where free white bread and herring was distributed to anyone who could prove their connection to the town.

Traditionally, the next night, October 3rd, was the evening when there was most likely to be trouble in the city. Many people, tired from the previous day and drunk for the second night in a row, would end up brawling. At one time, these rowdy Leideners had made targets of the city's students. During freshers' week, those who wore glasses had always been warned to leave them at home during the October 3rd celebrations so they would look less conspicuously like students. Fortunately, those days were long gone, but for many, what could often still be a much grimmer atmosphere on the second evening was reason enough to stay home.

Judith and Peter walked onto the Beestenmarkt, a triangular plaza with a fountain bordered on one side by a canal. There were smaller fairground stalls here, like a shooting gallery, hook-a-duck, and tin-can alley, which would usually be aimed at children, but today, the booths were surrounded by adults in various stages of inebriation attempting to knock over pyramids of cans, or fish brightly coloured ducks out of a plastic moat filled with flowing water.

'What do we do now?' Peter asked as he crushed his empty plastic beaker.

'Let's stay here a bit longer. I think that's probably the best thing to do for now. We can go to my house in an hour or so. You know where the Sionshofje is?'

'Behind the Kijkhuis cinema?'

'That's right. It'll be midnight in an hour, and the fair will be closing down. If they know who I am, they'll have been to my house already, and I'm sure they won't come back tonight. We'll have time to look at the photos we've taken when we get there. I'd rather go home straightaway, but I think it's probably a good idea to put them off the scent for a while. They probably won't be expecting us to be here right now.'

They had reached the end of the Nieuwe Beestenmarkt, a broad street lined with shops and restaurants, and emerged onto the Lammermarkt, which was dominated by the De Valk windmill. They were in the heart of the fairground now, caught up in a dense crowd of people that slowed them to a shuffling pace.

'Make sure you keep a tight hold of your bag,' Peter warned.

Judith blinked reassuringly.

They inched past the bumper cars where packs of teenagers had gathered. There was a chill in the air, but many of them were coatless. The music was so deafening that conversation required cupping a hand around someone's ear and yelling into it. There were all kinds of rides on the fairground. One that spun riders around dizzyingly fast while a giant arm slowly lifted them upwards. There was a sort of long pendulum with a cage at the end that whirled its strapped-in passengers around as it swung them upside down. Peter felt nauseous just watching it.

Judith stopped at the Ferris wheel which, at more than fifty metres tall, towered over all the other rides. 'Let's go on this,' she said. 'Leave all our earthly cares behind for a while, literally and figuratively.' She bought two tickets, and they joined the queue of people waiting to get on.

Peter was surprised that Judith seemed to have taken charge from the moment that... Actually, when had that happened? From the moment she'd taken over opening the casket, he realised.

It was their turn to board, and they stepped into the gondola together.

Peter thought about how his parents had met, just like this, on a Ferris wheel. A smaller one, of course, but still... His father had been queueing for the ride with two friends at the fair in Delft, standing next to his mother and her two girlfriends. Their friends had all rushed to clamber into gondolas, leaving them alone next to each other. The ride's owner had pushed them both into the next gondola without so much as a by-your-leave, and so fate had brought them together. At least, that was the way his parents had always told this well-loved family story. It had often made Peter think about the role chance had played in his life. He and his brothers and sisters would never have been born if his parents had gone to the fair just a few minutes later. How often had we missed out on something by being somewhere at the wrong time? Or unwittingly saved our own lives by leaving home a few moments later, narrowly avoiding being involved in an accident? What might have happened if Thomas had called just a minute or two earlier? Judith wouldn't have arrived at his office at that point, so she wouldn't have gone with him to the dig site, the casket might have remained undiscovered, and he wouldn't be sitting here with her now. Were humans merely insignificant cogs in a bigger machine, unable to avoid their eventual fate? Did it matter what decisions you made? Or was everything predetermined?

The ride started to move.

Out of the corner of his eye, Peter noticed someone standing near the Ferris wheel, staring at him. Judith squeezed his arm tightly. She had seen him too.

'Is that him?' she whispered it softly, even though no one else could hear.

Peter tried to reassure her. 'No, I don't think so.'

As their gondola moved further and further away from the ground, and the man gazing up at them grew smaller and smaller. He appeared to be gesturing at them, pointing the index and middle finger of his right hand at his eye and then at Judith and Peter.

'How did he know we were here?' Judith said. 'That man is driving me nuts.'

'He must be the person Professor Hoogers let into the institute earlier. But I don't understand how the professor is involved in all of this. Perhaps he threatened him too? No, Hoogers seemed to be at ease in his company. So what does he have to do with it? And that man, he must have walked around the institute and then followed us at a distance. I can't think how else he would know we were here. And now he's letting us know he's watching us.'

After the wheel had rotated a couple of times, Judith and Peter's gondola stopped at the very top where it dangled, swinging them gently back and forth. They had a fantastic view of the city and the brightly lit square below them. A strong breeze blustered around their faces. Peter suddenly felt ridiculous with the big cowboy hat on his head, and Judith was looking much less self-assured than she had earlier.

The wheel didn't stand still for long, but it felt like an eternity, dangled between heaven and earth, between life and death.

Peter realised that this might be the last normal moment of his life as he knew it. He thought of the commotion that was certain to break out once they arrived back on the ground. They would lose the casket and probably the photographs too. For a moment, he had a flash of hope: there was no way the man knew about the photos. But ... no, there was. Professor Hoogers was sure to have seen Verbeek's cabinet in Peter's office and worked out what they were doing. But even if they were acquitted of Thomas's murder, he'd still taken something from an archaeological dig, and that would inevitably be exposed. Plus, his reputation would be tarnished forever by the fact that he'd gone on the run from the police. And who knew how much influence Hoogers had? Or how ruinous that influence could be? He could probably forget about his academic career after this.

The Ferris wheel started to move again, and all too quickly, the gondolas were lowered back to the ground. The man hadn't taken his eyes off Peter and Judith the whole time, and now he moved closer to the ride's exit gate.

When their gondola came to a standstill, they were reluctant to leave it, but the fairground worker waiting at the bottom hurried them to get out so that his next customers could take their seats.

For a moment, Peter considered buying another pair of tickets and going around again, but he knew that this would only postpone the inevitable. They stepped off the platform next to the ticket booth and back onto the street. The man was calmly waiting for them, knowing they wouldn't be able to get past him. He put his hand in his coat pocket as if to tell them that he still had a gun. It was like a scene from a western with a faceoff between two gunslingers.

Peter leaned over to Judith. 'Maybe this would be a good time to get the attention of that policeman over there.'

'No. They'll lock us up, and we'll be stuck there all night. They'll make us hand in everything we have on us now, including the photographs, and all this will have been for nothing. We can smooth everything over tomorrow morning. Right now, I want to go home and look at what was written on those scrolls. But we'll have to get rid of him first.'

To Peter's astonishment, rather than walking away from

the man, Judith walked straight up to him. This also seemed to catch the gunman off guard.

Peter could clearly see the wound on his jaw where Judith had hit him with the casket earlier that evening. As she approached him, Judith unbuttoned her coat. She rammed her body into his, and then she started to scream.

'Get off me, you drunken idiot!' she shrieked.

The man flinched, and within seconds, a circle of people had gathered around them. Peter moved closer, and now he could see that the top half of Judith's blouse was hanging open as though it had been violently snatched at. The top two buttons had fallen to the ground.

She kept shouting. 'Were you trying to grab my breasts? What's wrong with you?'

She gave the man a hard shove, and he staggered backwards, bumping into a group of teenage boys who were clearly not about to come to his aid. One of them even grabbed his upper arm. Judith moved closer to him.

'Leave me alone!' she shouted. 'It's over! Why won't you just accept it?'

Some of the bystanders started to laugh. The boy who was holding the man by the arm tightened his grip.

'Did you hear her, you tosser?' he shouted in his ear. 'She doesn't want you anymore. You had your chance. Now get lost.' He yanked at his arm, forcing him to turn around.

The boy turned around and grinned at Judith. 'He can come with us for a bit. Give you a chance to make yourself decent,' he said as he cast a quick glance at her breasts, which were now partly exposed. His friends laughed and moved away with the man trapped in between them. He had no choice but to go with them.

Judith held the top of her blouse closed with one hand. A girl came up to her and said, 'I would report him if I were you, you know. Like, seriously. It's happened to me as well.'

But Judith politely brushed her off. 'No need. I think he's learned his lesson now. He's not that bad, really. But thanks for your advice anyway.'

She returned to Peter, and he put his arm around her. They walked like that together, passing through the narrow Lange Scheistraat that connected the Lammermarkt with the Oude Singel. On their right was the old Lakenhal, once the guild hall for the city's cloth merchants. They crossed the little bridge over the Oude Vest canal and walked past the tightly packed houses on the Lange Lijsbethsteeg until they reached the Groot Sionshof, where Judith lived. Just before they rounded the corner, they heard a voice coming through a two-way radio, crackling and hissing in a way that Peter had only ever heard in films.

Judith peered cautiously around the corner and saw a policeman getting into a car and closing the door behind him. The flashing light was turned off, and the car drove smoothly away.

'All right, so they know who I am and where I live. But now they've established that I'm not at home, they're not likely to come back for a while.'

She walked up to the courtyard's heavy outer door and opened it with a large, old-fashioned key that she took out of her bag. As silently as they could, they walked through the courtyard garden until they came to a door with *J. Cherev* painted on it in swooping white letters.

As they went inside, Peter noticed that next to the front door, there was a mezuzah, a cylinder containing verses from the Torah that Jews traditionally fixed to their doorposts.

Judith flipped a light switch in the hall. 'Wait here, will you? I'm going to change my blouse.'

She left Peter standing in the hall while she went into the living room where she closed the curtains and turned on the lamp over the dining table. Some clothes that she must have worn earlier were slung over a dining chair. She kept her back to him as she removed her coat and blouse and loosened her bra. She seemed completely at ease. Peter stared at her bare back but then took a step backwards so that she was out of his line of sight.

She emerged from the room a few moments later. 'Let's go,' she said, 'we're going to see Mark.'

'In the middle of the night?'

'Mark's a night owl,' she reassured him, 'just like me, so he often studies late into the night. He lives in the house opposite, and I can see him working from my bedroom window. I usually turn my light off and on a couple of times before I go to bed to say goodnight. Then he does the same with his desk lamp.'

They walked around the courtyard's garden to Mark's house, where the lights were still on. Through the net curtains, Peter saw a young man bent over a desk, writing. Judith tapped three times on the window. Mark looked over his shoulder. He didn't seem surprised to have visitors at this late hour. He stood up and disappeared into the hall.

'Judith?' came the curious-sounding voice from behind the door.

'Hey, Mark,' Judith said affectionately. 'Can we come in?'

The door opened.

'Of course, come through,' he said, stepping aside in the narrow hallway to let them in.

Judith kissed his cheek, standing on her tiptoes to reach. Peter watched as he put his arm around her. They stood that way, in a kind of half embrace, for a moment or two until Peter cleared his throat.

'Let me introduce you two,' Judith said when she'd pulled away from Mark. 'This is Peter de Haan. He is a lecturer at...'

Mark shook his hand. 'I know Peter,' Mark said. 'I know you,' he said again, to Peter this time. 'Archaeology department, right? And history?'

Peter nodded.

'I've got your book. That overview of the history of Leiden. Although I have to confess that I've not got around to reading it yet. But come on in.'

They went inside, and Peter closed the front door behind them.

Judith took off her coat and shoes and gestured to Peter that he should do the same. Mark walked ahead of them into the living room, which was sparsely furnished and scrupulously neat and tidy. A bookcase covered an entire wall, and the books wedged into it were all arranged by colour.

Peter raised his eyebrows in amusement and looked at Judith, who smiled back at him.

'To what do I owe the pleasure of this nocturnal visit?' Mark asked Judith.

'You might want to sit down, Mark,' she replied. 'Because I'm about to tell you an unbelievable story.'

While Judith sketched a picture of what had happened over the last few hours, Peter let his gaze wander around the room. A sofa, an armchair, a coffee table. This was the home of a very well-organised person, he thought. There wasn't a thing out of place, not a scrap of paper nor any opened mail or old newspapers anywhere. On a table pushed up against the desk was a hefty-looking typewriter with a sheet of paper sticking out of it, half-filled with text.

When Judith finished her account, the room felt strangely quiet. Mark stared into space, as though he'd fallen into a sort of trance. A frown appeared on his forehead, but still, he said nothing.

'You're right, that is quite a crazy story,' he said suddenly. 'But that doesn't mean one can assume, a priori, that it's untrue, of course.' And once again, he seemed to sink into a state of deep contemplation.

Peter looked at Judith, who shrugged her shoulders and surreptitiously shook her head. The silence that hung in the room was almost tangible.

Peter decided to break it. 'How far along are you with your degree?' he asked Mark.

'I'm almost finished,' replied Mark, coming back to life,

but he still looked distant and dazed. 'I'm working on my dissertation.' He nodded towards his desk.

'And what's it about?' Peter asked.

'How the synoptic gospels relate to a legendary manuscript called "Quelle" or "Q", which is believed to have been the source for part of the gospels of Matthew and Luke,' Mark told him. Talking about his dissertation had brought him back to familiar territory, and he seemed to have recovered from his reverie.

'But "Q" is just something that Bible scholars have hypothesised, isn't it? Or do you think that something like "Q" really does exist? An actual written collection of Jesus' sayings?' Peter asked.

'I think such a thing did indeed exist, and there are many who agree with me. All kinds of people have reconstructed "Q", but I'm conceited enough to think that I could do it better. So that's what my dissertation is about, in brief.'

He smiled almost apologetically, as if he was afraid of boring his listeners with even this short summary.

Peter noticed a picture frame on Mark's desk. Instead of a photograph, it contained a text written in ornate letters: PUNCTUATION IS FOR DUMMIES. A joker had stuck a yellow post-it note in the corner with the text GODISNOWHERE.

'That sounds more like a PhD thesis than a dissertation,' Peter said.

'My dissertation really only focuses on one aspect of it, namely the parables, and the linguistic differences between the versions told in the synoptic gospels of Matthew, Mark, and Luke. And as well as being my dissertation, it's going to form the basis of my research proposal for a PhD position after I graduate.'

Peter nodded approvingly. 'So what do you think?' he wanted to know.

'About the scrolls you found in the ivory box? If the letters really were written by Saint Peter and Judas Iscariot, why are they in Greek?'

'They might have dictated the letters in their own language to an assistant, a secretary. Not many people were able to write then, so it wouldn't have been unusual to have someone else write your letters for you. But they would have written them in Aramaic. They may well have decided to translate the letters into Greek at a later time since Greek was more widely spoken.'

'But it looks like these documents weren't intended to be read by the outside world, doesn't it?'

'Not by the outside world that their writers were living in at the time. But who knows what other issues were at play? Perhaps their author or authors thought these letters were very important, and they were worried that they would somehow get lost. They decided to have them translated into Greek so that they'd have a wider reach. Who can say? And who says this is the only copy? If they are transcribed letters, then perhaps the original letters still exist.'

Judith nodded as if she was convinced.

'I see that you're not using a computer, by the way,' remarked Peter.

'No. I did try working on a computer in the university library, but I was forever losing my work because I kept forgetting to save it. I think that this' – he pointed to the typewriter – 'suits me better. My tutor has given me permission to hand in a typewritten dissertation. I think he actually found it rather amusing. I know I'll probably have to make the switch to using a word processor, eventually. I don't think I'll be able to avoid it forever.'

'I typed the first draft of my dissertation proposal on that, actually,' Judith said. 'Mark read it and made some comments. I incorporated his ideas, and then I typed it up again on the computer before I sent it to you.'

Peter nodded. The image of Judith working in this room and Mark enjoying the pleasure of her company... It made him feel a little envious.

'But what if these letters *are* authentic?' Peter said. 'Just think! Judith and I have seen the names Cephas and Judas in them already. If what we've found really is an exchange of letters between Saint Peter and Judas Iscariot, it would be incendiary, wouldn't it?'

'It would certainly be extraordinary,' said Mark cautiously. 'Whether it would actually be incendiary remains to be seen. It could have been written by other people using Judas and Peter's names. That would make it just another manuscript that we can add to the long list of apocryphal gospels. And even if they were written by Peter and Judas, we still don't know how much of what they say differs from the accounts that were passed down and eventually formed the New Testament. Show me the photos, and I'll see what I can make of them.'

Peter took the Polaroids from his inside pocket but didn't hand them straight over to Mark.

'There's something that's always puzzled me about the gospels,' Judith said.

'What's that?' Peter asked.

'The role Judas played. I've never been able to understand it. He was one of Jesus' closest disciples, part of the inner circle who were there from the start. Jesus apparently trusted him enough to make him his treasurer, so it seems unlikely that Judas, of all people, would be the one to betray Jesus, and for a paltry handful of silver coins at that.'

'Coins that weren't even in use at the time,' Mark added.

'No?' she asked, surprised.

'They used drachmas, didrachmas, sickles, denarii, and other currencies in those days, but not silver coins. They fell into disuse three hundred years before Jesus was born. It's just another detail that reminds us that we shouldn't always interpret the gospels historically,' Mark explained. 'The sum of thirty pieces of silver goes back to a prophecy made by Zechariah, and that was simply added to the story to show that Jesus was the Messiah. Matthew mistakenly thought the prophecy was made by Jeremiah, by the way, but that's not relevant here. Unless you believe that the New Testament is literally the Word of God, which would make that kind of mistake more difficult to explain away.'

'But apart from that,' Judith interrupted him, 'if Judas hadn't betrayed Jesus, then Jesus wouldn't have been arrested or crucified. So surely the role Judas played was essential to the whole story? And Jesus himself knew what Judas was going to do. He told Judas so himself at the Last Supper: "Do what you are here to do." I've always thought it was unfair that Judas got such a bad name when he was only helping Jesus to carry out his plan. And then, after Jesus was arrested, he went back to the high priests to return the money because he'd realised how grave the situation actually was for Jesus. They refused to take the money, so he threw the coins at their feet...'

'Maybe he'd just found out that they'd not been valid currency for the last three hundred years,' Peter quipped.

Judith ignored him. 'He threw the coins on the ground,' she continued, 'and then he hanged himself. I always thought that was so tragic.'

'Or, alternatively, he threw himself off a cliff, landed on the rocks, and his intestines burst out of him,' Mark suggested. 'The way Judas met his end depends on which Bible book you're reading.'

'But if these letters are authentic,' Judith went on, 'then we know Judas didn't commit suicide.'

Mark agreed with her. 'Personally, I believe he didn't commit suicide. In his first letter to the congregation of Corinth, a port in ancient Greece, the Apostle Paul writes that Jesus appeared to Cephas after his resurrection, and – take note – to the twelve apostles. That was before the Ascension, which means that, according to the account given in Acts, it was before they'd chosen a new apostle to replace Judas, who had supposedly killed himself. Paul must have been completely unaware of this suicide because he doesn't write about Judas at all. So when he writes that Jesus appeared to the twelve, Judas was still one of them. Maybe Judas did hand Jesus over to the Romans, as the Greek word used in the gospels suggests, but that wasn't seen as a betrayal at all, originally. If it had been, it would make what happened at the Last Supper quite unbelievable: Jesus tells the disciples that one of them will betray him. They're all shocked by this, and ask: "Surely not I, Lord?" And then Judas says: "Surely not I, Rabbi?" and Jesus confirms that Judas will indeed be the one. And after that exchange, they all just let Judas leave! So it's clear that they all understood that one of them would have to deliver Jesus to the authorities, but none of them wanted to do it. I think the role Judas played has been distorted over time. Later history, which was often deeply anti-Semitic, portrayed Judas as the archetypical Jew, willing to betray anyone, even his master, for money. Who knows, maybe we're about to learn more about what his role really was. It would make sense if Judas returned to the group after he'd accomplished his task.'

'Why did Jesus have to be betrayed, then?' Judith asked.

'You could fill a library with everything that's been written on that subject,' Mark said. 'It's possible that they expected God to intervene as soon as the Romans arrested Jesus and show that he truly was the Messiah.'

'And that didn't happen,' said Judith.

'That did not happen, no – quite the opposite. Jesus was crucified as a criminal. His words "My God, my God, why have you forsaken me?" might well be the most authentic words spoken by Jesus in the whole of the New Testament.'

Peter looked at the painting above the sofa, a reproduction of Rembrandt's *Two Old Men Disputing* which depicted Saint Peter and Saint Paul in conversation. A local artist had painstakingly copied it, and the impressive result was now hanging prominently in the Pieterskerk. Although the church was named for Saint Peter, not many people knew that it was also dedicated to Saint Paul. For Peter, the most interesting thing about the painting was that Rembrandt had clearly made Saint Paul the image's focus. Not Saint Peter, who Jesus himself had said was the person upon whom he would build his church. That's why Jesus even changed his name from Simon to Petrus, meaning 'rock'. But here, Paul was brightly illuminated at the centre of the canvas, while Saint Peter was seen only from behind. Saint Paul occupied a higher position, literally sitting above Saint Peter, who was made to look slightly submissive. It had always seemed to Peter that there was no discussion taking place in the painting at all. Rather, Paul was lecturing Peter, telling him that he was wrong about something.

What might they have been talking about? Perhaps one of the Old Testament prophecies about the Messiah? Saint Peter is pointing at the pages of a book, perhaps to emphasise the strength of his argument. But what could a simple fisherman like Peter have to say to a dyed-in-the-wool orator like Paul, who would have been skilled in the finer points of theological debate? Had Rembrandt known something that the general public didn't know? Could he have been the guardian of a secret passed down from generation to generation?

'Well then,' said Mark, 'I'm going to make a start on this. Do you think you could make a pot of tea?'

Judith got up and motioned to Peter that he should follow her.

He gave the photos to Mark, who took them from him

with two hands. Peter noticed that his hands were trembling slightly.

Before he closed the door, Peter looked back at Mark, who was already sitting at his desk. He had put all the photos down except one, which he was holding in his hand and staring at in astonishment.

With a sudden, growing sense of uneasiness, Peter followed Judith into the kitchen.

Chapter Nine

J udith filled the kettle with water and put it on the hob.
Peter saw her reflection in the kitchen window with
the deep darkness of night beyond it. He leant against
the doorframe.

Judith stared at the kettle. 'Mark was admitted a while
ago,' she said.

'Admitted? What do you mean by that?'

'He's really brilliant, possibly a little too brilliant. I've
always taken extra classes in theology, and he was two
years above me when I started my degree. Everyone in the
Theology department knew him. He was a rising star. He
even took over for one of the lecturers once when they were
off sick. Always organised, always so laid back. At least,
that's how he came across to everyone. I liked him
straightaway. I felt really comfortable around him. Never in
a... How should I put it? I was never in love with him. He
felt more like a big brother to me. And he still does, really.
We had lunch together in the café in the LAK, studied in

the library together. People thought we must be a couple, or they saw it as inevitable that we eventually would be, but it never happened. Not in the way people expected, anyway.'

Judith rinsed out a teapot and assembled some cups. The ease with which she opened the cupboards, obviously familiar with where everything was, told Peter that she was quite at home in Mark's kitchen.

'We talked a lot, discussed religion a lot, obviously. The more I studied, the more Jewish I felt, and the more deeply I began to explore my background. But the more Mark studied, the more conflicted he felt about the faith he'd been raised in.'

The sound the kettle made as it heated on the hob started to change tone, indicating that the water was coming to the boil. Judith grabbed the handle with a tea towel.

'It's fairly common among theology students,' she continued. 'I've seen it happen with lots of people, a crisis of faith brought on by studying religion. Before he started his degree, he'd always been a dedicated member of his church, and like most other churchgoers, he just accepted whatever was preached from the pulpit. But the more he studied theology, the more troubled he became about the inconsistencies between the gospels.'

'Which inconsistencies?'

The water was boiling now, and the steam streamed through the whistle. Judith quickly flipped the cap open, halting the shrill sound. She poured the hot water into the teapot, and for a moment, as she stood shrouded in a cloud of steam, Peter thought she could have been a high priestess who had just thrown a sacrificial offering onto a fire altar.

'Well, those things you told me about in the hospital chapel, for example. What were Jesus' actual last words? Who was there when the tomb was opened on Easter morning? It became an obsession. Mark was searching for the truth, so to speak. So you could see his dissertation in that light. And his doctoral research too because he's more or less been promised a PhD place. He wants to see if he can create a definitive reconstruction of "Q" and uncover the true story and true words of Jesus. Ideally, he'd like it to be the version used in church services from now on, but I think he's given up on that goal for now. Things started to go wrong for him when he was writing his own version of one of the Gospels, the Gospel According to Mark.'

Now Peter was ashamed of how sermonising his tone must have seemed during their conversation in the hospital chapel. She'd turned out to be much more well informed about all sorts of subjects than he had assumed.

'Things went wrong for him?'

'Yes, it started to go wrong then. His behaviour got stranger and stranger. He could be quite disruptive, challenging lecturers in front of the whole class with questions that got more and more complex and detailed. Lectures had to be ended early because of him, more than once. Eventually, the staff held a meeting about him because the other students were lodging complaints about the way he was disrupting lectures, among other things. He just functioned on a different level to most of the rest of us. Mark suddenly stopped coming to lectures, and it got harder and harder to contact him. He was the one who helped me to get a house in this hofje, but it got to the point where he wouldn't even open the door to me. Said it would be better if I left him alone. So that's what I did.'

She put three cups on a tray, placed spoons next to them, and put the teapot next to the sugar bowl.

'A few weeks after I'd last tried knocking on his door, I got a phone call from Endegeest psychiatric hospital saying he'd been admitted. They'd picked him up off the street. He'd been standing on a box outside Central Station preaching to people, reading from his own gospel.'

'Wow, that sounds very distressing. And he still wants to do his PhD on the "Q" Gospel? Is that a good idea?'

'It was distressing, yes. He's all right now, but it was a difficult time for him. I visited him every two or three weeks. We went for walks around the hospital's grounds, and that was always lovely, actually. He's been back home for a year now, and he's picked his life back up again. The Theology department expressed their confidence in him, and that was very important to him.'

'That's good. And that bookcase? It's a bit unusual, isn't it?'

'Ah, his books,' she laughed. 'You mean how he's sorted them by colour? That started out as a bit of a joke. It began with the old-fashioned Dutch spelling book – you know the one, *The Little Green Book* – and he arranged his other green books next to it. It went on from there, and he decided to keep it that way. I never know where to find anything on his bookcase, but Mark knows exactly which book is where.

It's not a sign of madness, you know... Well, maybe it is just a little bit.'

She picked up the tray and nodded to indicate that they were going back to the living room. Mark hadn't moved from the position they'd left him in when they'd gone to make tea.

Peter found it slightly unnerving, but Judith didn't seem to notice. Perhaps she'd grown used to Mark's eccentric behaviour.

Judith poured out three cups of tea and spooned a carefully measured amount of sugar into Mark's cup. She brought it to him at the desk and then stood there for a few moments with her hand on his shoulder.

Peter spooned sugar into his own cup and stirred it mindlessly as the steam swirled upwards.

Judith resumed her place on the sofa next to Peter, sitting a little closer to him this time. Their thighs touched, and Peter felt the pleasant warmth of her body against his. He looked at her and smiled. She smiled back.

Peter stretched out his arm on the back of the sofa behind her.

Suddenly Mark, who was staring at the photograph and still hadn't spoken, broke the silence.

'I've seen this text before,' he said.

Chapter Ten

'What?' Judith and Peter both exclaimed at once.

Mark buried his face in his hands, rubbed his eyes, and then he looked at them and said it again: 'I've seen this text before.'

'But ... but that's...' Peter stammered.

'That's impossible,' Judith said, finishing his sentence.

'How on earth do you know it already?' Peter asked.

'It's a long story,' Mark sighed. 'Or a short one, depending on how you look at it.'

He stood, picked up his cup and came over to sit with them in the armchair next to the coffee table. He sipped his tea slowly, as though he was trying to buy time.

'Do you want to tell us?' Judith asked. 'Are you going to tell us?'

Mark gave them a penetrating look. 'I will tell you. You're both mixed up in it now, so you have a right to know what I know.' He put his cup down. 'It's an unbelievable coincidence, you coming with this. Coming to *me* with it, I mean. It's actually spooky,' he began. 'If I'd not lost my faith in God, I would have to conclude that this is divine providence. When you told me what had happened to you, Judith, I thought: this can't be true. But I took a good look at the first photo while you were in the kitchen, and then I was absolutely certain that I'd seen it before. I know what's in these letters without having to translate them. You're right. They were written by Saint Peter and Judas Iscariot.

'But...' Peter began, but Mark held up his hand, asking Peter to let him finish.

'Judith,' Mark said, 'do you remember Meneer Eco?'

'Meneer Eco,' Judith repeated the name uncertainly. Peter heard her make a quiet smacking sound, as if she was literally tasting the word on her tongue.

Then her face suddenly lit up. 'Oh, of course, the old librarian at the university. You used to have a bit of a thing going on with him, didn't you?'

'Yes, the librarian. And yes, I did "have a bit of a thing going on with him,"' he said, mimicking Judith's words with amusement. 'There was some gossip about it, all a bit unpleasant. People thought it was odd that someone as young as me should want to spend so much time with someone as old as him. We used to have lunch together sometimes, and we went for walks in the botanical gardens. He was an extraordinarily erudite man. A little odd, perhaps, but I enjoyed his company. Maybe he saw something of himself in me. At least, he said something along those lines once or twice. I think he enjoyed spending time with a younger version of himself.'

'And what about you?' Peter asked. Of course, Peter

knew who Eco was. The man had been a living legend, although Peter had never had much to do with him himself. He had seen him in the corridors of the faculty sometimes, paying a visit to Professor Hoogers.

'Me? You mean what I thought of him? As I said, he was an extraordinarily erudite man. I got on with him very well, and I loved listening to him. Meneer Eco had an international reputation as one of the leading specialists in Aramaic, the language spoken by Jesus and his disciples. He had this archaic way of speaking that fascinated me. He could deliver these long monologues, so eloquently and fluently, as if he had written them out at home before he actually said them out loud. Eco was a kind of mentor to me. In the East, they would probably call him a guru.'

A fleeting smile spread across Mark's face, like sun briefly breaking through clouds.

'Was his name really Eco?' Judith asked curiously. 'I always thought it was a kind of nickname or a shortened version of something else. Wasn't he Italian?'

'No, he wasn't. Eco is Old Frisian, I believe. It means something like "sword". When he was at school, the other children teased him and called him "Eco homo"... but I digress. Meneer Eco – we were always very polite with each other. We used formal pronouns and always addressed each other as "meneer" – he was rather an unusual librarian. He... How shall I put it...'

'Aha, now I remember him!' Judith said animatedly. 'Wasn't he the man who didn't want the library to lend people books?'

Mark smiled. 'Oh, he was worse than that. He would

rather not have let anyone into the library at all. He was responsible for the library's collection of ancient manuscripts, and he treasured them, almost regarded them as his personal property. Actually, I could probably leave that "almost" out. If it had been up to him, he would have kept his books away from the prying eyes of any researcher, whether they were from here or abroad. He would tell me stories about the people who had dared to touch a manuscript without protective gloves or who – oh, the horror! – sneezed at the dust that escaped when they opened an old book. He nearly had a heart attack when things like that happened. He would have liked to lock himself inside his domain like a modern monk and keep the evil world outside at bay. He was notorious for hardly ever granting anyone access to his collection. He was reprimanded by his manager several times for it, and even by the university's Executive Board.'

Peter shifted in his seat slightly, but not so much that he moved his leg away from Judith's. He could feel himself growing impatient: Mark really was digressing now. But Peter suspected that if he interrupted him, he might stop speaking.

'Anyway, to cut a long story short,' Mark continued. Peter exhaled a sigh of relief. 'He was prepared to let me into his sanctuary. Sometimes he hinted that he saw me as his ideal successor, but it's never been my ambition to become a librarian. I'm a theologian, just as he had been originally, and I want to be a part of the world, not shut away from it like he was. He could have been a professor, but he wouldn't have been able to cope with the pressure of lecturing. Besides, teaching was something that would have taken him away from what he saw as his real work. Being a librarian was the ideal occupation for him, especially when he allowed so few people into his sanctum that he could study uninterrupted for days on end.'

'There was something a bit suspicious about his death, wasn't there?' Peter asked.

'There was,' confirmed Mark. 'I'll come to that in a moment. But you knew him too?'

'Knew? No, not really. I knew who he was, of course. He sometimes came to the faculty to talk to Professor Hoogers, and I'd see him in the library, walking through the stacks. I don't recall ever actually speaking to him. I know he was found dead in his study in the library, and that the room had been turned upside down.'

'That's right, but ... I'll get to that shortly,' Mark said, and then he continued with his story. 'So I spent quite a lot of time with him, sometimes walking in the botanical gardens, as I said, but in the library's basement too. He kept his collection in a room down there where the temperature and humidity are precisely controlled. He'd show me the rare manuscripts, and when he told me about them, he was always so passionate. Sometimes he'd gloat about having refused to allow another famous academic to see a particular text. These were people who'd have given almost anything to have those works in their hands.'

Mark poured himself another cup of tea. Judith and Peter had let theirs get cold. Peter got the impression that Mark was about to get to the crux of his story.

'One day,' Mark told them, 'or rather, one evening after

the library had closed and we were the only ones left in the building, he confided to me that he'd come into possession of a certain text. He said it could shake Christianity to its foundations in a way that had never been seen before in all of history. And not just Christianity, but perhaps even the whole of Western civilisation. "The end of the world as we know it," he called it.'

'And that text was...' said Judith.

'And that text was, or appears to have been, the one that Thomas found yesterday. I know...' – he raised both his hands to stop Peter and Judith from interrupting him – 'I know... It doesn't seem possible, but listen. That evening, Meneer Eco also told me he'd been approached a few years earlier by someone asking him to look at a text. They were very secretive about it. The person he was dealing with didn't want to say who he was acting for, but money was apparently no object, and he gave away just enough to pique Eco's curiosity. Eco dealt with this sort of thing fairly regularly. He was often approached by people wanting him to look at a manuscript or a fragment of paper from a codex to determine its authenticity, and it was always done in the utmost secrecy. So this wasn't a routine request, but it wasn't out of the ordinary either. In this case, it concerned an ancient Aramaic text that this client, or the organisation they belonged to, had had in their possession for many years. Essentially, it had already been translated, but that had been many years ago, and the person making the request described the translation as being "very outdated". The way it was explained to Eco was that, in the same way new translations of the Bible are made all the time, the client wanted a new translation of this text written in more modern Dutch. Its contents were controversial, but it was very likely that it wasn't actually an original manuscript from the first century, but a forgery made at a later date. And since Eco was the world's leading authority on the Aramaic language, they'd come to him. He worked on the assignment almost incessantly for months. He'd had to swear to secrecy, and then when the translation was finished, things took an unpleasant turn. There was a narrowly veiled threat that something would happen to him and his family if he told anyone about what he'd been working on.'

'So he was taking an extraordinary risk by telling you about it,' said Judith, who, like Peter, had been riveted by Mark's story.

'There was a certain element of risk, yes, but at the same time, he didn't appear to take the threat seriously.'

'And did he take the text seriously?' Peter asked.

'No, he didn't appear to be taking that entirely seriously either. The contents were fantastic, almost too good to be true. But Eco broke his agreement with the client and made a secret copy of his translation when he was done. He pretended he was handing everything over to the contact person, including the notes he'd made over the months as he'd been working on it, but he kept a handwritten copy of the translation for himself. Maybe the threats had left him with a bad feeling about the person he'd been dealing with. But he let me read the text that night. So when I saw those photos just now, when you were in the kitchen, I could see from the first lines that this is the same text I read a translation of that night.'

He got up and crossed over to his desk to get the photographs.

'Look, this is the first photo. This text is in Ancient Greek, but its contents are the same as what I read then. It would take me months to translate it, but I can remember the first line, and I recognise it now in this text. He held the photo out in front of him and read the text aloud, first in Greek and then in Dutch. 'Cephas, a servant and apostle of Yeshua, greets you, good Judas.'

Judith and Peter looked at each other.

Mark put the pile of photos on his lap. 'I can't remember the contents word for word, of course, but I can tell you that it contained a very different version of events to the one that's given in the Bible. Meneer Eco made light of it, but it had quite a profound effect on me. I had been shown a possible alternative account of Jesus' final days and hours... That thought knocked me completely sideways. And that gospel of mine...' – he said, turning to Judith – 'the reason they put me away in Endegeest, that was largely based on what I could remember from the translation he let me read that evening.'

Judith looked at him, wide-eyed.

'I had to tell the world, but during my time on the secure ward it became clear to me that no one would believe me. They'd think I was a raving lunatic. And Meneer Eco died while I was there, so I lost my only chance to prove that I wasn't just babbling nonsense. Because this really could mean the end of the world as we know it.'

Mark took a breath as though he was about to elaborate – at least, that's what Peter assumed –

but just then, there were three hard raps on the living room window. Almost immediately afterwards, someone pressed the doorbell, holding it in.

All three of them froze. They heard the letterbox in the front door being opened.

Someone shouted: 'Meneer Labuschagne, could you open the door, please? We know you're home. This is the police.'

Chapter Eleven

Mark and Judith crept into the hall. Peter picked up the Polaroids but then decided not to take them with him. He opened the top drawer of Mark's desk, put the photos inside and shut it again. Then he joined Judith in the hall. She was waiting impatiently for him, clutching her shoes and coat. He grabbed his own shoes and coat too.

'I'm coming!' Mark shouted to the policeman through the closed front door. 'Just getting my keys.'

He rattled a bunch of keys exaggeratedly as he nodded towards the stairs.

Peter and Judith tiptoed upstairs. They heard the front door open, followed by Mark's calm voice talking to the policeman – or policemen.

The first floor of the little house had just one large bedroom and a bathroom, which was really more of a cupboard with a shower inside.

They would be able to climb out through the window, but they would have to jump down into the alley below.

The window was at least three metres from the ground, and there was a good chance of them twisting an ankle. Someone jumping out of a window was bound to attract attention. And who knew how many policemen had been sent to the house?

Panicking now, Judith scanned the room, trying to find a place to hide, but there weren't many possibilities. Along one side of the room was a large built-in wardrobe. The space behind its doors extended out beyond the bedroom walls, under the eaves on either side. Judith gestured to Peter that he should get inside the wardrobe and sit on the floor in the corner. He crawled in and sat with his back against the short side, under the roof's slope. There were some blankets stored inside the wardrobe, and Judith draped one of them over Peter before sitting down opposite him. They sat in the dark, legs stretched out in front of them – his on the outside and hers on the inside. Then Judith managed to pull the door shut until it was almost completely closed.

They heard footsteps on the stairs, and as if by some unspoken agreement, they both threw the blanket over their heads.

Peter realised that their hiding place would be useless if the policeman actually bothered to take more than a glance around the room. He tried to breathe without making a noise, but that was difficult with the itchy blanket covering his face. Drops of sweat started to bead on his forehead.

They heard what sounded like multiple people coming up the stairs and a man's voice saying: 'Don't worry, sir. This is all just a routine search. One of our colleagues has been attacked, so, as I'm sure you'll understand, everyone's on high alert.'

It sounded like they had stopped when they reached the landing. The officer continued. 'It looks like Juffrouw Cherev has been home. The caretaker let us into her house, and we found the clothes she was seen wearing on the hospital's security cameras earlier this evening. If she's not involved in any way, it seems odd that she would feel the need to go home to change her clothes.'

Now the voices came into the room.

'As I've already told you, I haven't seen her tonight,' Mark lied. 'I've been working on my dissertation all night, and I've not noticed any unusual activity. It's so quiet here after dark that I would definitely have heard if she'd knocked on my door.'

'But you didn't hear her enter her own house either,' the policeman challenged him, 'when we know she was there.'

They stood still. The wooden floorboards creaked under the two men's weight.

Peter began to pray silently, words rising to the surface of his mind that had been buried since the day he saw the pope riding around in his new Popemobile. 'Hear my prayer, O God; give ear to the words of my mouth. For the insolent have risen against me, the ruthless seek my life; they do not set God before them. But surely, God is my helper; the Lord is the upholder of my life. He will repay my enemies for their evil. In your faithfulness, put an end to them.'

Suddenly, a feeling of deep calm washed over him, a serenity he'd not felt in a very long time. 'With a freewill-offering I will sacrifice to you; I will give thanks to your name, O Lord, for it is good. For he has delivered me from every trouble, and my eye has looked in triumph on my enemies,' he recited silently, his lips brushing against the rough wool of the blanket.

Someone was walking towards the wardrobe. Miraculously, Peter didn't feel any panic at all.

The door opened, and the inside of the wardrobe grew lighter, even through the thick blanket.

Mark's voice sounded very clear now. 'If I see her, I'll let you know, officer. I've known Judith for a long time, and I simply cannot imagine her being involved in any of this. I can see how it looks, but I'm sure there must be another explanation.'

The policeman took another step closer.

Peter imagined he could hear Mark holding his breath. 'I believe your colleague is calling you,' Mark said.

Peter could actually hear someone shouting up the stairs, but he couldn't make out exactly what was being said.

The policeman in the bedroom sighed audibly and called down to his colleague that he was on his way. For what appeared to be form's sake, he pawed through the clothing in the wardrobe. Peter heard the hangers rattle against each other briefly before they came to a standstill.

The policeman's footsteps moved away.

Just before the wardrobe door was closed again, Mark whispered: 'Stay in there for now. Don't leave the room until I come and tell you it's safe.'

Neither Judith nor Peter responded.

Mark closed the door, and the darkness returned.

Peter threw off the blanket. He was sweaty, and his hair was sticking to his forehead. It was then that he heard Judith sobbing, very quietly.

'Judith? What's wrong?' Peter whispered. He grabbed her foot and gave it a gentle squeeze, trying to encourage her. 'Hey, everything will be all right, sweetheart. It really will. I know it looks like we've got ourselves into an impossible situation, but we're going to be able to explain everything eventually. We'll prove that we're innocent of anything they think we've done, and then we'll be able to get on with our lives.'

'I know that. That's not why I...'

They heard Mark and the policeman talking downstairs. Then the front door slammed shut. Peter had the urge to get up, but he thought better of it and did as Mark had instructed. Despite the darkness in the wardrobe, he could see that Judith had covered her face with her hands. She began to sob again, more intensely now. But after a while, she calmed herself. She drew up her knees and rested her head on top of them.

'Are you okay? What is it, Judith?'

Without lifting her head, she began to explain. 'My grandparents died in a concentration camp. And so did lots of my mum's side of the family. My dad and his brother, my uncle, escaped because they were sent to the countryside in Groningen before it was too late. That was in 1942, so my dad was just five when he was separated from his parents – forever, it turned out. They were taken in by a farmer and his wife in East Groningen. Communists who had no children of their own. My dad...'

Judith stopped speaking. She sniffled for a moment, and then she raised her head again and wiped the tears from her eyes and face.

'When it was clear that their parents were never coming back for them, my dad and my uncle stayed on the farm permanently. No one from that side of the family came back alive, so my dad and my uncle had no one else.'

'Oh,' Peter said sadly. He didn't know what else to say.

'Aaltje and Fokko, the couple were called. Good people. They saw it as their duty to give the children a home and didn't think of how much danger it put them in. My dad and uncle both lived there until they were eighteen. My uncle was older, so my dad lived alone with them for a while, until he left to study in Amsterdam. My dad and his brother went back to see them nearly every month, and they'd stay all weekend to help run the farm. They slept in their old rooms, which had never changed since the day they'd arrived. Naturally, Fokko and Aaltje were like parents to them.'

'What a story,' said Peter. He couldn't think of anything better to say.

'They died very shortly after each other in 1965 and left the farm to the two brothers. My mum and dad seriously considered moving there. This was a few years before I was born in 1970. Have you ever been to East Groningen?'

'Not recently, no. Never, in fact.'

'It's beautiful but very remote. At the time, my parents were hippies, more or less, and they imagined themselves starting some kind of self-sufficient community there with like-minded people. But they gave the idea up in the end. I think that was probably for the best.' She smiled.

'Life in those idealistic communities often turns out to be less than idyllic,' Peter said.

'You're right, it does. And anyway, my mum had grown up in Amsterdam, so she was really too much of a townie. She was born in England, though. Her parents had gone there in the late 1930s because they'd seen the threat from Germany coming closer and closer. The rest of the family thought they were overreacting, but in the end, my mum's parents were the only members of her side of the family to survive. They came back to Amsterdam after the war, but their house had been expropriated, and they had enormous trouble getting it back. Other people were living in it, and they proved difficult to remove. My grandfather once told me he got the distinct impression that the people occupying their house were full of resentment towards them. It was like they were silently reproaching them for having actually survived the war.'

A pensive hush fell over them.

Then Peter asked, 'Why are you telling me this story, Judith? I mean, why are you telling this story now?'

Peter wanted to crawl over to sit beside her, but the space inside the wardrobe was too cramped.

'My grandparents on my dad's side went into hiding in Amsterdam. By the time it was clear what the Germans were really planning to do, it was too late for them to escape. Amsterdam had been turned into a huge open-air prison, and there was no way out. Their downstairs neighbour was willing to help them, provide them with food and drink, but the plan was doomed to fail from the start. They moved up to the top floor of the house, and they let the neighbour and his family use the first floor. They'd created some extra space inside a wardrobe up there, and the only thing they could do if there was a raid was hide inside it.'

'Oh... So that's why...'

'Yes, that's why... I've been told the story all my life. We don't know exactly what happened, but eventually, one day, the house was raided. The neighbour and his family were out that day, so they had a narrow escape. But my grandparents were found in their pathetic, useless hiding place, and taken away. They were deported to Auschwitz and went to the gas chamber on the same day they arrived.'

'Oh, Judith...'

'My dad went back to the house later, and the neighbour was still living there. It was suspicious, obviously, that he'd not been at home on the day of the razzia, but the neighbour swore he'd had nothing to do with it. Dad believed him. People who helped Jews were in danger of being deported themselves, so they'd have caught him eventually, whether he'd been at home that day or not. When they got home and realised that their house had been raided, he and his family fled to relatives in The Hague. He was sent to Germany later in the war for *Arbeitseinsatz*, forced labour. They grabbed him on the street. His wife and two children suffered horribly in the famine in the winter of 1944 and '45. My dad saw the wardrobe his parents must have been hiding in when the house was raided. He said that it would have been obvious from the outside that people were hiding inside it. It might as well have had the words "Jews hiding here" written on the door in big letters.'

She adjusted her position. Peter's legs had fallen asleep, so he drew his knees up to his chest.

'And just now, when that policeman came walking up the stairs, the footsteps, the creaking floorboards, the voices nearby... I... I just lost it, Peter. I just saw myself in my grandmother's position, as if I were sitting there in her place. Of course, this isn't the same thing at all. I know that. If we'd been caught and arrested just now, we'd be able to explain our way out of trouble eventually. And that's what we're going to have to do, sooner or later. But my grandparents knew that the second those wardrobe doors were opened, their lives were over.'

'What a terrible story, Judith. I've read about these things, and I know they happened. But hearing it directly from someone whose own life has been touched by it... I can't put it into words,' Peter said. He was happy to be able to say something more than just 'oh'.

'Christ-killers,' Judith said suddenly.

'What?'

'Someone shouted that slur at my grandfather in the street. It happened more than once. My maternal grandfather told me about it. This happened before the war, before anyone knew the full extent of the Holocaust. After the war, people tried to pretend that sort of thing only happened in Germany, but my grandfather said that he was often called "Christ-killer". It usually happened on the way to the synagogue on Fridays, or on Sundays when church services ended, and rowdy groups of boys roamed the neighbourhood throwing stones at Jews. "Jew badgering" it was called, and it the police always dismissed it as kids getting into mischief, but there was a whole world of hate behind it. It was always the worst at Easter when their sermons emphasised that Jews were responsible for Jesus' death. And regardless of whether that was true or not, as a child, I thought that, if those Jews hadn't betrayed Jesus, he wouldn't have been crucified, and the whole plan would have failed.'

'But now we know it might not have happened the way we've been told it did. I would love to be able to read those letters right now.'

'Me too. And that's why I want to keep going,' Judith said. Peter detected a steely determination in her voice. 'I was about to crawl back out of this wardrobe when that policeman was here, but now I want to see this through. This might be our only chance.'

'Let's wait for Mark to come back.'

There was a long pause, and then Peter asked, 'Is this why you're so interested in Rabbi Zevi and the stories about the Messiah?'

'Ah, so you're an amateur psychologist too...' she said, and there was a hint of mockery in her voice. 'But the answer is yes, and I don't think you'd have to dig very deep to uncover that. After he visited my grandparents' house, my father started to look into Judaism more deeply. So did my mum, actually. For him, I think it was a sort of early mid-life crisis. This came shortly after they'd decided not to live on the farm in Groningen, and they'd abandoned the hippy lifestyle too, although I'm not sure they'd ever truly been committed to it. My dad and uncle had sold the farm and the land, so they had some money. My parents were both high school teachers. They started working less but didn't stop completely. My dad mostly used his extra free time to study Hebrew and Jewish writings and go to Shul. My mum devoted herself to cooking and sewing, but to literature too. She read a lot. Still does.'

'And how does Rabbi Zevi fit into this story?

'Very easy, actually. Jews live in anticipation of the Messiah's arrival, so we discussed that topic at home. We often talked about religious issues. We kept Shabbat – or at least, we kept it as well as we could. But the belief that the Jews murdered Jesus was an important subject for my dad. It wasn't just because he was Jewish. It was because the idea had been at the root of the persecution of all Jews over the centuries. "His blood be on us and on our children" and all that. But if you look at Jewish doctrine, you'll see that Jesus fulfilled virtually none of the criteria for being the Messiah. The fact that he died on the cross without freeing the Jewish people and restoring the throne of David was probably the biggest clue that he couldn't have been the Messiah.' She let out a cynical laugh. 'And then on top of that, you've got the accounts of Jesus' arrest and trial which, from a historical perspective, are completely inaccurate...'

Judith abruptly stopped talking. Someone was coming upstairs. She threw the blanket over her head again, but Peter didn't bother. He would have liked to tell Judith about the experience he'd just had, about the deep sense of peace he'd felt when he'd begun to pray.

The wardrobe door opened.

'They've gone. I waited a while before I came up in case they came back.'

Judith crawled out of the wardrobe on all fours. Now that she was standing in the light, Peter saw that her eyes were rimmed red and her eyeliner had run, leaving two streaks of black on her cheeks.

Mark looked at Judith with concern. 'Do you want to go and freshen up a bit?' he asked.

'I think I do, yes.'

A little later they heard the tap running and water splashing.

'She's been crying?' Mark asked.

'Yes, hiding inside the wardrobe reminded her of what happened to her grandparents, and she got quite upset.'

'Poor thing... I have to say, that story did cross my mind when I was standing there with the policeman. History repeats itself, but never in exactly the same way, fortunately.'

When Judith came back from the bathroom, she looked much better for having washed her face.

'What did the policeman say?' she wanted to know.

'He said that there's a warrant out for both of you. If it's any comfort, he did let slip that he didn't believe that you actually killed Thomas or knocked out the policeman who was guarding his room. They found a nurse gagged and bound and locked inside a storage cabinet at the hospital. So their attention seems to have shifted to a third person, the man who was chasing you. That's who they think did it now. But the police still think your behaviour was suspicious, you understand. And, obviously, because you seem to be doing your best to avoid them, that suspicion is only growing.'

'And what did you think when you were standing in front of the wardrobe with him?'

'It was absurd, Judith, but I wasn't at all nervous. I felt completely calm, as if a voice was telling me not to worry.'

'I had that too!' Peter exclaimed, and then he clapped his hand over his mouth because he had said it much too loudly. 'I had that too,' he repeated, more quietly this time.

Judith gave him a questioning look.

'When they were standing in front of the wardrobe,' he began to explain, 'I said a prayer. A psalm about facing your enemy without fear. A feeling of deep peace came over me, and all of a sudden, I knew that even if they did catch us right then, it wouldn't be the end. It was strange, Judith. I think it was one of the most spiritual moments I've ever experienced,' Peter said.

Judith nodded but said nothing.

'Well, I wasn't the slightest bit worried,' Mark said. 'Not even when he opened the door and pushed the hangers aside. I thought, if he just looks down, he'll see that there's something not quite right in there. But it was as if he didn't want to see you. It was so strange. And then his colleague called him from downstairs. They've given me a telephone number, and I'm supposed to call it if I see you.'

'What do we do now?' Peter asked. 'I'm sure they'll be watching the courtyard door.'

'There's a much simpler solution,' said Mark. 'Why don't you just climb out of the window?' He pointed to the bedroom window that opened onto the street. 'We'll go for the classic escape with knotted bedsheets.'

'But where can we go?' Judith asked. 'The game's already over, isn't it? Peter and I should just go to the police, turn ourselves in, and clear everything up. We'll hand over the casket, but we'll make sure there are plenty of witnesses so it can't just vanish. Nobody knows we've got the photographs. Professor Hoogers might, but he can't do anything with that information because it would reveal that he's involved in all of this. You can translate the scrolls over the next few months using the photos, and we'll decide what to do with it when you're finished.'

Keen to put these words into action as soon as possible, Judith pulled on her coat.

Peter looked defeated, not entirely convinced that this was the best thing to do.

'I have a better plan,' Mark said, breaking the silence. 'It's...' he said hesitantly. 'I haven't told you everything yet. I think you should sit down.'

Judith and Peter sat down on the edge of the neatly made single bed. Judith unzipped her coat again.

'So, obviously, I always wondered what happened to the translation that Eco made. His death was shrouded in mystery... On the one hand, the autopsy showed that he'd died of a heart attack sitting in the chair in his study. He died with his boots on, so to speak, at the desk where he'd spent so much time doing what he loved. It must have happened in the evening. He wasn't found until hours later when his wife realised that he hadn't come home. Mevrouw Eco usually goes to bed late, but she fell asleep watching TV in the armchair that night. She woke up just after midnight and realised that her husband wasn't there. She phoned him, and when he didn't answer, she called the police. They found him in his study, slumped over his desk. So, as I said, it looked like a heart attack.

'But the strange thing was that his study had obviously been searched. "Ransacked" is a strong word, but someone had disturbed the strict order that he'd always kept in his room. Books had been moved from their proper places, drawers pulled out, papers strewn over the floor. There were no signs of forced entry, so the case was closed. One theory was that he'd created the mess himself shortly before his death. Perhaps he did it in a moment of madness or panic, as though he'd felt the hour of his death approaching, and he was desperately trying to find something. Maybe he was looking for his heart medication. But then, that's another mystery. He always kept a pot of pills for his heart condition on his desk. He had to take them twice a day. The pills were gone, and they've never been able to find them. The police couldn't think of anyone who would have wanted to hurt Eco. He didn't appear to have any enemies. Of course, there were people who were angry with him, like the frustrated academics who'd been denied access to his collection umpteen times. But that was hardly a motive for murder. So it was recorded as death by natural causes, and the case was closed. And although people at the university talked about it when it happened, they soon lost interest. A new librarian was appointed, someone with more modern views who actually allowed people to access the books, much to the relief of the academic community.'

'But you thought it was suspicious...' Peter started.

'No. More than suspicious. I'm absolutely convinced Eco was murdered. And I've always thought it must have had something to do with that translation he'd done. That "they", whoever they were, had grown nervous. Maybe they suspected that he'd kept something from them. And that was the death of him.'

'Where do you think that text is now?' asked Judith.

'I don't think he would have kept the text in his study at the library. I think he hid it at home. Actually, I'm almost sure of it. I got in touch with his widow, but I didn't dare ask her about it directly. She was very sad, but she seemed to accept that her scatterbrained husband must simply have misplaced his heart pills. She knew that his weak heart would kill him sooner or later, and unfortunately, that was sooner rather than later. I didn't want to ruin that illusion for her by suggesting that dark forces might actually have been behind her husband's death.'

'And...' Peter said.

'And...' Mark repeated, sounding slightly irritated. He seemed distracted and paused for a moment before continuing. 'I get on well with her, and I still visit her quite often. She's in her early seventies but still very active for her age. I pop in for coffee or a glass of port at the end of the afternoon sometimes. She likes to talk about her husband, of course. He's become something of a saint in her mind.'

'So...' Judith asked, 'what are you suggesting we do?'

'Go and see her. Right now. I think it's time she revealed

what she knows. She's occasionally said things that have come over as a bit ambiguous. By that, I mean hints that she knew something but wasn't ready to tell me about it. If I ever pressed her, she would pretend to be confused, as if I'd misunderstood her. I'll give her a call. It's the middle of the night, but I know she'll be awake. She still goes to bed late. Old habits die hard.'

Mark went back downstairs, resolute, even though Peter and Judith hadn't yet agreed to this new plan. They heard his muffled voice downstairs as he made the phone call.

'What do you think?' Peter asked Judith.

'Pfff...' She puffed out her lips a little and let some air escape, as though it might release some of the pressure that had built up inside her. 'Let's do it,' she said eventually. 'This might be our last chance to find out the truth. Who knows what forces we've unleashed? And suppose Mark's right and this old lady does know something? I think we should pay her a visit, and if we don't find out anything useful, we'll go straight to the police station.'

'Okay,' he said. 'Let's do that.'

'She says you're very welcome to go and see her,' they heard Mark say as he came up the stairs. 'She lives on the Oude Rijn canal.' He told them the house number.

'But first, we have to get you out of here.'

Chapter Twelve

'D o you really think that's going to work?' Judith asked. 'Knotting bedsheets together and climbing out of the window?'

'It's only a three-metre drop,' Mark reassured her. 'You'll manage.'

He took two clean white sheets out of the wardrobe, shook them open, and began tying the corner of one sheet to the other.

'Listen,' Peter said, and Mark stopped knotting and looked at him. 'Listen, we'll go and see the old lady. I think that's a good idea. And you can go to the police afterwards, Judith, no matter what we find out there. But first I want to do something else, on my own if I have to.'

'Do what?' Judith asked.

'If we're lucky, Eco's widow will be aware of the translation. She may even know where it is,' said Peter. 'But when this all gets out, people might still think the letters are forgeries. Clever forgeries, even, perhaps dating from the first century, but still forgeries. So far, we have absolutely no proof that they really were written by Judas and Peter – the real Judas and Peter, Jesus' disciples. And Thomas was convinced that he'd found Saint Peter's grave at Matilo. There wasn't a shadow of a doubt as far as he was concerned. "I found him," he said. So the key to all of this must be at the excavation site. I'm absolutely convinced of that.'

'Saint Peter's keys?' Mark said drily.

'There's got to be something there,' Peter persisted, 'that would make a seasoned archaeologist like Thomas one hundred per cent sure that this was all real and not fake. And I'm going to find out what that something is, even if it's the last thing I do.' Perhaps realising how dramatic his words sounded, he toned them down slightly. 'I mean even if that's the last thing I do before I go to the police, obviously.'

'Are we leaving the casket and the photos here?' Judith asked.

'Yes,' Mark and Peter said in chorus.

'I think that's for the best,' Peter continued. 'No one will be expecting everything to be here.'

'Good idea,' said Mark, pulling the knotted ends of the sheets tighter. 'This should be enough.' He pushed his bed over to the wall and opened the window. Then he tied the end of one sheet to the bedframe and tossed the rest outside.

'Come on then,' he said. 'Who's going first?' Mark sat down on the bed to weigh it down.

Judith went over to the window, gave Mark a quick hug,

then sat down on the sill and swung her legs outside. She wrapped the sheet around her arm a couple of times, yanked it to make sure it was secure and then slowly lowered herself down. She made it look easy.

Peter leaned over the sill and saw Judith standing in the street a few metres below. He shook Mark's hand and climbed out of the window. As soon as Peter reached the bottom, Mark quickly pulled the sheets back inside, but he left the window open.

They had landed in Klooster, a small alley next to the Sionshof. Shouting and discordant singing came from the Harlemmerstraat a short block away, probably people stumbling back from the fair after it had closed.

Peter and Judith had only gone a few paces when they heard footsteps behind them. They both froze. When they turned around, they realised that Thomas's killer was approaching them, slowly and deliberately like a predator stalking its prey. In his right hand was a gun with a silencer attached. He held it with the barrel pointing downwards, but as he came closer, he raised it and aimed it at them. He stopped just below Mark's bedroom window.

'Meneer De Haan, I presume,' he sneered. 'I'm going to count to three, and one of you is going to put the box down in front of me. Both of you will walk away and disappear around that corner. Then this will all be over, and we can get on with our lives again.'

'We don't have the box, it's...' Peter tried to tell him.

The man fired at the ground next to Judith's feet.

There was a short, dull bang. A piece of cobblestone flew into the air. Peter and Judith ducked.

'One...' he started counting.

Judith shouted: 'We don't have it! We left it in the—'

'Two...' he continued coldly. He pointed the gun at Peter and Judith in turn, smiling and clearly enjoying himself. This time, he was in complete control, and there was no chance of them pulling any clever tricks. He heaved an exaggerated sigh like a parent reluctantly disciplining a child.

Judith looked desperately at Peter. 'We don't have it anymore!' she screamed. She closed her eyes and put her hands over her ears. 'It's at—'

Just then, Peter saw a flash of something white tumble out of the window above the gunman's head. Mark threw himself downwards, holding onto the sheets with one arm. He struck the man hard on the head with both of his feet at once. The gunman collapsed to the ground, and his pistol skittered over the cobbles. He lay moaning and holding his head in his hands.

Mark grabbed the gun and launched it in a perfect arc through his open bedroom window.

'Run!' he yelled. Judith's eyes had been so tightly screwed shut in fear that she had missed all the action, but now she opened them and realised that the tables had turned in their favour.

The gunman was still on the ground, curled up in the foetal position.

Mark's attack had taken him completely by surprise, like a *deus ex machina*. Peter and Judith dared to move again at last.

'But what about you?' Judith whispered loudly.

'Don't worry,' said Mark. 'He'll be out for a while. I'm going to go back inside to call the police. I'll tell them there's a drunk passed out in the alley.'

The man groaned; he could have easily been mistaken for a drunk. Peter almost felt sorry for him lying there. Failed again...

'Go! Now!' Mark urged them again, as he wrapped the sheet around his arm.

Before going around the corner, Peter and Judith looked back and caught sight of Mark climbing back up the wall towards the open window like an experienced cat burglar.

They walked through the Sint Ursulasteeg, which led to the Haarlemmerstraat where small clusters of people clutching beer cans shambled past the closed shops, shouting and singing. They crossed the high street and went down the narrow Kennewegsteeg, emerging next to the canal on the Apothekersdijk. The streets were empty here.

At the end of the Stille Rijn, they went over the spindly Waaghoofdbrug and turned left. They walked along the Hoogstraat, above the subterranean vaults that housed Annie's Verjaardag, one of the city's most popular café bars. They were almost there. They turned right onto the Oude Rijn canal. Neither of them had spoken since leaving the alley behind Mark's house.

Peter had felt a distance opening up between them ever since they had come out of the wardrobe. He guessed it had something to do with the way Judith had so intensely relived her grandparents' experience. The steps they had taken so far had been too predictable, Peter thought, too obvious. The killer had somehow always kept pace with

173

what they had done or planned to do. But now they had the advantage – he'd been put out of action, at least for the time being, and he couldn't possibly have any idea that their next stop was the widow Eco's house.

They stood outside her front door. It seemed odd to be ringing an elderly woman's doorbell at this late hour, but what *was* normal in these circumstances?

The nameplate below the doorbell still read H. ECO.

Judith rubbed her thumb over the name and smiled. There was a golden knocker on the door in the shape of a lion's head, and Judith let it softly fall three times against the door. 'It's like he still lives here,' she said, and it was clear that the thought moved her.

As she knocked for the third time, the door opened as though Mevrouw Eco had been waiting behind it. Perhaps she actually had.

She gestured that they should enter quickly and hurriedly closed the door behind them. The only light in the hallway came from a small wall lamp that burned wanly below a mirror. In the gloom, it was difficult to see the woman's face. But they could tell that Mevrouw Eco was a diminutive lady, at least physically.

Wordlessly, she passed Peter and Judith in the hallway and led them into the living room. This room was also dimly lit, like a museum gallery where priceless artefacts were protected from the bright daylight.

'Take a seat,' she said. Mevrouw Eco lifted a teapot from a trivet where she'd been keeping it warm over a tealight and poured out three cups of tea. Without asking, she scooped a spoonful of sugar into each one and placed them on coasters in front of them.

She was a thin, frail-looking woman with neatly coiffured hair that hung in grey curls about her shoulders. There was a hint of lipstick on her lips, and her eyes were bright and alert. She had the slightly upper-class accent of someone who had moved in genteel circles from an early age.

'Mark telephoned me,' she said simply when she had settled herself in her comfortable armchair, 'so I know you're good people. Mark is... I suppose telling you he's like a son to me may seem a little pathetic, but I do enjoy it when he occasionally honours me with his company. Now then, I don't know exactly what it is that you have found yourselves caught up in, and it may be that I don't want to know at all.'

Peter smiled contritely and held up his hands as if to emphasise an unspoken apology. 'It is very kind of you to allow us to come at this late hour,' he said. 'And to be honest, we don't know exactly what we've got ourselves involved in either. The short version of the story – and I think it will have to do for the moment – is that we've come into possession of a text, and certain people are, let's say, very interested in it.'

'More than very interested,' Judith added.

Peter put his hand on Judith's thigh, but she moved it back to his own leg.

'And now, in a remarkable coincidence, Mark has told us that he's seen this text before,' Peter went on, 'in your late husband's room at the university.'

'God rest his soul,' Mevrouw Eco said, almost automatically.

'God rest his soul,' Peter repeated. 'Your husband died while Mark was in Endegeest, and—'

'My husband was a good man,' she interjected. 'A good man, who never hurt so much as a fly in his entire life. As long as he had his books, his research... I know that he... How should I put this?' She smiled. 'That he was somewhat unorthodox. He was reprimanded on more than one occasion for not allowing somebody to see a manuscript. But in his eyes, very few people were, as he put it, committed enough to deserve access to them. That notwithstanding, he was obviously doing something right. I doubt he would have been able to hold onto his position for so long otherwise. And I know that he was given assignments from time to time that were shrouded in secrecy. I never questioned him too closely about them, but they usually involved determining the authenticity of a manuscript that was about to be auctioned, or a document that needed to be translated. I suspect he enjoyed it more than he was willing to admit, all that mystery... Anyway, I'm sure you haven't come here to listen to an old woman reminisce...'

Peter smiled, partly in an attempt to deny this and partly because she had read his mind.

'Can you tell us anything more about this text?' he asked hopefully.

Mevrouw Eco stirred her tea pensively, and for a time, the tinkling of the spoon in her cup and the dull tick of the grandfather clock were the only sounds in the room. 'I don't want to speculate about whether his death had anything to do with that translation,' she continued as if she hadn't heard Peter's question. 'Mark has never dared to ask me about it, although I can tell that the question is on the tip of his tongue sometimes. But it is what it is. He's no longer with us, and even if we did know exactly what had happened, it would change nothing. After he died, a week or so after the funeral, a moving van came to pick up the books from his study. He'd bequeathed it all to the library; that way, he could be sure that they'd be put to good use. Apparently, this wish was so strong that he was willing to allow other people to rummage through his books without his explicit permission. Anyway, I knew about it beforehand, and I didn't mind. What would I have done with them all? I just hadn't expected the university to be quite so eager about it. They were usually so slow about everything. But they showed me all kinds of official-looking papers, complete with stamps and so on. The two removal men had laminated identity cards clipped onto their breast pockets, and I assumed that everything was entirely above board.'

'Oh no,' Judith said, 'I can see where this is going.'

'I went to see my sister for a few hours,' the old lady went on. 'The men were traipsing in and out, stomping up and down the stairs with those big boxes... It was all rather chaotic, and I was glad to be out of the house, away from the mess. But more than that, it was painful, of course, to see them emptying that room where he'd sat working just two weeks earlier. When I came back, the removal men had already gone. To my great relief, I must admit. I had already been thinking about what I might do with that room; I thought I might rent it out to a student to bring some life back into the house. But I hadn't made my mind up at that point. When I opened the door to my husband's study, I couldn't believe what I was seeing. The room was empty. Com-plete-ly empty.'

She was a good storyteller, pausing at just the right moments for dramatic effect. Peter felt a shiver go down his spine, and he noticed he had goosebumps on his forearms.

'Com-plete-ly,' she repeated. 'They hadn't left so much as a scrap of paper behind. All that remained was his desk, and all of its empty drawers were strewn about next to it. Oh, and it was flipped upside down with the desktop on the carpet. They must have been looking for a hidden drawer... Even the magazine rack where I kept my embroidery magazines – I enjoyed sitting next to him, you see, doing my embroidery while he worked. It was something we both found very pleasant – they'd gone through that and taken my magazines. The whole room had been stripped as thoroughly as if they had been getting ready to paint it. I really did find it all very odd. I went back downstairs, and there were things out of place in the living room too. We didn't keep any books there, but the cabinets had all been emptied, and their contents were lying all over the floor. All the furniture had been moved away from the walls as if they had been trying to see if there was anything behind it, and the sofa's seat cushions had all been flipped over... It was a terrible state of affairs, I can tell you. Well, I'm sure you get the picture.'

'It must have felt like you'd been burgled,' Judith said.

'Exactly, my dear,' she said, nodding emphatically. 'Like I'd been burgled. Now, that seemed most unconventional to me. I was furious, as I'm sure you'll understand. So, of course, I telephoned the library to complain. When I finally got through to the right person, they said that they had just been about to call me to arrange a time to pick up my husband's books!'

Despite the dim light in the room, Peter could see that Mevrouw Eco's cheeks were flushed with indignation. 'Which means...' Peter said.

'Which means that those removal men were not from the university at all!' the widow exclaimed.

'The library didn't know anything about it. They hadn't engaged a removal firm or hired a van. Nothing. They were still trying to decide what to do with all those books because they weren't actually sure they could take the whole collection.'

Judith's hand flew to her mouth. 'And then?' she managed to say.

'I reported it to the police, of course. As soon as I realised what had happened, I called the detective in charge of my husband's case. He had two police officers here within a quarter of an hour, but nothing came of it in the end. I hadn't memorised the licence plate number, of course, or even paid attention to the sign on the van. I doubt I would have been able to pick those men out of a police line-up. How could I have fallen for it?' She slapped her knee in frustration.

'Ah, but anyone could have fallen for that, couldn't they?' Peter said soothingly. 'They did it so cunningly.'

That seemed to reassure her.

They all fell silent for a while.

'But,' Mevrouw Eco said suddenly with a triumphant tone that contrasted sharply with the note of dejection in her voice just moments earlier, 'perhaps not all is lost. There was something I never told Mark because I was afraid that it would shatter the peace that had returned to our lives. I didn't want him to get drawn into something too big for him to cope with.'

'And that was?' Peter asked.

He watched her lips curl in a satisfied smile. If this had been a cartoon, her eyes would have sparkled like diamonds.

'There's one place they didn't look,' she said.

Chapter Thirteen

Mevrouw Eco stood up, and Judith and Peter followed her into the corridor and up the stairs. When they reached the landing, she turned on the light, which seemed startlingly bright after the gloom of the living room. She opened one of the doors on the landing and went inside. 'Wait there a moment,' she said without turning around.

They heard her moving around inside. Illuminated only by the streetlamps, the room was surprisingly light. But it grew gradually darker as she closed the curtains. She came back to the door and turned on the ceiling light.

The room was almost entirely empty except for an easy chair in the corner, the desk, which was now the right way up, and the chair in front of it.

'After those "removal men" left,' she said, and the words had a caustic undertone, 'I didn't do anything in here except I asked my neighbour to set the desk the right way up. I didn't have the heart to rent the room to anyone. And

181

besides, I still like to sit in here to do my embroidery or read,' she said, pointing at the easy chair that was set at an angle in front of the window. 'Sometimes, I imagine that Huibrecht is still here, writing at his desk, just like always, and that brings me some comfort.'

She disappeared into her thoughts briefly but then realised with a start that this wasn't what her visitors had come for.

'I've never told anyone this,' she said, 'not even Mark. Perhaps I was afraid that he would stop coming to see me if I told him about it. I've become very fond of him. He never questioned me about how much I know, but the time has come for me to break my silence. I can see that. You'll probably find it hard to believe that I've never done what I'm about to do now.'

She walked over to a wainscoted wall. 'But I thought...' she continued as she ran her hand gently over the moulding that ran around the top of the panelling. 'I just thought that... Either there's something here, or there isn't, and opening it...' Her hand stopped abruptly, as if she had found what she was looking for.

'Here,' she said. 'This is where it is. Would you give me a hand, Meneer De Haan?'

Peter went over and stood beside her.

'And opening it would put an end to that uncertainty,' she said.

She pulled a section of the moulding away, and Peter saw a space a few centimetres deep between the panelling and the wall.

'Huibrecht told me about this eventually,' she explained.

'If he was working on something that he'd promised to keep secret, he usually hid it here. He had to tell someone about it in case anything happened to him. Would you please lift off this panel? I don't have the strength for it in my hands.'

Peter jiggled the wood back and forth a little and realised that it moved. He pushed the panel upwards until he could lift it free of the grooves on either side, then removed it and placed it on the ground. He felt an intense disappointment when he saw that there was nothing behind the panel but the wall. The wall was covered with plastic bubble wrap, and behind that, there appeared to be some sort of stone wool insulation.

'There's...' Peter gulped, trying to overcome his disillusionment. 'There's nothing there. No door or hatch, no safe... Nothing.'

He looked sideways at Judith, who tried in vain to give him an encouraging smile.

Mevrouw Eco stepped in. 'You need to turn the panel over. There's nothing in the wall. The bubble wrap is just insulation to keep out the cold and damp. Go on. Turn it over.'

Fresh hope surged through Peter's body, and he turned the board over expectantly. Now he saw a thin join running down the middle of the panel from top to bottom. He pried at it with his fingers, but it was no use.

'Just a moment,' the old woman said, and she left the room.

'What do you think?' Peter asked Judith.

She shrugged, but before she could say anything,

Mevrouw Eco came back with a set of screwdrivers in one hand and a hammer in the other.

She handed the tools to Peter. 'These should do it.'

Peter pointed at the wooden panel. 'Have you ever seen your husband open this?'

'He showed it to me once,' Mevrouw Eco replied. 'After he told me he had a secret hiding place, he demonstrated how to remove the panel and open it at the back.'

Peter laid the wooden board on the floor and knelt down next to it. His heart pounded, and his chest felt tight.

'Look,' Mevrouw Eco said. 'There in the middle, at the bottom. See that little notch? Use the smallest screwdriver. Stick it in there and then give it a little tap with the hammer. You should be able to pop it open.'

What if this turns out to be a huge disappointment, Peter thought. He found the screwdriver with the thinnest blade and inserted it into the notch. The gentle tap he gave it echoed around the empty room. He looked up in panic, but the old lady blinked slowly to reassure him.

After a few more taps, the tip of the screwdriver had disappeared into the join. The thin board covering the back of the panel popped up, and Peter found he could remove it easily. Its construction was as simple as it was clever. Two hinged wooden boards had been attached to the reverse of the panel, creating a space a couple of centimetres deep, just enough to hide something like a writing pad.

Peter opened both panels, and Judith and Mevrouw Eco came closer and leaned over to watch.

Peter smiled. *It looks like I'm getting my Indiana Jones moment after all*, he thought.

Behind the panels was a plastic zip-locked wallet containing an old-fashioned school exercise book. Peter removed it and held it out to Mevrouw Eco, but she indicated that he should open it himself.

'Well, it's something, anyway,' he said hopefully, as he got back to his feet. His knees ached from kneeling on the wooden floor, and he noticed how tense his neck and shoulders were.

Peter unzipped the plastic wallet and removed the notebook. The smell of dust penetrated his nostrils. Just as he was about to open it, a small sheet of paper swirled from the notebook and landed at his feet.

Judith bent down and picked it up.

'Oh!' said Mevrouw Eco. 'That's Huibrecht's handwriting.'

Judith passed it over to her, and Mevrouw Eco read the short note in silence.

Peter burned with longing to open the book properly. However, not wanting to disturb this moment, when a widow was receiving a message from the other side, he waited patiently for her to finish. Only when she finally looked up again did he ask: 'What does it say?'

'At the same time, pray for us as well,' she read out loud, 'that God will open to us a door for the word, that we may declare the mystery of Christ, for which I am in prison, so that I may reveal it clearly, as I should.'

'Sounds like Saint Paul,' said Peter.

'Colossians, chapter 4, verse three, it says at the bottom,' she replied. 'It is Paul.' She smiled. 'Now, open the notebook,' she told him.

Peter opened it up and realised that the notebook itself was empty, and instead of pages, it contained a collection of loose sheets of lined paper covered in the neat writing of a meticulous scholar.

'And?' Judith asked. 'What does it say?'

'Peter tilted the page towards the light and read: '"Cephas, a servant and apostle of Yeshua, greets you, good Judas. To begin with, my fellow traveller on the Way, I cannot continue without first expressing what great sorrow your departure from Jerusalem has brought me." My God.' A shiver ran down his spine, and the hairs on the back of his arms stood up.

'This is it,' Judith said simply.

Mevrouw Eco stood beneath the glare of the ceiling light, clutching her husband's note in both hands. She looked exhausted.

'Let's go downstairs,' Judith suggested. 'We can read everything down there. Would that be all right, Mevrouw Eco?'

'Yes, all right, dear,' she said, sounding incredibly tired. 'It's very late and this...' – she pointed to the pages in Peter's hand – 'I'm sure this will all go over my head. I don't know if... How should I put it? I don't know if I actually want to read it. Or if I want to know what's in it. I'm going to go to bed. This is unusually late, even for me.'

She moved towards the study door. As she passed him, she briefly put her hand on Peter's arm. 'You may reveal this clearly, as you should,' she said, and she sounded sad.

In the doorway, she turned to look at them, still holding her husband's note with both hands. 'I hereby entrust these papers to your care. I'd like you to tell me how it all turns out later... For now, you are very welcome to spend the night downstairs. You can let yourselves out whenever you want. I would advise using the back door, just in case. It will bring you out next to the Burcht.' She turned again and left the room. 'I bid you goodnight.'

'Good night,' Peter and Judith replied together. They heard Mevrouw Eco's bedroom door close.

'That was a bit odd, wasn't it?' Judith remarked. 'Almost an ... an anti-climax... We find the manuscript, which could have been the reason her husband was killed, and she just walks away as if it were nothing more interesting than a book that needed returning to the library.'

'She's just very tired, I think,' Peter said reassuringly. 'She's old, and old people surprise less easily. Maybe being unexpectedly confronted with her husband's note has unsettled her. Who knows?'

'Let's go downstairs. Come on,' Judith said. Her tone was somewhat cold, as it had been ever since they had almost been discovered by the policeman at Mark's house.

She turned off the light in the study and went downstairs ahead of Peter. In the living room, Peter turned on some lamps so that they would be able to read the text more easily.

They sat next to each other at the large dining table.

Peter opened the notebook again, removed the sheets of paper, and put the pile down on the table between them. 'Nothing is covered up that will not be uncovered,' he murmured to himself, 'and nothing secret that will not become known.'

Chapter Fourteen

C ephas, *a servant and apostle of Yeshua, greets you, good Judas.*

To begin with, my fellow traveller on the Way, I cannot continue without first expressing what great sorrow your departure from Jerusalem has brought me. I understand that you had no choice but to leave the city and our group after the accusations that were made against you.

My thoughts frequently return, as I'm sure yours do too, to the last time we ate together in the garden of Gethsemane, under the canopy of the heavens as we had so often eaten together before. The stars twinkling in the pitch-black sky have always made me feel insignificantly tiny and yet still a part of G-d's mighty creation. The long cloth on the grass, the mounds of unleavened bread, the wine. The gentle breezes carrying the scents of nature's budding and blossoming. The spring has always been my favourite time of year, between winter's chill and the heat of summer. Seeing nature coming back to life, feeling the sun warming my skin...

I still remember the excitement of that day in the Temple when Yeshua overturned the money changers' tables and gave them that lecture. How angry He was. 'Get out!' He cried. 'My Father's house is not a marketplace! The house of G-d is a place of prayer, but you have made it a den of thieves!'

Seldom had we seen Him so angry. I must admit that it astonished me at the time, and I was not alone. Had not G-d himself ordered that animals should be sold in the courtyard? Where else were people to buy their sacrificial offerings? And was it not so that these money changers were there for the pilgrims' convenience? After all, everyone was required to pay the Temple tax in the correct currency, and the Court of the Gentiles was the place where people could exchange coins from their own lands. This had been so for hundreds of years. Yeshua undeniably acted in ways that sometimes seemed strange to us at the time. We came to understand his actions much later. This was surely also the case on this occasion, or so I told myself.

Of course, He had succeeded only in overturning just a few of the tables on that immense square. Thousands of pilgrims and vendors were gathered there, and few would have seen or paid any attention to the commotion He caused. But to us, it felt like the start of something bigger. How elated we were when the Temple guards arrived and failed to break through the circle the twelve of us had formed around Yeshua.

And I saw the disappointment on your face, Judas, when our Master gave us the signal to leave the courtyard. You, and perhaps indeed most of us, had assumed that this riot would be the beginning of the great rebellion. This was the moment when Yeshua would demonstrate that He was the promised redeemer, the Messiah who would restore the Kingdom of G-d and deliver us from foreign oppressors.

But the skies did not open that afternoon – nor the following afternoon.

Perhaps Yeshua had different expectations. Which of us can say?

We can no longer ask Him. Perhaps He saw it as a rehearsal for something much greater that was yet to come. But, needless to say, it never came.

We had entered Jerusalem so full of bravado that afternoon, and I remember all too well how little was left of it then. It had been your idea, hadn't it, Judas? To set Him upon a donkey to show that when Zechariah prophesied that the king would arrive in Jerusalem on a colt, the foal of a donkey, he was speaking of Him? I remember how people looked upon us with amazement when we laid down our cloaks on the ground before Him as He entered the city. Some of the women waved palm branches, and we all cried out 'Hosanna, hosanna! Blessed is He who comes in the name G-d.' Few of the bystanders paid any attention to what was happening, and many of them quickly went back about their business again. But for us, it was like starring in the opening act of a drama.

Going to the Temple was supposed to have been the next step on our path, but it took a different turn to what we were expecting. Yeshua had narrowly escaped arrest in the Court of the Gentiles that day, but we all knew that the Temple guard would not be content to let the matter drop.

No matter how unimportant Yeshua was in their eyes or how minor the offence of knocking over a few tables seemed to be, such things could not be allowed to happen. They were afraid that the

Romans would take advantage of this small disruption to strip them of their powers. With tens of thousands of pilgrims coming from far and wide to celebrate Passover in the city, the Romans were already on alert.

The Temple guard was anxious to deliver Yeshua to the Roman soldiers to prove that they were capable of maintaining order. After all, it was better for one man to die than for all the people to suffer. So had it been done in the past, and so would they do it again.

And the Romans were indifferent about whom they crucified. The loss of a life was of little concern to them. They knew every crucifixion sent a clear message to the people about who was in charge, and it would put any ideas of disturbing the peace out of their heads for a while.

Some of us were disillusioned after we left the courtyard. I know that, Judas. You could hear them thinking, was that it? You were not the only one among us who realised that something would have to be done to force events. But you were the only one who dared to say this to Yeshua, who dared to suggest it to Him. No doubt He had already thought of it himself. No doubt the incident at the Court of the Gentiles had been a disappointment to Him too. Where was the multitude of angels who were to have accompanied the act with their clarion call?

That is why, I think, He was so in favour of your proposal to instigate a great confrontation by leading the Temple guard and the Romans to us in Gethsemane. Surely G-d the Father would have to intervene?

I saw Yeshua growing increasingly enthusiastic about the plan you put forward.

The crucial question now was: who would take this role upon

themselves? After all, whichever one of us did it risked being arrested and executed himself if Yeshua was not with him.

And what if the plan failed? That man would surely go down in history as the greatest traitor of all time.

And then there was the supper, which turned out to be our last. Yeshua told us the story of our forefathers' exodus from slavery in Egypt in his own words. He compared it to the oppression we suffered under the Romans. He said He expected that this would all end soon. The tremor that went through the group, Judas. I remember it so well. We had the sense that we were part of something big, something bigger than ourselves. We were all part of the great plan that the Eternal One had for his people.

He held up a roast leg of lamb and explained that we could live because this animal had given its life. The lamb had given its body so that we could eat and live on. He said that each of us should be prepared to give his own life to protect his brother or sister's life – to die so that another could live.

I remember how we sang together, Yeshua's voice warm and deep: 'Tremble, O earth, at the presence of the Lord, at the presence of the God of Jacob who turns the rock into a pool of water, the flint into a spring of water.' And: 'O give thanks to the Lord, for He is good; his steadfast love endures for ever!'

Tears well up in my eyes when I think back on it. He blessed all four cups of wine before we passed them around the group. And He took the bread and broke it and told us that, whatever might happen afterwards, we should continue to do the same in remembrance of that evening, in remembrance of Him.

I remember the hush that fell over the group when He said that one of us would betray Him.

We knew that one of us would have to do it. But, until that moment, we had not been fully aware of the danger.

'Surely you don't mean me, Lord?' we all asked Him in turn.

'Perhaps he will wish he had never been born,' Yeshua said, referring to the punishment and torture awaiting the traitor if he was put on trial in Yeshua's place.

And you got up then, Judas, threw the moneybag at us as if you expected never to return, and simply walked away. This was the sacrifice that the Master had spoken of.

We ended the meal in silence, and Yeshua asked me, James, and John to go into the garden with Him to pray. We waited for Him at a distance, and so we could not hear his prayer, but we thought that He suddenly looked distressed and sorrowful, as if He was afraid of the consequences of what He had just set in motion.

We laid down to rest and must have fallen asleep; He had to wake us up. He was disappointed that we had not stayed awake with Him.

We returned to the group in a state of anxiety caused by both fear and anticipation. Would you return, Judas? And if you did, would you be accompanied by the Temple guard, by Roman soldiers? Who could have imagined that things would go so wrong? If only we had fled then. You might have suffered no more than a flogging, and we could have gone back to our lives in Galilee.

Not long afterwards, you did indeed return with a small group of Temple guards. They were surly and brutish, knowing they enjoyed the protection of the Roman soldiers who had come with them. There was so little light in the room that they had trouble distinguishing the person they had come for from the rest of us.

But when you walked up to Yeshua, they followed you, and just before you reached Him, they knew He was the one they had come for. They shoved you aside. Then, the soldiers grabbed Him, much more roughly than was necessary, and bound his hands behind his back.

Some of us believed that this was the moment when the clouds would part, and an army of angels would descend and come to Yeshua's aid. Or that Yeshua himself would demonstrate the Messiah's true power and might. And when that did not happen, we were sure it would happen at His trial instead. The trial could not take place that evening, of course, and probably also not the next day, so close to the Sabbath. We thought that He would be tried after the Sabbath.

I remember, Judas, how we stood and watched as our rabbi was taken away. We felt a strange combination of impotence on the one hand and absolute faith on the other that his arrest would be the beginning of a final victory and the restoration of G-d's reign over Israel.

I remember that you, Judas, began to sing that Psalm, haltingly at first, your voice growing more powerful as the rest of us joined in. One of the two Romans holding Yeshua turned his head and looked at us as if we had lost our minds:

> *Why do the nations conspire*
> *and the peoples plot in vain?*
> *The kings of the earth set themselves,*
> *and the rulers take counsel together,*
> *against the Lord and his anointed, saying,*
> *'Let us burst their bonds asunder*
> *And cast their cords from us.'*

He who sits in the heavens laughs;
the Lord has them in derision.
Then He will speak to them in his wrath,
and terrify them in his fury, saying,
'I have set my king on Zion, my holy hill.'

I will tell of the decree of the Lord:
He said to me, 'You are my son;
today I have begotten you.
Ask of me, and I will make the nations your
   heritage,
and the ends of the earth your possession.
You shall break them with a rod of iron,
and dash them in pieces like a potter's vessel.'

Now therefore, O kings, be wise;
be warned, O rulers of the earth.
Serve the Lord with fear,
with trembling. Pay homage to his son with a kiss
or He will be angry, and you will perish in
   the way;
for his wrath is quickly kindled.

Happy are all who take refuge in Him.

We kept on singing, long after the Romans and the Temple
guards were gone. I felt such energy among our group then. Some
of us looked up to the clouds in anticipation, waiting for the army
of angels that would surely arrive soon.

But how mistaken we were! That night, Yeshua was thrown

into a dungeon. Early the next morning, He was flogged and then, already half dead, nailed to the cross on Golgotha alongside ten others. It all happened so quickly.

There was no trial, no charge, nothing. And above all, the clouds did not part, no heavenly host appeared, there was no display of divine power. There was nothing at all.

Only his mother and wife had the courage to watch from close by. Oh, the heartbreaking expression on the face of a mother who saw her son suffer so horribly.

Just before his spirit left Him, He screamed out, 'My God, why have you forsaken me?'

This was no angry rebuke to G-d. Later, Mary said that it sounded as if He was genuinely shocked that nothing was happening, and dismayed too, that He was about to die.

It was only when he was dead and had been taken down from the cross that James, John, and I dared to come nearer.

Joseph of Arimathea had brought linen winding sheets to wrap Him in. We laid Yeshua's body in Joseph's new family tomb so that the women could wash and embalm Him after the Sabbath, away from the grim presence of the bones of Yeshua's father.

Afterwards, we were to carry Him to the tomb that his own family had owned for centuries.

Joseph and his men wrapped Him in the winding sheets and carried Him quietly away, leaving us standing next to the cross. They bore Yeshua so gently, as if He was not dead but sleeping, and they were afraid to wake Him.

The despair we felt at the idea of Him lying there in that dark tomb, already cold and stiff, having died in disillusion. Something that we had thought would be great and glorious had ended so abruptly. And so unnoticed: barely anyone in Jerusalem was *aware that He had been crucified. After all, men were crucified all the time.*

You weren't there. But I was resolved even then that I would write everything down. So that we would not forget Him and his stories and the things He did. So that no one would be able to distort his memory.

I am conscious that what I have written above differs from what I wrote in the source, but I have my reasons for that. I think I can predict how you will feel about that, but it is the way it must be.

Because, when all is said and done, the other story is the one we want to tell. Saul has convinced me that this is the right thing to do. I will give him this letter to pass on to you when he visits you in Damascus.

I know him well enough to predict that he will try to persuade you to overcome our differences of opinion and join us once more.

This letter has ended up being much longer than I intended, yet I feel that I have written down but a fraction of what I wanted to say. I hope that Saul finds you in good health. Receive him as a brother. He has never met the Master, and yet he talks about Him as passionately as if he had been in his presence every day as we were.

Accept my greetings, Judas. I hope to be able to speak to you in person in the not too distant future. A brotherly embrace, Cephas.

'This is so huge,' Judith whispered when they had read the last line of the first letter. 'I'm having trouble getting my head around it.'

'And what a translation!' said Peter. 'It really is a masterpiece, so smooth, so ... modern. As if Saint Peter himself were speaking to us from down the centuries.'

'If this is all true...' Judith said, 'about Jesus being put to death without any kind of trial, the failed plot with Judas in the leading role ... then it means rewriting history. Just for the story of Saint Paul alone, who was still called Saul at the time... Contrary to what we're told in the Bible, he didn't persecute Christians or go to Damascus to arrest Christians... He was in contact with the Apostle Peter and went to Damascus to deliver a letter to Judas Iscariot!'

'Entering Jerusalem on a donkey,' Peter added. 'Overturning the tables in the Temple, the arrest, the crucifixion... It all happened, but hardly anyone noticed it. That's why we find no evidence of it outside the biblical account. This is enormous. And at the same time...' He searched for the right words. 'And at the same time, when you read this, you feel like you're there in person, getting a clear picture of what Jesus was like...'

'Of what the man Jesus was like, yes,' said Judith. 'A man with all his plans and doubts, his despair and sadness.'

'You can't get closer to Jesus than this,' Peter said. There was real emotion in his voice.

Judith turned the page. 'Let's read on,' she said.

Chapter Fifteen

J udas, the true servant and apostle of Yeshua, greets you,
Petrus. I am in good health here in Damascus and have
found peace. I have lived here for more than ten years now,
ever since I had to leave you all.

As you may know, at first, I considered going back to Kerioth,
but the lies about my role in Yeshua's death had already reached
my hometown. The decision to go away was the right one,
although it broke my heart to leave the eternal city behind me, and
to leave you, my brothers, even though most of you no longer
considered me a brother.

Do you know that you are the first to write to me in all these
years?

After he delivered your letter, Saul stayed with me for a few
days. He had suffered one of the seizures that so often torment
him, and he was exhausted. He had fallen from his horse this time
and could have been badly injured. His travelling companions
watched helplessly as he lay shuddering on the ground, foaming at
the mouth. But as is usually the case with these attacks, all he

himself was aware of was a bright light and the sound of voices. The man sees himself as a prophet, and he believes that G-d speaks to him directly during these fits. I see the man as a charlatan, one who wishes to appear far more significant than he actually is. If you and the others are not careful, he will take over the Way completely. He will infect you with his own ideas about how Yeshua's message should be brought to the people.

But remember that Yeshua stressed time and again that He had only been sent to gather the lost sheep of Israel. And that He did not wish to change one letter of the Jewish Law. The Jewish Law, Petrus. Jewish!

As for your letter, in truth, there is little I can say in response to it. I think you've given a fairly accurate and faithful account of events as they happened.

What you don't know is that when I left you in Gethsemane that night to fetch the Romans and the Temple guard, I turned around several times and almost came back to call off the whole plan. But I couldn't do it. Yeshua himself had entrusted me with the task.

I think that He too had imagined that things would turn out very differently after our arrival in the city. Riding into Jerusalem on a donkey was an entrance deserving of a much larger audience than a few tired people resting by the roadside and a handful of giggling children skipping along in front of the ungainly beast.

And I was surprised by his outburst in the Temple courtyard. How many times had we ourselves bought animals there in the past? Or exchanged the foreign coins we'd earned from selling our fish, grain, and cattle on the market? As He went to upend the third table, the furious merchants and money changers charged at Him so threateningly that He was forced to stop after knocking over just two tables. The fact that we only barely avoided being arrested was perhaps the most shameful thing of all.

Where was the blast of trumpets that was supposed to have liberated us? Where was the blinding light? Where was the thundering voice from on high, admonishing the people who had gone astray and scorching the uncircumcised rulers with an all-consuming fire? There was none of any of that. And so off we slunk with our tails between our legs.

That night, on my way into the city, I turned around several times and started to walk back, back to all of you. I had already reconciled myself to the possibility that when G-d intervened, it would be in a different manner to what we had been imagining. We had all been ready for the final battle that day, prepared to lose our lives in it. If that had not been the perfect moment, then when?

But in the end, I continued on to the city, picturing what was about to happen. I imagined how Yeshua would be brought before the Roman court after the Sabbath; how just one look from Him would reduce the judge to a pile of ashes; how the shields and helmets would clatter to the ground when the soldiers were struck down as if by an invisible hand; how the ceiling would be torn open and the majesty of the Lord would be revealed; how afterwards, every unbeliever would fall on their knees, screaming and begging for mercy, realising that the G-d of Israel would no longer be defied. I was convinced that the time had come for the Anointed One to return to his rightful throne and rule as priest and king over the lost sheep of Zion.

And so, encouraged by these thoughts — even now, I get goosebumps when I recall my state of mind that night — I eventually ran to the Temple ... headlong towards our downfall.

But the Temple guards seemed to have forgotten all about the matter, and they showed a distinct lack of interest when I presented myself to their commander. I had the good fortune, or so I thought, that this commander had just been engaged in discussion with some of the merchants and money changers who were aggrieved by what Yeshua had done. They had been unable to find all of their money, and one of them had complained that some of his sacrificial doves had escaped. The merchants' incessant whining was clearly irritating to the commander. When I arrived, they became even more irate, having recognised me as one of the rabbi's followers. The commander gratefully seized this opportunity to put an end to the dispute.

I told him that we had no idea what had got into Yeshua and that we were also troubled by his behaviour. I said that Yeshua was planning to create havoc the next day too.

Now I had his full attention. He was anxious to avoid any disturbance on the day of Passover.

The merchants saw their chance and pleaded their case again, urging the commander to arrest the troublemaker. What were the Romans going to do with this rabble-rouser? What if overturning those two tables was his way of gauging the reactions of the Romans and the Temple guard? What if He managed to mobilise more people to join Him? The commander was receptive to these arguments, which I stoked by being somewhat cryptic about what might happen the next day.

A detachment of Roman soldiers happened to be passing by just then, and they stopped to find out what scheme this small group of people was cooking up. The commander briefly explained the situation and was quick to exaggerate the danger that threatened the city, as well as his own role in uncovering Yeshua's plot. Perhaps the Romans were bored and seeking distraction, because this vague story was enough to spur them to action. Since I was the one who knew where the rebel could be found, the commander introduced me to the Romans in broken Latin. A few Temple guards were hastily rounded up to come with me, carrying torches to light the path to Gethsemane.

In that moment, it felt like everything was coming together. It was as though it was meant to have happened this way: the disgruntled merchants and money changers, the commander who wanted to ingratiate himself with the Romans by showing that they could rely on him, the Roman soldiers who just happened to be passing by and were eager to see some real action at last.

I will never be able to forget what happened next. When we arrived in the garden, I saw you all standing there in a row like a human wall with the Master, the smallest of us all, in the middle. I remember the look in the Master's eyes as I approached Him. His fear and doubt seemed to have vanished, and now I recognised the determined look He used to have when He was sparring with the Pharisees. But I also sensed great tenderness and gratitude towards me for taking on this task. I realised that his eyes were wet, glistening in the torchlight. I saw Him glance up briefly, just once, as if He too expected that help would indeed arrive soon.

But I was pushed aside, and Yeshua was swiftly taken away. We all stood there beneath the trees in the garden where it had suddenly become very dark without the light from the torches.

And I began to sing the psalm: 'Why do the nations conspire and the peoples plot in vain?' And you all joined in with me.

You, Petrus, were the only one who went out and followed the group of men who took Yeshua, staying at a safe distance. And we all know the story of how you managed to escape arrest three times by denying that you were a disciple of the Master.

I've spoken to Saul several times. I don't know what story he will tell you. He is so cunning with words, and I am sure that he will twist it to suit himself, as he often does. That is why I've chosen to give this letter, which Saul is unaware of, to a courier. It's the only way that I can be sure it will reach you unread and unchanged.

I still cherish the hope that Yeshua did not die in vain. He may not have been the Messiah, the liberator of the Jewish people on whom we had all pinned our hopes. But He has made me a better man.

I still tell my children the stories He told. On the surface, they are so simple. When you look into them more deeply, they are always so much richer and more complex than they at first appear. Often, while I'm telling a story, I suddenly begin to see it in a different light to the way I'd seen it in dozens of earlier retellings, and I realise that I finally understand its true meaning. It's as if the stories change along with the phases of your life. I miss how He could make up a story on the spot and how it would be so relevant to the situation, so relevant to the question that someone had just asked Him. I miss His humour, the way He radiated such lust for life, the jokes He made, jokes that could sometimes only be understood when you got to know Him as well as we did. And I often think of the people who were spiritually blind and could suddenly see again, who were sick but saw their confidence and self-worth return because of the way Yeshua ministered to them. Do you remember that man who was lame, but believed so fervently that he could walk because Yeshua said he could? How, as if by some miracle, he managed to take a few steps?

If we can hold onto these memories, tell these stories, pass on something of the faith He had in G-d, then his life here will have meant something. He has shown us what a life dedicated to serving the Eternal One might look like, what it should look like. And until the day comes when the true Messiah arrives to deliver us, then we will continue to pass on the message of his stories and his deeds. If, from time to time, some crumbs should fall to the ground for the dogs, then they can be content with that, but we will focus on the lost sheep of Israel.

But I must confess to you, Petrus, that I am very conflicted sometimes. The hopes we had pinned upon Him, our conviction that He was the one who would come, as foretold by the prophets centuries ago, only to realise that He was not the one after all, and He did not fulfil any of the prophecies made about the Messiah. King David's dynasty was not restored, the twelve tribes of Israel were not reunited, there was no peace between all nations, and nor was the Temple rebuilt. Saul tried to convince me that Yeshua will return one day and complete all the work that He was forced to leave unfinished. But nowhere in our Torah does it say that the Messiah needs two lives to accomplish everything. You know this to be true, Petrus. The nonsense I've had to listen to over the last few days...

Do not trust Saul, Petrus. He is misappropriating Yeshua's story. He never even met Him, so how can he possibly know what he is talking about? I believe he's trying to take the sting out of the truth about Yeshua by telling his own versions of the stories. And by making us all wait for Yeshua's return, he's distracting us from what actually matters: living according to the examples set by people like Yeshua, giving glory to G-d and waiting for the true Messiah who will come to restore G-d's kingdom.

But at times, I am so troubled... When I think of that Sunday after He was crucified... What sort of person could invent such a horrible way to die? It pains me to think of how He hung there naked, struggling, and gasping for breath as the blood poured from his wounds. Perhaps, even then, He expected angels to come down and lift Him from the cross.

I heard that a soldier stabbed his spear into Yeshua's side to put an end to his suffering, and I was so grateful to him. Perhaps he only did it because his shift was over and he wanted to go home, but it still felt like an act of mercy. It was quicker than breaking his legs, in any case, which they also often do.

And then that first day, after the Sabbath, when we all unwittingly went to his family's tomb. I think we were all still numb with grief. His mother and his wife went in and found the tomb empty. They saw only Joseph's shroud, left behind after his bones were collected and transferred to an ossuary. The expression on Mary's face... it was just a fraction of a second, but it betrayed her hope that Yeshua was not dead after all, that He had somehow survived. Then, the awful realisation immediately afterwards that we were at the wrong tomb.

It was as if He had died again, right before our eyes.

We sent someone to fetch Joseph of Arimathea because none of us knew where the new tomb was. He came straight away and led us there. If any one of us was still holding on to the hope that Yeshua would be alive after a day and a half, it was surely dashed when we opened the tomb. The stench took our breath away. And the flies that buzzed around us! I could not help vomiting, and I was far from being the only one.

His wife pulled back his winding sheets – and, oh, I have never before seen such great grief in a face. To see Him lying like that, *his body so battered and bloody, covered in open wounds, and the gashes left by the whip, the blood, the pus... His face no longer looked human: the closed eyes, the cracked lips. The fractured arms, his injured hands that had once moved so gracefully when He was absorbed in the story He was telling.*

And then, suddenly there were the screams, the silence of the tomb shattered by the women's wailing when it dawned upon them that it truly was Yeshua lying there. Some were so overwhelmed by grief that they collapsed, no longer able to stand.

And yes, Petrus, I know how disappointed we were. The hope that we had briefly cherished, the hope that death had not come for our rabbi, and that He had escaped – that hope was dashed. And to have to see Him like this...

The women washed Him, took care of Him, anointed Him with oils as if He were a newborn baby. It was the most moving scene I have ever witnessed. His wife Mary could not stop crying, but she performed her ministrations steadfastly and with such tenderness. It was as though she hoped that her touch might bring Him back to life. His mother sang the songs she had sung when she rocked Him to sleep as an infant... We wrapped Him in a clean shroud and carried Him to his final resting place, dead among the dead. I remember how we laid Him to rest with his ancestors, with his father, Joseph. How we prayed before we finally closed the tomb and surrendered Him to the darkness.

How we cried when we joined hands and sang: 'The Lord is my Shepherd, I shall not want...', our voices so choked with tears that at times barely any sound left our throats.

How we walked to Jerusalem, and that fair city shimmered in the morning sun, unchanged, as though it had not just witnessed the greatest tragedy. Jerusalem, the city that kills the prophets sent to her. Mary Magdalene thought she saw Yeshua on the road. She ran ahead of us, stumbling and crying so pitifully, and grabbed this man, a complete stranger, throwing her arms around his waist and pulling him to the ground as she fell. The man's shock as he lay there covered in dust, pinned down by this strange woman who was shrieking incoherently at him. How it took two of us to pull Mary off him; she refused to let him go and kept on crying, 'Yeshua, Yeshua'.

But more than once, we thought we saw Him in the crowd too. Usually, it was someone glimpsed just disappearing around a corner, or a figure in the distance that resembled Yeshua. We talked to each other about how difficult it was to believe that He was no longer with us, how it always felt like He might reappear at any moment, just stroll in, laughing, as usual, embracing us and slapping our backs, telling stories and singing. But that was merely a dream from which we all awoke into the nightmare of reality.

Even then, I felt the rest of you silently reproaching me. Even then, I must have known, deep down, how this was going to end. And it started with you. When we carried Yeshua's washed and embalmed body to the family tomb, you were the one who walked beside me, whispering that you had thought the plan to hand Him over to the Temple guard and the Romans had been a terrible one from the start.

I was silent at the time, and you took that as an admission of guilt. But I didn't want to cause any upset. It was too sorrowful a time for that. You had already forgotten by then, and you all forgot later, that Yeshua himself had fully embraced the plan. You all forgot how, after those two pathetic tables had been overturned, we had sat dejectedly with each other, not knowing what to do next. We were just a small group. What could we do without heavenly help? Then we thought that perhaps heaven could be compelled to help us, and then we would act in accordance with G-d's will, vanquish the uncircumcised ones and re-establish his rule.

The weeks that followed were the strangest days of my life. We were still brothers, bonded in mourning, sharing memories that sometimes gave us the powerful feeling that Yeshua was with us. One day, two men knocked on our door, saying they had met a follower of the Way on the road to Emmaus. They had spoken with him and gone on to share a meal with him, all the while feeling so strongly that they were in Yeshua's presence that they came to tell us about it.

And I think that might be the most beautiful illustration of how I imagined it would be. That we would feel his presence when we talk together, when we tell the stories, and when we follow Yeshua's example. This would be how we could honour Him. This was how we could believe that He was still alive, that G-d was in our midst.

And one day, one day when the Messiah eventually comes back to restore all Creation and return the Jewish people to their rightful place, everything we hoped would unfold in our lifetimes will come to pass.

But I began to see that the group was gradually ostracising me. Conversations abruptly ended when I sat down to join you, and I was increasingly excluded from meetings. Of course, it was easy for you all to make me the scapegoat, put the blame on me so you could all be free of blame. When I came in that day and saw Matthias sitting in my place... You all looked at me in silence, and I looked back at you in silence.

It felt like I stood there for hours, but in reality, of course, it was no more than a few seconds. I knew then that you had all completely shut me out.

I went home to my wife. We packed up our possessions on two donkeys, and we left. My wife had a distant relative in Damascus, so that was where we decided we would go.

Now, more than ten years later, you have written to me, and it has filled me with delight. Your letter gives a truthful account of what happened, and for that, I am glad. But I am worried about the other story you are going to tell. I suspect that it has been written under the influence of that snake Saul, and his arguments are so clever that it is difficult to refute them. He always has a rebuttal ready, and he can even twist your own story so artfully that you begin to doubt your own words.

I hope we will meet again one day, Petrus. I have forgiven you now, just as the Master taught us to forgive each other.

Next year in Jerusalem? Perhaps.

I have been fully accepted into the small Jewish community here. They know about my background, but it does not seem to matter to them. Apparently, I am not the only one to have followed a man believed to be the anointed one. There have been others, and more will surely follow.

May we live to see the return of the true Messiah. I live in hope, and so I close this letter in anticipation of that day.

With brotherly love, Judas.

'Poor Judas,' Judith stammered. 'Poor, poor Judas...' She rubbed her eyes with the back of her hand, clearly upset by what she had read. 'And all the sorrows of my ancestors, the pain suffered by all the generations that came before me, all the persecution and murder, it was all because ... because the wrong story was passed down. The Jews had nothing at all to do with Jesus' death. The Romans killed him.' She sighed heavily.

'I understand now why some people would go to any lengths,' Peter said, 'to stop this being revealed to the public. It's so easy to imagine them going to the wrong tomb, still in shock at what had happened, and how their hopes would have soared when it was empty. You can understand them wanting to pass that same hope on to future generations. You can see them telling themselves that their rabbi hadn't died, after all, feeling his presence almost tangibly when they were together. It's all so easy to imagine, so understandable so...'

'Logical,' Judith said. She sighed again. 'This is heartbreaking, truly heartbreaking. We just can't keep this to ourselves.'

She turned the page.

Chapter Sixteen

Petrus, the true and genuine servant and apostle of Yeshua, greets you, Judas. More time than I would like has passed between receiving your letter and sending my reply. You can imagine that Saul was not a little upset when he learned that you had not entrusted your letter to him but given it to someone else to deliver. He swore your name would not pass his lips again for as long as he lived. An overreaction, in my opinion, but I know him to be a stubborn man, and I recognise something of my own fervour in him.

I did not let him read your letter, although he was very insistent that I should. You are right that he is a vain man; he burned with curiosity to read what you had written about him.

My heart broke for you, Judas, when I read that you almost came back to us several times that final night after supper. Of course, I too often wonder how we might have done things differently, but we were in a situation where creating a crisis seemed like the best solution. So I cannot criticise you for that, Judas. But I am also aware of what happened afterwards, and why some of us thought your plan had not been well thought out. It may have found favour with the Master, but He was also at a loss. I'm sure He imagined it would play out in a similar way to the incident with the money changers in the Temple.

When He was dead and buried, the blame was naturally laid at your feet. After all, it had been your idea, and you were the one who had pointed Yeshua out. Your sudden departure stirred up bad blood; some of us took it as an admission of guilt. You had been Yeshua's treasurer, and some considered the coins that were still in your moneybag to be unclean, not even good enough to give away. In the end, it was used to buy a plot of land. They call it the Field of Blood because they think your hands are stained with the rabbi's blood, and the money was contaminated because of you.

I know you have suffered a great injustice, but so it must be, Judas. By blaming you, the others imagine themselves absolved of blame. You understand how that works, surely? How often have we witnessed it ourselves at Yom Kippur, when the priest burdens the goat with the sins of our people and sends it into the desert to die of hunger and thirst so that we can start the new year with a clean slate? That is just how it goes. Someone takes the blame so that others can be free of it. The odd thing is that, in your case, nobody was grateful to you for taking the blame. But perhaps that was because you did not do so voluntarily but had the burden placed upon your shoulders without having asked for it.

It is strange, Judas, how these stories take shape, just as they did that morning after the Sabbath when Yeshua was crucified. The story of the first, empty tomb has taken on a life of its own in a way. And there are others who believe they have seen Him, just as his wife did. Some are even convinced that they have spoken to Him!

I have often felt his presence very strongly, Judas, thinking that if I only reached out my hand, I would be able to touch Him. At prayer, I have imagined that I might see Him standing before me if I opened my eyes.

And I know what you will say. Yes, I saw his body, battered and bloody. I smelled the nauseating stench of his rotting flesh. I know that after He was embalmed, we carried Him to the tomb where He was reunited with his father, Joseph, much earlier than He could ever have imagined. And yes, a year later, we collected his bones and put them in a casket. So I do know. I know that He is dead and no longer with us.

But I have come to believe that this was not the end, Judas. Not the end of our community, because it has only grown stronger since you left. And not the end for our Master, either.

I have talked a great deal with Saul lately. He goes by the name of Paulus now. We talk about many things, and so naturally we talk about this too. I must credit you with a certain amount of foresight regarding Paulus and his role. He has indeed become more important within our movement, but I question whether this influence is as negative as you think. Certainly, we have had our differences. In the beginning, our tempers flared so much during our discussions that the others had to step in to stop us coming to blows. In the beginning, because I had been so close to the Master, and Paulus wanted to learn more about what He had said, I often had the upper hand in our debates. But this changed over time. Paulus seemed to grow less interested in Yeshua's life and more concerned with his ideas. And on that subject, I could not compete with him. You know that he was taught by the great scholar Gamaliel, who also secretly became a follower of the Way.

In conversations, Paulus is a formidable opponent. When you talk with him, you eventually reach a point where you can no longer recall exactly what you have said, and after a while, you find yourself agreeing with him. It is a pity: perhaps your conversations with him would have been different if you had spent more than just a few days together.

Paulus sees the dangers that lie ahead of us. We are still being oppressed, and our situation is not improving. All sorts of trouble are brewing. Attacks on Roman soldiers are common; if things get out of hand, I fear the Romans will retaliate by destroying the whole city. It will take only a small spark to ignite the flame.

This is why Paulus is convinced that we should expand. What if the unthinkable happens and our people are driven away from here? What then?

Paulus says that our message and our group have a better chance of survival if we place less stringent demands on the new followers than we do on ourselves. He believes that certain rules should be discarded.

We recently had an important meeting. There were some men there who had come to Jerusalem from Antioch. Several people suggested that, according to the Law of Moses, these men should also have themselves circumcised. Had you been there, you would no doubt have agreed with them. However, upon reflection, I am sure that you would have taken an even more fundamental stance. I know that it is your opinion that we should not allow anyone to join us who was not born of a Jewish mother.

But you must understand that much has changed since you left. You must understand that we have brought Yeshua's good news to many people since then. We have told them about his love, his stories, his new interpretation of the Law, and how we can feel his presence when we talk about Him.

We gather together often now, not just at Passover, and we eat as we did on the last night. We break the bread as He broke it. We bless the wine and drink it. We talk, sing, and pray together. We tell each other the stories Yeshua told us, laugh when we recall memories of his playfulness and the jokes we shared.

We still miss Him every day, Judas, but by coming together in this way He remains in our midst, and his message lives on.

Surely, Judas, you cannot be against that? Our community continues to grow. People are attracted to the warm, brotherly atmosphere that exists between us, and we welcome women too, Judas. We especially welcome women because the rabbi so often took care to speak directly to them.

People come to us who have almost nothing, and yet they still want to contribute what scant bread they have to our love-feast. We turn no one away. There are lepers, cripples, blind people, servants, tax collectors, and whores, but also women of high rank, judges, scholars...

This is all exactly what Yeshua would have wanted, don't you think? I know you will argue that, when Yeshua was alive, He was only concerned with such people if they were also Jewish. But Paulus takes a very different view. He thinks that we may not always have understood Him correctly. Why should we keep his stories about living according to G-d's will to ourselves?

I believe that Paulus is right when he says that we should share Yeshua's story and open it up to other people. Paulus has also impressed upon me the importance of making plans for the future. What if there comes a day when we can no longer live here? Then we will be forced to live among the Gentiles. So why not make our group bigger? It could make the world outside our group safer, should we ever need a place of refuge. And as well as that, Judas, would it not be a fine tribute to our Master if we brought his message to more people than he could ever have dared dream of reaching? Why should we keep something so beautiful to ourselves? That would be like hiding food in your kitchen that is far better than what you serve to guests at your table. If you have a light, surely you don't hide it under a bushel basket or put it under the bed? Paulus says that Yeshua's light can be a light to all the nations of the earth.

And how many stories do the pagans have about people who appeared to have died but turned out not to be dead after all? You have surely heard those stories too? Osiris was dead and then brought back to life. And what about Tammuz and Dionysus? Yeshua may not actually have risen from the dead, but nor did Osiris, Tammuz, or Dionysus. Yeshua is risen in our hearts, Judas, and we arise with Him. This is what Paulus teaches us: we die with Yeshua, but we can also rise again with Him. Through Him, we return to G-d, who is now G-d for all the peoples of the world, not just us. We have made a new covenant that applies not only to Jews but also to the Gentiles.

Do you remember the hope that was in our hearts when we found the tomb empty? A hope that was dashed shortly afterwards, I know. But the hope we'd felt before that moment, that is what we want to pass on to future generations.

What do you think, Judas? Wouldn't that be a great legacy? One that would honour Yeshua's memory? The generations that come after us might still be talking about Him long after we are gone. Imagine that! Imagine them following his example and *trying to live as He did, honouring the Eternal One of Israel. Imagine them eating together, breaking bread and drinking wine, confirming the new covenant with G-d over and over again.*

I recently had a vision, Judas. I didn't know what was happening to me.

I was in Jaffa, and I had gone up onto the roof to pray. The spirit is willing, but the flesh is weak, Judas; I grew hungry and wanted something to eat. While my food was being prepared, I stayed on the roof, and that was when I saw the heavens open, and a large linen sheet being lowered to the earth by its four corners. And on that sheet, I saw all the four-footed creatures and reptiles of the earth and the birds of the air. I heard a voice saying: 'Get up, Petrus; kill and eat whatever you wish.' But I did not want to because I had never eaten anything that was forbidden by the laws of Moses in my life. Then I heard the voice a second time: 'What G-d has made clean, you must not call profane.' I heard it three times. Then the sheet was suddenly taken back up to heaven. Do you not think that wonderful, Judas? Was this not a sign that what Paulus says is correct? A sign from G-d to tell us that the old laws about what we are allowed to eat or drink no longer apply? Do you understand what opportunities this can bring us? How it will open up the Way to so many more people, people for whom it has always been closed off?

Our group's chances of merely surviving in our current situation are so slight, Judas. Consider that. The Romans will not leave our region any time soon. Meanwhile, all sorts of trouble are brewing among the people, and there are rumours of uprisings. And you know how ruthless those soldiers can be. Because, when you think about it, what had Yeshua actually done wrong? Knocked over a couple of tables! The Temple guards had already forgotten the incident entirely. Had it not been for you, and for those Roman soldiers happening to come along, the commander would no doubt have sent those whingeing merchants away. He might even have had them flogged for being such a nuisance. But he saw a chance to ingratiate himself with the Romans, and that is how everything got out of hand.

So you can imagine what might happen if a group of people took it into their heads to start a real rebellion! That could well have been the end of us.

So, Judas, when those men from Antioch came to us, we were so happy to learn that the Way had reached so far north. There was some dissent because a few of us believed that new people should also be circumcised. However, to demand that would have prevented many from joining our community.

Paulus and Barnabas thought it was no longer necessary. Real circumcision is spiritual and not literal. What is important is that you take Yeshua into your heart and live according to his example. Instead of being merely circumcised, you yourself are entirely cut away, as it were, no longer relying on your own blind obedience to stay in G-d's grace but putting your faith entirely in Yeshua. Like Paulus, who says he died on the cross with Yeshua and yet he is still alive. But what lives in him now is not his own self, but Yeshua. Yeshua lives within him.

You must see why I became more strongly inclined to see things Paulus's way after my vision in Jaffa. At the meeting in Jerusalem, when the argument between the two sides became heated, I spoke up. I, who was once just a simple fisherman. I felt the Spirit inside me, giving me the strength and courage to speak. I explained that we can all be saved by Yeshua's grace, and there was no need to burden the newcomers unnecessarily with a heavy yoke. Paulus and Barnabas agreed with me and told me about all the signs and wonders that G-d had done through them among the Gentiles. And Yeshua's brother James quoted the words of the prophets and showed that we should not impose too great a burden on non-Jews, as long as they do not fornicate, steal, lie, or serve idols. At the end of the meeting, we decided unanimously that they need not be circumcised if they want to follow Yeshua and join our community, nor are they bound to comply with any of the other commandments our forefathers had to obey. There is a new covenant, a new relationship with G-d.

Several people were disappointed and chose to leave us and return to the elders in the Temple. I fear that we will be split into two separate factions from now on.

And I know which group you would choose if you were here. Even if you believe we are debasing our Master's legacy, please try not to think badly of us. I am now confident that we have found a way to reach more people than we ever dared dream of, and we will be able to tell them about the love that Yeshua showed us, that He showed everyone.

Why should we not fulfil it now, Judas, the promise our ancestors sang of? That Israel would be given as a light to the nations? That, one day, every knee would bow before our Lord? Didn't Isaiah say that all the ends of the earth must turn to G-d, and He would save them? One day, all the nations will say: come, let us go up to the mountain of the Lord, to the house of the G-d of Jacob; for out of Zion shall go forth instruction. The time is coming to gather all nations and tongues; and they shall come and see the glory of G-d. Why should we not say that the time is now? And that Yeshua leads us in spirit, that everyone should know of

Him and live according to his example? And one day, perhaps, Yeshua will come back. Who can say that this is not true?

This is the hope, Judas, in which I too now live. Perhaps not even Yeshua fully comprehended or even realised how far his message could reach. Together with many others, I am now willing to follow Paulus and say: yes, we can bring this message of love and the hope that one day, everything will be whole again. We must bring it. We cannot keep this good news to ourselves, even if that is what Yeshua originally intended for us to do.

Yeshua died on the cross, and He paid the price for what we did. We were spared. Even though we shared the blame. He was a better man than we could ever be, but because He loved us so much, He died for us. Paulus teaches us that if we tell all the nations about Him, He will not have died but will live through us, and we through Him, as if He truly is risen from the dead after all. As if the first tomb had been just as empty as it had appeared that morning when we opened it, and He was more alive than He had ever really been in life.

Judas, I hope this letter finds you in good health. I know that our paths have separated and that they may never cross again after this letter. Still, I firmly believe that the old way is dead. Yeshua's new Way will lead to a brighter future. One day, all nations will sit at the Lord's table together, breaking bread and drinking wine to commemorate Him, united in seeking the Lord.

I have decided to withdraw from the movement and leave everything to the others. I will continue to live in Jerusalem, but I will no longer involve myself in any debates about the Way. Initially, we agreed that I would preach to the Jews, and Paulus would go out among the Gentiles, but it did not take me long to abandon that idea. I shall now leave it all entirely to Paulus,

Barnabas, James, and whoever else wants to contribute. I have already made my own contribution, and I have no more role to play. G-d will judge the choices I have made.

With brotherly love, Cephas.

I am sending you a copy of the Source, the story of Yeshua's life, which I have committed to paper. Those who come after me should use it to write their own stories.

Judith put her hands in her lap, resting them on top of the unread pages. 'Saint Paul must have been a very persuasive man,' she remarked.

'And a prescient one, too,' Peter agreed. 'He realised that they would be driven out of Israel eventually and that the movement's best chance of success was in making the group as large as possible. So all the barriers that might have prevented new people from joining the group had to be removed. Like circumcision.'

'That sounds surprisingly modern, actually. Rational... Improving their odds through a sort of risk management,' Judith said.

'There's one letter left, Judas's reply. I'm very curious about what he's going to say.'

Chapter Seventeen

J udas, the only true and genuine servant and apostle of Yeshua, greets you, Petrus. Much time has passed between the arrival of your letter and my reply, which will be the last I ever write to you as far as I'm concerned. I have read the Source, which you sent with your last letter. It is an incredible mixture of things Yeshua actually said and did and many other things that happened only in your imagination.

I don't know what could have got into you, Petrus, to make you write such a misleading account of events. And yet, in your two letters, you also tell the truth, especially about that final, fateful night. I do not even know where to begin. A refutation of all your falsities would result in a book twice as long as what you have written. So I will not trouble myself to do so. One day, I may write down my own version of the good news that Yeshua brought. The Good News According to Judas. I can see it already...

I will address only your description of the last night, and in particular, the way you portray me. I comfort myself with the thought that no one is likely to believe your version of how I betrayed Him.

Everyone will see that if Yeshua's death had indeed been foreseen by Him and others, my actions must have been an essential part of a divine plan. If I had not reported Yeshua, He would never have been arrested. And then none of the events you imagine happened afterwards would ever have taken place. Since I was the only one who had the courage to set the divine plan in motion, I should indeed be revered in your community as Yeshua's most faithful disciple.

I am not the traitor. You are the traitor, Petrus. Who swore up and down that he didn't know Yeshua? And six times at that! Who fled when he saw the net closing in? Your description of yourself as a man who shed bitter tears is quite brilliant. But what really happened? Did you not confess to betraying Him yourself that night? Did you not weep and beg us to forgive you? You denied Him to the doorkeeper, and when you sat by the fire, and to the slave girl. And then – just as Yeshua predicted according to your own account – after the cock crowed, you denied Him three more times! At the front porch, then to the same slave-girl again, and an hour later, you denied Him to a servant of the high priest. Then the cock crowed for the second time.

You told us this in meticulous detail, and we did not hold it against you. We wept with you, Petrus. We understood your fear and your shame. Weren't we also afraid? Shouldn't we have been ashamed too? Looking back, did we not all abandon Him? You at least followed Him after He was taken away, which is more than any of the rest of us did. We stayed behind in the garden, and we did not run away as some have claimed.

The Romans had no interest in us at all; they wanted Yeshua.

And I had completed my task, pointing Him out in the garden at dusk as I had promised them I would. And as Yeshua had told me to do! I only did what He asked of me, Petrus, as I have always done and would still do now if it had not all gone so horribly wrong.

But now I see what you are trying to do. You cannot bury the fact of your own betrayal, your own treachery, your denial that you knew Yeshua – not even in your version of the story – because everyone already knows about it. And everyone has already forgiven you for it. So instead, you paint me as a devilish traitor, the disciple who betrayed his master to the Romans with a kiss. A kiss! That you could even imagine such a detail! There was no kiss. I simply walked up to Yeshua, and then the Romans took Him away. Not one of us put up any resistance...

You have given yourself a heroic role, I see, grabbing a sword and slicing off a Roman's ear, which Yeshua reattached... Where do you get these ideas? You never touched a sword that night, and if you had, the only person you would have been likely to wound with it was yourself. And how could Yeshua reattach someone's ear? Did He have a needle and thread with Him?! There was no fight, Petrus. We were all waiting for something to happen, waiting for the imminent moment when G-d would demonstrate his mighty power. The atmosphere was one of triumph rather than defeat. Everything was going as we had intended. The Romans had fallen for our trick. There was no panic, no one ran away, and no one put up a fight because we knew that this was part of the great plan in which Yeshua was to play the leading role. When the Romans and their torches vanished into the night, you were the only one who left us and stealthily followed them back to the city...

We stayed behind in Gethsemane, praying, thanking G-d for

his wisdom. *After you left, the rest of us lifted our voices and sang the words of the well-loved psalm: 'Why do the nations conspire and the peoples plot in vain?'*

And I sit here now, weeping as I sing these words to myself, and suddenly I can see that this is where that kiss must have come from. And that makes it so much worse. You have twisted the psalm's words 'Pay homage to his son with a kiss,' we sang. 'Pay homage!' Not: 'Betray Him.'

I don't know where to begin, Petrus. You've allowed yourself to be beguiled by Saul or Paulus, or whatever his name is these days. That man is so slippery that he can't even be pinned down on the name his parents gave him.

But that the pair of you should distort Yeshua's message so outrageously! Oh, if only He were still here. How I would have loved to watch Him throw your Source into the fire, to hear Him scolding you. 'You scoundrels! This was not what I meant!' Did He not say that He had not come to abolish the Law or the prophets? And that every letter of the Law would remain in force as long as heaven and earth existed? Where did you get these notions that people are allowed to eat what they want now or that there's no more need for them to be circumcised? Not to mention your description of our last supper together in which Yeshua apparently told us to pretend the bread was his body as we ate it? I couldn't help laughing when I read that. Especially when you then wrote that, from now on, we would be drinking his blood when we drank wine...

Have you forgotten how many laws we have against consuming blood? Have you forgotten that whenever Yeshua ate an egg, he first broke it into a glass and held it up to the light? If there was even a tiny speck of blood in it, He would throw away the whole egg! How many times have you and I witnessed this? And now you say we should drink his blood? For crying out loud, Petrus!

Did Yeshua not say that whoever breaks one of the least of these commandments and teaches others to do the same will be called least in the kingdom of heaven? And that anyone who follows them and teaches them to others would be called great in the kingdom of heaven?

You were there when he spoke these words, words that are utterly incompatible with your claim that the rules should be relaxed for new members. And did He not decry as hypocrites those who crossed land and sea to make a single convert to the faith of our forefathers? Did He not say that, if such a newcomer failed to follow the letter of the Law, he would be doubly lost, made twice as much a child of hell as the one who converted him?

It is simply preposterous, the idea that Gentiles in Roma or Hispania or Gallia will soon be singing about how G-d led them away from Egypt. Of what concern to them is the history of our ancestors? Of Abraham, Isaac, and Jacob? Or David, Saul, and Solomon?

Did Yeshua ever say anything positive about non-Jews? He warned us not to pray as the Gentiles do, endlessly mumbling a torrent of words in the hope that some of them might be heard. They worry about tomorrow and do not know that tomorrow will bring worries of its own. But our Heavenly Father knows what we need. Today's trouble is enough for today. And did He not command us never to cross the borders to preach but only to go to the villages and towns in Israel? He told us emphatically to go nowhere among the Gentiles, and this was a rule He also followed. He was the shepherd who was, above all, concerned with restoring our people and gathering the lost sheep of the house of Israel. That is why He chose us twelve, Petrus. He chose twelve disciples, not eleven or thirteen. One of us for each of the twelve tribes of Israel.

I feel such despair, Petrus. It is a despair perhaps far deeper than what I felt on the day our Master was crucified, and when we carried Him from the tomb of Joseph of Arimathea to his father's tomb a day and a half later. I despair because you have so utterly obscured his message that even his awful death has become meaningless, no matter how you twist it.

Are you and Paulus really suggesting that He was a son of G-d? We all know that Joseph was his father. Hear, O Israel: The Lord is our G-d, the Lord alone! Have you forgotten even this? How can G-d have a son if He does not have a wife? How can you bestow a son upon the Merciful One when He is too sublime to have a child? Or is Paulus trying to give his story a pagan veneer to make it more appealing to the Gentiles?

And then there is that entire story about his trial. The Sanhedrin is not permitted to convene after sunset if they are ruling on a capital case. No trials may be conducted on the Sabbath, on holy days, or even the eve of a holy day. A death sentence must not ever be passed on the day of the trial itself; the judges are supposed to sleep on their decision for another night. Under Jewish Law, remaining silent, as Yeshua did, should not be taken as a confession of guilt. And I could go on.

You even bring Pilate into it. Do you think this callous man had shown any interest in our Yeshua's fate for even one moment? And did Pilate suddenly speak our language? Or did Yeshua suddenly speak Greek or Latin? And your account has Pilate ritually washing his hands in accordance with Jewish custom – it is all too ridiculous for words.

Who knows what misery you will bring upon our people in the future with your description of the crowd of Jews baying for Yeshua's crucifixion? 'His blood be on us and on our children...' G-d forbid!

And all of this was done to get on the Romans' good side? The Romans crucified Him. They alone had the authority and the power to carry out that horrific sentence. So no one will believe the obvious lie that the Jews are behind Yeshua's death.

Petrus, oh, Petrus. You have betrayed Yeshua once again, but this time you can expect no forgiveness from me. Yeshua was sent only to us, the lost sheep of Israel.

I will close this letter by reminding you of three incidents, which I take from your own Source. These events were, of course, too well known to be left out of your account. You could not weasel out of including them. But, despite what you say, Yeshua was not in the habit of ever healing anyone who was not a Jew.

I was there during that incident with the Syrophoenician woman who asked Yeshua to heal her daughter, who was being tormented by a demon. How many times had we seen people healed when Yeshua merely touched them, spoke to them, paid them a little attention? He made them whole again, gave them back their humanity. Yeshua did not judge this woman worthy of so much as a glance, and he told her: 'I was sent only to the lost sheep of the house of Israel.' We wanted to send her away because we knew she would only continue to cry out to us and following us. You and I tried to grab her, but she threw herself at Yeshua's feet and said: 'Lord, help me!' And Yeshua did indeed reply as you have written in your account: 'It is not fair to take the children's food and throw it to the dogs.' Then, when she said that even the dogs eat the crumbs that fall from their masters' tables, Yeshua said that her words showed great faith. And, from that moment, her daughter was healed. But Yeshua would never have actually touched the girl himself. He didn't want to be defiled. And the crucial words were spoken not by Yeshua himself, but by her mother.

It was the same in that other case when the centurion in Capernaum begged Yeshua to heal his slave who was paralysed and laid up in bed in agonising pain. Again, afraid of being made unclean, Yeshua didn't go to the house but acted on the faith demonstrated by the centurion. After the description of this incident, there is another passage of pure fantasy in your Source in which He says that all the nations will sit with Abraham, Isaac, and Jacob at the feast in the kingdom of heaven. But everyone will easily recognise this fabrication as a falsehood. I cannot begin to understand how you can dare to put into Yeshua's mouth so many words that He never uttered. Yeshua was a Jew who worked among the Jews and only ever wanted to work among Jews.

And so to the third and final example from your Source, which will ultimately also be detrimental to you. I am referring, of course, to the healing of the Gadarene madman. I remember it as clearly as if it happened yesterday. Before we had even moored our boat, he approached us, coming out from where he had been living in the tombs. His hands and feet were covered in wounds from the fetters and chains he kept managing to remove. He threw himself down before Yeshua, and Yeshua said to the unclean spirits inside him: 'Leave him and enter that herd of swine there.' The unclean spirits entered the swine, and the animals went completely mad. At least two thousand of them, the whole herd, rushed down the steep bank into the lake and were drowned in the water. And good heavens, the looks on the faces of the swineherds who saw all their *pigs killed in one fell swoop! How angry they were with Yeshua! They knew that, as a Jew, He was forbidden to eat pork. But to actually destroy their pigs, their only source of income... They demanded that He go away, and so we left.*

Now tell me, Petrus, did Yeshua then allow the man He had healed, a Gentile, to join our group? Of course not! He wouldn't even hear of it. I can still see that man standing on the lakeshore, his eyes bright and clear once again but filled with tears because we had left him behind. I have often wondered what happened to him. I am sure those swineherds would have felt precious little gratitude for the expulsion of his demons...

And I could go on in a similar vein for many, many more pages, Petrus.

But I suspect there is no use in trying to disprove all these lies and half-truths of yours. I cannot imagine that anyone would swallow them, but who can tell? You have a convincing advocate for your cause in Paulus. A man who never met Yeshua nor ever heard Him speak.

But I concede defeat and acknowledge that you are the winners in this battle. I comfort myself with the thought that not only do I know what really happened, but you do too – and that you will have to learn to live with your lies.

I have sung this beautiful psalm so many times: 'Hear a just cause, O Lord; attend to my cry; give ear to my prayer from lips free of deceit. From you let my vindication come; let your eyes see the right.'

Greetings from Judas, perhaps the only remaining true follower of the Way.

Judith flipped over the last page to check that there was no more text, and then they both sat quietly for a while, thinking.

'It all sounds very plausible,' Judith said, breaking the silence. 'It's clear when you read the Gospels that Jesus was completely uninterested in any nation but Israel. He'd followed the Jewish Law all his life and had no intention of changing it...'

'He wanted a less stringent interpretation of the Law, I think,' Peter said.

'So he was all right with curing a cripple on the Sabbath or stoning an adulteress when the Law specifically demanded it. But actually changing the Law? No. And when he was alive, he'd only ever concerned himself with the Jews. He didn't travel to any other regions... The views he expressed about the Gentiles were mostly negative. And then the Source... My God! That must be the document Matthew and Luke referred to when they wrote their gospels. What a pity that wasn't in the casket too.'

Peter thought for a moment, and then he said, 'It's all so different to what we thought we knew, to what we've been taught. All of it... And Judas's account does seem to make a lot of sense. The role he played in betraying Jesus, what Jesus did in the Temple, Paul...'

'When I think of how many wars have been fought in the name of that other story,' Judith said, 'and of all those religious councils endlessly debating Jesus' true nature, all the books that have been written on the subject of the empty tomb, enough to fill a library! And how puzzling Judas's role has always been... but above all, those words, "His blood be on us and on our children." My God...'

She began to cry again.

Peter felt useless, sitting there beside her. What they'd just read had made a great impression on him too.

'So what now?' he said eventually. 'What should we do? I'd still like to go back to the dig. I don't think the police will have got around to removing all the evidence from the tent yet. They might have an officer posted at the site to make sure nothing is removed from it, but if we tell them we're willing to turn ourselves in on the condition that they let us look inside the tent first, I think they might let us in. There's got to be something there that can give us some sort of concrete proof.'

'You know, it's three o'clock in the morning already,' Judith said. 'I'm done in, to be honest with you. I don't mind going to the site, but I need to close my eyes for a couple of hours first. Is that all right?'

'Of course. Why don't you have a lie down on the sofa? It looks just about the right size for you. I'll take the armchair and see if I can manage a nap there.'

Judith didn't even have the energy to argue about who should sleep where. She kicked off her shoes and lay down. Peter folded the pages of Eco's translation in half and put them back inside the plastic wallet without their cover. He slipped the wallet into his inside pocket.

Even before he had installed himself in the armchair, he could tell from Judith's steady, regular breaths that she was already asleep.

A noise startled him awake. It was still dark, and it took him a fraction of a second to remember where he was: in an armchair in Mevrouw Eco's house on the Oude Rijn. He heard another noise. It sounded like footsteps. Worried now, he stood up and shook Judith's legs to wake her up.

She sat bolt upright. 'What's wrong?' she asked sleepily. There was no need for him to answer because now she could hear it herself.

Footsteps. On the staircase.

Chapter Eighteen

They were both still too drowsy, and perhaps also too surprised, to move. Peter felt in his pocket to make sure that the translation was still there.

When the door finally opened, they were both overcome by a feeling of immense relief. Mevrouw Eco appeared in the doorway wearing a long white nightdress.

Peter and Judith had both been holding their breath, and now it escaped in a long, simultaneous sigh.

Mevrouw Eco seemed as surprised as they were. 'Oh!' she said when she'd recovered. 'You're still here. It was so quiet, I thought you'd already left. But I noticed the living room lights were still on when I went to the lavatory, so I went downstairs to turn them off. No need to get up, either of you. I'm going straight back to bed.'

'Mevrouw...' Peter was just about to say, but before he could get the words out, she had already closed the door behind her. He gave Judith a puzzled look. 'She didn't even ask if we'd read the letters,' he said in amazement.

'Hmm...' said Judith. 'I think she genuinely doesn't want to know. That is quite ... odd.'

Peter glanced at the clock. It was quarter past six now and still dark outside. 'Judith,' he said. 'I'm just going to cut to the chase here. I know we've got a lot of things on our minds, and I'm sure we're going to need some time to work through it all, but I have to ask you something. You'll probably think it's silly considering everything we've just been through, but ... I get the feeling that ...'

'You get the feeling that there's a distance between us,' Judith added.

'Er ... yes. I do.'

Judith pulled up her legs and crossed them. 'There is a distance. I'm really terrible at hiding my feelings, apparently. At least, that's what Mark's always telling me. He says I'm not much of a challenge to a scholar who loves unravelling mysteries.' She smiled.

'So what's wrong?' Peter asked.

'Look, Peter... Hiding inside that wardrobe was a huge thing for me. Really huge. I grew up hearing the stories about my grandparents, and I've always tried to imagine the fear they must have felt. There's a story my mum told me... I'd completely forgotten about it myself, but she said my little brother and I pretended to be them once. The two little boys who lived next door to us played the "nassies", as my little brother called them...' She smiled in spite of herself. 'They pretended to be the Nazis who found us in the wardrobe. My mum thought we were just playing hide-and-seek at first, but when she heard us screaming and crying, she came running upstairs and realised what we'd been up to. My little brother cried, but only because I was crying. I was absolutely beside myself, apparently, but the strange thing is that I really have no memory of it. And I must have been at least seven or eight at the time.'

Peter nodded.

'I've hardly told anyone that story about my grandparents. Just a few close friends. And Mark, of course. But otherwise...'

Peter got up and sat down next to her. He gently put his hand on her knee, and she allowed it. 'The story you told me about your grandparents really had an impact on me. So did your reaction when you relived what happened to them. I realise you've told me things that you don't just tell anyone. I know how special that is, and it felt like a special moment for me too. I'm aware that what I experienced was in complete contrast to what you had just experienced but ... I felt such peace come over me then, a feeling of total serenity. I can't think of any better way to describe it. I stopped praying years ago, gave up on the idea that God intervened in people's lives '

'Who says it was God?' Judith said, interrupting him. 'Why couldn't this feeling of peace and serenity simply have come from inside you?'

'I suppose it could have,' he admitted. 'But it felt like it came as an answer to my prayer. It was an extraordinary experience for me. And for Mark too. Didn't he say that he felt something similar at the same time?'

'Yes, he did say something like that. But why didn't I feel it too, then? Why wasn't I reassured when I needed it most?'

Peter had no answer for that.

She was about to get up, but Peter stopped her.

'As long as we're sitting here,' he said. 'You hadn't quite finished telling me your story back there in the wardrobe.'

'What story?'

'About you being so interested in Sabbatai Zevi because so many people believed he was the Messiah. And that turned out not to be the case. Just like Jesus couldn't have been the true Messiah, according to the Jews.'

'Ah, yes, that's right. I think that probably is what interests me most about it, yes. And it feels like my dissertation is somehow being pushed in that direction, towards the story's Messianic aspects. It was – and still is – my intention to write about the history of Judaism in Leiden. But then I stumbled upon Moshe Levi's papers in the archives. This was a man who sold everything he had to follow a rabbi, so when you read them, knowing that the rabbi wasn't the Messiah, you find yourself wanting to warn him: "Stay here! Don't go!"' She cupped her hands around her mouth like a megaphone. 'Because you know what's about to happen. Sabbatai Zevi turned out not to be the Messiah, and Moshe left his home and everything he owned for nothing. I hope I'll be able to find out what happened to him and his family one day, but I doubt the answers to that question are in the Leiden archives.' She looked disappointed.

'But the parallels with Jesus are so obvious,' she continued. 'When I hear Christians claiming that their Jesus fulfilled all the Old Testament prophecies about the Messiah, I'm always taken aback. I can't help thinking that they have no idea what they're talking about. Anyone who doesn't just blindly parrot what they've been told by other people and actually looks into it for themselves will soon find out that Jesus didn't fulfil *any* prophecies. That subject alone would be enough for a dissertation or even a PhD thesis. Jesus didn't restore King David's dynasty...' Judith said, counting on her fingers. 'He didn't bring world peace. He didn't convert the people of all nations and cultures to Judaism. He didn't reunify the twelve tribes of Israel. He didn't rebuild the Temple. When the Messiah arrives, there's supposed to be no more hunger, no more death. Every weapon will be destroyed. The Nile will dry up, the trees will bear fruit every month, and so on and so forth. The list is almost endless.' She put her hands back in her lap. 'None of that has happened. And I know Christians will argue that those things will only come to pass when Jesus returns, but that's just a pathetic attempt to try and make sense of it. The true Messiah would do the job properly the first time. He wouldn't need two lives. There's nothing anywhere in the Torah about Him living twice.'

'The subject really gets you wound up, doesn't it?' Peter said.

'Yes, it does get me wound up, but it confounds me too. If Christians simply took the trouble to read the list of prophecies made about the Messiah, surely they would immediately be able to see that Jesus simply wasn't the one? That there's just no way he could have been?'

'And that...'

'And that winds me up, and it confounds me. But it's not just that. Throughout history, Jews have been accused of being Christ-killers, and it's that sort of thinking that makes atrocities like the Holocaust possible. The Nazis were only harking back to a centuries-old anti-Semitism that had been constantly fuelled by the Catholic and Orthodox Churches, and let's not forget, that other famous anti-Semite, Martin Luther. It was all based on a misunderstanding about who Jews think the Messiah is... But the result was that people have persecuted Jews so they could go to church to worship a Jew who, according to the Jewish prophets in the Jewish holy books, was sent by God to restore the Jewish people to their rightful place as a light to the nations.'

Judith was on her feet now.

Peter stayed on the sofa. He tried to conclude the discussion with a light-hearted remark. 'I think that might be a bit too much for one dissertation.'

To Peter's relief, she laughed. 'Yes, it's more of a book, really. Or even a series of books.'

'So are we okay now?'

She smiled. 'Of course,' she said, and she shook Peter's hand with mock solemnity. 'But in those moments after we crawled out of the wardrobe, the contrast between what you'd experienced and what I'd experienced was just too much. I'd been so afraid, feeling just a little of what my grandparents must have felt, and then you started going on about how peaceful and serene you'd felt, like you'd been touched by God. But... Anyway, let's move on.'

'The strange thing is,' Peter said, 'and I'm sorry to bring it up again, but the strange thing is that I think that might have been a turning point for me in terms of my own faith.

It really felt like God was with me. And now that we've read these letters, I feel closer to Jesus than I've ever been.'

'I can understand that Peter, I really can,' Judith said.

And with that, the peace seemed to have been firmly re-established between them.

'Shall we go?' Judith asked.

'All right,' said Peter, and he went into the hall to get their coats. 'Let's leave by the back door, just to be on the safe side.'

The sun was already coming up. The clock struck seven. After they'd put on their coats and shoes, they walked through the perfectly ordered kitchen to the back door. There was a key in the lock, with another identical key attached to it on a ring.

Peter tried the second key in the lock. It worked.

'We'll leave one of these on the counter,' he explained as he removed a key from the ring. 'And we can lock the door behind us with the other one. I'll bring it back later today.'

Peter and Judith left the house and locked the door. Outside, they found themselves in a small garden where a tall fence separated them from the lawn around the motte on the other side. On top of the motte was the Burcht, a circular castle keep about six metres high, complete with battlements. The man-made hill the keep stood on was a popular spot for sunbathers and picnickers in the summer. Now there wasn't a soul to be seen.

The garden gate was open, so they went through it onto the wet grass around the castle. At that moment, the gate at the back of another house opened about ten metres away, and a man stepped through it. Peter and Judith were so taken aback that they stood absolutely still.

A flame leapt up from the lighter the man was holding, and their panic subsided. Just as they were about to turn around and continue on their way, Peter heard someone calling his name – not loud, but very clearly.

Peter turned back around and put a hand on Judith's arm to stop her from going any further.

'Who is that?' Judith whispered.

'That's Luuk. He's a friend of mine, a doctor,' Peter replied. 'He lives in that house there with his family. He's up early... Luuk!' Peter waved and started walking towards the man.

Now it was Judith who grabbed his arm to hold him back. 'What are you doing?' She spoke quietly, but there was a hint of exasperation in her voice.

'Let's go and talk to him,' Peter said. 'He's a good guy, I promise. And seeing him has just given me an idea. Trust me, this is the best thing that could have happened to us right now. He's a Knight of the Teutonic Order,' Peter told her, whispering very quietly, as though he was afraid Luuk might hear him even from so far away.

Judith gave him a confused look.

'I'll explain later. Come on.' He held onto Judith's arm as he began to walk towards Luuk, and she followed him.

'Hey, Peter, it's good to see you!' Luuk said when they reached him. He shook Peter's hand. 'I've been worried about you. Both of you.' He looked at Judith.

Peter introduced them to each other.

'Worried? Why were you worried?' he asked.

'Pieter called me last night,' Luuk said. 'Pieter Hoogers. He sounded pretty agitated. Wanted to know if I knew where you were... Either of you. Thomas is in a critical condition in the hospital, and the police are looking for you in connection with the attack. I had no idea what he was on about.'

'It's a long story...' Peter began.

'Let's go inside,' Luuk suggested. 'It's freezing out here.'

They followed Luuk through the garden and into his house. In the kitchen, a coffee machine was already percolating on the counter, and the thing intermittently belched out great clouds of steam.

Peter rubbed his hands together with anticipation. 'Ah, coffee!' he sighed. He opened a cupboard, grabbed three cups and lined them up on the countertop. 'You're up early, Luuk.'

'I know. And Anne and the kids are all still sleeping like logs. I was going to go to the Van der Werffpark for the hymns, but then I decided I'd rather stay here and work on an article I'm writing. I want to be in the Pieterskerk for the service by ten though.'

'The service?' Peter asked, but then answered his own question immediately afterwards. 'Oh, the remembrance service.'

Judith looked at him quizzically.

'There's a memorial service in the Pieterskerk every year on the third of October,' Peter explained. 'The citizens of Leiden gathered to give thanks to God for liberating them from the Spanish after the siege. That was in 1574, and the tradition is still kept today.'

'I feel I have an obligation to go every year as a member of the Order,' Luuk said. 'Anyway, that's not important. What is important right now is what is going on with you two. Should I call Pieter and let him know you're here?'

'No!' Peter said.

It came out a little too emphatically, and Luuk raised his eyebrows and stared at him.

'No,' Peter repeated, more calmly this time. 'It really is a long story, Luuk.'

Peter poured the coffee and told Luuk about everything that had happened to them since the previous afternoon. When he got to the part about the casket, Judith's eyes grew wide with panic. She opened her mouth to cut him off, but he held up his hand to stop her.

'Luuk and I have known each other for a very long time, Judith,' he explained. 'Ever since freshers' week in 1978, in fact. We were in the same group for induction, and we were inseparable after that, all the way through university. We've been friends for nearly twenty years.'

He told Luuk about the casket but not that they had opened it. Nor did he mention the strange encounter with Pieter Hoogers at the faculty. He did reveal that they'd had another confrontation with their attacker at the fair, and that they'd visited Judith's friend Mark in the Sionshof before spending a broken night sleeping on the sofa of an old lady who lived a few houses away.

Unconsciously, Peter put his hand over his inside pocket where the translation was.

'You mean Eco's widow?' Luuk asked, surprised. 'But why would you...?'

'Long story,' said Peter, deciding that his old friend didn't need to know absolutely everything. He explained that he and Judith had reason to believe that the ivory box Thomas had found was linked to Saint Peter in some way, and that they had been on their way to the dig site to look for evidence to prove it.

Peter also told Luuk about the man who had broken into his house, the confrontation in the hospital, Thomas's murder, and how they'd been on the run ever since. It all formed a cohesive story that Luuk seemed ready to believe.

Luuk was quiet for a moment. Then he looked at Judith and Peter in turn. 'So why don't you just go to the police?' he asked. 'If you had nothing to do with it, then there's no need for you to be on the run, is there? Can't you just hand the casket in to the authorities? You did take it from the site illegally, and...'

'This isn't the time for legal niceties, Luuk,' Peter said with irritation.

'So where's the casket, now?' Luuk asked.

Peter looked at Judith. She shook her head, almost imperceptibly. 'Listen, Luuk, that's not something you need to know just now,' he said. 'It could put you in danger too.' He paused for a second or two, and then he continued. 'Obviously, I realise that we could have gone to the police, and we probably should have. As soon as we're ready to, we will. We just need a bit more time. Once we've handed the casket in, what happens to it will literally be out of our hands.'

Now Judith spoke for the first time. 'Someone might purloin it,' she said.

Luuk couldn't help an amused grin. 'Purloin?' he said. 'I think you might have been reading too many detective novels or watching too many thrillers about conspiracy theories. This is real life we're talking about. Here in the Netherlands, if we hand something over to the authorities, we can trust that it will be dealt with appropriately.'

Judith said nothing.

Peter hadn't known her for long, but he already knew her well enough to tell that, right now, she had plenty to say but was choosing to keep her mouth shut.

'It's a bit more complicated than I've made it seem,' Peter said. 'When this is all over, I'll tell you everything, but right now it's better if you don't know all the details.'

Luuk seemed riled, now. 'Well, that seems a bit fishy to me, Peter. Let me call Hoogers. He was worried about you. Surely you don't mind me putting his mind at rest? Or is it better if he doesn't know all the details either?' The question sounded distinctly sarcastic.

'Actually, yes, it *would* be better if he didn't know all the details either,' Peter said calmly but firmly. 'Really, Luuk, just trust me. Trust us. You and I have known each other for years, and I would never try to deceive you, but I'm asking you now to please just be patient.'

'All right, then. What about you?' He looked at Judith.

'What's the Teutonic Order?' she asked.

Luuk looked at Peter for a moment, took the last sip of his coffee, and said, 'Let's go up to my study.'

Luuk led them upstairs. Halfway up, he turned and put his finger on his lips, telling them to be quiet.

At the end of the landing, he opened a door into an

elegant, classically furnished room. An oak bookcase on one wall reached the ceiling, and every shelf was crammed with books. In front of the window stood a huge, solid-looking desk made of dark wood. The desktop was empty except for a lamp and a few hand-written sheets of paper lying on the leather desk pad. What looked like an expensive fountain pen had been put down on top of them.

A large window offered a magnificent view of the castle, which looked especially majestic from this low angle. Two brown leather wing-back chairs stood at one end of the room. In front of them on a small glass table was a beautiful Bible with a ribbon marking a page somewhere near the middle. A sticker on the front read: *Fully Revised 1995 Willibrord Translation of the Old and New Testament*. Standing between the armchairs was a tall, silver-coloured ashtray with a push-down top. The faint smell of cigar smoke hung in the air.

Luuk motioned them towards the armchairs. He sat down on a leather desk chair that had a bulky wooden base.

Peter picked up the Bible and said with genuine surprise, 'I hadn't expected you to have a Catholic Bible.'

'Ah,' said Luuk, 'well, a Bible's just a Bible, isn't it? And the advantage of the Catholic editions is that they're longer than the Protestant ones.'

'Who's that?' Judith asked, pointing at a painting hanging on the wall behind them. It showed a man in late middle age. Slung over his shoulder was a white mantle embroidered with a blue cross, and a similar blue cross framed in silver hung from a gold chain around his neck.

He looked directly at the viewer and held an open book – presumably a Bible – in his hands.

In the top left corner of the canvas was a coat of arms, or perhaps it was two coats of arms arranged closely together.

'That's our land commander,' Luuk told them. 'Not the current head of the Order but the one before him. It's a real painting rather than a print, but it's not the original, just a copy. The paint is literally still wet. The original is at our headquarters, Teutonic House, in Utrecht.'

'Right,' Judith said. 'So tell me, Luuk. What does your Order have to do with the Pieterskerk or with Saint Peter?

'Maybe more than you think,' Luuk replied. 'And perhaps more than even I know,' he continued, looking at Peter. 'I think I'm starting to get an inkling of what might be going on here. And if I'm even vaguely right, Peter...' He let the rest of the sentence hang in the air.

'Yes?' Peter asked. 'What if you are?'

'Then your attacker was probably right,' he replied.

Judith was sitting on the edge of her seat. 'Right about what?' she asked.

'About you not knowing what you've got yourself into,' Luuk said. 'But above all' – he paused dramatically like an actor heightening the suspense in a play – 'he was right when he said that neither of you has the slightest clue who you're up against.'

Chapter Nineteen

'Do you mind if I smoke?' Luuk asked Judith.

She shook her head.

He slid open a desk drawer and took out a glossy wooden box, which he opened and presented to Peter. Peter got up and picked up a cigar from the box. He passed it beneath his nose and inhaled pleasurably. Luuk chose a cigar, then he took a slender strip of cedarwood and lit it, holding the spill pointing downwards until it developed a slow, steady flame. Peter put his cigar in his mouth, held the end in the flame, and puffed a few times before sitting back down with it glowing between his fingers.

Luuk also lit his cigar, waved his hand to extinguish the spill, then closed the box again and put it back in the drawer.

Both men took a few short puffs on their cigars to get a good, even burn, and then leaned back contentedly in their chairs. The blue smoke swirled smoothly towards the high ceiling.

'We've spent many happy hours in this room,' Peter said to Judith. 'Smoking cigars with a good glass of whisky or wine. It's led to some of our best conversations.'

'Well, gentlemen, this is all very nice,' Judith said sarcastically. 'Meanwhile, we still find ourselves in quite a bizarre situation. Although we're innocent of any involvement in Thomas's death, the fact remains that we've stolen something from an archaeological dig. We're on the run from the police, *and* we're being chased by a madman who's shown himself willing to kill in order to get his hands on that casket... You two might be quite content to sit here smoking cigars and reminiscing about two decades of friendship, but I think we might have more urgent matters to discuss. What did you mean just now, Luuk, when you said that we don't know who we're up against?'

Luuk looked at her with amusement, as if he found it funny that she had spoken so sharply, but then he apologised immediately. 'Sorry, Judith, you're right. I'm probably not taking this seriously enough. I've not been through what you two have just been through. I'm only coming in in the middle of your adventure. But listen...'

He drew thoughtfully on his cigar, puffed out his cheeks a little, and let the smoke slowly escape from his mouth before continuing. 'Some things are beginning to fall into place for me too, although I'm not sure about the finer details. I only have suspicions. We – my father, my grandfather, my great-grandfather, and so on – have always been part of the Teutonic Order, otherwise known as the Bailiwick of Utrecht of the Teutonic Order. The Order has always been part of my life. When I was a little boy, my father would take me to the meetings in Utrecht. It found it fascinating, listening to all those conspicuously aristocratic gentlemen. They were discussing what I later understood were requests for financial assistance from all over the country. They were good people, they really were. They all had a wonderful sense of humour, loved a good glass of wine ... and they'd sit and consider these letters they'd received from people asking for their charity. They were concerned with using their funds for "individual exigencies", as they called it then. They dealt with what were often quite distressing cases, people who had got into trouble through no fault of their own because of illness or accident or some other bad luck. The Order would provide a one-off grant, give a lady in need so many thousands of guilders, pay for a stairlift, fund an orphan's education. All very worthy work, of course, so as you can probably imagine, the atmosphere was always pleasant.'

'I'm sure it was. It's easy to give money away when it doesn't personally belong to you,' Peter said.

'That's right,' Luuk agreed. 'But even then, they always had to reject a huge number of applications. They prided themselves on being able to justify why a particular application had been unsuccessful. And if they were in any doubt, they always dispensed the funds anyway. I've had the honour of being able to continue that work. When my father retired, I automatically succeeded him. The task was bestowed on me by fate, but I've carried it out to the best of my ability.' Luuk tapped the ash off the end of his cigar.

'Where does all that money come from?' Judith wanted to know.

'The money, well…' Luuk said. 'It's important to know that our Order goes all the way back to 1187 and the time of the Crusades. We, or my predecessors I should say, founded a military hospital in what's now Akko in Israel, where they nursed the sick and wounded crusaders. The founders were merchants from Bremen and Lübeck, so that's why our organisation is also known as the "German Order". The priests who belonged to the Order expanded their work to Europe, and they gained many admirers who gave them money and land, quite a common thing back then. The Bailiwick of Utrecht was founded in 1231 when a supporter donated a building just outside the city. Later, we moved to the city centre. Those headquarters had to be sold almost 200 years ago, but we managed to repurchase the building just last year.'

'Are you an aristocrat too?' Judith asked him.

'One of the membership requirements is that both your parents should be of noble birth,' Luuk replied. 'So, yes, I am. I come from an old family, and we've always had a connection to Leiden, going back at least as far as it's possible to trace these things.'

'And what does the Teutonic Order have to do with Leiden?' asked Judith.

Her tone betrayed a combination of curiosity and increasing irritation.

Luuk wasn't allowing himself to be rattled by her questions. 'The city and the Order have an ancient and close connection.' He took a languid puff of his cigar, watched the smoke circle upwards, and then he began expounding. 'Our Order was founded somewhere around the year 1190.

Originally, we were a religious military order, like the Knights Templar, which makes me a Knight, officially. We're headed by a land commander, who has the highest rank, with twelve commanders below him. Then there are twelve knights or "associates", as we call ourselves. That puts me at the bottom of the hierarchy. Like the Knights Hospitaller and the Knights Templar, we were originally established to join the Crusades and help recover the Holy Land from Muslim rule. As you know, the Crusades ended in a fiasco, so the Order began to focus on converting Northern Europe to Christianity. They were quite successful, especially in Prussia.'

'I forgot to bring my notepad, Professor,' Judith said sardonically.

'Yes, yes, just listen,' Luuk responded irritably. 'You were the one who wanted to know about the Order, weren't you? Then you need to know something about its history, or you won't be able to understand what might be going on right now.'

'Sorry,' Judith mumbled. 'My apologies. You're right.'

'Peter will be able to tell you much more about Leiden's history,' Luuk continued calmly, 'but it's always been centred around the Pieterskerk. The Counts of Holland settled here in 1100, south of where the Breestraat is now, and they built a tiny chapel dedicated to Saint Peter and Saint Paul. That was in 1121. Much later, in 1268, Count Floris IV bestowed the right of advowson or patronage on the Order, which meant it could appoint priests. Until then, that had been the exclusive right of the Counts of Holland. That was the start of a relationship between the Order and the Pieterskerk that lasted hundreds of years. During the Reformation in the sixteenth century, the Teutonic Order converted from Catholicism to Protestantism. Critics claimed that this was done only because the Order wanted to protect its property from confiscation – but who can really say what the reason behind it was? The Pieterskerk didn't come through the Reformation unscathed either. The people of Leiden destroyed many of its sculptures and paintings during the Iconoclastic Fury in 1566. Lucas van Leyden's *The Last Judgement* was spared, fortunately. After the Reformation, the Pieterskerk was used by the Protestant Niederdeutsche Church, and so the Order was able to stay connected to it.'

'Why wasn't the church's name ever changed?' Judith asked. 'Surely Saint Peter is more of a Catholic saint? After all, the legitimacy of the Pope's authority is based on the claim that he's Saint Peter's heir.'

'That's a bit of a mystery,' Peter said, joining the discussion. ' I've actually always been surprised by that too, although I only seem to be realising it now. But maybe...'

'But maybe you're both on the verge of finding out the answer to that question,' Luuk mused. 'What if you and Thomas aren't the first to have discovered something that could be a direct link between Saint Peter and Leiden? What if people have always known about it, and that's why the name was kept? The Pieterskerk shares its name with the Basilica, the papal church in the Vatican. And that brings me back to the point where I started my story.'

Luuk put down the small stub that was all that was left

of his cigar. Peter did the same, mirroring Luuk's gesture in a sort of pantomime for two gentlemen.

Luuk stared up at the ceiling, clearly trying to decide whether he should say more. Then, without looking at either Peter or Judith, he began to speak. 'There have always been stories about an order within the Order, the *Ordo in Ordine*. I've always dismissed it as an unsubstantiated rumour. If you give rumours like that any credence, before you know it, you end up with nonsense like that book that came out in the early eighties. What was it called again?'

'*The Holy Blood and the Holy Grail*?' Peter said. 'By those two English authors. What were they called again? Michael Baigent and Richard Leigh.'

'Yes, that's the one,' Luuk confirmed. 'My God, what utter nonsense they spouted in that book. If they're to be believed, Jesus married and had children, and after his death, those children fled to the south of France with Mary... And there was a secret society called the Priory of Sion, whose members were supposedly some of the most influential people in the world. They dragged Victor Hugo into it, and Leonardo da Vinci, who they claimed had left coded messages in his paintings... If you ever want to try your hand at writing a thriller, Peter, you couldn't find a better place to start. I bet people would love it.'

'But when they wrote that book, it was already a well-known fact that the Priory of Sion was a hoax dreamed up by Pierre Plantard de Saint-Claire,' said Peter. 'He eventually admitted that he'd forged the documents about the Priory's history and smuggled them into the French

National Library in Paris, which is where Baigent and Leigh found them.'

'God, I got so annoyed about it,' Luuk said. 'Suddenly, people were investigating our Order because it was founded around the same time as the Knights Templar, so obviously, there *must* have been something mysterious behind it... And the fact that the Order shies away from publicity, to put it mildly, only fed the conspiracy theories, of course. Fortunately, they lost interest fairly quickly, but if I'm honest, I'd have to say that there's always been a seed of doubt in my own mind.'

'You never told me about that,' Peter said, sounding more astonished than reproachful.

'No, I ... I've grown up with the Order, of course. My father and his ancestors all served, so I'm following a long family tradition. Who am I to start doubting the Order?'

'But now...?' Judith asked.

'But now I'm not so sure. My father said something to me once that I've never forgotten. I was still quite young, maybe twelve or so. One of my uncles went to Russia and brought me back a set of *matryoshka* dolls. You know what I mean, little wooden dolls with more little wooden dolls inside. I'd taken them all apart, and I thought I'd opened them all, but then my father picked up the smallest one and showed me that it opened too. It wasn't easy, but he eventually removed that last doll. He showed it to me with a triumphant flourish and said: "Remember this, Lucas..." – he often used my official name – "remember that what you see isn't always everything there is to see. There is often still something hidden from view. And that that hidden thing is perhaps more important than what you thought you saw."'

'And you thought he was talking about the Order?' Judith asked.

'Now that I think about it...' Luuk said carefully. 'When he made that remark, he was looking very deliberately at the big portrait of the land commander that hung in a prominent position on in our sitting room. As if he was trying to tell me something.'

'And now?' Judith said.

'Now I think there could well be something in those rumours. I can't quite put my finger on it, but the way they're coming after you, so persistent and so violent... If whoever it is has anything to do with the Order within the Order, then you're dealing with some very powerful, rich, and influential people. They won't ever let you win.'

'But what makes you think your Order has something to do with it?' Peter asked. 'Surely there's just as much chance of it being some other group? Maybe the man who is after us deals in antiquities and knows that what we have could fetch a lot of money on the black market.'

'But, Peter, wasn't he the one who told us that we don't know who we're up against?' said Judith. 'I took that as an empty threat, but maybe he really meant it.'

'Even if he is connected to Luuk's Order,' Peter protested, 'it doesn't prove that they're behind all this.'

Now Luuk stepped in. 'Now just hang on a minute,' he said. 'It's not "Luuk's Order". What I said was that it could be an Order within our Order. I'm almost convinced that it must be. We've always had strong links with Leiden, and especially with the Pieterskerk. It is odd that our Order was given the right of patronage for the Pieterskerk in Leiden when our headquarters were in Utrecht. It makes me wonder if our Order has some sort of knowledge that gave it its privileged position. And then there's the Order's wealth... I've always been told the money comes from donations made in the past and smart investments being made now. But what if there was another source of income? They were in the Promised Land. Who knows what they might have taken from there? Similar stories have been told about the Templars. They carried out excavations under the Temple Mount, and then they suddenly became fabulously wealthy, which suggests that they'd unearthed a fantastic treasure.'

'Or it could have been something that didn't have much monetary value,' Peter suggested, thinking along the same lines as Luuk. 'Something that would have shaken the Church to its foundations if it was ever made known. The Vatican might have paid huge sums of money to keep a secret like that hidden. Jesus' remains, or a book written by Jesus himself... Who knows?'

Luuk enlarged upon Peter's idea. 'Suppose,' he said, 'and in my opinion, the idea is too absurd for words, but let's suppose you're right. Suppose my Order found out, either via the Knights Templar or simply through one of its own members, that Saint Peter didn't die in Rome, but here, somewhere near Leiden, and that he had a little casket with him, a casket with secret contents...' He looked at Peter meaningfully.

Peter's ears flushed pink, but he said nothing.

'So suppose,' Luuk said, continuing this train of thought, 'that they knew Saint Peter must actually have died in this country...'

'Then Thomas's find will have set off alarm bells,' Peter said, finishing Luuk's sentence for him. 'They must have been involved in the dig at Roomburg from the start. Maybe they even helped finance it.'

'But how did they know...' Luuk began.

'There was a young man working at the dig,' Peter told him. 'A bit of an oddball. German accent. Thomas didn't really trust him. He often caught him snooping around the dig outside of working hours. Thomas spent a lot of his weekends doing research there, and this German man started turning up all the time. Herman, that was his name. He followed Thomas like a shadow. Maybe he was some sort of mole. He must be our gunman. He has a German accent as well.'

They heard a door open on the landing and the thump and patter of children's feet on the stairs. Luuk looked at his watch.

'It's past eight-thirty,' he said. 'I know you were on your way to the dig, but I think I have a better idea. The service in the Pieterskerk is at ten, but if we go there now, we can have a look in the parsonage before it starts.'

'Now?' Judith exclaimed in amazement. Then she clapped her hand over her mouth because she knew she had spoken too loudly 'Now?' she said again, more quietly this time.

Peter seemed surprised too. He looked at Luuk dubiously.

'You know the Pieterskerk underwent a major restoration between 1977 and 1982?' Luuk said. It was more of a statement than a question.

Peter nodded.

'The parsonage has original copies of the reports that were made during the restoration,' Luuk told him. 'But they're kept under lock and key. Now, that's something I've always thought was odd. I asked the custodian about it a while ago, and he said he did have the key, but he wasn't allowed to let me see them. I was disappointed, and I thought it was unusual, but I just accepted it. Now I'm wondering if there was more to it. So I think it would be a good idea to try to get a look at those reports and see if there's anything in them that could help us. Maybe something was found during the restoration work that will turn out to be another small piece of your puzzle. I'm on fairly good terms with the custodian. I think I can convince him to let us look. Afterwards, you can go to the dig and then you can go to the police.'

Peter and Judith looked at each other.

Judith shrugged her shoulders. 'Fine by me,' she said. 'as long as it doesn't take too long. Who knows, there might be something there. I don't think it will make much difference if we get to the site an hour or so later than we'd planned to.'

Peter didn't appear to be convinced. 'I don't know if it's a good idea to go to the Pieterskerk. There'll be hundreds of people there soon.'

'All the better,' said Judith, and Luuk nodded in agreement. 'In a crowd, we'll be more anonymous and less likely to stand out. And best of all, they won't be expecting us to go there.'

Judith looked at Luuk and said, 'I would really like to change my clothes before we go, if I can. Does your wife maybe have something I could borrow? And if you have anything resembling hair dye in the house, I could change my hair colour. Peter, you should wear something else too. Luuk, do you have a hat or something for him?'

Luuk smiled. 'Yes, I do. Good idea. Come on.'

He stood up, and Judith and Peter did the same. Just as Luuk opened his study door, a woman in a bathrobe walked across the landing. She stopped short and looked at Luuk with surprise.

'You have visitors?' she asked. 'I thought I smelled cigar smoke, but that seemed ridiculous at this time in the morning.'

She carried on walking, and only then did she see Peter.

'Hey, Peter!' she said warmly. 'What are you doing here so early?'

Peter walked towards her, revealing Judith, who had been standing behind him.

'Oh! And you have a woman in there too? Luuk,' she laughed, 'are you hiding anyone else from me?'

'Not at all,' Luuk said. 'My lover climbed out of the window, just like she always does.'

Luuk's wife winked at Peter.

Luuk introduced Judith to Anne. 'I know this is a bit of an odd request, darling,' he asked his wife, 'but would you happen to have any hair dye?'

Anne raised her eyebrows and looked at her husband

curiously. 'Intriguing... Are you two on the run?' She asked the question jokingly, but when it was answered with serious faces, she stopped talking.

'It's a long story, darling. I'll explain later,' Luuk said. 'For now, what's important is that Judith changes the colour of her hair and maybe pins it up, and puts on some of your clothes and one of those adorable hats of yours. It's only for a few hours. That's all they need.'

Anne seemed reluctant at first, but Judith smiled at her apologetically, which appeared to persuade her.

'Okay. Come with me,' Anne said to Judith, and she opened the bathroom door. 'I'll give you a hand. And Luuk, can you sort Peter out? We'll have you ready to go in thirty minutes.'

Luuk led Peter up to the next floor where he picked out some clothes for him. Blue trousers with a matching jacket, a new shirt that was still in the packaging, light grey socks, and even a smart, perfectly polished pair of shoes with wooden tensioners in them.

When Peter had changed into Luuk's clothes and checked his appearance in the mirror, his reflection looked back at him with satisfaction. They could hear the women in the bathroom on the floor below, talking and even laughing. The atmosphere might have been mistaken for cosy domesticity if the situation hadn't been so critical.

Luuk changed his clothes too.

Less than half an hour later, they heard the bathroom door open again. As the men walked downstairs, Judith emerged with pinned-up, freshly blow-dried hair in a shade of dark brown that was almost exactly the same as Luuk's wife's. She was wearing a simple skirt suit with an elegant belt. The sight of her took Peter's breath away. Luuk also seemed to be impressed.

Judith smiled and struck a graceful pose with one leg forward and a hand on her hip. She looked approvingly at Peter.

'Very nice,' Luuk said. 'Now you just need a nice hat and some shoes, and you two will look just like a couple off to church in their Sunday best.'

They went down to the ground floor, where Anne found some shoes to match Judith's outfit. She chose a hat from what looked a large collection of headgear on the coat rack.

She handed Peter a hat too, brown felt with a broad brim. He pulled it far down over his eyes that they would be obscured from anyone standing directly in front of him.

'Perfect,' said Luuk.

'Listen, darling,' he said to Anne. 'I'm going to walk to the Pieterskerk with Peter and Judith. Then I'll come back and pick you up, okay?'

'All right,' Anne replied.

She turned to Judith. 'I hope we can meet again under different circumstances soon. This was a bit of a strange way to get to know each other.'

Judith agreed.

The two women gave each other a quick hug, and then Luuk, Peter, and Judith stepped out into the street.

'Wait,' Judith said. 'You two go on ahead of me, and I'll walk behind you. If they're searching for us, they're more likely to be looking for a man and woman together.'

'Smart thinking,' said Luuk, said, nodding in agreement.

'We'll meet you at the entrance on the square. You know where it is, don't you?'

Judith stood at the front door and watched the men walk away along the canal. Peter turned around to take a last look at her. Somewhere inside him, a vague feeling of dread began to grow

Chapter Twenty

Peter and Luuk walked around the corner onto the Nieuwe Rijn canal where they crossed the Koornbrug. This stone-built, cobbled bridge was popularly known as the Pilarenbrug or Pillar Bridge because of its thirty-two columns, sixteen on each side, giving the bridge its distinctive, graceful appearance.

The streets were still relatively empty and quiet. Here and there, traders were setting up food stalls, and a small truck was delivering big barrels of beer to a bar. Students pushing bikes walked by them with their ties loosened and their shirts untucked.

An alley brought Peter and Luuk out onto the Breestraat beside the grand city hall. They crossed the street, walking past the high street stores' darkened windows into the Pieterskerk-Choorsteeg, a narrow lane of small shops leading to the Pieterskerkhof. At the end of the lane, the Pieterskerk rose up gloriously before them, splendid and colossal, a rock that had stood immutable for centuries in the ever-changing urban sea around it.

They went left around the church. Luuk stopped for a moment to look at the memorial plaque to the Pilgrim Fathers on the outside of the baptistry.

'That's another strange story, the Pilgrim Fathers,' Luke mused.

'They're not somehow mixed up in all of this too, are they?' Peter asked him, and there was a perceptible hint of derision in his voice that he wasn't able to suppress.

'No, that's not what I mean. Or maybe I do. My father was fascinated by the Pilgrims. George Bush visited Leiden a few years ago. He's descended from the Founding Fathers himself.'

'What are you trying to say?'

'I'm saying that for such a small town, Leiden has played a pretty big role in world history, hasn't it? The men and women who founded the United States lived in this city. They worked hard and saved hard until they had enough money to sail from Leiden to Delfshaven and on to England, where they set sail for America. So, the foundations of the most powerful country in the world were, in fact, laid here in this town.'

'Don't you think that's exaggerating it a bit?'

'Well, maybe. But what surprised my father – and he was not the first or the last to think this – was that they chose Leiden as their departure point. And that's quite odd because the much more obvious choice would have been an actual port like Amsterdam, Rotterdam, Antwerp, or even somewhere in Zeeland. There must have been something in

Leiden that attracted them to it; they must have had another reason for choosing Leiden. At least that's what my father firmly believed.'

'And that's where Saint Peter comes in?' Peter asked. He started to walk on, but Luuk held him back.

'Who knows what they knew, Peter? I know it sounds mad, but how can anything seem normal after what you and Judith have been through? And after what Thomas found? Look at it like this: the Pilgrim Fathers broke away from the state religion in England because they thought the Reformation hadn't gone far enough. They could have gone anywhere they wanted, but where did they choose? Leiden, of all places! Don't you think that's strange?' Luuk was impassioned now, completely absorbed in his own argument. 'They went to Amsterdam first,' he continued, 'but there were all sorts of religious squabbles going on there, so they moved to Leiden. And where did they settle in Leiden? Here, in the Kloksteeg, as close as they could possibly get to the church dedicated to St. Peter, the very disciple who gave legitimacy to the pope they hated so much.'

'Where are you going with this exactly, Luuk?'

'Where am I going with it? What if the Pilgrims' spiritual leader, John Robinson, didn't just choose Leiden randomly? What if he knew there was something here that would completely destroy Rome's power once and for all? They lived here for eleven years, and then, all of a sudden, they left. Or at least, some of them did. Most of them, about two hundred of the three hundred Pilgrims, stayed behind. And it gets even stranger.'

Now he had piqued Peter's interest. 'Go on,' he urged him.

'The practice of burying people inside churches began in the early Middle Ages. Originally, it was a privilege reserved for nobility and high-ranking members of the clergy. But about a generation before the Pilgrims settled in Leiden, around 1550, they started allowing the town's wealthier citizens to be buried inside the church too. Even John Robinson was buried here, and many other Pilgrims were buried alongside him.'

'I still can't quite see what you're getting at.'

'Do you know what helped bring about this practice of burying people in the church itself?' Luuk asked him. He allowed a dramatic pause to fall before he told Peter the answer. 'The presence of a saint's tomb.'

'But...' Peter started to protest. 'You're not trying to tell me Saint Peter was buried here, are you? Surely he couldn't be here? He died more than a thousand years before Leiden was even founded. That's why Thomas spent so many years looking for P—' Peter stopped himself, aghast. 'I mean, that's why Thomas and I... That's why Thomas spent all these years looking for an explanation as to why Saint Peter...' He tried to regain his composure. 'We used to talk about how remarkable it was that they chose Peter and Paul as the Pieterskerk's patron saints because, at one point, the two of them were even in direct opposition. At least, according to the Book of Acts they were. Why not choose someone like Saint Willibrord, who came to convert the Low Countries to Christianity and landed on the beach near here at Katwijk?'

If Luuk had noticed Peter's slip of the tongue about Thomas's true purpose, he made no mention of it. 'He might not actually be buried here, but what matters is that there were probably people, like the Pilgrims, who thought he was. Who believed that his grave had been found here in 1100 and that his bones were reburied on this spot. The town sprang up around a little chapel dedicated to him. The city of Leiden might literally have been built on Saint Peter the Apostle. There was probably a tradition known only to a few insiders based on the idea that Peter didn't go to Rome but breathed his last in this region.'

'Okay, now you sound like the authors who wrote *The Holy Blood and the Holy Grail*,' Peter laughed.

Luuk was stone-faced. 'But this theory could actually be based on facts,' he said earnestly. 'You said it yourself. Weren't you and Judith on the way to the Matilo dig because you thought you might unearth something to connect Saint Peter to the casket you found?'

'That is true. And we still intend to do that as soon as we're finished here. Although if I'm honest, I don't think we're going to find anything in these reports.'

'I don't even know if we're going to be able to get a look at them, but there are some other things I want to show you inside the church. You'll already be aware of a lot of it, but I think you might see it all from a different perspective now, after everything you've found out over the last few hours.'

They walked around to the square in front of the church, where Judith was waiting for them. She was trying to appear calm and composed, but it was obvious even from a distance that she was unsettled. Suddenly Peter felt guilty that he and Luuk had stayed out of sight talking for so long when Judith might have been anxious.

She was visibly relieved when she saw them. As he approached her, Peter saw that she was wringing her hands and her cheeks were bright red.

'Where have you been?' she asked with a mixture of relief and annoyance.

'We were just around the corner,' Peter reassured her. He put his hand on her shoulder and felt her relax at his touch.

'Nobody followed you?'

'I don't think so. The streets are so empty that I'm sure I would have noticed. But let's go inside. We're too easy to spot out here.'

The church door was already open. Inside, a few volunteers were bustling about, preparing the church for the service. It looked like a large number of people were expected to arrive, judging from the sea of chairs that had been neatly arranged in rows.

They entered through the large doors and walked down the aisle towards the choir. Luuk pointed out some of the graves on the way.

'That one there, and that one... This one here and this one as well... There are a couple more over there, too...' he said.

'What do you mean?' Peter asked.

'There are explicit instructions on each of those graves that they must never be opened or sold. Never. Do you know how unusual that is? It used to be common practice to "shake" graves, as it was called, to make room for a new grave. If you had a burial vault, your grave was dug up and sifted, and any bones, teeth, nails, and other remains were transferred to an ossuary and placed in the crypt. The bones in most other graves were usually moved to a common charnel pit. So it seems pretty strange, doesn't it, for a grave to never, ever be opened? Even when the church underwent that major restoration, these graves were left undisturbed. What secrets might be hidden inside them? Why would someone keep a promise made by people long since dead to people who turned to dust centuries ago? And look up there. What do you think of that?'

They were standing still now, while the people in the church continued about their business around them, seemingly oblivious to their presence.

Luuk pointed to the top of one of the many massive pillars inside the church.

'What about it?' Judith said.

'These pillars support the roof of course, but as you can see, the top of each one fans outwards. That part doesn't provide any support. It's purely decorative. During the last round of major repairs, they discovered, quite by accident, that those sections weren't solid wood as they'd thought, but hollow.'

'Really?' Peter said in amazement.

'Yes, really,' Luuk replied triumphantly. 'And they found all kinds of things inside those hollow spaces. It was mostly everyday stuff: broken tools like chisels and hammers, lengths of rope, clothing, some coins, scraps of paper from what had probably been a Bible... I wanted to make an overview of everything they'd found in there, just out of curiosity really. But I was refused access to the reports. Ever since then, there's been a nagging voice at the back of my mind telling me that something was off. I decided just to leave it at the time, but now that same voice is back again. Do you understand what I'm telling you?'

'Yes,' Judith and Peter replied in chorus.

'It's as if... I'm sure you'll have experienced this too: a quiet little voice in your head or a feeling in the pit of your stomach... You can't quite work out where it's coming from, and eventually, it fades into the background, but it never completely goes away.'

Peter nodded. His own feeling of uneasiness had now returned in full force.

They walked on.

Luuk stopped at the pillars around the choir, where the faded remnants of religious paintings could still be seen on the stone.

'Many of the paintings here were covered up with a thick layer of whitewash in the Iconoclastic Fury. But in the end, that was a good thing because they were better preserved than they'd have been if they were exposed to the ravages of time. But look...' Luuk pointed to a rectangular image on the first column on the north side of the choir. 'On this one, can you see what looks like two sections with four saints in each one?'

Peter and Judith nodded attentively as if they were visitors on a guided tour.

'On the top row, from right to left, you can see Saint Peter, Saint Andrew, John the Baptist, and Saint James the Less. Below them are Saint Norbert of Xanten, Saint Cornelius, Saint Christopher, and Saint Anthony the Great.

And this is another odd thing, Peter.' Luuk looked directly at Peter, perhaps referring to the conversation they had just had outside the church. 'Almost all the paintings were covered up with whitewash, but they left Saint Peter untouched. And here, come and look at this,' Luuk said, leading them to the fourth pillar on the church's south side. 'This one shows two angels floating above a forest. There would have been a statue here once, and they're holding a halo above where its head would have been. Sadly, the statue is lost now, but who might it have been? Saint Paul? Who knows?'

Now he looked at both of them.

'Maybe it was Saint Paul,' he went on. 'After all, this church is dedicated to both Peter and Paul. And Paul went down in history as the victor in the battle between them. Peter vanishes about halfway through the book of Acts, and after that, we're only told about Paul, who goes on to put his own, indelible stamp on Christianity. But what if...' He paused for a brief moment, effectively building up the suspense again. 'What if there were people who knew that Saint Peter's original argument had been right? That Jesus only ever intended for his message to be given to Jews? Might that explain why, for example, they left the painting of Saint Peter untouched on that pillar, but smashed the statue of Saint Paul on this one?'

Peter exchanged a knowing glance with Judith, as if they both wanted to say, 'If he only knew how close to the truth he was.'

'And then there's this...' said Luuk. He walked towards the sacristy. Hanging next to the door was a large reproduction of *Two Old Men Disputing*, Rembrandt's painting of Saint Peter and Saint Paul.

'Hey,' Judith said in surprise. 'Mark has a copy of this painting in his study! What a coincidence! I never noticed this hanging here before.'

'It's not been there long,' Luuk said. 'It was a gift from an enthusiastic amateur artist. They painted it by projecting an image of the original onto the canvas and meticulously copying it, but it's been beautifully done.'

He motioned them to stand closer to the painting.

'Rembrandt painted the original in 1628. It's in Australia's National Gallery in Melbourne now. There are several different ways of interpreting it. The most popular interpretation is that the apostles are just talking to each other, probably discussing a passage in the Torah. Or maybe they're discussing what Saint Peter has on his lap, the lost document in which he wrote down his memories of Jesus. Who knows? In any case, these two disciples are obviously having quite an intense conversation.'

'Or maybe Saint Paul is telling Saint Peter what to say in his letter to Judas,' Judith whispered, so quietly that only Peter could hear her.

He gave her a surreptitious nod.

'But I don't know what's going on with me,' Luuk continued. 'When you came to my house this morning, and we started talking, the puzzle pieces all seemed to start falling into place. It was like I'd been looking through a misted-up window before, and now I can see things clearly. Do you understand what I mean? There's another way of looking at this painting, which I didn't take seriously when

I first read about it, but now it suddenly makes more sense. The other explanation is that Saint Paul's greater importance is illustrated by his position in the centre of the canvas and the fact that he's illuminated much more brightly than Saint Peter, whom we only see from behind, literally sitting below him. It looks like Paul is lecturing Peter. Paul has never met Jesus, and Peter is one of the most important disciples, and yet it looks like Paul is explaining the scriptures to Peter and telling him what Jesus really meant. Maybe they're discussing the Old Testament prophecies about the Messiah, and Paul is explaining how they all point to Jesus, and how God's old covenant with the Jewish people has been replaced by a new one made with the whole world, both Jews and Gentiles.'

'It's a shame we can't see Saint Peter's eyes,' Peter remarked. 'What we might have seen in them?'

'It is,' Luuk agreed, 'but his posture alone speaks volumes. He seems to radiate an air of resignation, don't you think? As if he's struggling to find the words to parry Saint Paul's argument. If we could see Saint Peter's face, we might have been able to read dismay or alarm in it, as if he was trying to say, "No! That's not what Jesus meant!"'

'That's a pretty bold theory.' Judith's voice was flat, but Peter was sure he heard something of a nervous quiver in it.

Peter had started to feel nervous himself now. From the moment they'd split up outside Luuk's front door, he'd felt ill at ease, and he wasn't sure why. The feeling had faded during the walk to the Pieterskerk and their conversation about the Leiden Pilgrims, but now it was as strong as ever.

Was Luuk really just speculating now, or was he playing

some sort of game with them? And was it really just a coincidence that Luuk's train of thought was leading him to the same conclusions he and Judith had drawn after reading the letters? How likely was someone to abandon a belief that they'd held their entire life after just one conversation?

'But there's something I don't quite understand,' Judith said. 'The Order doesn't appoint priests these days, does it?'

Peter was glad Judith was still asking questions; it gave him some time to try to relax.

'No, not for many years now,' Luuk admitted. 'After the Reformation, the Pieterskerk was used by the Niederdeutsche church, which later became the Dutch Reformed Church. So there were no priests after that. The last services were held here in 1971, and the church was deconsecrated in 1976 and transferred to a foundation set up by the city and the university. Since then, it's only been used for events, like receptions, special PhD ceremonies, awarding honorary doctorates, that sort of thing.'

'But...' Judith started to ask, but she didn't get a chance to finish.

'But our Order,' Luuk cut in, answering the question that he thought Judith was about to pose, 'has always been connected to the Pieterskerk. You could say we've evolved alongside each other. The Order will be celebrating 750 years of its association with the church in 2018, on July 13th to be exact.'

'And that's a Friday,' Peter joked.

'Indeed. Quite a coincidence, eh? Not really an auspicious day, Friday the 13th,' Luuk replied earnestly.

'However, some say it marks the beginning of a special era, a time when our trials and tribulations will end.'

'In what way? Peter wanted to know.

'Personally, I think it's a bit far-fetched,' Luuk said cautiously, 'but a few of my fellow knights are intrigued by what you get when you add up the numbers in the date that our connection to Leiden and the Pieterskerk began. If you add together 13, 07 and 2018, you get $13 + 07 = 20$ and $2 + 0 + 18 = 20$. Together that makes 40, which, as I'm sure you both know, is one of the most important numbers in both the Old and New Testaments. It's the number for tests and trials, the time in days or years that God takes to decide if a person or even a whole people is worthy of being entrusted with an important task. Think of the forty years that the Hebrews wandered in the desert, or the two times that Moses fasted for forty days on Mount Horeb where he was given the Ten Commandments. Or Jesus fasting for forty days and then being tempted by the devil before he began his ministry. What mission might our Order be given in 2018 if we show ourselves to be worthy?'

Peter was curious now. 'Do you have any ideas about what that mission might be?'

'Let me put it this way: I'm beginning to develop a theory about the true task that has rested on our shoulders for centuries.'

Luuk unhooked the latch on the sacristy door and pulled the door open towards them, indicating that Peter and Judith should go ahead of him. He followed them and closed the door behind him.

They found themselves in a long and surprisingly bright

and spacious room. Dozens of baskets filled with flat white loaves of bread were set out on tables along the wall. There were several dozen carafes filled with wine too – Peter and Judith spotted the empty 3-litre wine boxes under the tables – and bottles of grape-flavoured cordial for the children.

'And I have an inkling,' Luuk concluded, pointing to a large, vault-like cupboard in the corner, 'there's something that will answer your question and prove my theory somewhere in this room.'

Chapter Twenty-One

Peter walked over to the two small windows in the room, which each had thick bars on the other side of the glass, and stared outside. Then he glanced over at the clock. Its loud tick was the only sound in the room.

Judith pulled out a chair and sat down to take off the high-heeled shoes she had borrowed from Anne. She grimaced as she rubbed the soles of her feet.

Peter walked over to where she was sitting. 'Are you all right?' he asked.

'Hmm,' she replied. 'These are just a bit too small.'

Peter looked around the room and noticed some bouquets of flowers that were being kept in buckets of water. He removed the flowers from one of them and set the bucket down in front of Judith's chair. A few green leaves floated on top of the water.

'Here you go,' he said invitingly. 'Put your feet in there. That should ease the pain a little.'

Judith looked at him in amusement but did as she was

283

told. As her toes touched the bottom of the bucket, the corners of her mouth turned up in a smile of pleasure. 'Aah... Gosh, that really is lovely. Thank you.'

'Sorry to interrupt this cosy scene,' Luuk said, 'but I'm going to see if I can find the custodian. I know him quite well, so I'm pretty confident that he'll give me permission to look at those report books this time if I explain the situation.'

'What kind of service is all this stuff for?' Judith asked him.

'What kind of service?' Luuk replied. 'Oh, the service is usually pretty ecumenical, but today, it's being performed by a Catholic, and he likes to try to evoke a more authentic Last Supper feeling. So he uses real wine – grape juice or cordial for the children – and fresh bread.'

'The only thing missing is the fish,' Peter remarked.

'White bread and herring, that's right,' Luuk said, smiling. 'They'll already have handed those out at the town hall this morning. But distributing fresh fish during the church service would cause a few logistical headaches, I imagine.' He nodded, then left, shutting the door behind him.

Judith lifted her feet out of the water and rested them on the edge of the bucket.

Peter looked around and saw a stack of towels under one of the tables. 'Come on,' he said, 'Let me dry your feet.'

He grabbed a towel and knelt down beside her. She pointed her foot gracefully towards him, and he gently dabbed it dry. She had beautiful, slim feet with perfectly neat, red-lacquered nails. Peter had to resist the urge to kiss her toes.

He lowered the dry foot and picked up her other foot, his fingers circling Judith's calf, which felt supple and relaxed in his hand. He looked up at her, and she smiled back with a wink.

'That's how I like my men,' she laughed. 'At my feet.'

Peter laughed too. 'At your service, milady,' he said with an exaggerated English accent. He stood up, folded the towel, and hung it over the back of a chair.

'I'm absolutely famished,' said Judith.

'Me too,' Peter said.

He grabbed a loaf of bread from one of the baskets.

'Here, take this and eat some of it. I'm sure they won't miss one loaf of bread.'

He tore the loaf in two and gave one half to Judith, who took in a satisfying sniff of the aroma of freshly baked bread before biting into it.

'I'm sure this is one meal we'll always remember,' Peter said. 'Would you like a drink?'

'It's a bit too early for wine,' Judith replied. 'I'll just have a glass of water.'

Peter rinsed out a glass that was standing next to the sink and filled it from the tap. He added a dash of grape cordial before he gave it to Judith. It sank to the bottom of the glass where it formed a thick, syrupy layer. Peter stirred the cordial into the water with a spoon, and it turned bright red.

'If someone comes in now,' he said as he gave the glass to Judith, 'they're going to think you're knocking back a big glass of wine, but who cares?' He made another glass of cordial for himself. 'Cheers then,' he said, and they clinked their glasses together. 'May this crazy day be the start of a new friendship.'

'Louis, I think this is the beginning of a beautiful friendship,' Judith said, doing a surprisingly good Humphrey Bogart impression.

Peter felt a warm glow flow through his body.

They sat quietly together, eating the bread and sipping the cordial.

'But,' Judith said, breaking the silence, 'I still wish we'd gone straight to Matilo instead of coming here.'

'In those shoes?' Peter pointed to Anne's high heels.

'Well,' she said, 'I probably would have taken them off at some point on the way there.'

'What are you thinking?' Peter asked.

'I'm not sure, Peter,' Judith began. 'I felt fine when we were talking to Luuk earlier. And when he suggested coming here, I was convinced it was a good idea at the time, but...'

'But...' said Peter, who was also feeling increasingly uneasy.

'But now I've had time to think about it, his story doesn't add up,' she continued. 'He claims that, somewhere in this room, we'll find some reports about the restoration of the church that could provide the evidence for his "theory". And this evidence *may* back up our story somehow. But we were already on our way to Matilo. Wasn't that actually much more urgent?'

Peter nodded soberly.

'You know,' he said, 'the thing is, I've known Luuk for such a long time, and I trust him absolutely, but there's something about this that I can't quite put my finger on either. It's like he bowled us over. We were so dazzled by everything he was telling us that we've just gone along with him. But you're right. Now it's just the two of us sitting here quietly, I'm starting to wonder. What could be so urgent or give us such convincing evidence that we needed to go and look for it straight away? Going back to the dig site and finding clear proof that the casket is linked to Saint Peter is defin—'

Peter stopped mid-word and turned as white as a sheet.

Judith sprang up from the chair.

'What's wrong?' she asked in alarm.

Peter's hand flew to his inside pocket. He suddenly realised that he had left Mark's translation in his own jacket and forgotten it in the fluster of changing clothes.

'The translation...' Peter stammered. 'I left it... I left it in my jacket pocket at Luuk's. How could I be so stupid!'

He leapt to the door, but when he tried to open it, it stayed firmly shut. Peter yanked at the handle, but the door didn't budge. He peered through the gap between the door and the frame and saw that it hadn't been locked but was bolted shut on the other side Peter turned around, leaned back against the door with his eyes closed. 'He's locked us in,' he said, so quietly that Judith barely heard him.

She stood in front of him and took both his hands in hers. 'Listen, Peter, we need to...' she started. But then she realised that she didn't know what to do either and stopped talking.

'He's my friend,' Peter said. He faltered over the words as if he were a foreigner practising his pronunciation of a sentence in Dutch.

'My God. What have we got ourselves into, Peter? How well do you actually know this Luuk?'

'I'm beginning to wonder about that myself. Remember what he said? Maybe he's in the Order within the Order. And all that talk about his doubts, what his dad said, the Pilgrim Fathers...'

'The Pilgrim Fathers?'

Peter waved her question away. 'Doesn't matter. Maybe all those stories of his were a smokescreen, and he had a far better idea of what's going on here than we do. Didn't he tell us that we didn't know who we were up against? What if he meant that it was *him* that we were up against?' Peter slipped his hands out from Judith's and held them over his eyes. 'He's my friend,' he said again. 'My friend,' he repeated, and the words came out in an almost inaudible sob.

Judith moved his hands away from his face, forcing him to look at her. She touched his cheek and looked at him tenderly. 'We'll find a way out of this together,' she said. 'We have to try to stay calm.'

Peter regained his composure, partly in response to her gentle words and touch. But above all, because he could tell that she was doing her best to quell a rising panic inside herself. She was locked up for the second time today.

Judith held her finger to her lips.

They heard the soft sound of feet shuffling on the other side of the door.

'Hello?' Peter called out. 'Is that you, Luuk? Whoever it is out there, could you open this door for us? Some joker has locked us in, and their joke has gone on just a bit too long now.'

There was no reply, but it was clear that someone was on the other side of the door.

Peter asked again, more softly now.

'It's me,' Luuk answered suddenly, sounding nervous and hesitant. 'It's not what you think, Peter. What either of you think, Judith. I'm just a simple knight, Peter. An underling in our Order. I'm just following orders. I can't tell you more than that.'

'Orders? What do you mean "orders"?'

'It's all so complicated,' he whispered, and his voice was so low that Peter had to put his ear to the door to make out his words. 'I knew that the police were looking for you, so I couldn't believe my eyes when I saw you at the Burcht. I invited you in, and I did as I'd been instructed.'

'Instructed?' Peter repeated angrily. 'What have you been instructed to do?'

'I was told to...' Luuk was clearly trying to find the right words. 'I was told to detain you somehow. I mean... There are some people who really want to speak to you, but you kept getting away from them. So everyone was asked to work together and make sure that the conversation could take place.'

'You're my friend, Luuk. Or you were my friend. I'm not so sure now. Surely you could have just told us that someone wanted to talk to us? Then we could have decided for ourselves if and when we wanted to talk to them.'

'It's too important for that. It's very urgent. I'm just a ... nobody. A small cog in a big machine. I don't know exactly which powers or forces are behind all this.'

'And all that talk about the Pilgrim Fathers,' Peter spat, 'and the painting of Saint Peter and Saint Paul, the hollow pillars – it was all just a ruse to—'

'No, that was all sincere. I really have wondered about all of those things. But I owe obedience to the people above me. I swore a lifelong oath. 'It's all so complic—'

Peter slammed the palm of his hand hard against the door. It made a dull sound. 'Rubbish!' he shouted. 'Open that door, or you're dead to me, do you hear?'

There was no answer.

'Do ... you ... hear ... me...?' Peter screamed at him, slamming his hand against the door with each word.

But Luuk was already gone.

Now panic seemed to be getting the better of Judith. She rattled the handle, but the heavy wooden door hardly moved a millimetre.

She stared at Peter, her eyes wide with fright. Nothing remained of the calm she'd radiated just moments earlier. She put her shoes back on and ran over to the window, but she soon saw that it would offer no escape either.

'We're stuck, Peter. The translation is at Luuk's house, and the casket and the photos are at Mark's. It's all over.'

'But that's a good thing, isn't it?' Peter seemed to have found some courage. 'Right now, we don't have anything they can take away from us. And they don't know where those things are. So, really, it was a smart move, leaving them behind.'

'But now we're locked inside this room.'

'Yes, but in a public place. There are plenty of people walking around behind that door. If the worst comes to the worst, we can start screaming. And remember, Mark's probably working on a new translation at this very moment. We have him as a witness.'

His words seem to reassure Judith, but not entirely. She walked back to the door and began to yank pointlessly at the handle.

'I think there's nothing for it but to wait, Jude.'

Suddenly they heard a noise on the other side of the door.

'Who's there?' shouted Judith.

'Excuse me?' said a voice they didn't recognise.

'Who's there?' Judith repeated, more calmly this time, putting her ear up to the door.

'I thought you'd already left...' the man said uncertainly.

'No, we're still here,' Judith replied. 'Could you please unbolt the door? Who are you, by the way?

'I'm ... I'm conducting the service today,' said the man. 'But I've just been told that I can't come in until there's no one left in the sacristy.'

'Who told you that?' Judith demanded. Then without waiting for an answer, she continued. 'Someone's locked us in here. There's been a misunderstanding. I don't know what you've been told, but my professor and I' – she looked back at Peter – 'but my professor and I came for the remembrance service at ten o'clock. We were a bit too early, so we ended up wandering in here. Someone, we don't know who, shut the door behind us. Maybe that person thought the sacristy was empty.'

'Well, I've been told that you—' said the priest.

'Come on!' Judith yelled. 'Let us out, damn it!' She slammed her hand on the door.

Peter thought he could almost feel the priest's reluctance through the wood.

'Listen, I ... I'm just doing what I've been told.'

'Oh, Father, this is just a misunderstanding,' Judith said. 'Truly. I'm sorry for getting angry just then, but I have claustrophobia. I've got to get out of here.'

There was a moment's silence. Then they heard the sound of the metal bolt being slid back.

Judith pushed down on the handle and threw her shoulder against the door with such force that it flew open and hit the priest on the head. The man fell to the ground, where he lay motionless. By the looks of it, Judith had given him a nasty head wound.

As they walked out of the room, Judith bent over the priest. Then she stood upright again and walked away. Peter stopped for a second, but when he saw the priest bring his hand to his bleeding head, he decided that the man hadn't been injured too seriously, and he followed Judith.

She headed for the door on the left-hand side of the church.

Peter looked around the church itself to see if Luuk was there, but he saw no one except for a few visitors arriving early for the service.

He caught up with Judith, who was breathless with

stress and excitement. They stopped at the door. Peter grabbed Judith's arm. 'Judith, this is really going too far. We can't just leave that man lying there...'

She pulled her arm away. 'I know that. You don't have to tell me,' she said. 'But we escaped, didn't we? And right now, that's all that matters to me. I'm not interested in anything else. For all I care, we can go straight to the police station. The most important thing as far as I'm concerned is that I'm not locked in there anymore, and I can decide for myself who I do or don't talk to.'

'We need to get away from here first, as fast as we can,' Peter said. 'Then we'll decide what to do next. Let's go somewhere where we can think more clearly.' He pushed the door open, and they walked outside. 'Come on.' He hooked his arm in hers. 'We're going to pretend we're just an ordinary, smartly dressed couple on our way to an event.'

They walked through Muskadelsteeg to Het Gerecht before going on to the Rapenburg canal where they crossed the bridge and turned left.

'Where are we going?' Judith asked.

'Hortus Botanicus,' Peter said. 'The Botanical Gardens. I go there quite often. It's the perfect place to think.

They walked along Rapenburg and soon reached the red-brick façade of the university's Academiegebouw, the oldest building in Leiden. Behind it, the Hortus was already open. A large sign outside announced that admission was free on October 3rd. They passed the ticket office – unstaffed because there were no tickets to sell – and strolled into the gardens.

'That was pretty awful, what just happened with that priest. The poor man is supposed to be conducting the service soon,' Peter said.

'I know,' Judith sighed. 'I'll go back to explain everything to him and apologise at some point. But I really got quite panicky in there.'

They continued towards the back of the gardens where the enormous greenhouses were. They stood there, not sure what to do.

Judith looked at Peter and smiled sadly at him.

And suddenly, although he hadn't planned it, Peter leaned forward and kissed her on the mouth.

She was taken aback at first. Even so, she seemed to quickly abandon any reservations she might have had and returned the kiss with enthusiasm. After a moment that felt like an eternity to Peter, she took his face in her hands and looked at him intensely. There were tears in her eyes. 'Oh, Peter, what are we going to do?'

They wrapped their arms around each other. Peter buried his face in her neck and inhaled the scent of her Magie Noire perfume – and as if the twenty years since had melted away, he was immediately transported to Ben Gurion airport, and it was as if he was holding Sabrina in his arms.

They stood that way for a while until a gardener pushing a wheelbarrow came by. He was accompanied by a woman wearing an apron printed with the logo of the Hortus Botanicus restaurant. Peter's eyes met the gardener's. The gardener winked at him as if to congratulate him on his conquest.

Peter took Judith's hand and led her over to a bench in front of one of the greenhouses. 'Do you mind waiting here for a little while? I hope you don't think me ridiculous, but I'd really like to go and sit down there on my own for a few minutes and see if I can come to a decision about what we should do. Maybe you could do the same. Is that okay?' Judith pulled her hand away from his. 'It won't be for long,' he said reassuringly. I just need a few moments to myself to consider our options.'

Judith nodded in agreement.

He walked away, and when he was not much more than a stone's throw away from Judith, he fell to his knees and began to pray. 'Heavenly Father, I know I've not been your most faithful servant in recent years, but now I come to you, humbly asking for help. I wish this all over. What should I do? What should we do? Is what we've discovered genuine? Is what we've discovered in conflict with your plan of salvation, or have we actually been wrong about your plan for the last two thousand years? Is it your will for us to reveal what we've found so you can carry out your true plan at last? Lord, help me overcome my unbelief, come and take away my doubt. Be with me, be with us, in this time of uncertainty, give us guidance. Heavenly Father, deliver us.' Peter hesitated for a moment, overwhelmed by despair. 'But not my will, but yours, be done.'

His nose started to bleed, something that had often happened at times of great stress when he was younger. But he'd not had a nosebleed for many years now. Thick drops of blood dripped onto the ground. He found a handkerchief in the pocket of Luuk's jacket. He tipped his head back and pressed it to his nose.

Peter got to his feet and turned to go back to Judith. He saw her slouched on the bench as if she had fallen asleep. Suddenly, he heard the crunch of footsteps on the gravel path. Two policemen were walking towards Judith's bench.

Peter froze. If he let them see him, he would give himself away. Then neither of them would have a chance of finding a definitive link between Saint Peter and the casket. But it was not this realisation that held him nailed to the spot.

Now he had a clearer view of the men who were advancing towards Judith. As he'd thought, the two figures at the front were policemen, their batons tapping rhythmically against their thighs. But it was the man he could now see walking behind them that chilled his blood.

Professor Pieter Hoogers, his old tutor.

Chapter Twenty-Two

J udith appeared to be fast asleep, and the two policemen were striding towards her at a rapid pace.

Peter took a step backwards so that he was partially hidden by the bushes but still had a clear view of what happened next.

The police officers shook Judith to wake her up. At first, she didn't seem to know where she was. But even from this distance, Peter could see that Judith quickly understood how hopeless the situation was and gave up her attempt to resist arrest.

He decided he would come out of his hiding place and allow himself to be arrested along with her. He even took a couple of steps forward but jumped back in fright when he thought he saw Pieter Hoogers looking at him.

It was clear that the officers were pressing Judith with questions, but Peter saw her pointing in completely the opposite direction to where he was hiding. He took this as a sign that she would forgive him if he stayed out of the way.

But if he left her on her own now, it would feel like a betrayal.

Slowly, he began to turn around, but his jacket snagged on the thorny shrub he was hiding behind. Not wanting to make any noise, he slipped out of the jacket and left it hanging on the branches. A cockerel scurried past Peter's feet with his brood of hens. *If that beast starts to crow, I'll wring its neck*, he thought grimly. He looked back again and saw that the officers had gone off in the direction Judith had indicated. Hoogers was still standing beside Judith, who was looking deliberately away from him.

Peter decided to walk towards the Witte Singel, the canal running along the back of the Hortus. He had walked less than a hundred metres when he met the gardener who had given him an amused wink when he and Judith had been in each other's arms earlier.

'Hey, where's your girl?' the gardener asked. 'Have you given her the slip?'

'Girl? What are you talking about?' Peter said, hoping to get away from the man as soon as possible.

'I mean that pretty lady you were just getting so cosy with.'

'Oh, her... We don't really know each other that well. Actually, I don't even know who she is,' Peter said, as he walked away from the gardener.

'Well, you're a fine one, aren't you?' the gardener called after him. 'Ditching a beautiful woman like that!' The jocular tone was gone from his voice.

Peter turned around and said, 'For God's sake, man! I

don't know her at all. Just leave it, all right?' He found himself having to try very hard not to shout.

Burning with irritation, he walked away. He passed the restaurant, where the woman he'd seen with the gardener earlier was setting up tables outside.

'Good morning!' she greeted him cheerfully. 'Was that your girlfriend that the police collared back there?'

'I don't know what you mean,' Peter said, and he carried on walking. But she wasn't going to let him get away from her that easily either.

'Didn't you see it?' she continued. 'Just after you two split up, the police came and arrested her.'

Peter closed his eyes and took a deep breath. He turned back to look at her and said, 'Honestly, it wasn't what it looked like. I hardly know her. I don't know what they want her for, but it's nothing to do with me. So if you don't mind, I'd like to be left alone. Please!'

He picked up his pace, walking past the large greenhouse and along some narrow pathways towards the water. He knew that it wouldn't take long for the police to realise that Judith had sent them the wrong way.

He knew that the Hortus had a side exit on the 5th Binnenvestgracht, a narrow canal on the other side of the gardens. As he walked along the path that ran next to the Witte Singel, he spotted a man mooring a kayak. He watched as the man carefully stood up, stepped out of the rocking boat and walked across the grass, unbuckling his belt as he disappeared into the bushes.

Peter didn't think twice; he ran over to the kayak and stealthily climbed in. A fly fishing rod had been ingeniously mounted on the side. What an interesting combination of sports, Peter thought.

He pushed off from the canal bank with the paddle. While the man was still in the bushes, Peter paddled away almost noiselessly, making quick, small strokes in the glassy surface of the water. That poor guy is in for a surprise, Peter thought. He imagined the astonished look in the man's face when he returned to the waterside.

The boat slipped smoothly through the water as Peter calmly paddled around the canal bend, fast enough that the kayak's owner would be unable to see him even when he returned to the spot where he'd moored it.

'So what's become of you my friend...' he sang softly to himself. 'And what's become of me?' he murmured. 'Maybe I should have been a fisherman. Going out on the water every day, working with my hands, bringing in a catch and putting an honest meal on the table. What have I become instead? Someone who fishes for opinions. Angling for recognition.'

As he rounded the bend of the Witte Singel, he hummed a psalm to himself. 'When I look at your heavens, the work of your fingers, the moon and the stars that you have established; what are human beings that you are mindful of them, mortals that you care for them?'

He continued to be amazed at how easily the words came back to the surface of his mind after having lain dormant for so many years. What had happened to him in the wardrobe at Mark's house? he wondered. What was that peace, that serenity that had come over him like a warm, comforting blanket, like the soft embrace of a mother soothing her child?

He paddled smoothly on, past the Leiden Archives where Judith had begun the research on Moshe Levi that had led her to him. One day, they would sail along here together, he daydreamed. When all this was over, they could pack a picnic basket, rent a boat, and explore the canals of Leiden.

That kiss – of course it had just been a one-off. It was an impulsive reaction, a way of releasing the tension he had felt between them, a response to the wild adventure they had ended up on together. At least, he assumed that the kiss had been a one-off. How much older than Judith was he? Fifteen years?

He turned left onto the Vliet canal and realised that he was following the route that the Sea Beggars had taken when they relieved the city in 1574. After they broke the dikes, they would have been able to sail over the flooded land to reach the city, bringing herring and white bread for the starving citizens. They entered Leiden via the Vliet canal, which was where the brothels happened to be.

If he hadn't been on the run, he would have enjoyed this, he thought. The splendid canal houses behind whose stately gables people were readying themselves for another day of festivities; the rippling reflections of the trees that lined the canal; the regular sound of the paddle dipping in and out; the droplets make little circles as they landed on the water's surface.

Peter went under the bridge at the end of the Vliet and turned right onto the Rapenburg canal. He was reminded of an evening when he and Thomas had met up for a drink in café De Burcht at the foot of the castle's motte. Thomas had talked at length about the history of Leiden.

'What could have been so important about Leiden that the Spanish wanted to lay siege to it? All that effort! The logistics of it all, all those men and their wages, all those provisions, and so on... All for Leiden! For Leiden!' he said, banging his beer glass on the table to emphasise his point. 'Leiden wasn't the least bit important then, you know. Yes, there would have been merchants' warehouses full of valuable stock here, and some of the citizens were rich, but there wasn't much in the way of loot in the city. There was no great treasure in Leiden. Or at least, there was nothing to justify laying siege to it, anyway. Do you see where I'm going with this?'

'Come on, let's hear it then,' said Peter laughing.

'Or,' said Thomas, drawing out the 'o', 'or maybe they knew there *was* something worth stealing here. Something big. Maybe something that was a threat to Christianity, that could jeopardise the pope's position. Something that those renegade Protestant heretics that the devil had led astray could use in their fight against the Vatican.'

'Saint Peter,' Peter said. Thomas had once told him in confidence about his suspicion that the connection between Saint Peter and Leiden might have been stronger than most people thought. Peter was fascinated by the way Thomas always managed to come up with some new and thrilling element to embellish his theory.

'Yes! Petrus. Saint Peter the Apostle. Suppose someone at the highest level knew that Petrus wasn't buried in Rome,' Thomas went on, 'but in Leiden or somewhere very nearby... Suppose, eh? Just suppose...'

Thomas took a swig of beer and continued on his train of thought. He was clearly enjoying this conversation. 'Take the Spanish king, Philip II, defender of the faith. He was a crusader, but this time, he wasn't fighting against the Muslims. He was fighting against the apostates within the Holy Mother Church, which he had sworn to defend with his blood, sweat, and tears to the bitter end. This King Philip—'

'To the k-i-i-i-ing of Spain,' Peter interrupted, raising his glass and singing a couplet from Dutch national anthem, 'I have granted a lifelo—'

Thomas waved his hand to dismiss this musical intermezzo. 'King Philip II,' he continued staunchly, 'saw himself as having been put on this earth and crowned by divine providence to defend the one true faith. He was fighting on two fronts. Firstly, with the Ottomans, who were actually a greater threat to him, although that was on a purely geopolitical basis. I'm sure he didn't actually care that they followed this Mohammed, a self-proclaimed prophet. Above all, though, he was fighting against the mud-slinging Protestants who had the gall to question the authority of the Holy Father, Pope Pius V—'

'Pies? Did he moonlight as a baker?' Peter quipped, rudely interrupting him.

Now Thomas was starting to get annoyed. 'Pies? What? Will you stop talking rubbish and listen? I've discovered something important!'

'Sorry. I'm listening.'

'Where was I?' Apparently, Thomas had literally lost the plot now.

'Pies V. Sorry, Pius.'

'That was it. Well, King Philip saw himself as the leader of the Counter-Reformation, sent to earth by God himself. His task was to gather all the lost sheep and lead them back to the flock to save them from eternal damnation.'

'Hey, shall we go for a kebab later?' Peter asked, interrupting him again.

'A kebab?' Thomas said. 'Erm, yes, fine. But back to those lost sheep. They had to be returned to the shepherd. As far as Philip was concerned, there was no difference between his interests – so Spain's interests – and those of the Catholic Church. No more *cuius regio, eius religio*, "the religion of the ruler dictates the religion of the ruled", as his father would have believed. Now it was simply *tutti catolicci*, or however you say it in Latin.'

'No idea,' Peter admitted.

'Anyway, it meant that everyone was a Catholic. And this wise king threw himself into attacking everything that he thought deviated from the church's true teachings. The Compromise of Nobles and their petition to end the persecution of protestants? Rejected! Wimps! Send in the Duke of Alba. He'll teach those Hollanders a lesson. It's a long story, and, as you know, it was all part of what led to the Iconoclastic Fury. But King Philip ruled over a huge empire that stretched as far as Latin America, and yet, despite that, he decided that the tiny town of Leiden was worth going to the bother of laying siege to. The man owned practically half the globe! So did he choose to secure Istanbul for Christianity and make it Constantinople again? Did he march his troops to the Holy City of Jerusalem and chase away those Mohammedan dogs? Did he spend his last ducats on hiring mercenaries and leading them to victory against the Moors in North Africa? No, he did not. Instead, this man decided it would be more worthwhile to lay siege to Leiden for an entire year!'

Thomas took a big gulp of his beer and shook his head as if not even he could believe it and was searching his mind for an argument that would convince himself. 'Leiden! Surely it could only have been worth it if there was something valuable here? Just imagine, Peter,' he said, putting his hand on Peter's thigh and letting it rest there. 'Philip II was on good terms with Pope Pies V, so imagine that—'

'Ha! Now *you're* saying it!'

'Pies, Pius, whatever. Imagine that the pope shared a shocking secret with him: that the entire story about Petrus being in Rome was untrue. All that about him going to Rome and being crucified upside down because he didn't think himself worthy of the same death as his Lord and Saviour Jesus Christ – it had never been anything more than a religious fable. And Rome had known it from the very start. Rome knew that, when Petrus disappeared, he'd actually gone to the West. And they knew for a fact that he died somewhere near where Leiden is now and was buried here. Meaning that St. Peter's Basilica was not built on Saint Peter's tomb, so he could not have been the rock on which Christ built his church.'

Peter nodded in wonder at Thomas's ideas. He never knew quite how much of his theories he should believe. But he had to admit that, although this was all speculation, it was well-founded speculation, and he found it fascinating.

'This pope – or perhaps his successor Pope Gregory XIII. It was, in any case, *a* pope. This pope tells Philip II that the Catholic Church will find itself in serious trouble if the true location of Petrus's grave is discovered by someone who doesn't belong to their faith,' Thomas continued. 'After all, if Petrus had gone to the West, he couldn't have passed the keys on to the second pope, the man who—'

'Linus!' exclaimed Peter, pleased he could contribute to the conversation at last. 'He was called Linus. Typical *Trivial Pursuit* question.'

'So no keys for Linus. I didn't know that was his name, by the way,' Thomas admitted, 'And, as you can imagine, that removes the very thing that underpins the legitimacy of the Apostolic Throne of Saint Peter. So Saint Peter wasn't in his grave in Rome, no keys for Linus. It was nothing but a legend. If the hoi polloi had got wind of this, particularly those bite-the-hand-that-feeds-you Protestants, it would have provided the heretics with more – and, I should add, very legitimate – ammunition. What would be left of the pope and his authority then?'

'But they gave up, didn't they?'

'The Spaniards? Yes, they gave up. In reality, they were simply defeated, of course. Apparently, God had ordained otherwise. Perhaps the Spanish realised that the Calvinists, those wreckers of religious paintings and statues, had no idea that their cowardly, pasty Protestant backsides were sitting on a potential goldmine. There's no other way to explain why the Spanish would give up so easily. The people of Leiden were at the end of their tether, utterly exhausted. So if the Spanish had wanted it, the city was theirs for the taking. But no, when the dikes were broken, they literally got cold feet and fled. Can you believe it? I think King Philip had told them: Hey, lads, the coast is clear. Those idiots don't have a clue about the treasure that lies within their walls. Never mind Leiden – we're off to conquer Istanbul and Jerusalem!'

'So, what about this discovery that you said you'd made?' Peter said.

'Did I say that?' Thomas had to think for a moment; then, he remembered. 'Yes! That's right!' he exclaimed enthusiastically, only now removing his hand from Peter's leg. He put his empty beer glass down on the table. 'I was reading about the popes of the period,' he said. 'Including Pope Gregory XIII... He was made pope in 1572, a year before the Siege of Leiden. Ten years later, in 1582, he implemented a new calendar, the Gregorian calendar we use today. It introduced the leap year system. He removed ten days from the calendar that year to align it with the astronomical solar year, deleted them from time as if they'd never existed. And which day do you think he decided to make sure was erased?'

'Well, that must have been October the 3rd or 4th.' Peter laughed. 'You're trying to connect everything with Leiden, right? I'm sure he wanted to erase the blot that was October 3rd, or better still, October 4th, the first day that Leiden was no longer under siege.'

Thomas looked at Peter triumphantly. 'Bingo!' he said in the manner of a teacher speaking to a student who had answered a question correctly. 'That's right. October 4th. He had 365 days to choose from, so why did he pick October 4th? It must have been meant as a signal to the hell-bound riff-raff of Leiden … to show them: we're in charge here. We even control time. If we say that October 4th never existed, then October 4th never existed.'

Peter smiled at the memory as he paddled sedately over the Rapenburg, under the bridge at the end of Doezastraat, and past the lush trees and grass of Van der Werffpark with the statue of the burgomaster it was named for at its centre. The man who, according to tradition, was willing to sacrifice his body and his life to save the people of his city.

Someone dies, sacrifices themselves to make life possible for others who would otherwise have died, Peter mused. *An old idea, probably from the time of the hunter-gatherers, who realised that their existence depended on the deaths of the animals they hunted. We've just translated all those primitive, primal feelings into modern life. We might look different now, wear clothes, eat with knives and forks, but not much else has changed. We still worship a man, an innocent victim, who gave his life to make our lives possible. But even so, even so… If none of it is true, if what we've always learned, what I've always been taught, is wrong and Jesus wasn't the Messiah, isn't the risen Lord... And the letters between Saint Peter and Judas Iscariot... If they really are genuine... Then where did that feeling of absolute peace and acceptance come from when I was hiding in the wardrobe?*

Peter had passed the Van der Werffpark now and entered the long, dark tunnel underneath the shops on the Breestraat and the pavement cafés on Gangetje that connected the Rapenburg canal with the water of the Nieuwe Rijn. When he reached the other end, he paddled with just the left oar, turning right onto the Nieuwe Rijn.

Peter realised that he must have been an odd sight to the people passing by. A smartly dressed man in his forties wearing a neatly pressed shirt and brown felt hat, kayaking along the canals early in the morning of October 3rd.

He glided under the bridge that spanned the Hooigracht, heading towards the Utrechtse Veer. No one would look for him there, he thought, feeling pleased with himself. They would search in and around the botanical gardens first. It would take them a while to realised he had escaped by water. That kayaker would have to get over his embarrassment before he could explain to the police exactly why he'd moored his kayak there, giving someone the opportunity to steal it.

It didn't give him much of a head start, but it would help.

How might it affect my renewed relationship with God, Peter wondered – because he felt in his heart that this was what his experience in the wardrobe had been – *if what Judith and I read in those letters is the truth? Will the facts affect my faith? Will they stand in the way of my belief? What is truth?*

At the end of the Utrechtse Veer, he went under the bridge on the Zijlsingel. He was reassuringly far from the city centre now.

He and Judith would have been at the dig a long time ago now if they hadn't fallen for the strange story Luuk had told them. In hindsight, it was almost impossible to understand how they could have gone along with Luuk's idea. But he and Luuk had been friends for so long, had spent so many pleasant hours smoking cigars and philosophising together... When he'd decided to approach Luuk after they'd left Mevrouw Eco's house, Peter had been hoping he would provide them with a change of clothes. And Luuk's willingness to help them disguise themselves had given Peter even more confidence in him.

But still. They had fallen into his trap with their eyes wide open, allowing Luuk to lock them in the sacristy, and had only managed to escape from it at that poor priest's expense... They had been lucky, but now, inevitably, their luck had run out.

God, where would she be now?

To calm his nerves, he sang an old hymn based on his favourite psalm: 'The Lord is my shepherd; I shall not want. He maketh me to lie down in green pastures. He leadeth me beside the still waters.'

He'd reached the end of the Utrechts Jaagpad, and now he turned right into the wide Rhine-Schie canal, where he suddenly found he had to contend with strong headwinds. The kayak wobbled dangerously from side to side. Some water splashed up and over the edge, landing in his lap.

'Yea, though I walk through the valley of the shadow of

death,' he continued, 'I will fear no evil: for thou art with me; thy rod and thy staff they comfort me.'

Now Peter had to concentrate. Small waves washed over the kayak's bow, at times almost threatening to submerge it.

'Thou anointest my head with oil; my cup runneth over. Surely goodness and mercy shall follow me all the days of my life.' Singing helped him to stay focused. Peter realised that the prayers he'd been reciting and the songs he'd been singing were all from the Old Testament. Could the God he'd felt have been the God of the Old Covenant? The God of Judith's people, not the one that Jesus' followers had claimed they were following? If Jesus hadn't been the Messiah, did that mean that the true Messiah would still return? That the Jews had been right? Had he actually been a Jew all his life?

In a moment of wild fantasy, he imagined Judith and himself, now a convert to Judaism, standing under a chuppah and stamping on a wine glass to shatter it.

He had arrived at the spot where he had planned to go ashore. Peter paddled to the other side of the canal and looked for a safe place to moor the boat. *If only I could walk on water*, he thought. *That would make everything so much easier*. At last, he found a suitable spot where the side of the canal sloped gently enough for him to get out.

He grabbed onto the long grass on the canal bank with one hand to help him stabilise the kayak. Then he crouched down in the cockpit until the boat was almost still before he attempted to climb out of it. He found a length of rope at the bottom of the kayak and used it to tie it to a sturdy tussock of grass. He hoped it would be strong enough to hold the kayak in place.

Cautiously, Peter crawled up the bank until he had a clear view of the field in front of him. He saw the large tent where he and Judith had found Thomas the day before.

There was no sign of any activity. There were no cars parked on the site, and his own car was gone too. It appeared to be utterly deserted, as it had often looked when he'd happened to drive past it on weekends during the previous summer. It looked like the police had finished examining the crime scene. Their investigation would undoubtedly have been focused on what had happened after the first attack on Thomas: their colleague being knocked out in the hospital, Thomas's death, Judith and Peter's repeated Houdini-like escapes, and now Judith's eventual arrest. Where had the gunman gone? Had he given up? Or would he have been arrested himself by now?

There was no other way to reach the tent than to walk over to it. Crawling across the field commando-style would be ridiculous; anything taller than a blade of grass would be immediately obvious here.

Peter took a few deep breaths, stood up, and set off. The tent was no more than five hundred metres away, but it felt like an endless distance. He walked in a straight line, his eyes fixed on the tent as if it might get up and walk off too.

'He alone is my rock and my salvation, my fortress; I shall never be shaken,' he said to himself, reciting the words like a mantra. He was convinced now that there was no one on the site at all. There was only one thing he wanted to know: was there anything here that might prove there was a connection between the little ivory box and the saint? If he could find out the answer to that question, he didn't really care what happened next. He would hand himself in to the police. He and Judith would be absolved of any guilt or involvement in Thomas's death and the attack on the policeman. They'd be reunited, and then they could go and see Mark. He was sure to have started work on a translation of the scrolls that would more than compensate for the possible loss of Eco's translation.

When Peter reached the tent, he flung the flap back from the entrance and went inside. Nothing seemed to have changed since the previous evening when they'd found Thomas lying here, battered and bloody.

He walked hurriedly through the tent, and within seconds, his gaze fell on a cloth covering an object that looked distinctly like a box of some sort.

Peter paused, briefly apprehensive, but then strode over and knelt down in front of it. He pulled the cloth away, and there, as he had known it would be, was a chest made of stone. There was no doubt in Peter's mind that this was an ossuary. Carved in clear, legible letters on the side of the chest were the words:

πετρος κεφας

My God, Peter thought. This is it. But can it really be this simple? He was almost disappointed that he'd found what he was looking for so quickly. He had imagined that when this moment finally came, it would feel more dramatic – but, this was it, then.

The lid was partly jammed inside the chest at a crooked angle and was difficult to remove. When he finally managed to lift it away, Peter peered inside. It contained what were obviously the remains of a human skeleton. In one corner of the chest was an empty space the same size as the casket that Judith had stolen.

From beneath the skull came a vague glimmer of something made of gold or bronze. Peering closer, he saw something that strongly resembled two large keys.

As he reached into the chest to move the skull aside, he was startled by a noise inside the tent. He looked up and found himself staring directly into the eyes of Pieter Hoogers, who had emerged from behind the long table.

The rictus grin of a madman spread across Hoogers' face.

Peter looked at him, too surprised to be afraid. He felt something hard hit the back of his head, and then everything turned black.

Chapter Twenty-Three

Notes made by Judith Cherev during her imprisonment

This is probably exactly what they want: for me to sit here and write. But what choice do I have? There's nothing else to do here, and I'll go mad if I spend all my time just sitting at this desk or lying on the floor.

I've taken off my shoes and my jacket and that belt that felt like it was cutting me in half. Strangely enough, it's neither cold nor damp here. I'm in a brightly lit room, a cell of sorts, about three by four metres, that looks like it's recently been swept clean.

Everything is made of concrete, like a bunker. I know that there are still quite a few World War II bunkers left along the coast. The irony would be stomach-churning: locked inside a German bunker...

There's nothing in the room except a chair, a table, and

this pen and paper. There's no bed, no cupboards of any sort, not even a mattress. But they've left me a big bottle of water, and there's a bucket in the corner with a lid on it, which I'm assuming is supposed to serve as a toilet.

The door looks new, clearly not as old as the bunker itself. I'll just call it the 'bunker', for want of a better word. There's an opening in the door with bars across it, but the hatch on the other side is shut.

When they brought me here in the car, they put a bag over my head. A man sat next to me in the back seat, and he forced me to lie down. The bag seemed a bit over the top to me. I had no idea where we were going anyway, but perhaps they only needed it when the car stopped, and I got out. It meant that I didn't see the surroundings outside the bunker, but on the short walk here, I think I heard the sound of the sea somewhere in the near distance, and I definitely heard gulls crying. The ground we walked on was soft underfoot, so not paved, but more like a rural path. The car journey took about twenty minutes, which also points to this being somewhere on the coast. Katwijk or Noordwijk would be the most obvious place, or maybe Wassenaar, near the beach at the Wassenaarse Slag.

Shortly after Peter left me sitting on that bench so he could go and quietly think things over – on reflection, not really the best time to wander off – I fell asleep. The tiredness, the emotion, the multiple narrow escapes... It had all got the better of me, and I passed out. At least, I'm assuming that's what happened because I wasn't even aware that I was falling asleep.

When I woke up and saw the two policemen standing

there with Peter's old tutor, I knew that I wasn't going to be able to get away this time. Maybe I could have tried giving the men a hard shove and running away, but it felt like something inside me had broken. I barely had the energy to sit up straight, so there was little chance of me being able to escape the clutches of two burly policemen.

Well, not actually policemen, as it turned out... The stupid thing is that it wasn't until they led me through the entrance gates, and I saw they were taking me to an ordinary car rather than the police car I'd been expecting, that it dawned on me that they might not be real policemen at all. Pieter Hoogers got into a different car, where someone was already sitting in the driver's seat waiting for him with the engine running.

As I was coming to the frightening realisation that the policemen on either side of me were imposters, I also remembered what Peter and I had told Luuk. Namely that we were going to Matilo to look for something to prove the casket was linked to Saint Peter.

I was in no doubt that Hoogers would know Peter was still intent on carrying out his original plan. And no matter how Peter managed to make his way there – even if he were to run across the water – Hoogers would always get to the dig site sooner, and he would be lying in wait for him. Peter would fall into their trap like a rat.

I think Peter was intensely focused on one goal, which was going to Matilo even if it was the last thing he did in this whole affair. It was his final chance because, once they'd caught him too, everything would be removed from the site, and the evidence would remain out of his reach forever.

And Peter must have realised how dangerous it was to go there when we'd revealed to Luuk what we were looking for.

After I sent the policemen in the wrong direction, I could see that Hoogers was growing increasingly agitated. 'You don't understand the first thing about any of this! Nothing!' he kept saying. 'If you had any idea what was at stake,' he snarled at me, just as his accomplices came running back after having realised that I'd literally sent them down the wrong path. I hoped I'd given Peter enough opportunity to escape and make it to Matilo in time.

It was at that moment that I knew, absolutely, that Hoogers hadn't come to the Hortus as a concerned tutor, worried about the fate of his former pupil who was accused of murder. I knew he had entirely different motives. Thoughts that had previously been strong suspicions now became firm convictions.

And everything fell into place.

The fact that he'd turned up at the university last night; the fact that he'd known something had been removed from the dig; the fact that he'd been at the botanical gardens at the same time as us. Luuk had gone to get him. I was sure of it. Hoogers must have seen Peter and me leaving the church after I hit that poor priest with the door. And then he and the two fake policemen must have followed us into the Hortus.

Hoogers just nodded at the policemen – or pseudo-policemen – and they ordered me to stand up. They stood on either side of me, each one grabbing me by the elbow, and forced me to go with them. Hoogers walked behind us without saying another word, as if he was silently hatching a plan.

Some of the visitors were staring at us, and I wanted to yell out that this wasn't what it looked like, that I wasn't a criminal. The real bad guy was behind me. But who would have believed me? Me, all dishevelled, with my sleepy face and tangled hair, being led away from the gardens like I was a vagrant they'd found sleeping in the bushes? Or him, well-groomed in his smart suit, walking calmly behind us?

As I said, I only sensed my impending doom when we got closer to the civilian car. Naive perhaps, but then I've never had anything to do with the police before. I tried to put up a fight until one of the men said in a tone so calm it sent chills down my spine: 'Nothing will happen to you if you cooperate, I assure you. But if you decide to be difficult, I'm going to kill you, here and now. Nobody will hear the gun go off, and all those people over there looking at us will just think you've fainted.

He moved the panel of his jacket aside, letting me glimpse a holster containing a small pistol with a silencer screwed onto it. It terrified me, but the strange thing is that the fear faded almost instantly, as if I already knew it wouldn't come to that. It was a strange kind of faith that wasn't actually based on anything – maybe it came from the same place as the serenity Peter experienced earlier today.

Strangely enough, I'm quite serene now, and it doesn't feel like I'm trying to drown out my fear or push it away.

And there's another strange thing. I can't stop thinking

about Moshe Levi and how he lived in the hope of the Messiah's arrival. How he longed for it so ardently that he allowed himself to get caught up in the hysteria around Sabbatai Zevi. Levi would have told himself that Zevi had been born on a Sabbath. And on the ninth day of the month of Av at that. This was the very day that, according to rabbinic tradition, the First and Second Temples were destroyed. According to prophecy, it was also the day on which the Messiah would be born. And hadn't Zevi been exactly forty years old – the biblical number for trials and tribulation – when this messiahship was definitively revealed?

I can imagine that Jesus' disciples found themselves in a similar position. They had also given up everything in the expectation that the End Times would begin at any moment.

What do I long for? What do I live for? For what or whom would I be prepared to leave my home and sell every last thing I own, burn all my ships behind me on the basis of nothing but pure faith?

Suppose Zevi really had been the Messiah. Just suppose. And that you had doubted him, that your faith hadn't been strong enough to follow him. What must that have felt like?

I wish I knew what eventually happened to Moshe Levi and his family. Did they return to Leiden, penniless? That doesn't seem likely to me. Did they make a new start in Israel or Turkey, or wherever they ended up? Perhaps his wife and children had already lost their faith in the rabbi. Perhaps Moshe held on to his conviction even after Zevi converted to Islam. I won't ever know for sure.

But I'm increasingly able to imagine it. At first, I'd

considered him to be something of a pathetic figure, tricked by the charlatan Zevi and his right-hand man, Nathan. Now, I'm beginning to understand the yearning behind his faith, this conviction. He lived in an environment that was always hostile to some extent, where attitudes towards Jews could change in a heartbeat. The Jews' history had proved that acceptance and tolerance were often nothing more than a thin veneer. It suddenly disappeared when there was a crisis like a crop failure, pestilence, or the unexpected death of a child... And then there was the longing to be free of it all, free of the never-ending suspicion, from the feeling of always being the outsider, the temporary citizen, the passer-by. The yearning for a life of freedom in the Promised Land, with the twelve tribes reunited under the rule of the Messiah who would sit on the throne of David...

I've never had to personally deal with the feeling of insecurity that must come from always having to have a packed suitcase ready, just in case. But the stories of my grandparents, my own parents, uncles, aunts, nieces, and nephews – who all experienced hatred and fear firsthand – have made it an ever-present theme running in the background of my life.

But to believe in the coming of the Messiah? The whole idea of a Messiah interests me from a historical and theological perspective. I enjoy looking into the stories around it, the ways in which people have tried to rationalise the fact that the Messiah still hasn't come. Followers of all faiths are waiting for a saviour in a way, and that fascinates me. Hindus await the final incarnation of Vishnu, Buddhists are waiting for the teacher Maitreya, Christians expect the return of Jesus, and Muslims hope for the reappearance of the hidden Imam...

And Peter? Of course, I'm thinking about him, too. But I've noticed that I shouldn't think about him too much. If I do, my fear for his safety threatens to overwhelm me. These people killed Thomas with no compunction whatsoever, and they won't lose much sleep over the loss of another life here or there. It's hard to believe that less than twenty-four hours ago, I was sitting at home, swotting up for the seminar that Peter, or Meneer de Haan as I knew him then, would be giving that afternoon.

And I know that he was attracted to me from the moment I stepped into his office, especially when he started talking about my perfume. I suspect it reminded him of someone. Besides, I know the effect I can have on men.

And that kiss in the botanical gardens... I don't regret it at all. It felt so right in the moment, and I enjoyed it too. What we'd been through in the hours leading up to it had been crazy, and we'd just had another narrow escape. The kiss was a kind of release, something we both needed. But I'm fairly certain that he was just acting on impulse too, and it was a spontaneous heat of the moment thing. I mean it was a one-off as far as I'm concerned, and from what I already know of him, I'm sure his heart won't break if I tell him that. But I don't think I'll need to tell him. It was very lovely, just then, to be held so tightly by someone, and yes, it was lovely to be kissed so deeply.

I can't help smiling as I write this... It would be nice if we could get to know each other in a more conventional way when this over. Perhaps it could develop into the kind of friendship I have with Mark. I can't see us ever running out of things to talk about, and we seem quite evenly matched despite the age difference.

This morning, I wasn't really open to the idea of us being friends. Quite the opposite, in fact. But now I'm looking forward to perhaps going to see a film at the Kijkhuis with him, with dinner afterwards in La Bota or Het Praethuys. Having long conversations about the religious experience he had at Mark's, and about many other subjects, like...

I have to stop writing. I just heard the door upstairs opening and at least two, maybe three people coming down the stairs.

Chapter Twenty-Four

P eter had regained consciousness but was only very vaguely aware of what was happening to him. He groaned as two men dragged him along a sandy path.

He heard keys jangling and a door being opened. The two men changed position, and Peter assumed this was because there wasn't enough room behind the door for three people to stand next to each other.

One of them grabbed him under his armpits, and the other took hold of his feet, and they carried him down a flight of stairs like that, with his back bumping painfully on the edges of the concrete steps.

When they reached the bottom, the person holding his top half laid him down on a cold floor, and Peter heard the rattle of keys again. A door was opened. In the distance, he heard Judith's voice. She was asking, loudly, what this was all supposed to be about.

She demanded they release her immediately, but the men didn't bother responding.

Peter tried to open his eyes, but it only made his head throb painfully, so he quickly closed them again. The two men dropped him roughly on the ground, and then he heard their footsteps moving away.

Someone lifted his head tenderly and shifted it onto something soft that felt like a lap. He assumed it was Judith's. He had seen Thomas's bloody head resting in her lap like this less than twenty-four hours ago, and now they were playing out the same scene... The door shut with a bang, and then he heard what sounded like a hatch being opened.

'We'll be back soon,' a loud voice said. Peter recognised it at once as belonging to his old mentor, Pieter Hoogers. The *Ordo in Ordine*...

Then he recognised Judith's voice, whispering sweet, comforting words to him as she gently stroked his hair.

He felt his pain being lifted away as he sank back into a fathomless darkness.

When Peter woke up again, he had no idea how much time had elapsed. He opened his eyes to a thin squint, and when he noticed that it didn't make his head ache too agonisingly, he dared to open them completely. He saw Judith sitting with her back against a wall, her eyes closed.

The room they were in looked completely empty at first. A hazy memory of being roughly bumped down a flight of stairs and the fact that he could hear no sound at all coming from outside told him that they were underground.

He tried to say Judith's name. It came out as not much more than a groan, but it was enough to make her immediately open her eyes and struggle to her feet. She approached him cautiously, as if sudden movements might make his pain worse. Very softly, she said his name.

His throat felt dry, and he found it difficult to swallow. He tried to sit up, but this attempt was immediately punished with a wave of nausea and a violent, pounding pain in his head.

Judith sat next to him on the floor and managed to heave him into a slightly more upright position. He did what he could to help, pushing himself up as much as possible so that he could lean against her. She unscrewed the cap from a bottle and carefully poured some water into his mouth. Some of it dribbled down his chin and onto his chest. The next attempt to slake his thirst was more successful, and after several further attempts, he was able to take a few gulps himself. Somewhat revived, he felt he could sit up unaided, so, a little regretfully, he pulled his body away from Judith's.

Now his eyes were completely open, and he was able to focus his gaze. He saw Judith's face close to his.

'Sorry' was the first thing he said.

'It's all right,' she said. 'It's all right.'

'I felt so stupid. Like I let you down. But it was...'

'I know,' she said soothingly. 'That's why I sent them the wrong way. I thought, if we still have a chance, this is it. Did you find anything?'

'Judith...' he said with renewed energy, sitting up straight now. 'I found Saint Peter's ossuary. His name was on it. When I got the lid off, I saw some bones and a skull inside it. But there was more than that: there were two keys! The keys Saint Peter carried to symbolise the ones Jesus gave him when he made him the keeper of the gates of heaven.

'What?' exclaimed Judith. 'You really saw them? So it is true!'

'It is true,' Peter said, taking her hands in his. 'It is true,' he said again, letting out a sigh of relief. At that moment, he felt as though a great weight had been lifted from his shoulders.

'It was almost too easy,' he continued. 'That should have been a warning.' Peter told her what had happened since they had lost sight of each other in the Hortus.

Judith listened, spellbound. She barely interrupted him, only asking for clarification now and then.

'When I knelt down next to it and pulled the cloth away,' Peter said, 'I saw his name on the chest, and I knew I'd found what we were looking for. I knew the ivory casket was authentic, that the letters really had belonged to Saint Peter and were written by him and Judas. I knew what I was looking at were the mortal remains of the man Jesus said he would build his church on, who had been at Jesus' side... If I touched those bones, it would be like reaching out through the centuries to touch Jesus himself. Only his skin and his flesh would have been between us.'

'And you saw the keys?'

'And I saw the keys. Imagine what they would have given to get their hands on this in the Middle Ages, Judith. To possess the apostle's bones and the keys that might have been handed to him by Jesus himself. And, of course, to have the casket and the letters. A king would gladly have given his entire empire for this. Wars have been fought for less...'

'This is going to turn everything upside down, Peter.'

'It is. It's the end of the world as we know it. If this is made public knowledge, not just that Saint Peter died and was buried in Matilo but what's said in the letters between him and Judas... If this gets out, then history will have to be completely rewritten. Who knows how much this knowledge will change our understanding of historical events? And who knows how many people were already aware of it? How many people knew about this fundamental threat to Christianity? Rembrandt, possibly, and Philip II. And, of course, the Vatican...'

Peter and Judith sat in contemplative silence for a few moments.

Then Judith spoke. 'You can see why there might be people would prefer that this information didn't get out.'

'Yes, that's right on the one hand,' said Peter. 'Suppose an order like the one Luuk belongs to, the Teutonic Order, had always been aware of what we've uncovered. And that the Vatican had always known that its claim to papal authority was built on quicksand, based on nothing but a legend. Then I can imagine that they wouldn't want this to be made public. Their whole world would collapse... But...' Peter looked for a way to put his thoughts into words 'But on the other hand... Having read the letters between Judas and Peter – words written by two disciples who were with Jesus every day from the very beginning on the Sea of Galilee until his awful death on the cross on Calvary, who were in despair after he died and waited in vain for him to come back as they'd been promised – I feel closer to Jesus than I've ever felt in my life. They've shown me a Jesus who was a man of flesh and blood, just like his disciples, with all their doubts and fears, their cowardice and anger.'

'I know what you mean.'

'It's strange to think that...'

'What's strange to think?'

'It's strange to think, looking back,' Peter went on, 'that the Jesus I read and heard so much about in my youth, and who was still an important figure in my life later, always in the background, but still present – *that* Jesus was a real person, just like you and me. Although he must have been a very remarkable person, and charismatic, like the Nelson Mandela of his time, he was still a human being. I wonder if he started to believe more fervently in the Messianic prophecies as he made his way to Jerusalem, even started to think he might be the Messiah himself. Hence his choice to ride into Jerusalem on a donkey, which, according to the letters, nobody really even noticed. And recklessly overturning the tables in the Temple, another event that would have been entirely forgotten if it hadn't been recorded in the gospels.'

'And now...'

'And now...' Peter said. 'Now, this has all made him feel closer and more real than he's ever been before. I feel like I understand him better than ever. He was a man on a mission, a man who fought against the overly legalistic interpretations of the rules that governed Jewish life. Why shouldn't he have been allowed to cure a blind man on the Sabbath? "The sabbath was made for man, and not man for the sabbath." He believed in living and acting in the spirit of the law, not following it mindlessly or slavishly. "Love the Lord your God with all your heart, and with all your soul, and with all your mind," he said, and he meant it.'

'I've experienced something like that too. Not that I've ever believed Jesus was the Messiah, of course, but I think I have a better understanding of how it was then. Yes, I think he was probably a very charismatic young man, good at telling stories that were simple on the surface but told deeper truths. Someone who spoke about love and forgiveness and gave people a glimpse of a world that would be possible if everyone lived according to his example. He seems more human to me now too, more believable.'

'When he was caught up in the euphoria of the moment, the euphoria of the procession to Jerusalem and the excited frenzy of all those pilgrims on their way to the Temple, he must have started to think: maybe it *is* me. Maybe I am the one the Eternal One promised would come to liberate the Jewish people, who would claim his rightful throne and gather all the tribes of Israel together. We know his outburst in the Temple was a complete failure, but he and his disciples must have thought it was just the beginning.'

'Exactly.'

'And those stories were told for decades before they were finally written down... How much of them would have been mythologised in the meantime? Although the letters between Judas and Peter weren't written by Jesus himself, they let us into his world. I don't think we could get any closer to the events that took place then.'

'And that's why I think it's such a huge shame,' Judith said, 'that there's a very real chance the world will never see them. I mean, look at us, stuck in here. We have no idea what's going to happen, but it's looking pretty hopeless, especially now we know what these people are capable of... And they won't give up until they get their hands on the casket.'

Peter suddenly started to feel something that resembled hope. 'But they don't know about the photos!' he said, interrupting her. 'Nor the translation. And they don't know where the casket is either.'

'But that's what I'm so afraid of, Peter,' Judith said. Now, for the first time, he heard fear in her voice. 'That they have no idea where it is, and they'll do everything they can to get that information out of us. And that I...'

Judith's hand flew to her mouth to stifle a scream. She stood up and began to pace around the room. There was nothing left of the calm with which she had previously seemed to face their situation.

'Calm down, Jude,' he said. He tried to get up, but it made his head pound again. He sank dizzily back to the floor. Helplessly, he reached out an arm towards her, but she didn't seem to notice.

Judith went back to the cell door and pounded on it but without much conviction. She held her face close to the bars over the hatch and cried 'Help!' a few times as loud as she could.

A shiver ran down Peter's spine.

He struggled to pull himself into a crouch, and then, very slowly, he tried to stand up. The throbbing pain in his head was so severe that it blurred his vision; Judith shifted in and out of focus.

'Judith,' he said tenderly. 'Judith.'

She turned around, and just looking at him seemed to calm her.

Judith walked over to Peter and took hold of his hands. He dropped back to the floor and closed his eyes, waiting for the pain to subside again.

Judith squatted down next to him, still holding his hands in hers.

'Listen,' he said, 'I think that we need to accept that we've lost the casket. They're always going to win, no matter what we do, and right now, there's nothing we *can* do. But we may still have the photos, at least, and the translation. And nobody else knows about that, apart from Mark.'

Although Peter was telling Judith this to reassure her, he began to believe it himself as he spoke. He shuffled into a more upright position. 'Let's assume,' he said when the worst of the stabbing pain was over, 'that they're going to come back and interrogate us. I think we should tell them where the casket is. With a bit of luck, they won't find the photos. They don't know they exist, so they won't be looking for them. But let's suppose they do find the photos and let's even suppose they catch Mark working on the translation – then they'll think they've found everything there is to find. But they don't know that there's another translation that's already finished.'

'Which we don't have,' Judith pointed out.

'No,' Peter said. 'We don't have that. But there's still a chance they'll overlook it.'

'I really hope you're right' Judith said, sounding unconvinced.

'We might have lost the battle, but we haven't lost the war. Once they've got the casket, they'll let us go. They think they've won, but we've still got an ace up our sleeve. They don't know everything, Judith. I imagine we'll be out of here by this afternoon, and then I'll go and pick up my clothes, and...'

'You're going to go and pick up your clothes?' Judith exclaimed in amazement. 'I can't believe you'd even consider doing that! How do you imagine that will go? You're just going to knock on your best mate Luuk's front door and then' – she sounded belligerent now – 'what are you going to say? "Hello mate, old pal of mine! How about we light a couple of those excellent cigars of yours, eh? All that unpleasantness this morning when you set us up and betrayed us? Oh, all water under the bridge now. These things happen. So anyway, what about that Patrick Kluivert eh? Should he have been allowed to go to England after that court case?"'

She was on her feet now, clearly irritated.

'Judith,' Peter pleaded. realising that his attempt to reassure her had failed. 'We've got to stick together. For heaven's sake, let's not fall out with each other now. You're right, my friendship with Luuk is over. That's very clear. I just wanted to... I was just fantasising about being able to walk around outside again and about ... about this all being over.'

'It's all right,' said Judith, more kindly now. 'It's all right. But Peter, haven't you ever noticed anything strange about Hoogers? I mean, he appears to be at the centre of an ancient, worldwide organisation. Maybe he's actually spent his entire career as a professor of archaeology trying to find Saint Peter's grave.'

'Maybe. I don't know. I can hardly believe it, even now. I've never been aware of him taking any special interest in religion at all, never mind Christianity. And obviously, he was involved in the excavations at Matilo, but not particularly closely. He's retiring tomorrow and...'

'Retiring? Tomorrow?'

'Yes. So although Hoogers was involved in the dig this year, it was less than usual because he was about to leave the university. But his role must have been much bigger than I realised. And now that I think about it, Thomas told me he was the one who recommended the young German man who joined the dig at the last minute.'

'The gunman who's been chasing us.'

'The gunman, yes. I hadn't thought of that before. Although now that I've said it, I'm already wondering if it's true. I know he appeared at the dig almost out of the blue. And that him being there annoyed Thomas right from the start. Thomas didn't entirely trust him. He did much more than was expected of him, even turned up at weekends when Thomas really wanted to explore the site on his own. At least, that's what he told me. Of course, I know now that Thomas was working on his own personal project at the weekends. Looking for Saint Peter. And so, apparently, was this German. It's certainly possible that Hoogers sent him there to be his eyes and ears. And since Hoogers is such a renowned professor of archaeology, I'm sure Thomas would have wanted to keep him happy. You never know when you might need someone like him to return a favour. But there's something else. Something that's bothered me from the very beginning, that's been nagging at the back of my mind. Maybe you didn't even hear it, but when we were about to leave to go to the dig, and I opened Hoogers' office door...

'He was on the phone, wasn't he?'

'Yes. He was on the phone. I said something like: "I'm going to Matilo. They've found a visor mask." And he started his answer with: "Yes, yes, I know..." as if he knew what I was about to tell him. Then I think he was going to say something else, but he stopped himself mid-sentence and said: "Good, good. Tell me about it later." But knowing what we know now, it looks like he already knew about the casket by then. Maybe that German man called him on the field telephone just before Thomas did.'

'Or it could have been Thomas who called him.'

'Yes, he might have done. To tell him about the mask... And Hoogers called his spy straight afterwards and told him to do some snooping around, and then he must have mobilised that whole invisible network that he probably controls.'

'Or he could just be another little cog in that machine too. Maybe his position is similar to Luuk's.'

Peter thought for a moment. 'No, I don't believe that,' he said, 'because it's no secret that Luuk belongs to the Order. The members' names are made public. There's no secrecy there. But Luuk may not even know that Hoogers is involved. All he did was tell someone within the organisation that he'd managed to detain us, and that other person may have informed Hoogers. And suppose Luuk saw Hoogers going into the Pieterskerk. He might have thought he was just there in his role as a professor who was worried about the mysterious fate of his colleague.'

Judith was about to say something, but before she could, they both heard a sound that made them prick up their ears. Somewhere above them, a door was opened and then closed, followed by at least two pairs of feet coming down the stairs.

Peter saw that Judith was starting to panic again. She went over to the desk, folded up the sheets of paper she had been writing on as small as she could and tucked them into the waistband of her skirt.

'Stay calm now,' he said reassuringly. 'We're together, and we'll stay together. Everything's going to be all right.' They fell into each other's arms and were still in that embrace when the hatch in the door was opened.

'Oh, how romantic,' they heard Hoogers say derisively. 'Let him kiss me with the kisses of his mouth! Aren't you embarrassed, Juffrouw Cherev, dallying with a man so much older than you? And you, Peter?... Although it's perfectly understandable... Breasts like two fawns, twins of a gazelle...' He laughed mirthlessly. 'But there's no time for pleasantries. We have serious work to do.'

Peter and Judith heard him turn the key in the lock. The door opened, and Hoogers came in with a linen bag slung over his shoulder. The man who had been chasing them came in after him, holding a gun in his right hand with a long silencer attached to it. In his other hand were two pairs of handcuffs and something that looked like an iron glove.

Hoogers closed the door behind them and looked at Judith. 'Well, now, Judith,' he said, 'You don't mind if I call you Judith, do you? I'm sure you've heard the phrase "to put the thumbscrews on someone"?'

Chapter Twenty-Five

Without a second's thought, Peter leapt up and rushed at the two men. But before he had even reached them, he felt his head burst in a splintering explosion of pain as the butt of the gun was slammed into his head, knocking him out cold. In the seconds before everything went black again, he heard Judith scream.

When he regained consciousness, he found himself lying on his stomach in an extremely uncomfortable position, his left arm twisted behind his back and his wrist handcuffed to his right ankle.

Peter turned his head to the side and saw Judith had been handcuffed in the same way. She looked at him helplessly with red-rimmed eyes.

'You filthy bastard!' Peter shouted. 'Take these handcuffs off, you...' Hoogers looked at him in amusement.

Can this really be the same man, Peter wondered. *The man I've spent so many hours with, talking about our work, the history of Leiden, archaeology, my career? Who I've shared so many personal stories with? Was it all just an act?*

'Ah!' Hoogers said simply. 'Our hero is awake again. Smart move you made just now. I was most impressed by your performance. What a man!'

His accomplice chuckled sycophantically, like an underling laughing at his boss's joke.

Hoogers gave him a nod, and as if he'd been waiting for this signal, he sat down sideways on Judith's back.

Peter tried to get his attention. 'Herman. That's what you're called, aren't you?' he asked. 'Thomas told me about you.'

'His name isn't Herman. Don't bother getting your hopes up,' Hoogers said, replying for his accomplice. 'Our man here has many names. He's just one of our anonymous foot soldiers, willing to lay down his life if necessary...'

'Come on, Pieter,' Peter said. 'You've got to stop this. What are you doing? This is utterly ridiculous. I don't know what you're trying to achieve here...'

'Shut your mouth!' Hoogers screamed, so completely unexpectedly and with such fury that it chilled Peter's heart. The scream echoed faintly around the room.

'Shut your mouth!' he said again, less viciously now, but still furious.

He walked over to Peter and planted a foot on his back, a hunter posing with his slain prey. Peter moaned.

'Oh, my boy,' Hoogers said, like a father gently scolding his son. 'This was a textbook example of being in the wrong place at the wrong time. If you had given Herman – let's just carry on calling him that, shall we?' he said, curling his lips into a sardonic smile. 'None of this would have had to happen to you if you had only given him five more minutes. This really has all been so unnecessary. And you helped him without realising it, too. Coming to your house was an act of desperation. He knew the casket was already gone. The empty space in the ossuary told him so. But then Thomas refused to tell him where it was. After you'd interrupted his search of the tent, he couldn't think of anything else but to go to your house and pretend he knew you had stolen something. And when you ran away, it confirmed to him that you actually had. He took another gamble by going to the hospital. But you were so predictable... This adventure could have ended there before it had even begun, but...'

He removed his foot, and Peter sighed with relief.

Hoogers began to pace back and forth, at least, as much as the limited space in the cell allowed. It was something Peter had seen him do many times in lectures, thinking out loud as he walked. Hoogers' students had admired him for it because it told them that this tutor, at least, wasn't just giving them the same lecture he'd been delivering for years. No, this was an inspiring professor, one who shared thoughts and ideas that he seemed to be coming up with on the spot.

'But the two of you stubbornly refused,' Hoogers went on, 'to give back what had belonged to us for centuries... Herman called to tell me what had happened, and I couldn't think of anything else to do but go to the faculty. I had to do something. And that also turned out to be a lucky guess... As I said, you've been so awfully predictable. And what a fuss about nothing in the end, Peter, because here you both are.' He briefly stood still next to Judith. 'You know, Juffrouw Cherev. Today is a joyous day for me—'

'Could this guy get off my back?' Judith interrupted him. 'If you don't mind.'

Hoogers continued talking as if he hadn't heard her. 'A joyous day, as I said. It's actually hard to believe. On the day before I become professor emeritus, I will set the jewel in the crown of my life's work. Gracious is the Lord... An anonymous jewel, admittedly, because the outside world will never know what a fantastic close this brings to my career, but nevertheless, it is extraordinarily satisfying.' He stood still again. 'I have never sought fame,' he said theatrically.

Peter let out a cynical laugh. Hoogers was known far and wide for his outrageous vanity. He always made sure he stood in the most prominent position in group photos, he signed letters to newspapers with the formal title 'Prof. Dr.', he didn't attend conferences unless he was the keynote speaker, and he would cause a fuss if his was not the first name credited as the author of an article, even if he had only contributed to it indirectly...

'For heaven's sake, what do you want?' Judith exclaimed. 'Do what you must but spare us the sermon.'

'Ah, my dear Juffrouw Cherev,' Hoogers said condescendingly. 'I think you have a right to an explanation, that's all. You've been on quite an adventure, haven't you? But don't worry, it's almost over.'

'Thanks, I feel much better now,' Judith said.

'Anyway,' Hoogers continued distractedly, as if Judith

was a student interrupting him with an irrelevant question. 'Where were we? Ah, yes... A joyous day. And not just for me, but for our whole Order, even though most of our members will be quite unaware of it. They, too, are ignorant... We, a select group of initiates – but I'm sure you've both worked that out by now – knew that Saint Peter's grave and the letters he exchanged with Judas would be found somewhere near Leiden.'

'What?' Peter and Judith both blurted out at the same time.

'You already knew about—' said Peter.

'About the letters, yes,' Hoogers replied.

'But how—' Judith began.

'Don't bother your pretty little head over it,' he answered without even looking at her. 'Listen, this knowledge has been in our possession for more than a thousand years, passed down from generation to generation. Our Order was driven out of Acre by the sultan's army in 1291. You know that story, so there's no need for me to elaborate. And so the last stronghold of Christianity fell into the hands of the Muslims. Centuries of effort and sacrifice made by the Crusaders, all devout men – and women too – had been in vain.'

Good God, Peter thought. *He really does think he's standing in a lecture theatre full of first-year students.*

'At least,' Hoogers continued, 'that's what most people think; that's the official history, and that suits us. But when we left, following in the wake of our brothers the Knights Templar, we were not empty-handed. And it didn't feel like a defeat at all. As you know, the Knights Templar went to

Cyprus, taking secret treasures with them. Not even I know exactly what those treasures were, but they brought the Templars fabulous riches and a privileged position within the Catholic Church.'

'Until...' said Peter.

'Until they got too big for their boots and overplayed their hand. They were completely eliminated, root and branch – at least, that's what the world believes, and who am I to try to disabuse anyone of their belief? Our Order has always been more modest in its ambitions. More political, you might say. We also owned a fantastic treasure. It may not have been as valuable as the treasure the Knights Templar owned, but perhaps that was our salvation. The attention has always been focused on them, and that has allowed us to operate in relative peace. I mean, how many people have even heard of our Order? The Templars have always held a particular fascination for the outside world, partly because their order ended so dramatically. Because of that, no one ever took any notice of us, quietly doing our good works in the background. That was, and still is, our reputation. But we also had information that would shake the church to its foundations; that could have changed the course of history, and still could change it.'

'Do you mean to say that you...' Peter was so astonished that he couldn't finish the sentence.

'Yes, that is what I mean to say,' replied Hoogers. 'Not only were we aware of the existence of these letters between Judas Iscariot and Saint Peter, but we had also known about their contents for a very long time. They had always been in our possession, and they were in good hands with us. We found the original letters – both the two from Peter to Judas and those from Judas to Peter – in an ivory box, hermetically sealed and well protected from the air and moisture. I'm sure that will sound familiar to you. Found by the Templars and some of my illustrious predecessors during the secret excavations on the Temple Mount. You may have heard about them.'

'I always thought the stories about those excavations were myths, conspiracy theories...' Peter had to admit that, despite the desperate situation they were in, he was finding Hoogers' story fascinating. Everything was starting to make sense.

Hoogers laughed. He was obviously enjoying himself. 'And we were happy to help those myths along. Some of my brethren have even published several books on the subject, which all flew off the shelves. Much of the information they presented was factually correct but so implausible that historians have never accepted it. We also copiously "leaked", as they call it, information to those two writers. What are their names? Michael Baigent and that other fellow. *The Holy Blood and the Holy Grail*. Enormously good read. People just adore stories like that.'

Herman was still sitting on Judith, who tried to move but quickly realised it was pointless and closed her eyes in defeat.

'There was just one little thing,' Hoogers said, continuing his lecture. 'A loose end, so to speak. Although ... actually, it was rather significant. We knew that somewhere around AD 70, before Saint Peter left Jerusalem for the west and headed for what is now England, he had the four letters transcribed so he could take them with him. But there was only one copy of the Source...'

'The Source,' Peter said.

'Saint Peter wrote about the events of Jesus' life in his own words. He left that manuscript behind for other people to refer to when they wrote their own versions of Jesus' life story.'

'The "Q" Gospel. Quelle! But that's...' Peter whispered.

'Indeed. Ironically, this document, the subject of historians' speculation for more than two centuries and which Luke and Matthew relied upon when writing their own gospels, is referred to by German theologians as Quelle, or "source". Unfortunately, we do not have it in our possession. This treasure, I am certain, was in the hands of the Knights Templar and they lost it after that fateful Friday the 13th in 1307 when they were arrested. Eventually, that document was placed in the vaults in the Vatican Library. However, that's not what this is all about. Saint Peter clearly refers to his correspondence with Judas in the Source. This is knowledge that the Knights Templar did share with us. He also refers to the fact that he'd had an exact copy made of the letters and indicated that he would take this with him on a trip to England.'

'But how did you know that he ended up here, near Leiden?' Peter asked him. He had become so absorbed in the story that he hadn't noticed that Judith had not spoken for some time. She was lying motionless, with her cheek resting on the floor as if in a deep sleep. He said her name, but there was no response.

Herman realised that it was no need to restrain her anymore and stood up.

Peter tried to move and felt his arm and leg cramp up. He rolled as far onto his side as he could in an attempt to restore the flow of blood to his limbs.

'It was obvious,' Hoogers said impassively. 'The most logical route that he and his companion would have taken – we don't know who he was travelling with, but we do know he wasn't alone – would have been northwards across mainland Europe, roughly along the border between what is now France and Germany. At that time, those areas would have been the least volatile. And who would hurt two innocent-looking old men on horseback? There was some unrest on the coasts of France and Belgium, so they headed for Brittenburg in the far north-western tip of the Roman Empire, where the Rhine flowed into the sea. There was a thriving sea trade with Britannia, sailing back and forth across the channel to England. If you had enough money, you could easily board one of those ships anonymously. They just wanted to be as far away as possible from Jerusalem, the city that had been reduced to ashes by the Romans two years earlier.'

'But they didn't make the crossing?'

'Very sharp of you. No, they didn't make the crossing. After literally centuries of fruitless searching all over Europe – what do you think those legends of King Arthur and his knights were about? They weren't about finding the grail that Jesus used during the Last Supper, I can tell you! – someone came up with the simple but brilliant idea that Saint Peter might not have made it any further than

Brittenburg. Shipping and trade had come to a standstill because of the Batavian and Cananefate uprisings, so that may have had something to do with it. The channel crossing was not without its dangers. Perhaps Saint Peter simply decided that it was too risky for himself and his companion and also for the precious object he was carrying with him, and he thought it best to stay here. So the obvious place for them to end up would have been Matilo...'

'With the Romans? Who had just destroyed their holy city?'

'Well, not in the military camp itself, of course. But as you know, a civilian village developed outside Matilo's walls, full of craftsmen and so forth. It's likely that they settled there.'

'Pure speculation.'

'Yes, but substantiated speculation. Look, if we had known for sure, we would have gone digging wherever we could, but that would have been too obvious. We weren't absolutely certain, but we had extremely strong suspicions. Incidentally, the search in England was continued, but it's been called off as of today. We searched in many other places. At first, we thought that Bérenger Saunière, a priest in the French village of Rennes-le-Château, had found what we were looking for, but that turned out to be something else. It was no less spectacular. However, it's not information that I'm at liberty to divulge right now. But Thomas's find brought an end to almost eight hundred years of searching... And thou Leiden, land of Germania Inferior, art not the least... When the first settlement was built here in the twelfth century, it would have been obvious that its chapel should be dedicated to Saint Peter rather than, let's say, Saint Willibrord, for example. Secretly, Bishop Godbald was a giant within our Order, and he took care of that. It was also Godbald who arranged for the Order to be given the right to appoint priests in the Pieterskerk; it marked the beginning of a link between the Order and Leiden that has lasted for centuries.'

'And how did you get involved?'

'I am but one in a long line of many eminent men of even greater renown than myself. It is a ... great honour, let me put it that way, to be invited to join. I personally know only our leader, and that is quite normal. Only he knows all the members. Our organisation is large, certainly, and international, but he alone knows how far it stretches. I myself do not occupy a high position within the Order. Not yet.' His eyes shone with ambition. 'But that will change after today.' He approached Judith. 'Now then...' he said, indicating that he was finished his explanation. 'Let's get down to business, shall we?'

He nodded to Herman, who opened out the iron glove. It collapsed outwards into two halves held together with a hinge that connected the ring and middle finger.

'Herman!' Peter said loudly, trying to stall for time. 'Where do you fit into all of this?'

Herman looked at Hoogers, who nodded. In an unmistakably German accent, he briefly told his story, as if he was glad to be allowed to speak at last. 'It was quite easy, really. The professor arranged for me to join the team, which allowed me to spend as much time as I wanted at the dig site. I soon realised that Thomas had what you might call a hidden agenda. I watched him like a hawk, as the saying goes, more often than he was aware of. Thomas called you when the visor mask was found, and then he called the professor, who immediately called me and asked me to go to the site and check things out. I live near Matilo, so I was there within minutes. There's a wide plank over the ditch that I use as a bridge... I ran across the field, and I could see Thomas standing in front of the tent, holding something in his hands. He seemed to be looking out for someone. As soon as he saw me coming, he disappeared back inside. It didn't take me long to reach the tent. I ran in and saw him standing in the middle of it, and now his hands were empty.

'I yelled at him: "What did you find? Give it to me! It's not yours!" But he didn't answer. I saw the ossuary with its lid half off. And he tried to stop me getting to it, so I picked up the field telephone and knocked him out cold. It took only a single blow. I looked inside the ossuary and saw that something had been removed. I panicked, and then I regretted knocking Thomas out because now he wouldn't be able to tell me anything...'

He paused for a moment as if he was expecting some sort of sign of approval from Peter.

'I looked and looked, and then I heard a car arriving in the distance. *Your* car. I had run out of time, so I threw a sheet over the ossuary and went outside. When I saw you two, I ran. I came back later to take your car keys so it would be impossible for you to get back to the city. If I had known that Judith was alone in the tent with Thomas at the time...' he said, sounding regretful. 'Anyway, the ambulance arrived soon after that, and I walked back home, making sure nobody saw me. I got my gun, called Hoogers. He gave me your address, and... You know the rest.'

Peter felt his blood run cold. Not just because he was thinking of Thomas, who must have realised how much danger he was in. It was worse than that. It was because Herman and Hoogers seemed so relaxed about revealing everything to them. They were both blowhards, so there was obviously a measure of smugness and vanity behind it. But above all, it showed that they knew their story would never go beyond the four walls of this cell. That their two prisoners would not be able to repeat it. Or that, even in the best case, it didn't matter what they told Peter and Judith, because nobody would believe them if they tried to tell anyone about it. Hoogers and Herman would get away with all of this scot-free.

Hoogers seemed to have read Peter's thoughts. 'So,' he said, 'now you know everything. Not that it matters, you know. Even if you two do make it out of here – and I mean "if" – you would still have nothing. Herman here flies very much under the radar, and at this very moment, I am clocked in at the university. Someone is working on my computer, making sure I send the occasional email. The last time I was seen in public was in the Hortus Botanicus. And then once more after that, but I'll get to that in a moment. And if I should need to state under oath that I innocently assumed that two men dressed as police officers must, in fact, be police officers, I'm quite confident my story will hold up in court.'

He put on a virtuous voice. 'I was only doing my duty

as a citizen, Your Honour. I was concerned about my colleague, Meneer De Haan, who had been accused of such awful things. And this was the day before I was due to retire. I was terribly distressed, Your Honour. I was glad that I had at least been able to locate his partner, Juffrouw Cherev. After handing her over to the authorities – at least, what I thought were the authorities – I went back to university to put the finishing touches to my farewell speech.' He laughed. 'Quite convincing, eh? You won't be getting out of here, but even if you did, you wouldn't have a leg to stand on.'

He put on an innocent face and laughed again, enormously pleased with himself. 'All right, that's enough chitchat. Come, Herman, we have work to do.'

Herman took Judith's free hand and put it in one half of the glove. He closed the other half over it, fastening the whole thing shut with two clamps.

'This is one of the Order's heirlooms,' Hoogers told her, smiling affably. 'Should there ever be a museum dedicated to the Order, then this will be the jewel of the collection... In the past, the accused person's hand was held over a smouldering fire, but we won't be doing that today. We're modern people, humane. Go ahead, Herman.'

Peter was horrified to see the screws on each side of the glove's fingers could be tightened to increase the pressure on the wearer's fingertips.

Herman began to turn the screws with no more emotion than if he had been tightening a screw into a wall. Judith was instantly roused from her lethargy. She opened her eyes and began to scream, a piercing shriek that sounded like a pig about to be slaughtered.

Peter rolled over to try to get closer to her, but Hoogers kicked him hard on the side of his head, and he lost consciousness again.

Chapter Twenty-Six

J udith was still screaming. Peter opened his eyes to narrow slits and saw that Herman was no longer sitting on her back. Now he was straddling the desk, watching Hoogers as he crouched down next to Judith's head.

'Just tell him, Judith,' Peter said. 'There's no point resisting him now.'

'Well now!' Hoogers said. 'Look who's decided to join us! Perhaps you can help us, Peter, because frankly, this is getting us nowhere. If we tighten the thumbscrews any further, we'll break her bones, and that would be rather a pity. And, above all, quite unnecessary. So I'm going to give the two of you one last chance.'

'The casket is at Mark's house,' Peter shouted. 'He's her friend. He lives opposite her in the Sionshof. Go there and get it, but for God's sake, let us go! You've won. Stop hurting her!'

This revelation seemed not to affect Hoogers, nor did it

spur Herman into action, which surprised Peter because he had assumed that this had all been about the casket.

'Honestly,' he said. 'I swear it. After we shook Herman off at the fair, we went to Judith's house. She changed her clothes, and we went to see Mark. He lives opposite her. Go over there or send Herman. Mark will give you everything you want. Then you can let us go. And we'll never tell anyone about any of this. I'm begging you, Pieter.'

Hoogers got to his feet and went over to the linen bag which he had put on the floor next to the wall. With agonising slowness, he picked up the bag, not once taking his eyes off Peter. Judith moaned softly. Beneath her face was a wet patch of floor where her tears had fallen.

Hoogers put his hand inside the bag and waited for a second or two like a conjurer reaching the end of a magic trick. Then he pulled out his hand to reveal the casket. 'Oh, you mean this?' he asked with exaggerated friendliness, as if he really was expecting an answer. 'Courtesy of your good friend Luuk, who told us that you had been to see Mark.'

Peter was dumbfounded. Even Judith, who had turned her head to see what was happening, stopped moaning for a moment.

Hoogers placed the casket on the floor and put his hand back inside the bag. He took out the Polaroid photos and scattered them on the ground like confetti. 'Very clever of you, Peter,' he said, and there was genuine admiration in his voice. 'When I saw these, I realised what you two had been doing at the institute, and why you were so reluctant to allow me in. Very smart.'

Judith lowered her head again and looked at Peter with her brow furrowed as if to say: 'So why all this theatre then?'

Hoogers put his hand inside the bag a third time and pulled out a sheet of paper. He let go of it, and it fluttered to the floor. 'Talented chap, your Mark,' he said. 'He'd already translated two or three sentences, and I must say I am impressed. The man's a genius. To be able to translate this ancient Greek into modern, readable Dutch so quickly... Well done and hats off to him, I must say.'

'But how...' Peter began.

'Listen carefully, Meneer De Haan. You two have underestimated who you were dealing with from the very start. You really had no idea. And you never stood a chance, either, I should add. Did you think we were idiots? We've been chasing this for centuries. Did you think we would let it slip from our grasp so easily? My God!' He threw his head back and roared with laughter. 'Then you really are even more stupid than I thought. We have eyes and ears everywhere. Ev-er-y-where. And Mark is no stranger to us, you know. In fact, I sit on the Doctoral Committee that will be considering his PhD application.'

'What did you do to Mark?' Judith cried out. 'We've told you everything! You've already got what you wanted, haven't you? What have you done? You bastards!'

'Oh, my dear, sweet Juffrouw Cherev,' Hoogers purred unctuously. 'You mustn't worry about your friend. He's being given the very best care he could possibly wish for.'

'Given the very best care?' Judith asked desperately. 'What's that supposed to mean?'

'As I already said, Judith,' replied Hoogers, 'Mark is well known at the university. In fact, great things are expected of him. People talk about him, express their admiration for the way he came back after his, how shall I put it, little breakdown. And now, Judith, it just so happens that I have a friend, a very bright fellow who is a Professor of Psychiatry. He was willing to take another look at the "Labuschagne case". When we began to strongly suspect that Mark had the items we were looking for, I contacted my friend and expressed concern at the possibility that Mark was heading for a relapse. I told him Mark had telephoned me in a state of confusion. He was threatening to hurt himself if I didn't immediately assure him that he'd be offered a research position at the university after graduation. He said his life would be pointless if he failed to get a PhD place, and he was raving about hellfire and damnation, quoting from the Book of Revelation, and blah blah blah... My psychiatrist friend and I have known each other for many years and, well, you know all about the strength of old friendships, Peter. So, given the urgency of the situation, he was prepared to call the mayor of Leiden, a good friend from his student days who would be sure to take his call, even on October 3rd. The mayor trusted his expert opinion and authorised Meneer Labuschagne's involuntary admission to Endegeest psychiatric hospital on the grounds of the sad and potentially self-injurious recurrence of his religious delusions.'

'You bastard... You bastard...' Judith muttered.

'Funny, isn't it, how quickly these things can deteriorate?' Hoogers said. 'Yesterday you would have addressed me very politely as "Professor Hoogers", and now all I get are profanities. Fortunately, however, I'm not a stickler for formality. So, as I was explaining, because I was accompanied by a respected psychiatrist and two policemen, I was able to enter Mark's house in my capacity as a concerned professor and colleague without arousing any suspicion at all. And believe it or not – God really is on our side – your bewildered friend Mark opened the door and had no choice but to let us in. While my psychiatrist friend explained the reason for our visit, I was free to go into the living room, and I saw the casket, the photos on the book rest, and the first lines of his translation all right there on his desk. Would you believe I was almost disappointed by how easy it had been? I put the casket in my bag before the others came into the room' – he pointed at his bag as if Peter and Judith would be fascinated by this detail – 'along with the photographs. Excellent images, by the way, very clear. What a clever contraption our colleague Verbeek has made. I showed my friend the translation Mark was working on as proof that he was indeed losing his mind again, just as he had been when he was found preaching his own gospel outside the train station. "Here," I said, "a series of letters exchanged by Saint Peter and Judas Iscariot. What more proof do you need that he's relapsing?"

'My friend took the papers from me and glanced over them, but he was convinced at once. "You're right, this is very worrying," he said. "This happens a lot, you know," he said to the policemen as if they still needed persuading. "Things might go well for a while, but sooner or later, their religious delusions return." As if those policemen gave a damn! The October 3rd festivities were in full swing by then, and I'm sure they would rather have been in town. But instead, they were in a musty room filled to the rafters with dusty books, dealing with a religious madman.'

'He's not mad,' Judith said angrily. 'He's actually been doing really well. You're not even fit to tie his boots.'

Hoogers smiled arrogantly. 'Sandals,' he corrected her. 'John the Baptist wrote that he wasn't fit to loosen Jesus' sandals, but you've given it a contemporary twist, which I must admit, I rather like. But in any case, it was all enough to justify taking Mark away for his own good. And now he's safely back in a familiar environment. He was rather taken aback, I can tell you. And do you know what the funny thing is, Judith?'

He paused for a second, but then he answered his own question, as had been his obvious intention. 'The funny thing is that all it takes is one telephone call from me to have your friend Mark released so he can continue his academic career. And because I and others in my circle know the right people, he won't ever take it into his head to tell anyone about what really happened. He knows that to let the cat out of the bag is to guarantee himself a one-way trip to Endegeest and end his academic career. To end his normal life, in fact.'

Like two boxers who had realised their fight was over, Judith and Peter lay defeated on the ground.

'But then I don't understand,' said Peter, 'why this whole charade was necessary. You've already got everything you wanted. Just let us go. It's over.'

'Not quite,' Hoogers said. 'After Judith was brought

here by our two... let's call them auxiliary policemen, and Herman and I had to collect you from Matilo, Peter, we still didn't know everything we know now. We've been very busy this afternoon, you know, you can't imagine. After we brought you here, we raced back to Leiden so we wouldn't be late for our appointment at the Sionshof. What a delightful place to live, by the way, Judith... And then we raced back here again. Pfff... And at my age! But we're almost finished.'

Judith moaned again, as though she'd only just realised that her hand was trapped.

'At least take those clamps off her fingers,' Peter said. 'This is ridiculous, Pieter.'

'Ah,' said Hoogers, almost affectionately. 'Our dashing knight in shining armour. Are you very much in love?' Hoogers laughed. He walked over to Judith and stooped over her, but it was soon horribly clear that he didn't intend to relieve her pain. On the contrary, he tightened one of the screws further, causing Judith to writhe in agony.

Tears sprang to Peter's eyes. 'Why are you doing this, you unbelievable son of a bitch!' he yelled. 'Haven't you already got everything? The casket, the photos... What more do you want? This is pure sadism.'

'What more could I want, my dear pupil? What I want is for you to be honest with me. My gut tells me that you're keeping something from me. And as you know, Peter, I am a very intuitive person. I know there's something else, but I just can't quite work out what it is.'

'You've got everything,' Judith moaned.

'What were you doing at Mevrouw Eco's house?'

Hoogers asked in a saccharine voice. 'It was terribly nice of you to visit that old lady. Awful, just awful, what happened to her husband, wasn't it? Taken from us so suddenly...' He contorted his face into a smile, which quickly faded again.

'Did you have something to do with...' Peter shouted.

Now Hoogers was suddenly incensed. 'Listen!' he yelled, bringing his face close to Peter's. Peter felt a few splashes of saliva land on his cheek. Hoogers' fury disappeared just as quickly as it had flared up, and he carried on talking, very calmly, as though nothing had happened. 'All those things are far above your heads, far, far above. I was opposed to having a new translation made from the outset. But my superiors insisted upon it. The other translation was so old that it needed its own translation, and very few of us are fluent in Aramaic... So I allowed myself to be convinced. And of course Eco was the obvious choice. I was already acquainted with him, and I knew he'd done this sort of work before. I hoped we would be able to trust him, but I was never entirely sure of it. We didn't find anything in his study in the library that night, nor did we find anything among the items we removed from his home, and yet, there was something that still wasn't sitting quite right with me. And when Luuk told me that he'd seen you both coming out of Eco's house that morning, I knew without a doubt ... we still didn't have *everything*. That man had kept something from us. Mark and Eco had been friends, and what other reason could there have been for you and Judith to go directly from Mark's house to Eco's? You don't bother an old lady late at night unless it's very, very urgent, now, do you?'

Peter wondered how Luuk would ever dare face him again. He would beat the man black and blue if he saw him.

'So I'll make this very simple, Peter,' Hoogers continued. 'Either you tell me right now what you were doing there, or we'll go and get Mevrouw Eco. Now, I think you went to Mevrouw Eco because you either knew or suspected that Eco had made a secret copy of the translation. She's an old lady, Peter. Like her dear departed husband, she may have a weak heart... It's up to you. Make your choice.'

'Loosen those thumbscrews, and I'll tell you where I left the papers,' Peter said.

'Do you actually think,' Hoogers asked, 'that you're in a position to negotiate?' He sounded genuinely surprised. 'Do you...' he repeated, but now he was shouting again, 'do you really think you're in a strong enough position to negotiate with me?' He grabbed Peter's collar with both hands, ripping his shirt open. 'How dare you insult me! You are my witness, Herman. Here! I'll show you how strong your position is!'

He bent over Judith and tightened another thumbscrew.

Judith only sobbed.

'Come on, Peter!' he bellowed.

A suspicion that had been at the back of Peter's mind now became an irrefutable certainty: his old mentor was going insane.

'Negotiating?' Hoogers roared. 'If I turn this screw just once more, the bone in her first finger will break. And, after that, I still have four more fingers to shatter. I'll do the others with my heel if I have to.'

He bent over Judith again. She tried to roll away, but

Herman sprang forwards and pinned her down with a knee in her back.

Judith opened her eyes, and Peter looked at her imploringly. She nodded once, giving him permission, to tell the truth.

'It's true, he did keep a copy of the translation for himself,' Peter admitted, realising that everything was already lost. 'He hid it behind the panelling in his study. We found it and read it. And then we took it, with Mevrouw Eco's permission.'

Hoogers' face brightened.

'Well now,' he said happily, 'wasn't that easy?' He walked towards Peter again. Hoogers looked so relieved that, for a moment, Peter was worried that he might try to kiss him.

'And where is that translation now?' Hoogers asked.

'As my faithful friend Luuk may have already told you, we changed our clothes at his house. I left it behind in a rush to get away. You'll find the text in the inside pocket of a jacket that I left in his bedroom.'

Hoogers stared at him in disbelief. 'That seems highly unlikely. You want me to believe that you found the text at long last, the text that your colleague sacrificed his life for, and you left it in the inside pocket of your jacket?'

Dejectedly, Peter lowered his head to the floor again and closed his eyes. It seemed that this was enough to convince Hoogers that Peter was telling the truth.

'Oh well,' he said triumphantly, 'why not? Sometimes the truth is simple. Besides, it would be easy to find out if you are, in fact, telling the truth, wouldn't it, Herman?'

Herman only smiled.

Hoogers nodded to his helper, who started loosening the screws on the iron glove.

Judith heaved a sigh of relief, and Peter sighed with her. 'Well,' Hoogers said to Judith. 'I think you got off rather lightly, don't you?'

'Lightly?' Judith started sobbing again.

'So,' Hoogers said, stretching out the 'o'. 'This is where we part ways.'

'What about us?' Peter shouted furiously. 'You can't leave us here like this. There's nothing we can do. You've made that abundantly clear. We have nothing to back up our story. Our only witness is locked up in a mental hospital and will only be released if we all keep our mouths shut. What more do you want?'

'I'm going to think that over,' Hoogers said pensively. 'Let's just say that I shall carefully consider my next step if and when I find the translation in the inside pocket of your jacket.'

He made it sound like the kind of reasonable proposal no sensible person would disagree with.

Peter shook his head. 'You can't be serious, Pieter,' he said.

'Time will tell,' said Hoogers, and he turned to address Herman. 'Are you going to write your letter?'

Herman nodded and sat down at the desk. He picked up the pen, and soon all that could be heard was the nib's scratch on the paper. When he was finished, he gave it to Hoogers to read.

'Excellent,' he said, nodding approvingly. 'You are a loyal soldier.'

He gave the letter back to Herman, who folded it up and put it in his pocket.

As if on command, both men got down on their knees. Herman bowed his head to Hoogers and muttered something as though he were making a confession. Hoogers put his right hand on Herman's shoulder and appeared to mumble a prayer. Both men kept their eyes closed, and Herman clasped his hands together. It was an absurd scene under equally absurd circumstances.

Hoogers turned to Judith and Peter. 'Our brother Herman will go to the police and confess to attacking the policeman at the hospital and to murdering Thomas. He will sacrifice himself to protect our Order.'

'But then the police will find out about all of this,' Peter said, confused.

'Not if they find him dead in his cell,' Hoogers replied as if he was trying to put Peter's mind at rest.

'And his motive?'

'All explained in the letter they'll find on his body. A crime of passion. A rejected lover, mad with jealousy, who killed the object of his desire to ensure that he was his and his alone, hoping to be reunited with his love in death by killing himself too.'

'That's absolutely ridiculous,' Peter said aghast. 'Nobody—'

'Believe me. The more absurd the scenario, the more people will be inclined to believe it. We are masters in the art of misdirection.'

Herman stood there, mute, as none of this was anything to do with him.

'And we're not actually evil. Both Thomas' and the policeman's families will be well taken care of. They won't know where the money comes from, but a scholarship will unexpectedly be granted, they'll win a competition that they didn't know they'd entered... Leave that to us; our resources are virtually inexhaustible.'

'You're all mad. Totally insane.'

Hoogers smiled superciliously. 'Come, Herman,' he said. 'Release this lady and this gentleman. We have everything we want now, and we shall torment them no more.'

Herman removed the handcuff from Judith's arm, and she clutched the hand that had been in the glove to rub her painful fingers.

She stretched out her leg, which Herman grabbed to attach the released handcuff to her other ankle.

Then he turned to Peter and did the same to him.

They had no choice but to cooperate. Peter immediately extended his leg, which was numb after being forced into an awkward position for so long. He rolled onto his back and stretched out his legs as far as he could.

Herman went back to the desk and picked up the pen and the remaining sheets of paper, then he went to the door and opened it. He disappeared into the hallway without looking back. Hoogers crouched down next to the casket, photographs, and paper and put them all back in his bag. Just as he was about to follow Herman out of the room, Peter called out after him.

'There's just one more thing.'

'What might that be?' Hoogers asked.

'If you know what's in those letters, then you know that Jesus didn't rise from the dead. You also know that even his followers knew he wasn't the Messiah. You know that, rather than being a traitor, Judas was carrying out a plan approved by Jesus himself... You know that Jesus only ever intended to preach to Jews, but Peter allowed himself to be persuaded by Paul that their movement should be turned into a sort of multinational corporation... If you already know all of that... Personally, I feel that reading those letters brought Jesus closer to me, far closer than the New Testament stories I've been told all my life. So why do you want to keep this covered up? Wouldn't that make you preachers of false religion? Why not tell the truth?'

Hoogers looked at Peter as if he was considering what he'd just said. 'What is truth?' he asked. 'What is truth, Peter?'

'I don't understand.'

'Honestly, Peter, I'm a little disappointed in you,' Hoogers said, still standing in the doorway with his hand on the door handle. 'You know the power of stories, don't you? You are a historian, after all. Listen, my boy. Over the last two thousand years, this story, by which I mean the official story of Christianity, has inspired billions of people to live better lives. Billions. Humans have sacrificed themselves for others, put aside their own wants and needs, done the right thing, become better people, transcended themselves. They've fed the hungry, clothed the naked, taken in strangers and more, all inspired by the life and the teachings of our Jewish rabbi. He takes away all our suffering, he who died for us, and whose resurrection demonstrated that he is more powerful than sin, more powerful than death. And what hope this has always given people! And still does! Today alone, two billion people call upon his name. He gives comfort and the hope of a better life in the hereafter. He is always there for us, completely understands us, forgives our shortcomings and mistakes, offers us a second chance. And he does this over and over again. No ordinary person could give us so much! He does not judge, but he is with us in our darkest hours, at our times of deepest doubt. He takes away our fears and asks nothing in return. Nothing! All we have to do is believe. This is an enduring message, Peter. Who are we to deprive people of it? It works, and that's all that matters. And, moreover, none of this detracts from who God is, my dear boy. God exists, and He is greater than anything our primitive human brains could ever imagine. Whatever people imagine God to be, if Jesus brings people to Him, he is just another way in which they can interact with the endless source of all that is, and surely there can be no harm in that? Doesn't the historical accuracy of how and whether something happened then become irrelevant? And even if we were to make the truth known, Peter ... for the majority of people, it would make absolutely no difference at all. The good news, the stories of Jesus, his death and resurrection are more or less embedded in the DNA of the human race... And what I have come to realise is that facts do not stand in the way of belief. On the contrary, many people see facts that contradict their belief merely as God's way of judging the strength of that belief. Seventy-five-million-year old dinosaur bones? Placed in the ground by God as a test of faith. Because according to the Bible, the earth is only six thousand years old – and isn't the Bible the word of God? Even if we were to make these letters public, and experts were to use carbon dating to confirm their age, even if handwriting experts and linguists were to establish their authenticity, it would make not a shred of difference to most people's faith. So why would we want to confuse these simple souls with all these complexities? Why not keep the yoke easy and the burden light?'

'But that's...' Peter began.

'But that's not fair?' Hoogers said, finding the words for him. 'Not truthful? Not the way it really happened? Not what Jesus intended? Listen, Saint Paul was the great saviour. He was the true founder of Christianity. He was brilliant, a visionary. What do you think would have become of the disciples after Jesus' death? After Jerusalem's destruction? Jesus' few thousand followers would have been scattered across the Roman Empire, and his teachings would have dissolved into the fog of history. We'd no doubt be worshipping Mithras by now, performing the Mithraic ritual with bread and wine, but we'd certainly not be following Jesus. Saint Paul was the first to realise this, the first to understand that expansion, making the group bigger, was the only way the movement would survive. He knew they would have to admit non-Jews, which meant not placing any additional burdens on them, like circumcision and dietary laws. And it is true that Saint Peter allowed himself to be persuaded by Paul that this was the right thing to do. They were the victors. And Judas went down in history as the greatest traitor who ever lived. Because history is written by the victors. You know that by now, don't you? And I like to think that if Jesus was somehow able to see what they did and what his message has become, he would be very pleased. Because now his message of love and forgiveness is no longer confined to a small, exclusive group in a remote corner of the Roman Empire but has been transformed into one that gives comfort and hope to billions of people. His mission had utterly failed, and his crucifixion was a non-event in his time; that is why we don't find anything about them outside the Bible. But they have taken on a scope and a meaning that he could never have thought possible. It's like investing in a fund that goes bankrupt. You think you've lost all your money, and then, suddenly, a benefactor appears, one with a vision, who offers new perspectives and invests his own money into the fund, and look! Your investment is eventually returned twice over. It's as though you've scattered seed on a barren field, but some of your seed blows onto your neighbour's fertile land, yielding a crop thirty, sixty, and even a hundred times greater than what was sown. Look at it like that, Peter.'

'The most bizarre thing is,' Peter growled, 'that you apparently have no idea how cynical the words coming out of your mouth sound.'

Hoogers said nothing. He only nodded and then closed the door behind him. They heard him turning the key in the lock. He slammed the hatch shut.

The cell was silent.

Judith had curled into the foetal position and was rocking gently back and forth.

Peter shuffled across the floor towards her. There was no way they could escape. The most important thing he could do now was comfort Judith. He manoeuvred his right arm under her head and lay down beside her.

Her rocking slowed, then stopped, and her breathing became calm and regular. It didn't take long for Peter to fall asleep too.

Chapter Twenty-Seven

Peter opened his eyes. He watched as the four long fluorescent lights on the ceiling began to simultaneously flicker as if they were all coming to the end of their lifespan. They cast eerie shadows of Peter and Judith and the few objects in the room.

Judith was still asleep next to him with her head resting on his arm, utterly exhausted. Her injured hand rested in the palm of her other hand.

All their effort had been in vain, Peter realised. They were no further forward than if Thomas had just handed the casket to Herman in the first place. Then, at least Thomas would be alive now. He, Peter, would have been strolling around the fair with a beer in his hand right now. But he wouldn't have got to know Judith as he had. That was really the only positive thing he could see in this whole wretched affair. But Thomas couldn't have foreseen that... And neither could they... And now they had nothing to show for any of it. Who would believe them? How would they explain the choices they had made?

'We stole an ancient ivory casket from the dig, and after Thomas was killed, we did everything we could to evade the police.'

'Which casket are you talking about? Which photos? Which translation? Oh, the translation that Meneer Labuschagne was working on... Hasn't he just been released from the psychiatric hospital?'

Peter looked at Judith's face. She looked so vulnerable as she lay there sleeping. Now he had all the time in the world to study her fine facial features, her neatly tweezed eyebrows, her sharply defined cheekbones, the perfect cupid's bow in the middle of her top lip, and the light, velvety down on her face. God, she was beautiful. He longed to caress her but resisted the urge. What an absurd situation this was ...

But something was nagging at the back of his mind. Something Hoogers had said. Peter couldn't quite put his finger on it. Of course, it had all been unbelievably cynical, he thought, the explanation that Hoogers had given them. Maybe that's how you saw things when you got closer to power, but it had contrasted so enormously with his own experience of reading the letters. For him, Jesus had truly become a man of flesh and blood, and so had the apostles Judas and Peter, with their very human doubts. It all made sense... That Judas wanted to return to the village where he was born but was forced instead to go to Damascus, where Paul visited him years later. Judas was able to predict even then that Paul would try to take over the Way and lead its followers in a different direction. And the Apostle Peter, who knew that Jesus had preached only to Jews when he was alive and had never shown the slightest interest in the Gentiles, in anyone who wasn't one of God's chosen people... And yet, he allowed himself to be convinced by the cunning, silver-tongued Paul. Peter, a simple fisherman, was no match for Paul... Ah, that was it! Hoogers had suggested that none of this changed anything about who God was. He said that God was greater than we were able to imagine with our limited brains. That Jesus was one of the ways back to God ... the endless source of all that is.

It struck Peter that this was precisely what he himself had felt as he read the letters between Peter and Judas. And he had felt it especially during that strange moment when he and Judith were hiding in the wardrobe. He had felt such tranquillity, perhaps even love. The only way he could describe it was that it felt like he was communicating with God or some divine being. His spiritual life had been at a dead end for years, but as soon as they got out of here, he would breathe new life into it, Peter resolved. If they got out of here...

Peter felt that he wanted to pray and closed his eyes. 'Lord,' he murmured hesitantly, 'I don't know exactly who I'm praying to now. I'm praying to the one whose closeness I felt so clearly last night when we were in the darkness of that wardrobe. I now know...' – he was looking for the words that would express his confused feelings – '...I think I have a better understanding now of everything I once blindly accepted, all those scriptures I listened to so mindlessly without truly understanding what they were about; all the prayers that I repeated verbatim but that didn't come from my heart, like a child reciting a memorised poem in front of the class... I felt your presence, and... How should I describe it? It made me long for more. Please, save us. Save Judith and me from the danger we're in. Please, Lord, have mercy on us.'

Peter didn't know what else to say. He wiped the tears from his eyes with his hands. Then he fell asleep.

———

A radiant light filled the room. Peter woke up. He kept his eyes closed, but the light was so bright that it shone through his eyelids. He cautiously opened his eyes and noticed that the four fluorescent lamps were no longer flickering but were burning brightly. Although it may have been an optical illusion caused by the contrast with the way they'd flickered so weakly before, they seemed to be shining more brilliantly than ever.

Judith's eyes were still closed, but her eyelids began to flutter. She was moaning softly.

Peter bent his legs, which felt stiff, and he realised that the handcuffs were no longer attached to his ankles. He put both his legs in the air. Very carefully, he removed his dead arm from underneath Judith's head and sat up straight.

The handcuffs were lying on the floor where his feet had been. Judith's legs had also been freed from the tight shackles. It was as if the cuffs had simply fallen off their ankles.

Peter put his hand on Judith's hip and shook her gently.

Now she opened her eyes completely and blinked at the blinding light. She looked dazed and sleepy, and there was a crease across her face where she had been lying on Peter's arm.

'The handcuffs are off,' Peter told her. 'They must have come back to remove them while we were asleep.'

Judith struggled into an upright position. She grasped her sore hand and began to rub it. 'Did someone come in then? I didn't notice anything.'

'Me neither. We must have been in a deep sleep. After all, both of us were completely exhausted.'

Judith stuck her legs in the air, bent them and then drew them back up to her chest as if she was working on her abs at the gym. 'What about the door?' she asked after she had done a few more stretches.

Peter got to his feet but immediately crouched back down again. Standing up so quickly had made him dizzy. He made a second attempt, and when the pounding in his head faded, he dared to walk over to the door, which was still closed. He stood in front of it, not moving, as though he had already given up on the idea of opening it before even trying the handle. If the door was locked, they would be no better off than if the handcuffs had still been around their ankles.

Peter pushed at the door. It creaked open.

Now Judith jumped to her feet too. 'What!' she exclaimed, 'Is the door open?'

'Apparently so,' Peter replied. 'Someone must have unlocked it. I suppose it might have sprung open on its own, but that's not very likely.'

Judith came and stood behind him.

'Come on,' Peter said. 'Put your belt back on, and your shoes and your coat, and follow me.'

Judith did as Peter instructed and followed him into a narrow corridor where a stone staircase led upwards. They climbed the steps and discovered that the door at the top was open too.

When they stepped outside, a gentle breeze blew in their faces. Peter and Judith took in deep lungfuls of fresh, cool air. They could hear waves on a shore somewhere nearby and saw what looked like a faint path formed by a trail of small hollows in the sand.

'I think we should head towards the sea,' said Peter. 'We'll probably be able to get an idea of where we are from the beach.'

Judith nodded, and they trudged through the loose sand to the dunes.

When they reached the top of the rise, they stopped to orientate themselves. On the far left in the distance, they could just make out the pier at Scheveningen through the mist, and on the right, much closer, were a white lighthouse and a little church.

'We're in Katwijk,' said Peter. 'They've only brought us just down the road!' He laughed with relief.

Peter walked down the bank and soon reached the firmer sand close to the shoreline. He looked back and saw Judith still some way behind him. Peter sat down, took off his shoes and socks. When he stood up again, the feel of the cold, damp sand between his toes sent a tingle of pleasure over his back.

He walked to the water's edge and stood still. The waves lapped gently over his bare feet, soaking the cuffs of his trousers. He wriggled his toes. Air bubbles rose to the sand's surface where they floated briefly before being washed away by the retreating sea. Peter stared into the distance, gazing across the water that stretched out endlessly in front of him.

As the wind tugged at his hair, he thought of the words of Psalm 104: 'Yonder is the sea, great and wide, creeping things innumerable are there, living things both small and great.'

Nobody was chasing them now, Peter thought. He looked over his shoulder and saw Judith on the sand next to where he'd left his shoes. She was sitting with her arms wrapped around her legs and her head resting on her knees.

A fragment of another psalm floated into his mind. 'You rule the raging of the sea; when its waves rise, you still them.'

It's funny, he thought, *that when you ask people to tell you about their happiest moments, they often come up with times when they were alone, surrounded by nature. Recreation, being created anew, a new creation. And they always describe that feeling of happiness as a fleeting moment in which time seemed not to exist.* Peter felt the same way now, absolutely peaceful.

'Make me to know your ways, O Lord; teach me your paths. Lead me in your truth, and teach me,' he sang softly to himself.

'Peter!' Judith called out. Startled out of his reverie, he turned around and saw Judith, standing now and beckoning to him. Peter raised his hand to signal that he was coming.

The sun was low on the horizon, and Peter guessed that it was late in the afternoon. He walked back up the beach to Judith and picked up his shoes. She held his hand, and they walked in silence along the water. The waves washed over the sand with their eternal rhythm as they had done since long before Peter and Judith had existed and would continue to do long after they were gone.

When they had almost reached the broad steps that led up to the boulevard, Judith let go of his hand. She smiled and said: 'Come on, I'll race you to the stairs.'

Judith started running, and Peter followed the trail of her footprints. And as he watched her long hair flowing in the wind, Peter knew that, if he was with her, he would be happy to run forever.

Chapter Twenty-Eight

A rchippus sat up in bed and looked around his little room. Apart from the bed, there was a chair, and a table upon which stood an oil lamp and writing implements, but nothing more. He was glad that, after today, he would be leaving this unholy place. It was always either wet or humid here, and often cold even in the summer months, with few opportunities to enjoy the simple pleasure of basking in the sunshine as he had done at home. And at this time of year, daylight grew scarcer by the day. But today, he would at last complete the task that had been given to him by the Lord.

It had been a year and a day since Cephas had departed this life, shortly after their arrival in Camp Matilo. Before his death, Cephas had given Archippus clear instructions: bury him in the earth and collect his bones one year later, clean them, and place them in a stone chest. Archippus had instructed a local craftsman to make the ossuary, but the inscription on the side he had carved himself.

That was one advantage of this damp climate: by now, Cephas' flesh would have almost completely rotted away. Back home, it all took much longer; the dry air could practically mummify a corpse, and the deceased were sometimes still recognisable long after their deaths. But that would not be the case today.

He would have two helpers to whom he had promised a generous reward. They had made it clear that they considered his request to be highly unorthodox, but their revulsion was more than assuaged by the money they'd been promised.

He got dressed and went outside, where, to his surprise, the two men were already waiting for him. The sun was not yet up, but after a year here, he knew the area like the back of his hand, and he could easily find his way to the graveyard in the gloomy twilight. They had prepared the ossuary the night before.

When they arrived at the place where Cephas was buried, the men unceremoniously plunged their spades into the ground and started to dig for his remains. It didn't take them long to reach the body. As Archippus had hoped, it was almost completely decomposed.

The men dug away enough earth to reveal all of Cephas' bones.

Archippus wanted to look away but forced himself to watch and make sure the task was carried out properly. Watching them scraping away the bits of rotten flesh that still clung to the bones made his skin crawl, but he kept watching, even as his eyes were clouded by tears.

The task took less time than he had expected. They

rinsed the bones and skull clean with the water they had brought with them in clay jars. Then they placed the stone chest in the emptied grave, facing the east where the Temple in Jerusalem had once stood.

Archippus thanked his helpers and even gave them a few more coins than he had promised. Then he sent them away, telling them he wanted to perform the next task alone. The two men had apparently already lost interest, and with a short, mumbled goodbye, they were gone.

Archippus got down on his knees. He picked the bones up from the ground and laid them gently inside the chest. 'Righteous are You, Lord, and Your judgments are just,' he murmured. 'You are the True Judge, who judges with righteousness and truth. Blessed is the True Judge, for all of His judgments are righteous and true...'

He looked over his shoulder; the men had already disappeared from sight. From beneath his cloak, he took the two large keys which Cephas said had been given to him by the Master. Archippus had never been able to establish whether this was really true or not. Cephas had always tended to exaggerate, embellishing his accounts of events and adding extra drama to his stories. He placed the keys near Cephas' skull.

'Let the favour of the Lord our God be upon us,' he sang quietly. 'Let the favour of the Lord our God be upon us, and prosper for us the work of our hands, O prosper the work of our hands!'

He looked over his shoulder again. When he was sure that there really was no one to see him, he put his hand inside his cloak once more and removed the casket that

Cephas had always been so anxious not to let go of. Archippus put it in the corner of the chest.

Before he placed the lid on top of the chest to close it, he sang: 'You who live in the shelter of the Most High, who abide in the shadow of the Almighty will say to the Lord: "My refuge and my fortress; my God, in whom I trust."'

When he had sung the entire psalm, he slid the lid into place. He had sung these words countless times, and yet they still had the power to move him. 'Those who love me, I will deliver; I will protect those who know my name. When they call to me, I will answer them; I will be with them in trouble, I will rescue them and honour them. With long life I will satisfy them and show them my salvation.'

The men who had helped him would keep his secret. They had given their word. But just to be sure, Archippus had told them that God would bring a terrible curse upon anyone who tried to open the ossuary, upon them and their children and their children's children.

He stood up, bowed his head and whispered: 'But you, go your way, and rest; you shall rise for your reward at the end of the days.'

Archippus picked up the spade that one of the men had left for him and threw three spadefuls of sandy earth onto the chest.

'And the dust returns to the earth as it was,' he said, 'and the breath returns to G-d who gave it.'

The grave was deep, and it was some time before he had filled it up completely. Archippus stamped the earth down well, and then he scuffed at the top layer to loosen the soil so that the grave wouldn't stand out from its surroundings.

'May it be Your wish,' he said, 'Eternal, G-d of souls, that the soul of Cephas be received by you in love and affection. Send your good angels to save this person from any suffering in the grave and send this person to the Gan Eden, the Paradise.'

Archippus sighed deeply. It was finished. He ended the ritual by singing: 'The Lord is my shepherd; I shall not want.'

He picked up the spade and a jar that was still half-filled with water. As he walked away from the grave, he murmured a prayer: 'Your dead shall live, their corpses shall rise. O dwellers in the dust, awake and sing for joy! For your dew is a radiant dew, and the earth will give birth to those long dead.'

At the edge of the graveyard, he stopped to wash his hands, reciting the words: 'He will swallow up death forever.'

He looked back one last time at the patch of ground that would be Cephas' earthly resting place until the day when G-d would resurrect the dead and pronounce his final judgement on them.

When he reached the house where he had spent a year and a day, he set down the jar and the spade. Inside, he collected the bag he had packed with his meagre possessions.

Archippus closed the door behind him and went to the stable where he saddled and mounted his horse.

Then, without taking his leave of anyone, he rode away.

A watery sun had risen in the east, the direction in which he would travel.

And just as he and Cephas had done when they left the beach to come here, he lifted up his voice and sang one of their favourite psalms: 'To you, O Lord, I lift up my soul. O my God, in you I trust. Do not let me be put to shame. Do not let my enemies exult over me. Make me to know your ways, O Lord. Teach me your paths. Lead me in your truth and teach me.'

Epilogue

T he next day was Friday, October 4th, and when Peter
arrived at the faculty at five o'clock that afternoon,
there was a small removal van parked next to the main
entrance. Two men were loading identical cardboard boxes
into it, while their two colleagues went into the building
and returned with a fresh load of boxes.

As Peter entered his corridor, he realised that Pieter
Hoogers' room was being hastily emptied.

Confused, he approached one of the removal men, 'I
thought he wasn't leaving until the end of December?'

'He was, apparently,' the man replied, 'but the office got
an urgent call early this morning asking if we could do the
job today. Makes no difference to us, either way. But if you'll
excuse me ... we've still got a lot to do,' he apologised.

Peter walked down the hall to Verbeek's room and
knocked on the door.

'Come in!' Verbeek answered.

Peter opened the door halfway. 'I'll go and get your

cabinet,' he said. 'Borrowed it yesterday for a rush job. I'll order a new pack of film for you.'

Verbeek had been engrossed in the book that was open on the desk, but now he looked up.

'That's fine, Peter. No problem.' He leaned back and took off his glasses, then stuck one of the arms in his mouth. 'Awful, wasn't it? What happened to Thomas? Just awful. But I just heard on the radio that they've caught the man who killed him. He turned himself in yesterday. Did you hear about it?'

Peter told him he had heard about it. After he and Judith had arrived back in Leiden, they had both gone their separate ways. But this afternoon, they had gone to the police station together. Although the inspector they spoke to was angry with them for having done their best to evade the police, they weren't charged with any crimes. The murderer had come forward the previous night, only to unexpectedly commit suicide once he was in police custody. A letter had been found on his body, but its contents would not be made public out of respect for his family. The case was closed as far as the inspector was concerned, although Judith and Peter would still be required to make themselves available in the event of any new developments. Oh, and Peter could collect his car. They had towed it away from the excavation site, but they had no further need for it. He would find it parked in the yard behind the station.

Mark had been released from the hospital that morning, and his psychiatrist had expressed confidence that, with the correct medication, the risk of another relapse was minimal. After they'd left the police station, Judith had spent the rest of the afternoon with Mark, whose temporary hospitalisation had clearly affected him deeply. But he still insisted that he would not take the pills. He confessed to Judith that he had never taken his medication because he knew with absolute certainty that he was sane. Whatever had led him to come up with an alternative gospel, it hadn't been religious delusions.

Peter had gone to see Thomas's widow, Suus. It was a sorrowful meeting in which they sat in silence more than they spoke, their cups of coffee growing cold on the table next to them. Suus had received a phone call from an insurance company she'd never heard of. They told her that Thomas had taken out a life insurance policy just a week earlier. It would pay his next of kin the sum of two million guilders in the event of his death. She was still so numb that she hadn't questioned how they could have known about his passing so soon.

'I heard about it, yes,' Peter said to Verbeek. 'Shocking state of affairs. I... We'll talk about it later, all right?' He paused, and then he asked: 'And Hoogers – why is he leaving today already?'

Verbeek shrugged. 'I don't know. Although he did give his farewell address this afternoon, of course. Had a decent turnout for it too. Thomas's death cast a shadow over it all, but Pieter wouldn't countenance the idea of cancelling. He dedicated most of the first part of his speech to talking about Thomas's life and work. And he did it very well; it was certainly very moving. Pieter choked up himself a couple of times. It was a fitting and memorable tribute to Thomas. You were missed, obviously, but everyone knows you have other things on your mind at the moment. And if you ask me, it's Thomas's murder that's made Pieter decide to bring his retirement forward. I imagine it's made him keen to start the next phase in his own life. He did seem very upset. Looked terribly tired too. But he'll have plenty of time for himself to recover from it all now. He's retreating to a monastery near Utrecht.'

Peter smiled, a little bitterly. 'I have to go now, but we can get back to this later. Oh, and I'll bring the cabinet back shortly.'

'No rush, no rush,' Verbeek said affably. He raised his hand to say goodbye and immersed himself in his book again.

Peter closed the door behind him and went to his own room, where everything was exactly as they had left it the night before. Someone from the security team had closed the window.

He crashed onto the sofa, took a cigarillo from a box and lit it. He was just about to open the window a crack when there was a knock on his door.

'Come in,' he called.

The door opened to reveal Judith standing in the corridor, smiling at him enchantingly.

'Meneer De Haan,' she said with exaggerated formality. 'I would be very grateful if you would be so kind as to give me your opinion on the subject I've chosen for my dissertation. Is this a convenient time for you?'

'Of course. Please, do take a seat,' Peter replied with equally exaggerated politeness. 'Juffrouw Cherev, I believe?

And on which subject do you intend to write your dissertation?'

Judith sat down while Peter waved the cigar smoke away with his hand.

'Well,' she said, 'I was considering writing about the ancient connection between Saint Peter the Apostle and Leiden, our beautiful City of Keys.'

Peter nodded approvingly. 'An excellent subject,' he said. 'Please, tell me more about it.'

Excerpts from Judith Cherev's dissertation proposal

Dissertation proposal
J. Cherev
University of Leiden
History Department
Student number 9087467
September 1996

SUBJECT
The Merchant Moshe Levi and Rabbi Zevi: A brief history of the Jews in Leiden

A brief description of the subject

In my final dissertation, I would like to explore the history of Judaism in Leiden. Sporadic references to Jews can be found in Leiden's archives from the sixteenth century onwards, although an established Jewish community did not begin to develop in the city until the eighteenth century. In 1791, Jews were given their own cemetery, and a synagogue was set up in a private residence a few years later. I intend to trace the history of Judaism in Leiden from those first references in the archives to the present day.

A separate chapter will be devoted to a case study focusing on the seventeenth-century merchant Moshe Levi, who came under the influence of the Turkish Jew Sabbatai Zevi, or Rabbi Zevi, whom, for a time, many European Jews believed was the Messiah.

RELEVANCE 1
Academic relevance

The history of Judaism in Leiden has so far not been the subject of detailed study. In part, this is because the city has never had a large Jewish community. According to the 1815 census, only 1 per cent of the population identified as Jewish (270 of its 28,528 inhabitants). However, a further challenge is presented by the lack of historical records. Leiden's Jewish community's archives were lost in the gunpowder disaster of 1807 when an explosion caused significant damage to the synagogue and the adjacent school. In my opinion, this only emphasises the importance of writing about this subject and also, of making an inventory of all the sources that could be helpful in the study of the Jewish community in Leiden.

In addition, by examining the life of a Jewish merchant and his family in the seventeenth century, I hope to provide more insight into the position of Jews in the rest of the Netherlands and Europe at that time.

Finally, by examining the influence of Sabbatai Zevi, I will show how intense the messianic expectation was among the Jews at the time, and the extent to which Jews were still strongly connected, despite being scattered over many different countries.

RELEVANCE 2
Social relevance

Judaism's close connection with the Netherlands spans many centuries. When Jews from the Iberian Peninsula – and later from Eastern Europe – were forced to flee their countries at the end of the fifteenth century, many found new homes in the Low Countries. However, influenced by their Christian beliefs, the attitude of the Dutch towards Jews has often been ambiguous. To some extent, an awareness that they were not entirely accepted by society was always present in the background of most Jewish people's lives.

Unfortunately, Leiden's Jewish community was no exception. This is evident in, for example, the restrictive regulations that were in force for Jews who wished to settle in Leiden. Even today, many Jewish people feel that they must always be cautious, always alert. Recently, the windows of the Jewish student halls of residence on the

Levendaal were replaced with bulletproof glass, and security cameras were installed both inside and outside. I have heard from several Jewish students that they remove their kippahs in certain areas of the city because they would otherwise have to deal with threats, insults, and, in some cases, even physical violence.

In my dissertation, I will show that the Jewish community has long been part of the city's makeup. I hope not only to help increase knowledge of the history of the Jews in the City of Keys, but also to contribute to an increased acceptance of their presence.

MOTIVATION
Personal motivation

I was born in 1970 into a Jewish family. My parents are both Jewish and belong to the Liberal Judaism movement. At home, we observe the Sabbath and keep kosher as much as possible, but exceptions are made, particularly outside the home, for example, when visiting non-Jews. Our kitchen also does not have separate meat and dairy areas, so my family could not claim to be strictly observant.

My father was born in 1937. Because he and his older brother were evacuated to East Groningen, he survived World War II. They lived with a communist couple who were posthumously given the Righteous Among the Nations award by Yad Vashem for saving them. The rest of my father's family died in concentration camps.

Almost everyone in my mother's family suffered the

same fate. In 1935, her parents fled to England, the only members of the family to do so. My mother was born there in 1940. They returned to the Netherlands, immediately after the end of the war and were able to move back into their home in Amsterdam after a short legal battle with the people occupying it.

Although I have never really personally experienced the feeling of being 'a stranger in a strange land', I have always been fascinated by the history, fate, and fortune of the Jewish people. The Holocaust is a fundamental and inextricable part of my personal history; as a Jew, it is impossible to escape.

I am a student in Leiden. When I discovered that this city's Jewish history has been somewhat neglected, I decided to apply myself to studying it. I would also like to look specifically at the merchant Moshe Levi's messianic beliefs.

My father became a student of the Jewish religion later in life, and he has always been particularly interested in the belief in the coming of a Messiah. It was from him that I first heard of Sabbatai Zevi. I stumbled across some documents in the Leiden archives concerning Moshe Levi, a merchant who sold everything he owned and travelled to the Holy Land to follow this supposed Messiah. Remembering what my father had told me, everything then fell into place.

The Jewish merchant Moshe Levi of Leiden
Some preliminary details

Moshe Levi (born in Leiden in 1626? died in 16?? in ?) was a Jewish merchant. He lived with his family in what is now a listed building on the Hoge Woerd, not far from the place on the Levendaal where Leiden's synagogue stands next to the Jewish student halls.

His ancestors were probably Sephardic Jews who fled Spain at the end of the fifteenth century and moved to the Low Countries. It is not clear whether they immediately settled in Leiden. There are indications that they initially lived in Antwerp but were forced to flee yet again after the Fall of Antwerp (17 August 1585). The fall of the city followed the fourteen-month-long siege led by Alexander Farnese, Governor of the Spanish Netherlands.

Ironically, the Jewish textile workers who fled from the Spanish were partly responsible for Leiden's eventual wealth and prosperity. They brought new knowledge and production techniques that would ultimately lead to Leiden's thriving weaving industry. By around 1650, Leiden was the largest producer of textiles in Europe, and half of its one hundred thousand inhabitants worked in the textile industry.

Moshe Levi was not a textile manufacturer. However, he was a cloth merchant, and this trade must certainly have been profitable for him. His surname, Levi, indicates a connection to the Tribe of Levi, one of the Twelve Tribes of Israel Levi was Jacob's third son.

The Levites were the only tribe who were not allowed to

be landowners in the newly conquered Promised Land (Canaan). Instead, their task had always been to care for the Temple. During the forty years that the people of Israel wandered in the wilderness after their exodus from Egypt (see the book of EXODUS in the Old Testament), the Levites were responsible for carrying the 'tabernacle'. This was the Tent of the Congregation, the first Temple dedicated to Yahweh, which was completely dismantled and rebuilt every time the Israelites moved camp. When King Solomon eventually built the first permanent Temple in Jerusalem, the tabernacle was no longer necessary. The Levites were appointed the priests, guards, treasurers, and musicians of the Temple.

It is unknown whether Moshe Levi played a religious role in Leiden, but this does not seem likely. At that time, there were no synagogues and no Jewish community of any significance at all. It is even questionable whether it would ever have been possible to gather a minyan in Leiden at that time. Among the documents I found in the archives were many business accounts, statements, letters, and order lists belonging to Moshe Levi. However, I also found several personal letters addressed to a man called Shmuel. Nothing is known about this man except that he apparently lived in Turkey. Moshe seems to have made copies of the letters he sent, but Shmuel's replies have not been preserved (in the Leiden archives).

It is upon these personal letters that I would like to focus particular attention. And also on one final bill of sale from 1666 showing that Moshe sold everything he owned, including the house on the Hoge Woerd, so that he and his family could follow Sabbatai Zevi to Turkey. Like many other Jews in the diaspora, Moshe was convinced that Zevi was the Messiah whom the Jewish people had been expecting for many centuries.

Unfortunately, it is not known how he fared after he left Leiden.

Among Jewish communities in Europe, there was a degree of hysteria surrounding this Sabbatai Zevi, who had been proclaimed Messiah by a young rabbi called Nathan. Moshe Levi was by no means the only Jew in the diaspora who sold all his possessions so that he could be nearer to the Messiah.

If he was indeed descended from Sephardic Jews, he was possibly influenced by the knowledge that his ancestors had fled both Spain and Antwerp. This might have contributed to a sense of insecurity that no doubt increased his yearning for deliverance by the Messiah.

Moshe Levi was exactly forty years old when Sabbatai Zevi's messiahship was revealed, and according to one of the merchant's personal letters, this fact played a major role in his decision. We can also assume from this that he must have been born in 1626, which, coincidentally, was the same year Zevi was born.

In the Bible, the number forty is associated with tests and trials. For example, the Israelites' forty years in the wilderness, the forty days and nights that Jesus fasted, the forty days that Moses fasted on the mountain before he received the Ten Commandments from Yahweh. Perhaps Moshe believed that he, like his namesake Moses, had been tested throughout the first forty years of his life, but now his ordeal was about to come to an end. The year 1666 was also significant for Christians because 1666 minus 1000 is 666, which, according to the book of Revelation in the New Testament, is the number of the Beast/Devil. It was a turbulent year and said by some to be pregnant with doom.

As already mentioned, the Leiden archives' sources do not tell us what happened to Moshe Levi and his family. Did they travel to Turkey to join the rabbi who had, by then, been arrested and imprisoned by the Turkish sultan? Did Moshe Levi ever actually meet Zevi? What became of his family? Unfortunately, we cannot (yet?) answer these and other similar questions.

However, this brief history of Leiden's Moshe Levi provides a fascinating insight into the broader history of Judaism.

THE RABBI
Sabbatai Zevi Rabbi Zevi

Sabbatai Zevi was born in 1626 in Smyrna (present-day Izmir in Turkey). According to tradition, he was born on the ninth day of the month of Av, the Jewish day of fasting that commemorates the destruction of Solomon's Temple.

He was the son of a simple poulterer who prospered later in life as an intermediary for Dutch and English trading companies. Zevi demonstrated an advanced knowledge of the Torah at a very young age, but his special interest seemed to be in the teachings of Kabbalah, esoteric Jewish mysticism.

From the age of twenty, his moods swung back and forth between euphoria and depression. Today, he would be given a diagnosis of manic depression. In his calmer periods, he made a great impression on people with the depth of his knowledge, serene manner, and reputedly beautiful singing voice.

He married twice, but both marriages ended in divorce before they could be consummated. His bizarre behaviour, which included marrying himself to a Torah scroll, led to his expulsion from Thessaloniki.

After his expulsion, he wandered around for a time, and his wandering took him to Istanbul and then Cairo, where he joined a kabbalist group. Following in the footsteps of the biblical prophet Hosea, he also married a prostitute there.

In April 1665, he arrived in present-day Gaza where he met Nathan, a twenty-year-old rabbi from whom he sought help for his fluctuating moods. This rabbi, half Zevi's age, was known for his ability to cast out demons. However, Nathan quickly ascertained that Zevi was not afflicted by demons. Zevi was, in fact, none other than the Messiah, the Redeemer promised by the Eternal One who would restore the Davidic kingdom and make the Promised Land purely Jewish once more.

Now, everything suddenly made sense for Zevi: the euphoria, the conversations he had with God in his head, the lack of recognition, the wandering. 'Foxes have holes, and birds of the air have nests; but the Son of Man has nowhere to lay his head.'

On May 31st, the Messiah's presence was announced in

Gaza, causing great excitement in the synagogue. Letters were sent to the Jewish communities in the diaspora calling for them to make atonement and have faith in Zevi. The letters promised that, within a very short time, the Messiah would remove the Ottoman sultan's crown without bloodshed and lead the Ten Lost Tribes back to the Holy Land.

Many people fasted to prepare for this new era, and Nathan warned that even the most righteous would be punished if they had the slightest doubts about this good news ('*eu-angelos*').

Sabbatai went to Jerusalem where he won some support. The most prominent rabbis opposed him, albeit with quiet discretion, choosing to banish him from the city but taking no further action against him. He journeyed north and stayed in Aleppo, where he gained an enormous number of followers. He travelled on to his birthplace, Izmir/Smyrna, shortly before Rosh Hashanah. During Hannukah that December, he entered the synagogue there dressed as a king.

Very soon, a rift developed in the community between those who believed that Zevi was the Messiah and those who did not. One Sabbath, he stormed into his opponents' synagogue and announced that he was the Anointed One of God. He repudiated those who did not believe in him, and distributed kingdoms to his followers.

A fit of mass hysteria followed.

People, men and women, old and young, fell into a trance and had visions of Zevi sitting on a royal throne, crowned King of Israel.

Strengthened by popular support, Sabbatai continued his journey to Istanbul, but in February 1666 he was arrested there and imprisoned. The Sultan was at war with Venice, so Zevi was transferred to a prison in Gallipoli on the European side of the Dardanelles.

By bribing the right people, the rabbi was able to turn his prison into a court where he received numerous guests. Pilgrims from all over Europe undertook the long journey to visit his cell. They held messianic rituals and exhausted themselves with penance and fasting. The news of his messiahship spread like wildfire through the Jewish communities in Europe and the Middle East. Hymns were composed to him, and new holidays proclaimed, culminating in the celebration of his birthday on the ninth day of the month of Av.

Eventually, the Sultan's patience was exhausted, and Sabbatai was transferred to Adrianople (now Edirne), where he was brought before a court and given the choice of either converting to Islam or being beheaded. Sabbatai chose to become a Muslim. He was given a Turkish name, an honorary title and a generous state pension.

The shock of his conversion brought an abrupt end to most of his adherents' messianic expectations. However, others quoted from the Bible, Talmud, Midrash, and kabbalist texts to prove that even this apparent conversion had been foretold. Hadn't Queen Esther also hidden her true Jewish identity to marry King Ahasuerosh and save the Jewish people from Haman's evil plans? Like Esther, Sabbatai Zevi had hidden his true nature from his opponents – like a spy in an enemy camp – and, albeit in a roundabout way, achieved a brilliant victory.

The rabbi lived alternately in Adrianopolis/Edirne and Istanbul and led a double life, outwardly living as a Muslim while also observing Jewish rituals. At one point, the Turks were so fed up with this fake convert that they transferred him to Dulcigno in Albania (now Ulcinj). His followers continued to visit him to hear him expound on his complicated kabbalistic theories.

He died in 1676, on the tenth day of the month of Tishri, or, in other words, on Yom Kippur, the Great Day of Atonement. On this day, Jews confessed their sins before the congregation and before God. The priest sacrificed a (scape)goat which took on all the sins of the Jewish people. This scapegoat was sent into the desert without food or water, where it died, symbolically taking away the people's sins.

For Zevi's followers, the symbolism of his death was blindingly obvious. Hadn't the rabbi taken everyone's sins upon himself as a suffering servant of the Lord, and had he not also died for their sins? The man who had discovered him, Rabbi Nathan of Gaza, declared that Sabbatai had ascended to the supernatural world.

After his death, few continued to believe that Sabbatai Zevi had been the Lord's Anointed One. But this short, intense revival of hope among the communities in the diaspora was unprecedented, as was the intense disappointment that followed, particularly after Zevi's conversion to Islam.

However, there were still followers of Sabbatai Zevi as

late as the nineteenth century, with groups in countries that included Poland, Germany and Italy.

Hope in the coming of the Messiah remains an important part of the lives of many Jews. Despite the disappointment caused by one man who claimed to be the Messiah and turned out not to be, this hope remains.

[Source: Robert M. Seltzer *Jewish People, Jewish Thought: The Jewish Experience in History*, Prentice Hall: New Jersey, 1980, pp. 467-474]

Acknowledgments

First and foremost, I would like to thank Evelyn de Regt of Primavera Pers, who saw the potential in the earliest version of this book's manuscript. That first draft was written over a period of just a few months, but in a way, it was the product of the books I had read over many years. I returned to some of these titles in the process of writing this story, and you will find them listed in the bibliography. Evelyn guided me through the publication of my first novel with great humour and patience, and thanks to her excellent advice, the story gained energy and momentum.

I would also like to thank proofreader Femke Foppema for making the final but vital refinements. Reader Godelief Mallee read an early version of the book, and I gratefully took her suggestions on board. Chief editor Theo Veenhof played a greater role than even I perhaps fully appreciate, going over the manuscript with both a wide and a fine-toothed comb and enhancing its readability. His enthusiasm for the book was enormously encouraging.

I would like to thank André van Dokkum, who spurred me on to focus and finally commit my novel to paper. His extensive knowledge of the Bible set me on the right path and led me to explore the conflict between Saint Paul and Saint Peter that was to become such an important theme in this book. My thanks also go to Rinus Vermeulen for reading the first chapters and helping me think of a good title. I would like to thank my wife Hamide, who always believes in me and my ventures, wherever they may take me. Every Friday, she eagerly awaited the latest chapter, which she then read with a critical eye. Her enthusiasm gave me the energy and confidence to keep writing. Finally, I would like to thank Dünya, our beautiful daughter, to whom this book is dedicated, the little sun around which my world revolves. *Canim benim.*